TAMING IVY

THE TAMING SERIES, BOOK ONE

APRIL MORAN

Cover by: Amanda Walker PA & Design Services

Formatted by: Christina Butrum

ACKNOWLEDGMENTS

Of course, my ever patient husband, James is the first to be thanked. And our daughter, Alyssa, the joy in my life - thanks for letting everyone know my books are your favorite books you'll never read. But the night you read my 7th-grade stories and poems aloud during a party will always be a treasured, hilarious memory.

My dear friend, Ladyne- I can always count on you to read the first draft, (and the second, third, on and on ...) then tell me everything wrong and right with it! I might not have finished it without you. Thanks for the encouragement and the moments of reality.

Gary, for your awful, inappropriate word suggestions. And equally inappropriate book covers. I'll never use them, but how you have entertained all of us!

My best friend of 40 plus years, Chris...you always have my back- I love you.

I could not have written this book without a little help along the way from some dear friends. My beta ladies- Ladyne, Gloria, Kelly, and Melody- thank you so much! For reading, encouraging and critiquing, every bit of it was invaluable, and I will be forever grateful. My sweet friend Karen, who always makes me feel I'm the greatest writer alive- and this was before she read a single word of my book, lol. You are always the first one to post a positive comment or a heart on my Facebook page. My mom and my two sisters, Jodi and Wendy, for sharing my love of romance novels. Jodi and Wendy—we can still do a Mountain Man and SueBee collaboration!

And special thanks to two people I've never even met... Amanda Walker and Christina Butrum. You ladies stepped up at the 11th hour and went above and beyond to help this new author get her novel ready for publication. Your assistance, advice, and patient understanding of my lack of knowledge is so appreciated. Thank you from the bottom of my heart.

For my husband, James, my love and best friend. Thanks for understanding why I'm sometimes still in my pajamas, staring at my computer when you come home for lunch. I love you madly!

CHAPTER 1

LONDON, ENGLAND 1839

*S*ebastian Tyler Sheraton Cain, eleventh Earl of Ravenswood and last of his line, did not believe in love.

Nor did he trust in a woman's ability to maintain an enduring faithfulness.

The notion of angels singing or being struck by lightning upon seeing a beautiful woman? Or having his composure rattled by a comely figure? Patently ridiculous.

And he most certainly did not believe in rekindling affairs. Friends and acquaintances joked that Lucifer himself stood a better chance of finding his way into Heaven. When Ravenswood decided a relationship was over, whomever happened to occupy his bed became something akin to hell-scorched earth. And like dead ground, nothing would grow there ever again. The affair was erased from memory and never revisited.

Never.

The flurry of emotions the earl's appearance triggered in Lady Veronica Wesley's foyer proved puzzling. He endured a half-hearted slap to his face and squeals of joy as Veronica launched herself into his arms. While the stoic butler ignored their passionate kisses, she dragged Sebastian upstairs, her schemes for

APRIL MORAN

his amorous entertainment described in exacting detail. Intrigued by her creative imagination, he neglected to mention the true reason for his afternoon visit.

For an hour, his former mistress fulfilled all whispered promises until Sebastian took control. Thankfully the bedroom walls were relatively thick, masking the sounds inside; harsh breathing, little cries of pleasure, the creak of the bed becoming louder as Veronica writhed beneath him, her jeweled fingers tangled in the open fretwork of the mahogany headboard. Her moans climbed in steady increments, higher pitched and desperate as the afternoon slipped away. Sebastian played with her forever, slapping her plump buttocks each time her pace slowed, his hands meshed in the long hair streaming down her back, anchored tight and controlling. Riding her with steady thrusts, he forced her to move faster, finally allowing her to tumble over the edge of satisfaction, her knuckles the palest shade of alabaster from gripping the headboard so hard.

Sebastian never gave her a moment to recover, tilting her hips aloft, rocking harder and deeper until she gasped. Veronica preferred it rough on occasion and this certainly qualified as such. After attending his needs in the most diligent of fashions, it seemed fair he fulfill a few of her preferences. Only he'd not taken into consideration Veronica's genuine delight in his return. She'd taken more of his time than anticipated. Another hour, possibly more, was lost while seeing to her pleasure. And although he did not mind making love all afternoon, it was not his intention.

Tugging her hair until she squealed Sebastian laughed softly, abruptly withdrawing to flip her over. When Veronica moaned in dissent, he kissed her hard and said quietly, "Hush...I'm coming back," just before thrusting inside her.

Veronica squeezed him tight, legs curled hungrily about Sebastian's waist, using her thighs and inner channel muscles until his shoulders contracted and his fingers dug painfully into the flesh of her buttocks. Their movements became almost violent until

2

another climax crashed over her and his own pinnacle was obtained in a blinding rush of sensations seconds later.

Dropping his forehead dropped into the curve of her shoulder, sweat from his brow mingled with hers. Veronica exhaled a shaky breath of blissful wonder.

"God, Sebastian, you've no idea how much I've missed this. No one else can..." She stopped herself, the breathless words dying as her damp palms skated along his flanks. Smiling softly, she continued, "You should not have stayed away so long, darling."

A low grumble rippled through Sebastian. He rolled away to prop himself against the headboard she gripped with desperation just moments before. Covering his nudity with a flick of the sheets, he raked a hand through his hair and waited for her to regain control of herself.

When Veronica's color back faded to a shade of fine ivory and her magnificent breasts no longer heaved, Sebastian's brow rose by an imperceptible degree. He gave a subtle clearing of his throat and she swung her legs over the edge of the mattress at the sound, pulling a velvet coverlet up from the floor to be fashioned into a makeshift sarong.

"Brandy or bourbon?" Her voice was subdued.

"Bourbon."

It was nearing three o'clock and a late February sun illuminated the lively street outside the townhouse on Piccadilly. But the murky interior of Veronica's luxurious bedroom suited her, lending a mysterious, dusky glow to her exotic features. Using the coverlet as camouflage she stepped to an ornately carved sidebar. Glass clinked as the bottle touched a crystal tumbler.

Sebastian's expression remained veiled. He understood why she pulled the drapes tight against the unforgiving daylight. Always curvaceous, Veronica was easing into plumpness, but he found no fault in that. That soft voluptuousness pleased him. And probably the other lovers she entertained in his absence.

Watching as she poured his drink, Sebastian felt a disappointing and infuriatingly familiar lack of fulfillment nag him.

Despite the rigorous sex, his release proved empty rather bland. Sprawled amongst the tangled sheets like an indolent tiger, he wondered if his remoteness confused Veronica. He might as well be a stranger lounging in her bed instead of a well-known lover.

He'd never treated her with anything other than a casual indifference. A self-conscious attempt perhaps to retain the friendship shared before their affair began. That aloofness was necessary to maintain distance and it was his habit, as he came and went as he pleased, to never make a woman privy to his affairs. Veronica once foolishly questioned his frequent absences and it was that distance which allowed Sebastian to easily smile and say, "Now, that hardly matters in our situation, does it, my dear?" She was intelligent enough to never ask again, because if she had, he would have responded by obtaining a new mistress. No matter the state of the relationship, he'd be damned if a woman questioned his actions or dictated to him. Not ever again. Not after what he'd been through with his former fiancée, Marilee.

Fortunately, within Sebastian's privileged world there was no shortage of willing prey. As he cut a wide swath through London and other cities abroad, the same women whispering of his atrocious habit of moving from mistress to mistress also sought his company, eager for the pleasure lavished upon them while they were his. Veronica resided happily in that category. Had he any intention of resuming their relationship, which he did not, Sebastian knew she probably always would. Hardly noble to think it but it was the truth.

She perched beside him, handing over a crystal glass. With burgundy velvet wrapped about her, a raven-hued lock of hair tugged between the fingers of one hand and a tumbler of bourbon twirling in the other, she presented an appealing picture. A huge mirror leaned against the far wall, reflecting every activity occurring in her bed and undoubtedly Veronica practiced this particular mannerism many times before it. She executed it perfectly. The precise, slow twirl of the drink, the perfect, sultry pout. The careful sip which drew attention to her full lips.

She broke the awkward silence first. "How did you find France, Seb?"

Sebastian downed the bourbon in one swallow. *Get it over with, selfish bastard. Do not keep her hoping.* "Quite easily once I crossed the Channel." Because his particular brand of humor always eluded her in the past, it was surprising that her russet colored eyes narrowed with injured annoyance.

"I meant…"

"I know what you meant, Ronnie." He chucked her under the chin, feeling slightly guilty when she brightened with the calculated use of affection. It was still easy to manipulate her. "I did not find much to amuse me there."

Exhaustion proved a more fitting description of his four years abroad, the remembrance of last month's liaison enjoyed with three (almost) famous ballerinas tamped down. That first year away from England, one spent romping on the beach with a forgettable mistress on a newly purchased sugar plantation in the Caribbean, proved wearisome. After her, during his aimless drift across different countries, a lovely, lady in waiting to the Queen of Spain held his attention for a time. Comfortably situated in an airy villa just outside the palace, Sebastian developed an appreciation for hot, strong coffee every morning and enjoyed fiery lovemaking with the dark-haired beauty. Until her irrational jealousy led him to break the affair. That she also found him in bed with the wife of a French ambassador complicated matters. Sandwiched during and between those mistresses, including Veronica, were women selected to ease the loneliness and hold his boredom at bay.

Frowning at the hollow depth of recollections, Sebastian rotated the empty tumbler between his palms. "I was not in France the entire time."

"I missed you, Seb. Terribly, I'm afraid." Setting her glass down, Veronica slid closer. Her fingers rested against the lower portion of his belly before twining with sly intent in the whispery black hair snaking a trail beyond the edge of the sheet. "Had you sent for me, I would have come to you. No matter the others warming your bed. A familiar face might have been welcomed in your travels."

"Perhaps." Taking a firm grasp of her hand, Sebastian removed it from his abdomen.

A small clock on the fireplace mantle chimed the hour. Damnation. Two hours wasted yet it felt like much more. Rolling from the bed, he remembered squandering days in Veronica Wesley's bed and quite happily, too.

That time in his life could be centuries ago. A lifetime ago.

Flopping against the abundant pillows in a huff, Veronica's pretty face turned sullen. Sebastian hunted for his clothes, feeling her hungry gaze devouring his naked form. Finding his shirt lying on the floor near the door, he gave it a slight shake.

"I saw your aunt a week past at the Hadderly ball." Her voice wobbled, thin and high. "It was her first social event after…everything."

Sebastian paused in fastening the ivory buttons. Veronica was not stupid. She was beginning to understand the purpose of his visit and would say damn near anything to delay his departure. He hauled on his breeches in silence, hoping to find his boots quickly. Earlier she had yanked them from his feet with the skill of a master blacksmith removing shoes from a racehorse, flinging each expensive boot over her shoulder without a care for where they might land.

"Was *she* there?" Overturning a velvet-tufted ottoman, he trusted his revulsion in the subject matter was not too apparent.

"Yes." Veronica seemed torn between wanting to say nothing more yet also wanting to please with information. Desperation to bind him to her by any means was chewing away the edges of her dignity.

Sebastian's mouth twitched with a ghost of a smile. Jealous women made excellent informants. And spies.

"Such a strange thing. Lady Kinley was ghostly white after speaking with your aunt. Everyone speculated as to their conversation, although none were privy to it." Her restless fingers plucked at the sheets. "Lady Garrett departed immediately. She missed the entire fiasco."

"Fiasco?" Sebastian murmured. Veronica held little fondness for the recent source of gossip in London's uppermost echelons of society. And it was disgraceful - men flocking to that girl simply because one mad, infatuated soul took his life after the loss of her fickle attention.

"One can hardly describe it as anything else. Quite appalling, even if the *ton* is clamoring for Lady Kinley, proclaiming her this Season's "Darling Incomparable." It was scandalous... enough to guarantee Lady Hadderly's ball would be declared a sensation." An unconscious thread of admiration curled into Veronica's tone. "Viscount Basford stepped in on Lord Walsingham and as they argued Count Monvair waltzed off with her. Basford stormed after the count, everyone began pushing and shouting. Lady Hadderly feigned a swoon, just after vowing to see them all banished for the rest of the Season from every ball. Not that she possesses that sort of power, but she does hold a rather high opinion of herself. In the midst of it all, Lady Kinley just vanished! While old Lord Hadderly shuffled about, howling about silly girls, fainting fits and ill-mannered men."

"Enough, Ronnie," Sebastian grated out between clenched teeth. Thank God. One elusive boot peeked from beneath a flowing puddle of burgundy-hued velvet drapes. A moment later, its mate was located behind a decorative screen close to the commode room.

He regained his composure by the time he shrugged into a forest green afternoon coat, one he tossed onto the floor with no care for its exorbitant cost. While checking his appearance at a vanity table, messy with cosmetic pots and perfume vials, Sebastian pulled a tiny box from his coat's inner pocket, placing it amid the clutter. Running a hand through his tousled black hair to bring it to some sort of order, he was amused by Veronica's reflection in the mirror. She was pinching her pale cheeks, biting her lips to bring some color to them.

7

Sebastian motioned her to come to him, planting a distant kiss to those reddened lips. "Thank you for an enjoyable afternoon."

"Will you come again tomorrow?" Her eyes held a shimmer of tears. She already knew his answer but was compelled to ask regardless.

"You know I won't, Ronnie." He lifted her chin with a forefinger. "However, we shall remain friends, if you grant me that honor."

Veronica accepted the official ending of their affair with admirable grace and pragmatism. "We've been friends for so long, something like this cannot possibly jeopardize it. I can give Lord Alimar serious consideration now, I suppose. He's been quite persistent to make more permanent arrangements. Told me I was foolish to wait for you, but I've had other lovers since you left."

Sebastian detested this element of affairs, the final chapter, this closing curtain. Although his mistresses praised his generosity and compassion, garnering accolades for kindness to a woman at the end of his use of her never failed to strike him as rather bizarre. Veronica was taking it better than most, but then again, she had years to prepare herself for this moment.

"Should you ever require anything, you have only to ask. I can arrange it so you would never..."

"You needn't even say it, darling," Veronica interrupted with a small, sad smile. "I know very well a kind heart exists in there." The palm of her hand pressed flat to his chest as she sighed. "Somewhere beneath all this glorious wickedness."

Their gazes held until Sebastian cleared his throat and turned to gather the remainder of his personal items.

It was too damn easy to shed the women in his life. A pretty bit of jewelry, a few kind words and he was free to carry on. It was almost embarrassing. Still, relief overrode the prick of shame when he glimpsed Veronica's dismal face peering down from the second story bedroom window.

She must believe he could not see her as she stood half hidden behind the wine-red drapes. Sebastian nearly raised a hand in farewell before thinking better of it. The stale air of London was hardly an improvement over the bouquet of sex, bourbon, and faint cigar smoke found within Veronica's suite of rooms, but it blotted his guilt until it eased. As his luxurious coach merged onto bustling Piccadilly Street, those drapes fell back into place.

Veronica probably facilitated between giddiness and disbelief over his parting gift. The golden topaz and diamond necklace with matched earrings cost a small fortune, a penance gladly paid for the failure in officially ending their affair four years before. Settling against the leather squabs, Sebastian shoved her from his mind. She was his friend, but also just another woman, one in a long string effortlessly replaced. It was a pattern often repeated in his life; a few coins spent, a meaningless token and an emotionless 'thank you' for hours wasted making loveless love.

Over and done.

~

"SHE'S LITTLE MORE THAN A HIGH-BORN, SPOILED COURTESAN."

Lady Rachel Garrett's shrill voice was as ear piercing as Sebastian remembered. Her hands twisted in her lap, making him want to give her something. A ball of yarn, a chicken that needed plucking. Anything to absorb that frantic energy and put it to good use.

"Perhaps," he replied.

"She'll bewitch you as she did my poor Timothy."

"Impossible."

"Men foolishly pursue her." Rachel clasped her gaunt cheeks in distress. "You'll be one of many."

Sebastian just spent the past half hour listening with a calm detachment to his aunt's histrionics. Now, his lips quirked. It was possible the young countess had done little to entrance his cheerful, romantically inclined cousin, but it did not absolve her guilt. Swirling his brandy, he contemplated various methods of escaping this dreadful meeting.

"She cares not that he is dead!" Aunt Rachel wailed.

"That, madam, is most likely true." Pulling a crumpled piece of vellum from a drawer of his desk, he wondered if Ivy Kinley cared that Timothy was dead. She *had* killed him, after all. Indirectly of course, but she was the instrument of his destruction.

Rachel watched him with shadowy eyes, perched on the edge of a leather club chair in Sebastian's study, her spine painfully rigid. She possessed the air of a small black crow, stricken with grief yet alert with private loathing.

Sebastian eased out the deep crinkles of the page before pinching the bridge of his nose. Thanks to Rachel's incessant despair upon learning his intentions, he now had one hell of a headache. And no matter how many times he read this letter, he'd come no closer to understanding his cousin's disturbing fascination with the Countess of Somerset. Nor to unraveling the mystery behind it. The anger contained within the tear stained ink was as bewildering as Timothy's chaotic swings between despair and adoration.

My Dearest Ivy,

I've called upon you countless times and still that damned butler won't allow me entrance! He treats me as if I'm the lowliest chimney sweep or a piece of rabble seeking your charity. It is unacceptable, but I know full well he only does your bidding.

I long to hold you, to feel the sunlight of your smile. You know I adore you. You know you are mine. Ivy, I need you. Without you, I am nothing. I feel nothing. Can you understand my simple words? I am nothing without you.

My sweet Ivy, my heartless, beautiful love. These past weeks have been hell. My headaches grow worse, my medication as useless as sugar water. But I think you do not care. Damn you, goddamn you! Do you see the depths I've fallen to? I curse your name and hate myself for it. Your cruelty blinds you to my suffering. Or do you know my torment and find this agony amusing? Does it please you? Knowing this wretchedness has beset me?

What have you done to me? God, what have I done to you? Ivy, I beg you to see me again. Today. Tomorrow. Now. I don't care.

This is torture and I cannot bear it. I am in Hell and you are the Devil's own angel, but I love you. I know you love me. Your affections could not have been lies. Please, before it is too late. What must I do? Tell me how to make you love me again. Because I must have you. I must. I simply cannot live without you. I love you. Yes. I love you. But damn you, damn you, you are killing me. As surely as if you twist all these knives in my heart...

~Timothy

His cousin died in his private rooms, here at sprawling Ravenswood Court on Grosvenor Square, his dark head of curls pillowed upon this very letter. A decanter of brandy teetered on the edge of his personal desk, the liquor forming a puddle on the expensive rug. Beside Timothy's stiff hand lay an empty bottle of laudanum and a bowl of sugar cubes. A writing quill, the silver nib crusted with dried ink, was still clutched within his fingers.

Lady Garrett's cries for justice resulted in the bobbies being called in.

"An unfortunate tragedy," Inspector Barrett declared. "I'm afraid nothing can be done in the matter, milady. No law exists preventing a young lady's refusal of a gentleman's courtship."

"An unintentional death," Old Doctor Callahan determined upon meticulous examination of the suite and Timothy's body. The official declaration guaranteed his cousin's final resting place in the family plot, complete with all necessary blessings of the Church. Rumors of suicide escaped nonetheless.

Sebastian shot his aunt a sharp glance when she sniffled. "You must trust my judgment on this matter, Aunt Rachel." He hoped she would not collapse into sobs again and sighed with relief when she did not.

"It's scandalous...this notion you have of courting her. After what she did." As if realizing the hysterics annoyed him, Rachel stated this in a more restrained manner.

His aunt was correct; it would be scandalous. But had he been in London, this whole madness might have been avoided. Shouldn't he bear a bit of the responsibility for the tragedy? From the time he'd

11

come to live with them at the age of four, Timothy idolized Sebastian. In fact, the boy emulated him and in the careless manner of an older brother, Sebastian loved his cousin as well. Much could have been done to alleviate the situation before Timothy harmed himself. How the carefree and jovial young man spiraled so quickly into such a dark pit over a woman was difficult to comprehend. And in just a few months' time according to Rachel. *Damn it, Timothy, you love-struck bastard. Did you not learn anything from my mistakes with Marilee? Now I'm left to deal with your irrational mother, all the damnable gossip. And the heartless little bitch who caused your downfall.*

The uncharitable thoughts of Aunt Rachel caused a stab of guilt. His father's eldest and only sister was suffering the loss of her sole child. For his father's sake, and Timothy's, Sebastian summoned forth his most sympathetic nature.

"There will be times you question my actions." His eyes flickered over the woman, evaluating her reaction. "I'll caution you not to interfere."

Rachel's mouth curved in a tight slash of disapproval. She'd lost a stone in the time he'd been gone. It did not compliment her gaunt face, marking her far older than her sixty years. Her husband's demise and the impoverished state due to his gambling debts had not aged her as Timothy's passing had. A haunted expression flitted in her blue eyes whenever she spoke of the girl responsible for her son's death nine months before and Sebastian thought his aunt's return to society was far too soon.

"I want Lady Kinley to suffer for what she did to Timothy."

"She will." The assurance was firm. "In a method of my choosing."

After Rachel exited his study Sebastian pondered the latest scandal involving the Countess of Somerset. A popular wager emerged in the gaming hells and private gentlemen clubs during the months following Timothy's death, a grotesque amusement for those with deep pockets and a sense of the macabre. Some fool, obviously lacking a clever bone in his body, devised the appalling title, *Taming the Countess.* The objective of the game hinged upon one's ability to withstand the charms of Lady Ivy Kinley. Ultimate victory was twofold; one could not end up as dead as the unfortunate Lord Timothy Garrett and one must capture the lady's hand in marriage. Of course, considering the size of the fortune in question, it was not simply the countess herself men were so eager to capture. *Survive her or win her…*

His family now the brunt of sordid entertainment, Sebastian had no sympathy for the girl caught in the midst of the scandal. It was incomprehensible the *ton*, notorious for its fickle nature, was fascinated with her.

It was seven years before when Sebastian first met the young countess. The day he arrived at the Somerset estate was one of his first social calls following a year of mourning his own father's death to a sudden illness. His recollection of that afternoon, and memories of a disagreeable twelve-year-old little girl crowned with frizzy brown hair, her face sprinkled with unfortunate freckles, were far from pleasant.

The visit was made with considerable reluctance, an onerous duty owed in part to the friendship his father shared with the Earl of Kinley. Sebastian came to pay respects on the recent passing of Kinley's wife, Caroline. Since Kinley held many of Britain's influential men in the deepest, darkest wells of his pocket, failure to convey personal condolences would have been considered a grievous insult. Having just turned twenty-two at the time, the reins of the Ravenswood earldom newly in his hands, Sebastian could not risk offending so powerful a man.

A dark-grey haired butler operating in a dazed fog failed to collect his coat and hat, leaving Sebastian awkwardly holding the items in his hands. Kinley's entire staff appeared stunned by the death of their lady. As the butler silently led the way down the hall, two downstairs maids wept into their handkerchiefs, not bothering to pretend otherwise when Sebastian's gaze swept over them. The house possessed an air of despondency, with dark gleaming furniture in want of dusting, the curtains drawn tight against the brilliant sunshine.

When Kinley joined him in the west drawing room Sebastian became privy to the unnerving spectacle of a notoriously self-composed man downing several tumblers of brandy. It was a peek into a private world not meant to be seen, the earl dropping the acerbic manner cultivated since his brush with financial ruin years before. This Kinley staggered about in a haze of grief. Lady Caroline's death was not surprising, having been ill for the past two years, but the earl's composure was one of a devastated man.

An hour of stilted conversation crept passed before Sebastian deemed it safe to depart. Kinley stared with blank eyes for the majority of the visit while his guest said all the necessary things and fidgeted at the slow passing of time. Checking his watch with a relieved sigh, Sebastian murmured his farewells, pausing when raised voices rose in the hall. Something heavy and probably very expensive crashed to the floor just outside the door just as a whirlwind of velocity burst into the room. An interloper, clad in dirty breeches and a yellowed linen shirt, slammed the door with such force the walls shook.

His dignified exit ruined, Sebastian sank into his chair by the fireplace.

"Were you going to tell me? Did you plan to roll me up in my bedsheets? Dump me in a coach to take me away? Without even a word from you? Is this what you planned? *Answer me!*" A shabby, gray tweed cap obscured any discernible features; the tattered bill yanked down so it hovered above the bridge of the wearer's nose.

Damn. A disgruntled servant had come to exact revenge against the earl. Or could it be some unfortunate soul from the nearby village who managed to barge his way into the house? Where were Kinley's servants? They ought to be rushing in to remove the intruder at any moment.

Kinley stumbled back against the sideboard. Reaching for the decanter of brandy, his hand quivered. "My intention was to inform you this afternoon."

Carefully crossing a leg over the other, Sebastian's eyebrow rose in faint horror. Kinley might be accustomed to strangers invading his wife's ancestral home but this ragged trespasser spoke with painful familiarity.

"You planned this. Weeks ago." The accusation was snarled. "Before Mama even died...admit *it!*"

The ragged creature possessed a feminine voice. Hoarse, broken but undeniably female. Ah, it was easy to see if one bothered to look close.

She scowled in fierce disapproval at the decanter in Kinley's fist. A scrap of black ribbon gathered a mop of brown hair at the nape of a sweaty, dirt streaked neck. Those knotted curls could use a comb and soap. For that matter, she needed a good scrubbing all over.

Failing to notice the third party observing the quarrel, her full lips lifted in a sneer. "It's not even noon, Father."

At the thread of violence in the girl's tone, Kinley spilled the majority of the brandy down his leg. Taking up a cloth, he blotted at the stain as something resembling gratitude flashed across his features. He waved a hand toward the fireplace. "My dear...the Earl of Ravenswood has come to offer his condolences. May I present my daughter? Lady Ivy Elizabeth Kinley. Now, Countess of Somerset."

Sebastian silently groaned. Escaping unnoticed from this little drama, or whatever one wished to call it, was impossible now. When she pivoted toward him, a whirlwind of feral heat, the tiny ripple of unease he felt embarrassed him. She was a child. Unable to do any real harm, but her battle stare rivaled that of a seasoned knight. Rising from his chair, he clasped his arms behind his back in afterthought. A simple precaution, in case the girl's teeth snapped in his direction. After all, it appeared wolves had raised her.

He bowed. "Lady Kinley." *Such a shame the old and esteemed title is wasted on this ill-mannered creature.*

Her spine jolted into a rigid line. Delicate hands with dirt tinged fingernails fluttered to the cap on her head before she reached back to smooth the frizzy tangles bunched at the nape of her neck. Indecision flickered in gold-flecked aqua eyes while she trembled with the panic of a cornered fox. She blinked. And blinked again.

Slowly, a devilish gleam lit those fascinating eyes, the corners of her full mouth twisting with slow contempt. She ripped the bedraggled cap from her head. Two russet-colored leaves drifted to the floor to blend with the intricate golden hued pattern of the Aubusson rug.

Her father winced, swallowed his brandy in one huge gulp and refilled the glass to overflowing with an even shakier hand.

The curtsy executed by Lady Ivy Elizabeth Kinley, the new Countess of Somerset in her own right and all of twelve years of age, was a rude mockery, made more so by the rough garments she wore. A flick of her wrist sent the cap sailing through the air to land on a marble bust of a nameless Greek god residing atop a marble pillar in the corner. The ragged piece of tweed swung three precarious circles before coming to rest at a haphazard tilt to obscure one vacant staring eye with rakish flair.

Her mouth formed a silent "oh!" of astonishment at the unintentional perfection of het aim and some devil within Sebastian longed to dare her to try such a trick again. It was a struggle to hold his tongue. The chit would no doubt delight in challenging him to a hat-throwing contest. And she would likely win.

With methodical preciseness Lady Ivy Kinley proceeded to scrape her battered riding boots against the beautiful rug, leaving a multitude of pungent smears. Was that dirt or something else? Did he really wish to know?

"Lord Ravenswood, is it?" Ivy's eyes flared in silent triumph at leaving him and her father speechless.

She managed to make his title sound like a curse word. Her manners were atrocious. While Sebastian did not usually condone such drastic measures, if Jonathan Kinley did not take a strap to his daughter's well-titled backside, it would prove an admirable exercise in restraint. A bit of discipline would do her a world of good.

Gaining her mother's inheritance, now a countess in her own right, Ivy surpassed her father in status and titles. A complete lack of parental guidance existed in this girl's upbringing; the formidable Earl of Kinley apparently had no bloody clue on how to handle his daughter.

Ivy swung toward her father, dismissing Sebastian while he continued examining her. Like bejeweled ornaments, a few burnished leaves hung ensnared in the web of her plain brown hair. Despite those god-awful muck-encrusted boots and her disinterest in soap, Ivy somehow carried the freshness of a summer storm sweeping through a meadow, the outdoors on and around her. The pungent earthiness of horse sweat accented the mix of contradictions. Shoving her into the usual pigeonhole assigned to children of nobility would be an impossible task. He wondered how past governesses might have dealt with the girl, for she was surely an apt student and one difficult to control.

As for her features, she was neither an attractive child nor an ugly one. Like a puzzle with missing pieces, leaving it impossible to create a pleasing image, nothing about the young countess fit together. With awkward arms and elbows, surprisingly long, coltish legs and a fat, frizzy ponytail of hair she kept tossing to one side as though it aggravated her to no end, she was at odds with herself. Her lips were too full in a face still round with the remnants of a baby's chubbiness. A smattering of buff-colored freckles danced across a raw, arrow straight nose; an unbecoming flush of crimson splotched her pale cheeks. Haunting blue-green eyes touched with gold were swollen and red-rimmed, but eyelashes resembling sable-hued spikey feathers lent a doe-like appearance. Streaked with dirt and faint tracks of either tears or sweat, her chin jutted out in a most stubborn manner. No, everything did not fit together in the girl's face, strong hints of maturity clashing with the features of an obstinate child.

Realizing she was under scrutiny, the girl swiped an arm over her face. The grimy shirtsleeve blotted the wetness away but added to the stains marring her cheeks.

"You've arranged to send me to that horrid place and Mama's dead scarcely a month." She no longer shouted and the clipped, moderated tones of her voice were pleasant to the ear. It was the voice of an adult trapped within a youth, a child left to fend for herself for far too long. "I need more time, I can't-" Chewing her bottom lip until it was crimson and plump, her eyes swelled with incriminating moisture. She inhaled, held it, before allowing the breath to whoosh out almost silently. "Father, I cannot go. I *will* not go."

With remarkable aplomb, she wrangled her emotions into check. Sebastian shifted his feet, uncomfortable with a sudden comprehension. She wouldn't cry. Not this one. Not in front of others. An element of ice lay inside her. This girl was strong. Perhaps more than her perplexed father could even begin to contemplate.

"I'm sorry, my dear," Kinley muttered in a gruff voice. "It's already arranged." He stared into his drink as if to find fortitude at the bottom of the glass. When he rubbed his eyes, Sebastian recognized the gesture of extreme weariness. He'd seen his own father do the same many times,

Tossing back his brandy, Kinley suddenly pinned Ivy with a bright blue gaze. "I've business to attend in Ireland over the next few months and you will not remain here with no female supervision. You shall love Miss Chase's Seminary for Exceptional Young Ladies. During breaks you may come here when I'm in residence, or you may visit Kinley House if I am in London. Now, might I suggest you pack a few of your personal things? You depart first thing in the morning. The stable master will have your mare delivered there by the end of the week. Or Heather can remain at Somerset. Regardless, *you* shall be at the seminary next week." A few spoken words and Jonathan Kinley regained control of the situation, his daughter and himself.

Ivy deflated, becoming very small and very young very

quickly. She was no match for a father who'd outwitted and outfoxed far more cunning opponents than one defiant, awkward daughter with horrid manners. The dizzying swiftness of Kinley's actions, using a pony as leverage, left no doubt his reputation was well earned. His brutality truly did extend to his own flesh and blood.

When the earl cleared his throat as a pointed reminder, his daughter offered a beautifully executed curtsy with downcast eyes. She might still plot revenge with the cunning of a well-seasoned royal courtier behind this dispirited façade, but she hid it well.

"Pardon my interruption, Lord Ravenswood." The cap was retrieved from the morose Greek god, smashed back onto the girl's head.

The door closed behind her with a soft click and Kinley's gaze shot to Sebastian. "The young have no idea what's best for them. Caroline's death has been very difficult for Ivy."

Sebastian waited for him to continue but Kinley stared off into the distance for a long moment. Maybe he contemplated the challenges faced in raising an ill-tempered, frizzy-haired daughter without a mother's tender guidance.

"I thought it best she spent some time with girls her own age. You see she possesses an uncompromising nature." Kinley gave a rueful bark of laughter. "Other than her beauty, I fear she bears none of her mother's gentler traits."

Lady Caroline Kinley possessed an enchanting loveliness her daughter failed to inherit. Apparently, the earl saw something only a father might. Sebastian nodded politely. "She is most certainly her father's daughter."

With an unusual gift for remembering details, he pondered his recollection of that day. He recalled his uncomfortable position in the chair, the tired despondency on Kinley's face. The desperate wildness of the childish, obstinate countess. Little suggested the girl would one day become the darling of London, nothing to hint Kinley's daughter would become a great beauty, twisting hearts about her tiniest finger until a man believed he must possess her or die trying. A woman held power with sex or the promise of it. Lord Kinley used his wealth to manipulate men; his daughter applied sex to the same effect. Was it the promise of satisfaction or the refusal of further encounters that spurred foolish Timothy to his demise?

Sebastian would not stand idle, could not allow yet another deceitful woman to make a fool of him or his family. Could not allow Timothy's death to go unavenged. Unfortunately, his gullible cousin followed Sebastian's own path when it came to falling in love with a heartless woman and had paid the ultimate price.

The memory of a forlorn, fierce little girl grieving her mother pinched him again. Sebastian shoved it aside. His hardened heart held no room for pity. Ivy Kinley's ruination was a necessity and would provide an amusing pursuit. Women were impatient to be used by him and like others, she would tumble into his bed. Revenge for Timothy's sake would be found between the countess's thighs. He'd find a bit of pleasure for himself there as well. If he were fortunate.

He would collect pieces of her, fragments held in his hand until nothing remained of the countess but an empty shell. At the end of the game, the tattered collection would be crumpled and discarded. Not in his usual manner, with kind words and an expensive trinket presented for time spent between the sheets. No, this would be different. When he finished with her, Lady Kinley would be acceptable only to the palest fringes of Polite Society. She would not be anyone's "Darling." There would no longer be sonnets to her beauty, no accolades of adoration. No more eager suitors vying for her heart and hand. She would be ruined and tamed and Sebastian would delight in the destruction.

I'm coming, Countess. Get ready for me.

CHAPTER 2

"*He's here!*"
"*-actually came. I can't believe it -*"
"*Ravenswood is on the hunt for Poison Ivy.*"

Panic battered Ivy, her heart pounding with the violence of it. Like a wildfire sweeping over her, the roar filled her ears until she could hear nothing else.

It was rude. It was deplorable. But if she did not get a breath of blessed fresh air, she would throw up all over her new dancing slippers. Or perhaps those highly polished Hessian boots Brandon was so bloody proud of. She abandoned the viscount, mouth agape in stunned annoyance, in the middle of the black and white marble floor, gaily-dressed couples swirling about him.

Open curiosity and murmurs of scandalized outrage rippled outward from the center of the ballroom. Ivy's pace increased as she reached the edges of the floor. A cluster of girls, clad in the identical white of freshly introduced debutantes, tittered behind pristine gloved hands, whispers mingled with their giggles. Those multiple-hued heads dipped together, while words so thick with cruelty they almost formed a cloud, drifted in Ivy's wake.

Gossip was her constant companion now, a bedfellow difficult to ignore. The miserable sting in Ivy's chest every time a barb found its mark was a harsh reminder she was far from immune. It hurt, but no one needed to *see* how deeply the arrows wounded her.

A few more steps to the nearest terrace doors and freedom would be hers. With stoic grimness, shoving through the maze of elbows and satin skirts, Ivy plotted escape. From the terrace to the gardens and from there to the front steps of the mansion. She could simply locate her coach, allow it to whisk her away. The curved handles of the terrace doors lay at her fingertips...

"Ivy Kinley, don't you dare run."

"I'm not running." Ivy's stomach flip-flopped with the denial. When champagne tinged bitterness rose in her throat, her teeth clenched against the choking tide. She would be sick, right there, in front of God and everyone. "I was-"

"You would make an excellent thief, darling." Linking their arms, Lady Sara Morgan spun Ivy away from the terrace doors. "Your abilities to escape are remarkable."

"You'll wish you'd let me go when I ruin your slippers as well as my own." Ivy pressed two trembling fingertips to her lips. "I feel quite ill."

Sara's blonde head tilted. She assessed Ivy then ignored the dismal confession, surveying the ballroom.

"Oh, dear. There's Count Phillipe Monvair. Someone ought to remand that man's valet to Newgate. Those color combinations are simply criminal. A violation to all the senses, don't you agree?"

Jostling his way through the crush of some three hundred odd people attending the Sheffield Ball, the dubiously dressed count held two goblets of champagne balanced high above his head. By the grim smile of determination splayed across his hawkish, bearded face, his path was evident.

Sara swallowed another laugh. "Such a gaudy little peacock. I've never seen a man strut with such a complete lack of humility."

"I rather like how the count dresses."

"Only because you believe it takes attention away from you." Sara stood on her tiptoes; the better to scan the entire ballroom.

22

"If I thought it would help my cause," Ivy grumbled, "I would gladly sponsor his tailor."

Rocking onto the balls of her feet, Sara shot her an exasperated glance. "Attempts to disappear only makes others that more rabid to seek you out. You might as well hang a sign about your neck begging people to poke and prod at you."

Ivy said nothing. Sara could not fathom the depths of her desire to escape, to become invisible to the threat stalking the elegant ballroom. Despite the feeble attempts at lightheartedness, dread prodded her. She should rip away from her friend's grasp. Run as though the devils of hell chased her. One hunted her now. What would she do if he caught her?

Her free hand twisted the folds of her skirt. Nervous energy brimmed and bubbled inside her, causing her stomach to rope and twist into hangman knots.

Candle light blazed from every available corner while high overhead enormous chandeliers illuminated the vast room in a romantic glow. Glittering people filled the space; some danced, while others stood in clusters, sharing on-dits of gossip. Liveried servants in red and gold slipped in and out of the crowd, trays of champagne held high overhead. In the midst of it all, the Earl of Ravenswood waited to materialize.

"Do you realize who is here?" Ivy muttered. Rumors galloped in wild abandon from one end of the ballroom to the other. It seemed impossible Sara did not know.

"Perhaps not..."

"Oh, he is. Somewhere. Much like the plague. Just because one cannot physically *see* the disease does not negate its existence." Ivy's foot tapped in agitation.

"That's hardly complimentary of you," Sara laughed softly. "While true he's not a man to be crossed, I doubt Lord Ravenswood has anything in common with infectious diseases."

"I'm not so certain. The rumor is..."

"I'm well aware of the rumors and *you,* darling girl, will not run. You have done nothing wrong. If you show even the slightest weakness, these heartless vultures, otherwise known as our friends, will rip you apart." A mischievous grin spread across Sara's lovely features when Ivy's tightly pressed lips acknowledged the wisdom of her words. "Besides, those doors there are locked. I witnessed three -" Sara held up three fingers, ignoring Ivy's tiny groan of frustration, *"three* -mind you, love-silly couples discretely attempting to pry them open. Just within the last five minutes. Lady Sheffield always locks them, remember? Lord, she is an eccentric creature, although I wonder how we might escape a fire or some other disaster."

"Locked terrace doors certainly impede our chances of survival," Ivy sighed. "Although such a distraction, while quite tragic, would be welcomed."

Sara's voice dropped to a conspiratorial whisper. "It's said she hides the key in the depths of that ample bodice of hers. No one, not even Lord Sheffield, dares any attempt to retrieve it."

Ivy's lips twitched with a reluctant grin.

Sara giggled. "See? A bit of humor exists in this deplorable situation. Now, chin up, darling. And won't you smile even a little for the poor count? Oh, blast it. Smiles for the entire Pack, for here they come running. I vow they track you with the bloodlust of a passel of prized foxhounds."

"Given a chance, I fear they would tear me apart and fight over the pieces." Smoothing her features into a cool mask of pleasant acceptance, the smile Ivy granted Count Phillipe Monvair was one that gossip columns recently declared to rival the sun. Which was utterly ridiculous. This smile was the same as her others. Only romantic fools saw a difference. "And does it matter if I smile? The entire lot of them can't seem to raise their eyes any higher than the area of my chest."

"That's not completely true." Sara grinned when Ivy's turquoise eyes narrowed. "Why, just the other day, I heard Lord McLemore comment what a lovely shade of gold your eyes are. Or perhaps he was speaking of your inheritance?"

"Mon chers, I bring refreshments," Monvair exclaimed in his

thick accent. He ignored the stoic servant standing nearly shoulder to shoulder beside him holding a full tray of beverages.

Ivy and Sara exchanged annoyed glances. The garishly dressed count proudly bore champagne as though it were fresh water in the depths of an endless desert. Six other men quickly completed the circle surrounding the girls, including the previously abandoned, fiercely frowning Viscount Basford. Since Brandon rarely moved at a pace beyond a dignified stroll Ivy knew he was truly vexed to have reached her in such haste.

The Pack overtook the conversation as Ivy accepted the glass Monvair offered.

"My lady, might I be so bold to request the next waltz when the orchestra returns? The viscount must have stomped your toes. I vow I shall not."

"Will you sing for us, Lady Kinley? Your voice is much sweeter than Lady Tremayne's daughters, lovely though they are."

What a boldfaced lie. Ivy knew full well she sang like a canary with tail feathers set aflame.

"You must honor me with your company at supper. Please, do not say no. You've denied me the last three times-"

"Lady Kinley, a bit of cake, perhaps? Some fruit? Champagne?"

Ignoring them, Ivy wiggled her toes, resisting the urge to pour champagne over the head of the man foolish enough to suggest more champagne. Maintaining a bland smile meant she was about to chew the insides of her cheeks raw. Lord, but these new slippers were a dreadful torture. She should make her way to the ladies' retiring salon to slip them off while the musicians took a moment to retune their instruments and the Tremayne Twins demonstrated how singing might possibly net one a husband.

A smile twitched the corner of Ivy's lip. What a perfect excuse to escape this madness. Even Sara would not suspect. Yes...she should do just that. After all, what choice did she have? Wait to be slaughtered by Ravenswood? Oh! What was she thinking, coming to this ball? Knowing the danger, knowing the earl would most likely attend, she should not have come tonight. She could not say why she had.

But that wasn't true. Curiosity and a perverse desire for punishment demanded attendance. Sooner or later, they would encounter one another. It was far better to face the man in this theater of war, where polite murmurs and courteous battle wounds could be exchanged in a civilized manner. At least in this setting Sara provided a shield against any unexpected assaults.

Only now, stomach roiling, hands sweating inside elbow-high silk gloves, Ivy wished she'd heeded her vastly intelligent inner voice. Her scar tingled where the silk clung to the moist surface of her palm and she resisted the urge to scratch it. Yes, she should have stayed home.

Someone pressed a second glass of champagne upon her. *Imbecile.* In a single fluid motion, Ivy's hands rose high, only to find both goblets snatched away.

Giving the glasses to a passing servant, Sara shook her head, frowning in amused exasperation while Ivy shrugged. To see the Pack scatter, yelps of confusion at the unexpected soaking would have been a welcomed distraction and a missed opportunity to disappear in the confusion.

"You are truly dazzling tonight, Lady Kinley." Lord Christopher Andry leaned in. "Prettier than the exquisite butterfly I only recently discovered."

Freshly graduated from Oxford, Christopher often floundered in painful shyness. It receded if the conversation turned to a scientific explanation of some unfortunate winged insect he'd captured and preserved under glass, stabbed into place with an ivory headed pin. Tonight, emboldened by champagne and a few tumblers of brandy, his hands barely trembled as he smoothed back his pale blond hair.

"What's this?" Sir Oliver Batten's smile lay partially concealed beneath a mustache of graying brown. "Andry is giving compliments instead of dissertations on a ghastly beetle collection. What's gotten into you, sir?"

"Half a bottle of champagne, I suspect." Monvair stroked the dark goatee lending a rakish flair to his thin features. A few chuckled at his dry humor while Christopher flashed the Frenchman a baleful glare.

"Lord Andry, we shall have a splendid time discussing this latest find over dinner." Ivy touched the crook of Christopher's arm before easing away. She'd grown much wiser during the course of this second season, and managing squabbling, jealous men now came as second nature. A shame she became so proficient after destroying one man with so little effort.

The others groaned while Christopher lit up like a firefly.

Although she returned his smile, Ivy intended on escaping long before the announcement of the midnight dinner. To give the impression one was favored over others was unwise, even if she held a soft spot for Christopher. He reminded her of Timothy before things went so dreadfully wrong, before Timothy decided she owed him more than her friendship.

Some manner of disturbance was causing a flurry of activity across the ballroom. It drew the attention of the crowd past the edge of the Pack as two men stalked toward the elevated terrace; an undulating sea of expectant faces bobbing behind the one in the lead.

Ivy's smile froze. Sara unceremoniously pushed past Christopher to take her hand, giving it a quick squeeze of encouragement as the Pack launched into a new squabble over who might procure fresh champagne for the ladies.

"He's coming," Sara whispered. "Dear God. I may be ill."

"Don't you even dare, Sara Morgan." Ivy was surprisingly calm. Her executioner *was* coming. He did not carry an axe, but the result would be the same. "One of us must keep our wits, and our heads, about us." Was it too late to escape? If only she possessed the strength to pry her fingers from Sara's grip. There must be a way to break through those damn terrace doors...with or without the key from Lady Sheffield's hefty bosom.

Sara's brilliant smile flashed from behind clenched teeth. *"We will not be ill!"*

"You're hardly convincing when you've turned a ghastly shade of chartreuse. I've seen that color once before. Came across Lord Paulson tossing his biscuits at the Searcy party a month ago. He lost a fortune at the hazard tables and I overheard him moaning how he'd ever explain it to his father and -"

"Shhh!" Sara's face took on an even greener cast. "You're only making it worse. Why are you suddenly so calm?"

Ivy almost laughed at that. Her? Calm? Oh, she was far from that. The nightmares suffered since news of Ravenswood's return swept through London were coming true. Ivy knew she should move quickly in the opposite direction and yet, a bizarre urge to see the approaching menace seized her. Gripping Sara's shoulder with one hand to maintain her balance, she lifted up the slightest bit on her tiptoes. And immediately sank back down, shivering, the breath squeezed from her lungs.

The man towered over those around him. Only the Earl of Bentley, almost lockstep beside him, possessed a similar height. *Oh God.* Sebastian Cain was terrifying. And brutal. A warrior hacking through bodies of vanquished mortals to reach his battle prize, the crowd falling to pieces behind him.

She was that prize. A sacrifice of blood in exchange for Timothy's young life. The sounds of the ballroom faded and an icy rivulet of sweat trickled down Ivy's spine to settle in the hollow of her back. She was definitely not calm.

"Damn Timothy Garrett," Sara whispered fiercely. "Damn him!"

Ordinarily, Ivy interjected. *"Have mercy for him,"* she would say, pleading for compassion. A prayer would be whispered for the charming, pleasant young man she once considered her friend, a hope his tortured soul found peace despite his sad, desperate actions.

Now, Ivy nodded in silent agreement.

Ravenswood was overwhelmingly male, all wide shoulders and lean muscles. He appeared to have no need for discreet padding to aid his form. In fact, it was indecent, the manner in which the elegant clothing clung to his body, stretching but snug in all the appropriate places. Realizing the path of her gaze, Ivy jerked her eyes back up, her cheeks on fire. The stark simplicity of his masculinity made every other gentleman seem a bit foppish by comparison. And his eyes...Good Lord. They were piercing and hot, glimmering silver with promises of sin and dangerous pleasures. And revenge. This man...he'd seen things. Done wicked things. Even in her innocence, Ivy recognized the sensuality burning within him like a lit flame.

Unwelcome memories from seven years prior rose in her mind. Enveloped by girlish purity and despairing grief, Ivy failed to recognize the young lord's splendid attractiveness that day in her father's drawing room. She noted it now. Despite her panic, it was impossible to ignore his devastating handsomeness. Thick ebony colored hair curled in ruffled waves against the tall collar of his black, cutaway evening coat. Lightly bronzed angular features were a study in rugged, male perfection, defined by high cheekbones and a bold nose. The square line of his jaw was fascinating, for although clean-shaven, the barest hint of a shadow lent a rakish air. He seemed immune to the women of varying ages trailing in his wake, many of them giggling and whispering, sometimes shoving to get closer.

He was danger incarnate. A predator who would think nothing of devouring her alive. He would wipe his mouth, lick his fingers and thank her for providing his breakfast. A sinful creature whose days surely began with a feast of virgins. Self-preservation screamed at Ivy to run, to get as far away as possible, but she found it *impossible* to move. Every muscle in her body ignored the mental commands to skitter out of harm's way.

Ivy swallowed past a lump of nausea. "Sara, I am terrified. What should I do?"

Sara blinked. "Now, I'm truly worried. I've never known you

to be afraid of anything so I can only tell you to have courage, darling."

Courage? Ivy possessed not an ounce of it so she formed a desperate strategy. Should she fail to acknowledge Ravenswood, perhaps he would do the same. They could slip past one another, each pretending the other did not exist. Remembering the devastating cut inflicted by Lady Garrett last week, a helpless sound, somewhere between a giggle and a sob, escaped her. Surprisingly, it drew a sharp eye from Brandon, and for a long moment, he considered her before resuming a disagreement with Christopher that *he* would most certainly accompany the countess into the midnight supper.

Ivy's jaw tilted. She must brazen this particular encounter out. Pray the earl held no interest in her. Gripping Sara's hand tighter, her gaze fixed on the musicians' loft. She could survive this and him. She must.

FIFTEEN MINUTES BEFORE, RAVENSWOOD AND THE EARL OF Bentley stepped into the Sheffield Ballroom, their progress delayed by several guests determined in their quest to personally welcome Sebastian back on English soil.

"Which one is she?"

"Oh, I forgot you've not been introduced," Alan grinned. "It won't be difficult to spot her. She's an uncommonly beautiful girl. Dazzling, actually."

"I've met her before. Just after Kinley lost his wife. A disagreeable chit with the manners of a sailor, frizzy brown hair and a face splattered with freckles." Sebastian's gaze dissected every female he saw. Young, old, plump, thin, some desirable, some not. Half possessed the plain brown hair of his memory. "And she was overweight."

Alan's eyebrow rose. "Freckles and fat? It is not possible we speak of the same Lady Ivy Elizabeth Kinley."

"Plump," Sebastian grumbled, accepting a snifter of brandy from a passing servant. "She was plump. I think. It's difficult to say. I believe her clothing was stolen from a stable boy. An overweight, filthy stable boy to be precise. Damnit, Bentley, at the very least, tell me what to search for now."

"You'll know her when you see her. Here now, I'll take pity on you. Look for an unusually high number of men accumulated in one spot, with two beautiful ladies at the center. However, the lovely, petite blonde who is surely with Lady Kinley has captured my interest, so I'll thank you to spare her in the carnage."

Sebastian scowled. "There must be three hundred guests crammed into this damned ballroom. What constitutes an abnormally high number of fools gathered around one woman?"

"Two women," Alan chuckled, giving Sebastian a friendly punch to the shoulder. "As we will soon join those fools, you might refrain from the derogatory characterizations."

With a snort of disgust, Sebastian scanned the room again. Only this time his gaze crashed to an abrupt halt. *There.* Across the swamped ballroom. It must be her. Standing on tiptoes, balancing herself with a hand on a blonde girl's shoulder, she surveyed the room in the same manner he did. Her eyes swept over Sebastian, halting for the briefest moment as their stares locked, and it felt as though a hundred, crushing jolts of lightning streaked through him. In absent disbelief, he rubbed the vicinity of his chest. It was her.

His prey.

What in the name of holy hell had become of the ungainly, awkward, neither pretty nor ugly child from seven short years before? This girl, this vision of absolute beauty, bore no resemblance to her. None whatsoever.

The discovery leveled Sebastian. He felt cheated. And holy hell...those could not be...were those damned *angels* singing? Lilting, beautiful...a chorus of melodic voices possessing the power to bring grown men to tears. Was it real? Or merely in his head?

No, thank God, not real angels. Just Lady Tremayne's pair of husband-hunting daughters providing a soaring a cappella performance while the musicians indulged in a short reprieve.

"Ah, you've found her." Alan's tone dripped with such sly amusement Sebastian realized he knew all along just where the countess stood in the crowded ballroom. "Well? What do you think?"

Think? Thinking was impossible. Sebastian could only feel, and what he felt must not be uttered aloud. It was too brutal, involved several crimes against God and Her Majesty's Crown - and all necessary for the ruination of a countess. And highly pleasurable for the man cruel enough to implement them.

Men swarmed about her, glazed adoration stamped on their features. Like drones surrounding a queen bee, their bodies clad in varying shades of colorful brocades and satins, they buzzed in a futile hunt for prime positions.

It was unfair to compare her to such an unworthy creature as a bee. Maybe a butterfly was a better analogy, or perhaps an exotic bird, beautiful and delicate, ready to flutter away at any moment. Fury sizzled through his veins but Sebastian welcomed it. It clarified his vision, sharpened things. God, her exquisiteness must have overwhelmed Timothy. No wonder his poor cousin succumbed to madness.

While Sebastian clenched his teeth, the angelic chorus created by the Tremayne Twins rose and fell as a backdrop. Damn, the girl positively glowed, like a flash of sunshine in a tawdry ocean of the artificial, her gown the palest blush hue, the exact shade of a red rose petal before it begins to fade to cream. He did not usually apply flowery tributes to women, no matter their attractiveness. It was difficult business to wring a compliment from the Earl of Ravenswood's lips; worshipping this girl in a moment of weakness made his anger swell to dangerous heights. What the hell was wrong with him? His particular brand of cold-blooded vengeance required unemotional reasoning and he'd never any trouble yielding it before. At least until now.

"Damnable Pack," Alan muttered beside him.

Sebastian was spoiling for a fight. The heat of it smoldered in the pit of his stomach, contracting with a violent need to confront the countess. He tore his gaze from the sunlight radiating on the upper terrace of the ballroom, finding it difficult to reconcile she was indeed his target. She required only a halo and a damned pair of wings to complete the illusion of absolute purity.

He felt dizzy. Off balance

"Why do you say that?" He pinned Alan with a penetrating stare. It sounded as if his old friend believed those men to be wholly responsible for the fashioning of the vain creature standing in their midst.

"Never mind." Alan swallowed back any further oaths.

Sebastian was hardly ignorant of Society's charming label for Lady Kinley's devoted band of followers, having learned of it upon his return to England. The knowledge Timothy participated in the sordid affair was infuriating. His jaw set at a grim angle, Sebastian made his way toward the countess, Alan falling lockstep beside him.

"Do try not to frighten off Lady Morgan, will you?" His friend's murmur was sarcasm at its best.

Sebastian managed a terse nod of agreement.

A mythical Pied Piper, he led the growing crowd. Upon guessing his intent, they now flowed in his wake, a herd of bleating, mindless sheep.

Sebastian considered the young woman standing beside the countess. Alan seemed quite smitten with Lady Sara Morgan and she was certainly a beauty. Her family was well thought of, the young lady herself described as kind and gentle. Sebastian found it perplexing she should befriend the likes of Ivy Kinley. His sources were quick to note the two girls' devotion to one another, their friendship dating back finishing school.

To the countess's left stood a dark blonde gentleman. Brandon Madsen, Viscount of Basford, considered himself the forerunner for Ivy's hand. Sebastian wondered how disappointed the man might be when her ruination was complete. The viscount appreciated the appeal of a fallen woman, doing his best to keep them occupied, although in the most secret of fashions. Quite a bit of the Basford inheritance was expended cleaning up behind the viscount and his pleasures.

Upon reaching the terrace, Sebastian did the opposite of what was expected. He promptly directed his attention to Sara as she yanked her hand from Ivy's tight grasp. Alan gave an exasperated shake of his head and politely greeted the countess.

"Lady Morgan." Sebastian brushed an impersonal kiss across Sara's gloved knuckles. "Lord Bentley's claims of your beauty have not been exaggerated."

Sara dipped a quick curtsy. "Such kind words, Lord Ravenswood."

"The truth is not always kind, but in your case, Lady Morgan, it is wonderfully so." He kissed her hand again before allowing her fingers to slide from his.

The moment Sebastian released Sara, Alan brushed past him. Placing his own kiss to her gloved fingers, Alan pulled her to him and that tiny bit of space enabled a different man to slip next to Lady Kinley.

Sebastian's gaze swept over his target, two gentlemen now flanking her sides. Like palace sentinels, they watched with mistrustful eyes while Ivy stood so rigid between them a slight breeze might snap her in half.

She studied the orchestra's loft with great intent. Indeed, her eyes traveled everywhere other than his direction. When she tired of staring at the musicians as they settled into their seats, her gaze drifted to various members of the Pack. Sebastian frowned. Should he be irritated or gratified? Was she frightened to death or *ignoring* him? She dare not snub him, not when half the ballroom just followed him to her feet. No. She was unquestionably terrified. An excellent start to things. She must be quivering with dread, although truthfully, she seemed merely disinterested by his presence.

Half the ballroom followed you to her feet... Sebastian's smile froze. *Goddamnit.*

In the haste to launch the first volley, he committed a grave misstep. He bloody well sought her out, like every other fool gathered so hopefully in this corner of the ballroom.

Basford leaned into Ivy, speaking low in her ear, his gaze locked on Sebastian. Sebastian ignored the viscount's challenging air, choosing instead to join Alan as he engaged Sara in casual banter. This allowed him to study Ivy and he took full advantage of the opportunity.

The top of her head would only reach the center of his chest should they stand face to face. It irritated him that she was not plump. Instead, she was lushly slender, with skin the color of cream roses, her cheeks the exact blush shade of her gown. The faintest of freckles lay scattered across her straight nose.

Sebastian nearly snorted aloud in disgust. Any other woman would move heaven and earth to be rid of that gold dusting. At the very least, she should pat her face with rice powder to conceal their existence. How could she appear sweeter with those freckles rather than hopelessly blemished?

Pinpointing her based on hair color alone would have given him a devil of a time. It was not the mousy brown of his memory, but a gloriously thick mass of chestnut, rich and glossy, brimming with hints of golden sunshine. Twisted into a stylish tumble, one silky ribbon of a curl trailed over a bare shoulder to grace the top of her décolletage.

And sweet fires of Hell, Ivy Kinley was blessed with curves no woman had a right to possess; all intriguing hollows and bends created for a man's pleasure. Sebastian's hand itched to touch the dip of her lower back, where the skirt of her gown flared away from a tiny waist. The modestly low bodice of the dress seemed to have no need for the additional padding some ladies used to enhance nature's gifts. Her breasts mounded above the neckline, tempting morsels he wanted suddenly to trace with his tongue. He

35

wanted to push that neckline down, to expose her. Taste her. Claim her.

It felt as if bonfires were lit all around him. Sebastian wondered if he could be the only one suffering the overwhelming, sweltering heat of the room. Was sweat beading up on his brow?

Viscount Basford touched the countess's elbow, a possessive brush of his hand she did not seem to mind. She smiled, her gaze shifting to Sebastian before darting away.

Sebastian's focus narrowed to a pinpoint. Everyone and everything faded until only Ivy stood before him. The other guests, the music, the sights, all sounds bleached into the background. There was only *her* and the unexpected flashing image of the countess pleasuring *him,* that beautifully full mouth wrapped about *his* erection, skimming up *his* naked body until their lips met in a heated kiss. The images searing his brain dazed him. Did other men contemplate similar fantasies? He almost could not *breathe* from the heat suffocating him.

A muscle ticked in his jaw, his glare turning to one of condemnatory fury. Of course, they did. They must be insane and blind if they did not. The girl was a contradictory mix of innocence and wickedness; judging from the disdainful tilt of her chin, she knew her power and gloried in it. Just when Sebastian thought she might be immune to the lightning crackling between them, the countess made an inarticulate sound and shifted her feet.

The countess was no humble bee. Far from it. She *was* a butterfly. Exquisite and bright, surrounded by male prowess and anxious to escape. To be elsewhere. These men hunting her could not capture or tame such beauty without crushing her wings beyond all repair.

But he would.

The Pack chattered on, oblivious to Ivy's discomfort. Sara and Bentley were so immersed in one another the earth might crack apart to swallow them whole with neither giving a murmur of protest. Lady Kinley's edginess was detectable only by him and Sebastian felt a small measure of his control easing back into his body, his blood cooling the tiniest bit. Enough so he felt more like himself, anyway.

He could seize her by the elbow, if he wished. Drag her from the guard dogs stationed at her flanks. While Sebastian contemplated the possibilities, that silly fop of a Frenchman nearly buried himself in the curve of her neck. Ivy's head inclined toward the count, eyelashes sweeping down.

Monvair's whisper went on and on. *Good God, what the hell is the bastard saying to take such a ridiculous amount of time?* A mysterious half-smile played across Ivy's rose hued lips, and her eyes, those huge, aqua colored eyes, smoldered. Any rational man, seeing her lips caught between her teeth to suppress a gasp, seeing those creamy cheeks blushing a particular shade of pink, might envision the countess sprawled across his bed. Flushed with desire, biting back cries, writhing. Moaning for more and more...

Sebastian wanted like hell to be the one providing that pleasure... He'd give her more. More than she'd ever had in her life, and he'd make damn sure she crawled back to him, begging for even more than that...

Again, Ivy glanced his way and averted her eyes, the turquoise depths flashing with something that would have looked like shy curiosity on any other woman. On her though - it was a blatant invitation. A tiny smile lifted the corner of her lips.

Something murderous flared within Sebastian. Something never experienced before. Something twisted and confusing. A flash of uncertainty he did not like.

"What is so damned amusing, Lady Kinley?"

The crack of his voice split through the chatter. The Pack, as one entity, turned to stare. While they gathering themselves, bristling and growling, Sebastian bared his own wolfish smile. Did this little viper of a countess require pups as protection?

Ivy's startled gaze flickered to him. "A private comment, my lord."

The emotions passing over her features was akin to a curtain falling at a theater play only to rise for the following act. Sebastian saw all her thoughts - revealed in those few transparent seconds. She'd been waiting for him, preparing herself. She would fight, regardless of the cost. And she was both terrified and excited to pay the price and play his game.

"I assume I am the subject." His hands flexed into fists, itching to smash into Monvair's nose when the man, with staggering audacity, grinned at him.

Ivy assessed him. "How you must despise hearing you are wrong."

"Do you believe the truth will offend me?" Based on Monvair's smugness, Sebastian knew the answer.

"The truth should never offend, my lord."

"Which can only mean you won't tell me."

"No." She smiled at his persistence. "Among friends, truthfulness is appreciated however…"

"We've not been formally introduced, is that it?" He interrupted with a slight bow. Her eyes were more intense than he remembered. Framed with long, lushly dark sable lashes, they contained a myriad of aqua swirls and flashes of deep gold deep. The full force of her beauty was enough to bring him to his knees. Now. Now, he finally understood Timothy's obsession. Ivy Kinley was a dazzling thing. A force to reckon with. When she arched a brow of dark chestnut, battle lines were officially drawn.

"We were formally introduced once before, Lord Ravenswood. It's foolish to believe that meeting in my father's drawing room is scored as permanently upon your memory as it is on mine." Even with its dagger's edge of sarcasm, her voice was husky and sweet, that distant smile surely reserved for the most persistent of suitors. "You forgot it, and me, before the end of that day."

Reaching out, Sebastian captured Ivy's gloved hand. His mouth hovered above her wrist before pressing a light kiss to her silk-encased fingers. She nearly shrank away before stilling the involuntary reaction.

"It would be reckless to forget someone like you." *Of course, I remember you. I've come to destroy you.* Cupping Ivy's elbow where the edge of the glove surrendered to bare skin, he inched her away from the dubious protection of the Pack. It was a calculated move, easily mistaken as a conciliatory gesture when she allowed it. "But then, you were merely a child. Graced with an innocence only the young possess and unable to do any real harm. Thank God."

Viscount Basford stared in stunned amazement, his attempt to drag Ivy back to safety stymied by her two raised fingers.

"Such a sad occasion your visit warranted that afternoon, Lord Ravenswood. My hope is you forgave any disrespect I exhibited in my grief. It was not intentional."

An image of dirty boots scraping against an expensive carpet flashed in Sebastian's mind, and when Ivy's face flushed a guilty pink, both realized they shared the same memory. How extraordinary.

"I forgave you." he purred, tugging her even closer. *I've forgiven nothing, Ivy Kinley…you don't deserve it.*

"Children are rarely noteworthy, but I was horrid." Ivy's voice was thin, but she stood her ground. "I pray I am unrecognizable today."

Seeing how much he unnerved her, Sebastian tightened his grip. Lady Morgan glanced at Ivy often, as if reassuring herself the countess stood whole and unharmed. The strains of another waltz drifted in the air, but it resonated with a muted tone. The musicians leaned forward on the railing with conspicuous nonchalance, watching the two combatants face off on the elegant expanse of the ballroom battlefield below.

"I would recognize you anywhere, Countess." It was vulgar to address her in such a manner, but the way her title rolled off his tongue gave it the cadence of both curse and endearment. He liked saying it. As if he both loathed and loved her and whatever emotion leaked out in the utterance of that word hinged on his whim at the moment.

Sara, her cheeks a distinct shade of white, edged closer. Did she think to rescue Ivy? If so, that was a pity. Sebastian was not yet ready to let her go. His smile was ruthless. "You see, Timothy's descriptions of your beauty, and your character, were quite exact in detail."

Timothy's final correspondence sought a loan to purchase his own lodgings; no reason behind the abrupt request, just an entreaty Sebastian failed to answer. His cousin's letters had slowly disintegrated until they were little more than rambling, petulant demands for greater allowances from the trust Sebastian managed on his behalf. During the last year of his life, the funds supported far more of Timothy's fondness for brandy, gambling and the high-priced whores at Madam Trudy's. He'd never mentioned Lady Kinley in his communications, however Sebastian was not beyond using a lie to his advantage.

Ivy gasped as the meaning of his words began to make sense.

Her involuntary sound drew immediate results. Alan swung about, brown eyes snapping. His muttered curse sounded suspiciously similar to a hasty plan of wringing his friend's neck. Howls rose from members of the Pack, passionate vows of defense for the countess tumbling forth in a heated muddle. Guests crushed forward like early morning hagglers at a fishmonger's stall. Two elderly women shoved through the crowd as if intent on refereeing the confrontation.

"Better than attending Drury Lane." One, crowned with an old-fashioned purple turban and wobbling against the uncertain support of a mahogany cane, chortled in delight.

"Ha! Better than Hadderly's last week!" The second woman elbowed Purple Turban aside in a particularly rough maneuver.

"See here, Ravenswood!" Monvair sputtered. Outrage thickened his accent, the silver buttons on the sapphire and fuchsia waistcoat strained to the point of bursting. His attempt to wedge between Sebastian and Ivy resulted in an encounter with young Lord Applegate, bristling with the same gallant intent. The two men crashed, bounced off in opposite directions, then reeled back together, gripping each other's arms in an awkward dance to maintain their balance. Gales of laughter swept the crowd.

Realizing the two men could collided with them, Sebastian released Ivy, muttering beneath his breath, "Bloody, fucking brilliant. A brawl ..."

"Outrageous!" Lord Batten's thick mustache quaked with the indignation of an irritated walrus, having overheard Sebastian's curse and he searched for a waiter to hand off his champagne, ready to join the fray should a full-fledged melee ensue.

Basford waited until Ivy was behind him before saying, "Ravenswood, your words are cruel. Hardly those of a gentleman." The declaration provided reason aplenty for a predawn gathering on a misty field in Regent Park. A few young women whispered of the viscount's courageous stand. Monvair and Applegate still grappled with one another, an unfair contest as the Frenchman was most concerned for his new waistcoat's survival.

Sebastian's eyes narrowed in cold warning. His mouth stretched into a hard line, transforming his features into a veneer of untainted emotion. Even the candles ringing the room seemed to dim, cowering before a man whose eyes flamed brighter than any light they could produce. Any gentleman eager to defend the countess was subjected to a brutal measurement. One by one, exposed to unflinching scrutiny by such a dangerous antagonist, each man deflated.

Lady Kinley was unworthy of the reckless devotion shown by these irrational men. Frustrated rage suffused Sebastian. Especially since she'd sidled out of arm's reach.

"It is no secret the lady and I share a mutual association by way of my cousin. All in the past, of course, circumstances being what they are. We are all aware Timothy is deceased." *Because of you...Poison Ivy.* The accusation hung, heavy, unspoken while Sebastian's gaze, hard and unapologetic, flickered to the countess.

She did not seem prepared for war after all. One little skirmish and she folded with astonishing haste. Her wide eyes reminded him of a panicked doe, a wounded shimmer in the aqua depths. Her bottom lip visibly trembled. Incredibly, *infuriatingly*, Sebastian wanted to press his mouth to hers to tame its lush quiver.

Goddamn, he'd forfeit his soul to taste the skin of that delicate collarbone, the nape of her neck, the soft underside of her breast... to soothe the hurt he just inflicted.

A tear slid down Ivy's cheek, its significance elusive to Sebastian, but the crowd hushed, the Pack gawking with such astonishment he wondered if wings were unexpectedly sprouting from the countess's back. Murmurs slowly built, rising until a deafening crescendo buffeted from all sides. Snippets of disbelief were already racing from one end of the ballroom to the other. Monvair and Applegate's half-hearted tussle came to an abrupt halt, each staring at the countess.

"She's crying..."

"Wouldn't believe it, had I not seen it myself."

"My God, did you hear what he said to her?"

"That sharp tongue failed her at last."

Basford bristled with fresh anger, to the point he practically vibrated. "I *cannot* allow this repulsive cruelty to continue, Ravenswood. This assassination of Lady Kinley -"

"- is none of your affair, Basford," Sebastian murmured, his eyes fixed on Ivy's face. One deceitful tear streaked down her pale cheek like a raindrop on glass. He tried not to let it stir him.

"But sir, you... this...." Christopher interjected, stuttering until Sebastian flicked him a cold stare.

Christopher's mouth slammed shut so fast and so hard, his teeth clicked.

Men grumbled along the edges of the group, their blind loyalty infuriating Sebastian beyond all comprehension. Like hyenas plotting to steal a fresh kill from a lion, they surrounded him. But he knew how to handle scavengers. No one would snatch this lady from between his paws.

"Kingsley?" Sebastian swept the crowd with a contemptuous glare. For God's sake, Lord Kingsley was older than Ivy's own father. "Shall you intercede? Or perhaps you, Montrose? Cavat?"

Those unfortunate enough to be singled out clamped their lips tight.

"Lady Kinley was the very soul of kindness to Lord Garrett," Basford bit out. "She's an angel to have tolerated his…"

Sebastian swung toward the viscount with such ferocity a collective roar arose from the crowd. Then people pressed closer, making it impossible to separate the Pack from those who'd come simply to witness the slaughter.

"Stay out of it, Basford." Sebastian welcomed the opportunity to settle the issue in the oldest manner available to men, if the viscount wished to press matters.

"I- I've got som-something to- to say!" Christopher barreled forward, filled with fresh determination to waylay Lady Kinley's tormenter. Basford turned, intending to halt his progress, but Christopher had a belly-full of being the shy, butterfly-collecting gentleman. He shoved the viscount aside, sending him stumbling into a curious footman who'd wiggled through the crowd with a platter of champagne goblets.

Christopher desperately grabbed for the tray while Basford clutched the servant's coat in an attempt to retain his balance. The three men fumbled about as the first goblet bounced in slow motion and began to slide from the platter. In quick succession, forty others followed, creating a glorious golden waterfall of champagne and glass. Basford collapsed in an ignoble heap, the footman floundering atop of him. Christopher ended up with the tray, juggling it and two surviving goblets. He skidded forward on a thin sheet of spilled champagne until colliding with a heavy *"Oomph!"* against a much larger, solid wall of iron. The tray, two crystal goblets and one young gentleman hit marble flooring with an ear-shattering clatter.

Teeth clenched tight, Sebastian reached down, hauling Christopher to his feet, ignoring the man's profuse apologies.

Bedlam erupted, with guests sidestepping splintered crystal, spilled champagne and a tangled heap of arms and legs comprised of the drenched Basford and a mortified footman. Numerous servants added to the chaos, darting here and there to blot frantically at splattered silks and satins. Someone finally extended a hand to Basford while Sebastian did the same to the footman. Muttering a slew of unintelligible curses, shaking off pieces of glass, the viscount glared at Ravenswood as though he were to blame for the entire disaster.

Sebastian searched for Ivy. She must have dodged the worst of it, no doubt pleased with the turmoil, those false tears quick to dry. Hell, if she wasn't doubled over with laughter, he'd be vastly disappointed. But, she was not in within the Pack's protective circle, nor at the edge of the boisterous throng. Fists clenching, he recalled Veronica's words; in sudden, vivid clarity, they burned his brain - *"In the midst of all that, Lady Kinley simply vanished..."*

His prey had flitted away like an elusive butterfly. Lady Sara Morgan was gone too. Catching Alan's eye, his friend gave an apologetic lift of his shoulders, and an infuriating thought struck Sebastian. Should Ivy find anything entertaining about this initial confrontation, it would not be Basford dropping like a stone, champagne spilling or even bumbling fools knocking one another senseless in romantic charges to her defense. It would be the effortless manner in which she won this skirmish. With the shedding of a tear.

He, the bloody Earl of Ravenswood, defeated by a single, glittering tear. In the space of a *bloody* half hour, she had gained the upper hand. In a game for which he made the rules.

CHAPTER 3

*W*hen a crash and roars of laughter sounded behind them, neither girl paused to witness the distraction. Sara pushed Ivy through a set of doors leading to the foyer and eased them shut. A quick glance about the hall confirmed they were alone. "Go, Ivy. Now, while Ravenswood's attention is elsewhere. Lord Bentley will delay him further, but you must leave before anyone realizes you've gone. Saints help us," Sara giggled. "I thought Bentley might actually throw you over his shoulder to carry you to safety."

Ivy gave her a fierce squeeze of gratitude. "I cannot leave you behind. What if…"

"Never mind me. I can handle myself, you know that." Sara tilted Ivy a rueful smile. "Who would have guessed Ravenswood could be so ruthless? I should have listened to you and allowed you to escape before he confronted you. Now, go. Quickly, before he comes searching for you. Do not stop for anyone." She blew Ivy a kiss and with a mischievous smile, returned to the ballroom through the same doors. A key turned in the lock with a soft, decisive click.

Ivy almost grinned as she hurried down the wide foyer. Should

45

Ravenswood try to follow her through that door, he'd find the way thwarted by a clever Sara. And later, the Sheffield staff would locate a key in the most unlikely of places. Either an urn or a window sash, if they found it at all. Knowing Sara, she'd simply take the key with her.

Collecting her cloak, Ivy thanked the two attending maids in the calmest of manners so that her departure would not attract unwanted attention. By the time she entered the expansive court-yard of the Sheffield mansion, her heart thumped so hard and fast she was dizzy.

More than two hundred conveyances waited patiently for their charges, a hopeless crush, but the Kinley coach stood near the front of the que. Once inside the dark confines of the coach, Ivy choked on a hysterical laugh. Her poor servants, she thought, recalling the alarm on the footman's face as he handed her up into the vehicle. She probably frightened them half to death, the way she rushed forward, pleading to be taken home immediately.

Oh…what was she to do? Ravenswood had returned. The earl's self-imposed exile from English soil was over. Because of her. He sought her out, taunted her, then with disgusting ease, left her in pieces. Lacerated by his cruel barbs.

With hands that shook, Ivy stripped off her white gloves. As the coach clattered along London's uneven streets, she stared at the half-healed puckered scar slicing her left hand into halves. Beginning in the valley between thumb and forefinger, a faint, blush-pink road tracked the hill of her palm before dipping to the paper-thin skin just above her wrist.

Ten petite dashes of thread. Thread that once held the sliced edges of her flesh together. Thanks to her butler's skill with a needle, eventually only an ivory-hued slash would exist as a reminder of Timothy Garrett's betrayal. If only she could explain to Lord Ravenswood the events leading up to the tragedy. If only the earl might listen. If only he would *believe* her….

Common sense said he would not dare follow, but Ivy's stomach roiled with nauseating uncertainty. The lengths the man

46

might go to avenge Timothy's death were uncertain. Those ruthless gray eyes did not lie; the Earl of Ravenswood meant to destroy her. She'd be a fool to ignore the danger.

∽

IVY MADE HER WAY TO THE DINING ROOM, CURSING HER MISTAKE IN oversleeping. Considering the lack of bravery the previous night, she refused to cower in her room. If she were fortunate, her father would already be gone and about his business for the day, unaware of the encounter with Ravenswood.

A peek into the vast room confirmed her worries. Hidden behind a sheaf of freshly ironed morning papers, Jonathan Kinley sat at the head of a lengthy rosewood table, a steaming cup of tea at his elbow. He'd finished his breakfast and awaited her arrival.

With a deep breath, Ivy approached the side buffet. Thomas, one of the underbutlers, stepped forward to assist but she waved him away.

Once, long ago, she and her mother shared breakfast with the earl in this very room. Once, long ago, her father swept Ivy into his arms, tickling her until she squealed in delight. "You've sprouted overnight, like the weed you're named for!" Jonathan would bellow in laughter while his wife frowned in mock disapproval.

"Jonathan," the countess rebuked in her sweet, even-tempered manner, "it's most unseemly for Ivy to shriek in such a tone. And even more so for you to cast her so high in an attempt to touch the ceiling."

"But Mama, I can touch the sky if I want to! Papa says so!" Argumentative even at the tender age of four, she wrapped her arms around the earl's neck, begging to be tossed even higher while Jonathan whispered they'd best give Mama many kisses as a distraction. Dipping his daughter toward Caroline, Ivy gave the countess the sort of resounding smack on the cheek children give as kisses. Then the earl gave his own kiss to his wife, which caused Ivy to sigh with impatience because that kiss lasted much longer and involved whispers and soft laughter she did not understand.

It was that way for the first six years of Ivy's life until matters drastically changed. She never learned the exact details, but she recalled her mother mentioning "bad investments and creditors," and perhaps she shouldn't pester her father to play with her. The earl was very busy, Caroline explained.

At that age, Ivy did not know what bad investments and creditors were. She only knew that her father, upon whom the sun rose and set, and who always had a smile for her and her mother, became short-tempered and impatient. The earl had no time for either his daughter or his countess. There were no more afternoon picnics or quiet evenings spent fireside. He was absent on business more often than he was at Somerset and when she and her mother came to visit him in London, they were virtually ignored. Caroline was left to her own devices while Ivy drifted about the partially unfurnished townhouse like a little ghost.

For unexplained reasons, Ivy did not comment upon the disappearance of the furnishings and the lovely paintings. Even when her toys vanished, she said nothing. When several carriage horses and her favorite pony were suddenly absent from the Somerset stables, she dared not question that either, although she cried for weeks over the loss of Zeus, her smart little chestnut gelding.

On rare occasions, the family shared a meal, her father at one end of the huge table, her mother at the other. Since her nanny's discharge many months prior and the staff's operating at a bare minimum, Ivy often joined her parents rather than be banished to the nursery. She would sit perched in the middle, stiff and proper, a tiny buffer between two adults once madly in love but now only sharing an awkward kiss on the cheek upon entering or leaving a room. Caroline mustered encouraging smiles, but Ivy recognized every teardrop of her mother's silent anguish. Entire meals passed with Jonathan failing to acknowledge his lovely wife and daughter were even present.

This morning, Ivy wished her father would resume such habits.

She slid into a chair several places away as Jonathan laid aside the papers, his vivid blue gaze sweeping her. His frown contained a shadowy concern.

"So, Daughter. What have you to say for yourself?"

"Good morning, Father."

"Do not avoid the subject."

"I'm afraid I'm unaware of the subject," Ivy cheerfully retorted, accepting the cup of tea Thomas handed her.

At fifty-two years of age, her father was an attractive man, his full mane of chestnut hair streaked with gray and a face that had weathered well. Women, some hardly older than Ivy, still hoped to become his next countess. Why he never remarried, she did not know. She could only assume he had no interest in another's needs outside of his own.

"What is this business between you and Ravenswood? I've been told you spurned his suit."

She choked on a sip of tea. "His *what*?"

"The gossips say he wishes to court you."

"That is far from what that man wishes," Ivy muttered. The earl craved nothing less than an opportunity to rip her to shreds. His aunt's very public social cut was painful enough, but Ravenswood, oh, the man was a veritable master of the game. He truly slashed for blood.

Her laugh was scornful. "The situation was comically misconstrued, Father. It's true Ravenswood introduced himself, but he conversed with Sara far more than me." The blueberry scone she nibbled on gummed about her teeth and suddenly tasted as dry as a chunk of wood. It was stretching the truth, but the man *did* speak to Sara first.

Before launching his attack...

A strange light entered Jonathan's eyes. "They say you fled the ballroom. Sobbing, no less."

Why her father sounded so oddly protective was unfathomable. Ivy gave an unruffled façade of a shrug. "How absurd. *They* have an overactive imagination."

Her nerves trembled like leaves in a high wind. How foolish to react so impulsively to Ravenswood's barbs. If only she'd kept her wits about her. Flung a witty retort in his handsome face instead of fleeing. For God's sake, it was surely on everyone's lips this morning. *It's true! Poison Ivy weeping!*

"Perhaps you are right. I cannot imagine you shedding a tear in public. As to the matter of Ravenswood and his courtship," Jonathan shook a warning finger as Ivy gave him a blank stare. "Will you ruin it as you have the others?"

"Will you never stop these tragic attempts at matchmaking?"

"I suspect you've tipped that pretty nose of yours up at every eligible gentleman in London, including those I've *not* personally selected. If the earl deems you worthy of his attention, you will think twice before discouraging him." Jonathan's fingers drummed the chair arm while considering his mutinous daughter. "His is an excellent bloodline. And Ravenswood is hardly the worst of the lot. There was that unfortunate business with the Earl of Landon, but men do foolish things when women are involved. I was friends with old Ravenswood and your mother was very fond of the countess."

"I was unaware you possessed friends." Another bite of scone promptly turned to sawdust in her mouth. "Just unfortunate souls you've taken advantage of."

Despite the taunting, Ivy's curiosity was aroused. Jonathan employed spies all over the country for various purposes. Should anyone be privy to the mystery of Sebastian Cain's flight from England four years before, her father would know the details. But there was little point in quizzing him. He would misconstrue it as a sign of her interest in the earl.

Ivy's head tilted. "And how would you know whom Mother was fond of? You rarely took note of her, except to check the profits of her estates. Or when it came time to pay the florist."

"Watch yourself, little miss."

Jonathan's voice trembled; whether from anger or shame, Ivy did not care. They were forever at cross-purposes, the chasm deep-

50

ening with each battle. Her father's chief interests were twofold - to see his daughter advantageously wed, and to increase his wealth and power beyond the obscene levels already attained. He would never understand her aversion to matrimony for he firmly believed in contracts and dowries and gains. He married Caroline for love, but her mother's estates proved a strong lure as well. In his view, love marched a distant second to position and power.

Following Timothy's death, Jonathan allowed Ivy to come and go as she wished. On occasion, she must answer his probing questions, but those inquisitions were shallow. Matters soon reverted to their previous state; her father away on estate business, mercifully absent and Ivy doing as she pleased with a blessed lack of supervision. His attempts at steering her toward marriage were strangely lacking these past eight months and Ivy imagined her whispered involvement in the scandal over Timothy's death cooled his enthusiasm. It appeared that reprieve was over.

She sipped her tea in silence. Her father believed she'd rejected many of England's most eligible bachelors, but if he knew how close she'd come to being married into the Ravenswood family, he would have stopped at nothing to make it a reality. Oh, he knew something occurred with Timothy; after all, it was the gossip of choice even now. It was impossible he could know the full extent of the matter, regardless the number of spies he employed. Neither she, Sara, nor Brody would ever speak of it.

Nor Timothy, for that matter.

"Maybe the tattlers have it wrong, but all the same, you shall not refuse his courtship." Jonathan's fist pounded the rosewood table in an unexpected burst of frustration. Delicate teacups clattered upon their saucers in noisy protest while from his post at the sideboard, Thomas slanted the earl a faintly exasperated stare. "Damn it, girl! You're nearing twenty years of age.... will you wind up an old maid to spite me?"

Ivy slid from her chair, gripping the back of it as if it were a necessary shield. "I have a dress fitting at Madam Jocelyn's this morning."

"Do you understand me, Ivy?" Jonathan scowled.

"Rest assured, Father, Ravenswood has no intentions of vying for my hand. His interests are far too bloodthirsty for such trivial matters."

Ivy swept from the room before Jonathan responded and upon entering the center hall, nearly collided with Brody. He carried a large bouquet of ivory-hued wild roses arranged with artful meticulousness in an expensive crystal vase.

"My lady, the lad delivering this informed me he could not, under any circumstances, have them refused. He proved so distraught, I had little choice but to accept." Brody's brow lifted in bemusement as he shifted the weight of the vase from one arm to the other. "Poor tyke. I wonder what manner of punishment he might have received if his mission failed."

Ivy grimaced in dismay. London's male population loved to send flowers and French bonbons to the opposite sex, especially to the women spurning their advances or to whom they offended in some way. During the final year Mother languished, her father had fresh roses delivered to her bedside every day. Even when he was away, the roses came without fail. Her mother adored them; the romantic blooms overflowed the grounds of Somerset Hall, the gardens inundated by them.

Ivy hated them.

They caused her head, and her heart, to hurt. She could barely stand to look at or smell them. But a crushing sense of betrayal swamped her anytime she considered having the flowers ripped out. She simply could not do it, knowing her mother's love for them.

"It's alright, Brody. There must be some way around this latest tactic of florists and foolish men."

Brody sniffed in agreement. "Shall I place them in the drawing room or the music room?"

"The music room, I suppose." Trailing behind, Ivy watched as he placed the vase atop a gleaming black pianoforte. The roses were flawless but uncultivated. Where exactly did one find wild roses in the heart of London?

"There is a card." The unconventional bouquet earned the servant's full disdain. "Should you care to read it, milady."

"If only to inform the gentleman not to bother in the future."

Brody reached into the flowers and drew back with a muttered curse. The square of creamy vellum fluttered to the floor.

"Whatever is the matter?" Ivy exclaimed in bewilderment as the butler examined his fingers. "Does a bee still make his home there?"

"Thorns, milady! They neglected to remove the thorns! It's fortunate you were not harmed by their stupidity."

Ivy inspected the damage; a few minor punctures to Brody's fingertips and a scratch across the top of his wrist. Dabbing at the drops of blood with a handkerchief tugged from his coat pocket, she said, "I'm sure it was an oversight."

Brody allowed her ministrations then took the cloth from her, muttering in agitation, "My best silk handkerchief. How the devil shall I get these stains out?"

Inside the envelope was a letter instead of the usual florist card. Ivy's gaze went to the scrawled signature. What bloody game was the man playing with her? Eyes narrowing, she unfolded the paper completely and began to read.

My dearest Countess,

Please accept these roses in humble apology for my abysmal behavior last night. In light of such boorish behavior, I cannot fault you for seeking to escape my company. Please understand had no desire to wound you. Although this is a paltry- and commonplace- offer of a treaty, it is one I offer just the same.

I shall call at two o'clock this afternoon to convey my sincerest apologies in person. If you wish not receive me, I will understand.

~ Ravenswood

The thorns were no mistake. They were a restrained cannonball in a burgeoning war. Her fists clenched with apprehension. Oh, this was going to get quite messy.

"An undesirable acquaintance, milady?" Brody asked, still disgruntled and now frantically blotting at the stains on his handkerchief with a cloth he'd found near the fireplace. "Obviously provincial, judging the manner in which he sent these roses. I wish to know the florist he used. I intend on sending a strongly worded letter. With your permission, of course."

"Undesirable, yes. Provincial, no." The delicate fragrance of the creamy blooms prompted memories of death and sorrow, stark reminders of her mother's illness and the long-standing rift with her father. "I don't believe he used a florist."

The roses were stunningly beautiful. There was something quite arresting about them, something intriguing. Perhaps because they were so different from what she typically received. As well as the manner received. Ivy almost smiled. "The Earl of Ravenswood wishes to call today. At two o'clock."

Brody's gray eyebrows flew upwards in disbelief. "The devil you say."

"The devil, indeed." How ingeniously the earl worded his challenge. He did not request permission; instead, he left the decision in her hands. If she refused, she'd be forced to act the coward, and he bloody well knew it. Ravenswood practically dared her not to receive him - a brilliant tactical move. One she might admire if it did not pose such impending danger. "I have no alternative but to accept."

"The scoundrel," Brody breathed in grudging admiration before continuing with precise briskness. "I shall remind your father of his club meeting this afternoon. Will you wish to receive Lord Ravenswood here? Or the front parlor?"

"This will be fine, Brody. Thank you." Ivy folded the letter, smiling when the butler chucked her under the chin. Such familiarity between servant and employer might be grounds for immediate dismissal in another household, but Brody enjoyed a highly trusted status.

"Do not fret, milady. I daresay His Lordship has met his match in you."

CHAPTER 4

*A*ntagonizing Ivy Kinley with such blatant animosity was a tactical blunder. And short-sighted. The path laid with such carelessness must be erased, and set again, this time with roses and persuasion. How could he claim victory if he hacked at her with such brutality? He must gain Ivy's trust and affection, all while maintaining distance. Not a drop of empathy for the countess was possible, not when her destruction was the goal.

Sebastian knew why things went awry. Her beauty caught him off-guard. She wore an air of sweet vulnerability like a warm cloak. Used to great effect, it made a man want to protect and shield her from all harm. She blinded him. For a moment. But, not now. Oh, not now. He knew what must be done, and he steeled his heart for the battle ahead.

He was prepared this time. She wouldn't see him coming until it was too late.

THE CLOCK STRUCK HALF-PAST TWO O'CLOCK WITH DUAL, SOLEMN

tones and along with it, the heavy notes of the Kinley House's door chimes echoed.

Standing on the front steps of the elegant townhome in Mayfair, Sebastian frowned when the doors did not swing open to admit him at once. Granted, he was a half hour late, but the butler should have been in attendance. There were the muffled sounds of footsteps moving away, the murmur of low voices from deeper within, and the tattoo of rapid, heavier footsteps hurrying toward the front of the home. They slowed to a measured pace, but several seconds passed before entrance was granted.

The very same Kinley butler from seven years before, now with a headful of silver hair and imperious eyebrows, bowed to him.

"Good afternoon, milord." Void of emotion, the man's tone was level, save for a curious, breathless quality to his voice. Sebastian did not know for what purpose, but the elderly butler had just raced to the end of the hall and back.

"Good afternoon." Handing over his card, Sebastian waited for him to move aside. For a good thirty seconds, the thick ebony square was silently studied and carefully examined as if it were evidence in a murder case.

Sebastian's brow creased.

"Very good, sir. I shall inform Lady Kinley you have... arrived." The slight pause indicated displeasure at Sebastian's tardiness, and without another word, the butler strode away, shoes clicking on the polished marble floor. Reaching a door at the far end of the spacious oval foyer, he gave the lightest of raps before swinging it open.

His boot steps deliberately silent, Sebastian moved into the foyer.

"My lady, His Lordship, the Earl of Ravenswood has arrived."

Music trickled from the room as the announcement went ignored. The butler repeated himself, louder and bit more dramatically.

"The earl?" Above the music, Lady Kinley sounded out of

breath. "Of Ravenswood? I'd forgotten he was to call, but I suppose you must show him in."

Standing in the center of the oversized magnificent foyer, surrounded by ornate, floor to ceiling columns, where masterpieces by the finest artists known to the civilized world adorned the walls, and priceless vases occupied solid marble display stands, Sebastian grinned with anticipation. Ivy's voice reeked of feigned boredom and disinterest.

So, she would play his little game after all.

"Milord, if it pleases you." Brody motioned for him to advance, stepping aside only when necessary to allow entrance to the music room.

Sebastian twisted to witness the wink the butler gave Ivy and her answering smile. In a repeat of seven years prior, his overcoat, hat, and gloves again went uncollected when he stood waiting like a commoner on the front steps. Now, he practically threw the items at the servant and with a tranquil smile, closed the door with a slow purpose in Brody's abruptly scowling face.

Alone with his adversary, his heartbeat accelerated with pleasant anticipation. Leaning his shoulders flush with the wood panels of the door, Sebastian watched her.

Ivy sat at pianoforte of gleaming ebony, staring at a piece of sheet music. She did not lift her eyes, and although prepared for it, her beauty struck Sebastian. Clad in a sage and cream gown, she was as light and cheery as England's emerging spring. The heart-shaped curve of her bodice dipped in a modest nod, revealing only the topmost swell of her breasts while a broad sash of pale lemon satin accentuated her tiny waist. Rather than a demure bun, a wealth of dark chestnut hair spilled down her back, almost touching the bow of the sash. Sunshine streaming through green and gold paneled drapes at the window caught her in shafts of light, illuminating all the honey colored tones in that beautiful hair. Without the romantic glow of the ballroom to lend a mysterious allure to her features, it was shocking to realize just how young the countess was. Ivy possessed the guise of a true innocent, an angel painted in a masterpiece, delicate and sweet, suddenly come to life.

Sebastian's lips tightened. He knew her *true* nature. This - *this scene*, staged for maximum effect, no doubt - marched in forceful contradiction to the truth.

He pushed off from the carved door, advancing with measured steps until he stood beside the bench. From this vantage point, he thought he could see her heart beating beneath the fabric of her dress. Ivy's breath quickened, but she still refused to lift her gaze. A strange sense of expectancy permeated the room. If only she dared peek up, it was possible the earth and everything in it might shatter.

"The roses are quite lovely in this room." *Look at me, damn you.*

"Hmmm. Thank you for sending the bouquet. It was very kind of you." Ivy's voice was soft but steady.

Where was the scathing wit of the woman in the reports he had received? This girl was too cowed to look at him. That challenging fire in her eyes last night must have been imagined.

Bach's *Italian Concerto Andante* flowed from the belly of the pianoforte, the notes echoing with a fitful melancholy. It reminded Sebastian of a funeral dirge. "I apologize for the delay in my arrival." He was too ruthless; he must gentle his approach after all. What a skittish little mouse she was.

"I did not remember you were coming." Ivy possessed all the sereneness of a nun during prayers, her fingers trailing over the keys. "Your tardiness is of little matter."

Sebastian's grin melted.

He itched to grab her shoulders. He wanted to shake her until she had no choice but to acknowledge him. He desperately wished to turn her over his knee and spank her little rump for the impudent manner she spoke to him just now. The salacious thought made his palm tingle.

"Terrible accident on Regent. I was forced to leave the carriage and make my way on foot. One can only hope my driver manages to find his way here before I must depart."

"I hope you have no trouble departing as well, my lord." The sly derision in Ivy's tone, hidden beneath a layer of unfailing politeness, drove him to distraction. "I'd hate for you to stay a moment longer, should you feel yourself unwelcomed."

Sebastian slid onto the bench beside her. It was large enough for two, but he spread his legs with deliberate intent, crowding her. With the pianoforte positioned close to a curved wall of windows, Ivy could not gracefully slip out the other side. Her fingers stilled on the keys when he pressed close enough to crush her skirts. It seemed an eternity, but finally, her eyes rose to clash with his. A scathing rebuke probably hovered on her lips, waiting to be issued with icy authority, but her mouth pulled into a thin line. He smiled at her veiled irritation, nudging her with his shoulder. "You must play exceptionally well."

"I beg your pardon?"

"You surely know this piece by heart, considering."

"Considering?"

He indicated the music holder. "The sheet music. It's upside down."

Ivy's fingers compressed into fists, dropping from the keys to her lap. "Do you play?" When Sebastian shook his head, her delicate chin tilted in the most stubborn gesture he'd ever witnessed on a female. "I've played since the age of four. I find this to be more challenging."

"How interesting." Her bravado was amusing even if her explanation was ridiculous. "I find the selection quite depressing for such a beautiful afternoon. Do you know something a bit more lighthearted?"

Just when he thought she might refuse, Ivy conceded with a stiff nod, launching into a lively concerto by Mozart. When necessary, she leaned across while Sebastian remained in his position with deliberate intent. He relished how her arm rubbed his, appreciative of the way her hair tumbled across her shoulders and down her back. A few of those glossy strands clung to his afternoon coat.

His close proximity flustered her. Each time she stretched to touch distant keys, Ivy chewed her bottom lip. Even if she was affecting him to the point of madness, he enjoyed her discomfort. The fragrance she wore, a questionable cross of oranges and lilies, teased his nose. He craved the opportunity to sink his hands into her hair. Would those unruly waves feel as silky as they looked? Would they wind about his fingers? Slide through his hands like heated honey? How many men had been entertained in this music room? How many sat on this same bench to gaze adoringly while she played? How proficient was she in other activities? Juxtaposed with this exquisite creature, the thoughts were ugly and black.

That her lovers' identities remained unknown was vexing. Whispered rumors and conjectures ran rampant, but thus far, no hard evidence existed to condemn anyone. The tight-lipped fools were surely the most loyal and discreet group of noblemen to ever grace English soil and Ivy's power ran deep to inspire such devoted silence. But he would unlock her secrets soon enough. With enough money and persuasion, it was possible to unearth any mystery.

Sebastian clapped with slow deliberateness at the end of the musical piece. Ivy's hands dropped to her lap, curling into fists again. Before he could set the tone of the conversation, she took control, eyes bright with caution.

"Why did you come here today, Lord Ravenswood?"

Damn, her skills at putting him on defense were impressive. The possibility she could possibly outwit him was most alarming.

"Do you receive so many bouquets you haven't time to read all the cards?" Sebastian teased. "According to society's guidelines, my intentions are quite clear."

"I read the card, after the tangling with the thorns."

"I'm sorry. Were you injured?" His satisfaction lurked behind a frown of concern. No doubt about it. The countess understood the subtleties of war, roses and thorns included.

Ivy blinked. "Oh, no, I was not hurt. However, Brody was quite vexed to come away with a handful of barbs. I'm afraid you've earned his displeasure for some time."

Sebastian hid the disappointment with an easy smile. "I prefer wild roses to those grown in such an orderly manner by the city's florists. And I tore London apart to find what I wanted. The woman from whom I purchased your roses thought me quite mad as I watched her cut each one from her own garden at an ungodly hour this morning. I confess I never understood this odd practice of shaving thorns off. After all, without its weapons, isn't a rose nothing more but an ordinary flower?" Leaning close, his voice a whisper of smooth velvet, he recited, *"Read in these roses the sad story, of my hard fate and your own glory. In the white, you may discover, the paleness of a fainting lover; in the red, flames still feeding, on my heart with fresh wounds bleeding."*

Ivy stared at him, wordless. All women, in Sebastian's vast experience, adored poetry and in particular, sonnets recited in homage to their beauty. It spun heads and possessed the power to shatter lingering resistance. The right one could pave the way to seduction and this bit of verse, Thomas Carew to be precise, was perfection. Destroying the existence of Ivy's splendor, and the *ton's* ability to wallow in it, was paramount to his plan. He'd have this countess's vain heart tattered, bleeding and devastated by the time he finished with her.

"I shan't keep them, you know." Ivy smiled, head tilting as if recognizing the strategic maneuver and contemplating her own.

"I beg your pardon?"

"You may beg it, but I probably shall not grant it." The smile continued to lift her lips. She found him amusing. "The roses. I never keep them."

"These you shall keep," he vowed.

"You don't understand. I never do."

"We shall see. I took the liberty of making a sizeable donation in your name to the church and to the orphanage you favor. As well as several other worthy institutions. You shall receive notes of gratitude in the following days." With his man, Gabriel Rose, on the lead, Sebastian had an extensive network toiling to provide such useful services and information. "On occasion, I shall give you gifts meant for you alone." He grinned suddenly. "Ah...unique gifts which cannot be given away. These will be things you will desire, I promise you."

Maybe it was foolish to think so, but the hypnotic tick-tocking of the clock seemed to count down the lowering of Ivy's defenses. Her body swayed, and Sebastian's blood spun into liquid fire as her perplexed gaze drifted to his mouth. Curses hung in his throat when her tongue darted out to moisten her upper lip. Bloody hell, ruining her was going to be tremendously enjoyable. But must she look so damn innocent, so clean and guiltless, he might dirty her just by touching her gown?

"Shall we call a truce, little butterfly?" Sebastian murmured, eyes lingering on the delectable fullness of her mouth. Should she lick her lips again, as a practiced seductress might, he'd take it as an invitation.

"A truce?" Ivy echoed with a soft breath. "We are not at war."

Maybe it was only nerves when she licked her top lip a second time, but as she caught the bottom one between her teeth, his eyes glittered with victory. She would not fight him. Sebastian leaned close until they were almost nose to nose. She was his. For the moment, at least, and he was dying for the first piece of her. The first taste.

"Aren't we? At war, that is?" It was the barest hint of a kiss, his mouth gently brushing her lower lip, but it ignited an unexpected blaze.

Ivy exploded off the bench as if fired from a cannon, her shoulder catching the underside of his chin. Things flew everywhere. Sheet music, a metronome, the candelabra...Sebastian...

He landed on his arse in an undignified heap of his own tangled limbs.

"Oh, dear!" Ivy cried. For several seconds, she frantically snatched at the paper drifting every which way before conceding defeat. A thunderous silence ensued as she dropped back to the bench, its sole occupant, a few leafs of paper clutched to her chest. Rotating the upper half of her body away from him, her shoulders shook the slightest bit.

The faint, metallic hint of blood seeped into the corner of Sebastian's mouth. He touched the spot with his index finger. *Damn, she split my lip.*

During the fall, his legs had become entangled with the bench's legs. As he now disengaged himself, the bench, with an abrasive, scraping noise, flew across the hardwood floor like a sled on thin ice. Ivy's shoulders shook even harder with the unexpected ride, a choked sound escaping her as she clutched the seat's edges, holding on for dear life. *Bloody hell, is she laughing?*

Brushing his breeches off, Sebastian stood and gathered more sheets of music from the floor. Ivy rubbed her knee while he replaced the pages into the music holder, then he pulled the bench, with her still seated upon it, back to its proper position.

"Are you alright?" The question was bemused politeness as he reclaimed his seat. That she found him so damned entertaining should be annoying as hell, but even he found it oddly comical. She knocked him to the floor *and* split his lip, then suffered waves of silent hilarity at his predicament. Incredible as it seemed, the countess was the first to draw blood.

"I'm fine. Certainly, I'm fine." A wavering tremor to her voice suggested she might burst into unrestrained giggles at any moment.

"I've never experienced such, ah, *forceful* reactions to my advances."

"You caught me unaware. I…I did not mean to knock you from the bench." Ivy finally let loose with a laugh that was like a summer breeze to Sebastian's ears. It was a tinkling, musical sound. "I must beg your pardon, Lord Ravenswood."

"Perhaps you shall have it. But first, I must ask. Is your knee injured?" Touching his fingertips to her elbow, Sebastian willed her to look at him. A smile of such transcendent beauty lit Ivy's face that for an awful moment, he faltered.

"It's fine. Just a little bump." Her eyes widened in alarm. "Oh, my God, Ravenswood, your lip…"

"A casualty of war." His hand waved in faint dismissal of the superficial wound, but his chest tightened with ridiculous spasms at the sight of her obvious concern. The ache only worsened as her smile faded, her aqua colored eyes turning misty. Strange, but he suddenly thought it possible to stare at her all day, even with the annoying pain in his chest and a busted lip.

Ivy abruptly bowed her head. She still clutched the crumpled sheet music to her chest, so she silently straightened them and replaced them on the holder. With nothing left to occupy her hands, she tugged a glossy curl over her shoulder to toy with. "A casualty. Our situation certainly begs for battle-weary descriptions."

"There's no reason it must be this way."

She shot him a look ripe with incredulity, watching as he blotted at his lip with a silk handkerchief procured from the inner pocket of his coat. "You cannot believe that. You've no doubt heard the rumors, what people are saying. Including," she added with painful bluntness, "your own aunt."

A twinge of pity shot through Sebastian. The underlying sadness and play of emotions across Ivy's expressive features tugged at hidden strings he could not control. She was ruthless, she was cold hearted, and she teased and enticed and flirted until men went mad from wanting her.

And yet…

There was something about her, an element at odds with his verdict of her wicked character. Could a woman fake such a guilt-less air? Could the straightforward shimmer in those hypnotic eyes be little more than a practiced sham? Could that smile lure men to their deaths, much like a spider? Weaving a web of such beauty that curious victims venturing too close found themselves help-lessly trapped and devoured?

His former fiancée sprang to mind. A curse whistled beneath Sebastian's breath. Yes, a woman could pretend. Ivy had prac-ticed on dozens of men for two London seasons. Hell, less than an hour in her pretty parlor and already, he merrily traipsed along the same path with the other fools licking at her heels. Yes, like Lady Marilee Godwin, Ivy could twist men into worshipping lapdogs, using them until they served their purpose and she wearied of their company. She merely studied *him* for the moment, determining what he might like best...what would entice him to chase her. *Innocent maiden or experienced mistress...*

Sebastian wrapped cold intent back around his heart. "I am aware of the gossip. Indeed, my aunt opposed my visit here today." Ignoring her ladylike huff of vindication, he continued to chisel away her defenses. "However, I am Ravenswood. I do as I wish. As bizarre as this may seem to you, and believe me, I find it inexplicable, I would like us to be friends."

It was possible Ivy correctly suspected his motives, but Sebastian saw a strange hope glistening deep in her eyes. Was she so eager to count him among her conquests she willingly disregarded the instincts keeping her safe? Her hands twisted in her lap in contemplation of this dangerous alliance.

"I'll have your answer. Friends? You will not regret it." He thought he had ensnared her already. Her eyes were huge mirrors to the inner workings of her mind and like a ripe plum, she was tumbling into his hands with barely a shake of the tree. The simplicity of it all left him somewhat ashamed. And it was disturbing, how easily Ivy shifted roles, how quickly she went from icy temptress of the evening to innocent girl of the afternoon.

"Very well, Ravenswood," Ivy said in a soft voice. "I accept."

Sebastian kept his features blank. "A wise decision. Now, indulge me. No more vanishing. Agreed? I abhor surprises. A quirk of mine." The handkerchief was tucked back into its pocket as he continued. "An operatic troupe arrives from Italy in two weeks' time to perform *Lucia di Lammermoor,* and I will escort you to the performance. It is short notice, but friends are permitted such concessions."

Ivy smiled. "The hour was late and you were discussing

matters with the Pack which did not require my presence. I simply went home."

"Speaking of the Pack…I would know what Monvair whispered in your ear." His gaze turned penetrating, noting Ivy's cheeks turning red. She was uneasy. With his demand or the answer?

"Nothing of importance." Ivy fiddled with the lace on the skirt of her gown.

"Then there is no harm relating it to me."

"I prefer not to betray his confidence."

"I do not know the man, other than making his acquaintance last evening. He will not know you told me." Sebastian leaned close. "I've no choice but to assume you discussed me."

Ivy's lips pursed. "Of course, we didn't."

"How can I know for certain?"

"You cannot be certain. You must take my word for it. However, if I told you, would you vow not to repeat what was said?"

"It is unlikely I would keep that pledge." His reply was honest. "Monvair appears harmless. Maybe I could be persuaded to swear an oath of silence."

Ivy searched his face then leaned forward to whisper, "He wanted to go somewhere alone. He said he…he wished to remove my slippers and rub my feet. Is that not an odd thing to request? There was something about ribbons and silk stockings, but I confess I was on the verge of bursting into laughter." Her cheeks flushed an even brighter pink. "Monvair can be so droll. I believe he was trying to amuse me. And himself."

Sebastian choked on an indrawn breath. *That reprobate.* Could Ivy have no idea what the Frenchman really wanted? Her elegant little feet were only the beginning. Surely, she was only toying with him now, playing this innocent act to the hilt. "I'll have his head on a pike for daring to suggest such a thing."

"Whatever is the matter?" Ivy frowned. "You swore your silence."

Sebastian shook his head. "I said *maybe.* But I cannot swear to this." The thought of that sly Frenchman gazing at, touching, or possessing any part of Ivy Kinley was abhorrent.

Ivy considered this. "Lord Ravenswood, you are newly returned to London following a scandal. Our connection to one another is circumspect and fragile at best. At the worst, the gossips will salivate for a reason to flay us both. Is it wise to provide fodder at this point? I beg you to refrain from engaging with the Pack on any level. They are a temperamental lot; it is a struggle to keep them from dueling one another over the smallest of slights, both real and imagined. Let it be. For my sake."

The countess was right, of course. Difficult to admit, but she was right. It went against every instinct he possessed, but he must accede to her wishes for the time being.

"Very well," Sebastian grumbled. "In compensation for my silence, I'll have your attendance at the opera.

Ivy shook her head. "Another already requested to escort me."

"You wound me." Sebastian laid a hand to his heart. "Rejecting me so soon after our avowal of treaty."

"I think you've rarely experienced rejection, my lord." Ivy needlessly straightened the pages of music again.

"Ah, so you've heard some tales, have you?"

She shrugged. "Your reputation is no secret, I'm afraid, notwithstanding your absence from England."

"One should not put much stock in gossip tattle." A hint of ice lurked in his words.

"I agree." A hard edge shimmered in Ivy's response. "However, your turn at rejection is the subject."

"Alright, it rarely occurs." Sebastian conceded with a reluctant grin. "To be honest, I'm not entirely sure how to react upon being spurned. Am I to beg for mercy and pray you reconsider? It would be best if you just agreed. To spare my tender feelings, of course."

"Other plans, my lord," was her breezy reply. "I fear I shall be quite tied up."

A rocketing, mental image of Ivy blindsided Sebastian. She lay sprawled on snowy white sheets. A silken length of black cloth lashed her in place, and she was unable to escape as he tasted her. Pleading, begging him to come inside, to enter her, to make love to her, she writhed against his mouth and holy hell, he wanted to slaughter, in the most violent manner possible, the fool brave enough to take her to the opera in his place.

With a slow deliberateness, he murmured, "I shall withdraw to lick my wounds, little butterfly."

Ivy regarded him for a long moment, her eyes big and soft. Without realizing it, she leaned closer to him, her gaze traveling over his features. Sebastian held his breath when she bit her bottom lip in concern.

"Why do you call me that, my lord?" Reaching out, she touched gentle fingers to the small cut on his lip. "Little butterfly?"

"Bloody hell." He froze in place as if struck by a sudden arctic freeze.

Ivy jerked away at his barely audible groan. "I'm so sorry. I shouldn't have done that."

Sebastian captured her hand, feeling her quiver as his thumbs smoothed over the softness of her palm. Another improper gesture he dared, but she did not stop him nor did she pull away. Why did she have to touch him? What was she thinking? He knew what *he* was thinking, and it was tying him into hot, twisted knots of lust. He needed to regain control of himself. "I think, just when a man believes he has captured you, you flit out of his reach. A butterfly no one has managed to cast a net over because they do not understand the damn rules for hunting butterflies. And there are rules, Countess."

Her eyes were round as saucers, her breath barely existent as he wove a spell about her. "What might those be?"

"Butterflies must decide to come to you. And when one flutters close, you patiently wait for her to land. You remain perfectly still and gain her trust before gently placing the net over her." Sebastian's voice was a deep, entrancing force of nature and she hung on his every word.

Ivy smiled. "I'm not sure if I should be charmed or alarmed."

"Tell me what concerns you."

"Perhaps the fact you might throw a net over me when I least expect it." Her eyes twinkled.

"I would take great care not to hurt you. You see, I've no interest in the destruction of beautiful creatures, and capturing a butterfly is an interesting prospect. A collection of delicate things gives a man pleasure." His hand lifted to cup her cheek. "The trick is to keep the butterfly alive while taming her."

Ivy's breath grew shallow. It was quick and warm where it feathered his wrist. Then she stunned the hell out of him.

"Would you like to know what I think, Ravenswood?" When he nodded, Ivy continued. "A friendship will benefit us both."

Did Ivy mean what he thought she meant? Damn it to hell. He was now unquestionably off balance. Her soft words scorched his body. Holding her hand, touching the silk of her cheek, and Sebastian knew he was in danger of going up in flames. Underestimating her allure was a grave mistake.

"If we are to be friends, I insist you call me by my given name," Sebastian managed to say in a normal voice. His fingers itched to plow through her hair, to hold her still while he kissed her until she forgot her own damn name in a whirlwind of pleasure.

A genuine smile spread across Ivy's face while he ground his teeth in frustration. How many men had she deployed this particular tactic against? It was a devastating weapon, used with tremendous skill. That smile of hers, men would kill for it.

Or die for it.

"We should not stand upon formality," Ivy said softly. "So, you must call me by mine."

"The more informal, the better." God, Ivy Kinley was enchanting and magical. She could not be oblivious to the sexual connotations of his statements, nor of how he touched her. He could pull her to him, crush her beneath his body. Rip her clothes away with his teeth, plunge between her legs. He'd never felt such an overwhelming attraction to a woman before. Perhaps it was the thrill of battle, but he wanted her with a bewildering intensity. All the advantage had shifted into her small, wicked hands and he wasn't quite sure what to do about it.

"Is your invitation to the opera still open? This is probably quite shocking, but I've changed my mind."

"Very little shocks me," Sebastian murmured with husky promise. "You will be glad you reconsidered. I'll make sure of it."

"I'm already glad... Sebastian."

She blushed as she said his name, and despite himself, he found it captivating. Would she blush so prettily when he kissed her breasts, when his hands slipped between her legs? Sebastian wanted to crow with victory and just barely restrained himself. Right now, it was necessary to distance himself, before he threw her to the floor, took her right then and there...revenge be damned.

Stepping clear of the bench, he pulled her along and noticed her wince. "What is wrong?"

Ivy shook her head, tried pulling away but Sebastian rotated her wrists until her palms fell open.

"What the hell." Gently, he traced the length of the pale pink scar. "How did this happen? Who did this to you?" Still holding her palm, he lifted her chin with his free hand. Sadness, guilt, and above all, an elusive glint of caution swirled in the aqua depths of her eyes. Sebastian's hand tightened. "I'd like an answer. Now."

Wide-eyed at the sharpness of his tone, Ivy murmured, "Perhaps I'll tell you someday, but it is an incident best forgotten. And already forgiven."

Bloodlust churned within him. An overwhelming need to protect her swamped him. Was one of the Pack, as Society so courteously called her admirers, responsible for this? Which one was it? He'd smash the man's face in; he'd slice him to ribbons; he'd—

The violence of his thoughts was astonishing.

Ivy sidled away from him with practiced proficiency. "Will I see you at the Quinn Ball tomorrow night, my lord? I shall save you a dance, should you care to have one." The teasing was hesitant, a fragile attempt to draw attention away from her puzzling injury. "I'll even remember my promise not to disappear when your back is turned."

Sebastian considered her for a long moment before nodding in agreement. Soon enough, all her secrets would come to light. When it became apparent he would not pursue an answer, Ivy's relief was instant, evident in the relaxing of her shoulders, the softening of her jaw.

"I will be there, butterfly, and I'll expect a waltz."

"You shall have one of your choosing." Ivy gave him such a sweet smile, it made his stomach flip-flop. She made the business of seduction incredibly easy. Ignoring such delicate invitations was impossible.

Later that evening, Sebastian stepped into Brookes, intending to meet Alan there. He flipped with idle curiosity through the wager books positioned at the front of the exclusive club. Grimacing at some of the ridiculous bets, he turned to the first page of the latest book only to have his name jump out under the bold heading of *"Taming the Countess."*

The original bet was thus: *Five hundred pounds a newly returned earl ruins a certain countess before Season's end.*

Met in the following manner: *One thousand pounds the prodigal earl gains only a broken heart and Poison Ivy emerges the unscathed victor.*

Capping matters off in a magnificently grand gesture, an extraordinarily confident lord answered both wagers in an equally outrageous fashion and no subtlety whatsoever: *Double that. Ravenswood shall accomplish the taming of Lady Ivy Kinley within three months' time. Or die trying.*

A muscle ticked along Sebastian's jaw.

Bloody hell. They sat atop the lists.

CHAPTER 5

"*I* don't like it." An anxious frown pulled Sara's brows together.

"You shouldn't frown so." Ivy bit into a teacake. "You'll wrinkle dreadfully."

"Do not change the subject." Sara replied, smoothing her brow. "You were desperate to escape him. Now, I'm afraid I don't understand."

Ivy shrugged. Sebastian's unexpected olive branch of a truce tossed her into a tailspin of confusion and hope. There was no understanding his offer or her acceptance of it.

"Ravenswood wishes to be civil, and I see no reason not to try." She recalled Sebastian's arm pressing with indecent heaviness against her shoulder, the warm smile crinkling the corners of his beautiful gray eyes. The crispness of his scent had imprinted upon her. If she buried her face in his chest and breathed deeply of him, what would he have done? If she turned her face to his, would he have deepened the kiss he brushed across her lips? "I was ready to do battle. It would have been quite bloody, you know."

"How you can take this so lightly?" Sara groaned. "He is not a man to be trifled with."

Ivy traced the rim of her teacup with an index finger. "If the earl wishes to end the speculation and gossip, I shall assist him. Perhaps even Lady Garrett will forgive me."

"There is nothing to forgive!" Sara's teacup slammed onto a delicate saucer. "If she would only accept the fact her son was unnaturally obsessed and hopelessly addicted."

"You believe I'm foolish to feel even the slightest responsibility. But, Sara, had I agreed to see Timothy, it might have prevented what occurred."

"God knows what he might have done if given a second chance. When I think of that night, it makes me ill." Lips pressed tight, Sara's fingers entangled with Ivy's as each recalled the incident. "What you have suffered since, what you've endured, I cannot bear how people whisper. If only they knew the truth. One day, I shall forget my promise to remain silent. And you will hate me for it." It was a miserable prophecy.

Ivy squeezed Sara's hand, her voice rising with excitement. "But Ravenswood is going to help in this! Oh, Sara, can't you see? He can end this! I know it's madness, but I find myself trusting him. Even after such a rocky introduction." Disentangling their hands, she ran a finger across the scar on her palm. "He asked me about this. I was so nervous about him prowling Kinley Court, I completely forgot to wear my gloves."

Sara's face drained of color. "Good heavens, Ivy. What did you tell him?"

"That perhaps one day I would explain. He did not ask any more about it."

There was an odd glow in the earl's eyes upon examining the wound, as if he yearned to punish the person responsible for such damage. He held no obligation to her; it was foolish to think he cared or was remotely interested in fighting her battles.

Sebastian was needed to champion her cause, to hold back the wolves. After all, there was that despicable game high on the books in the gambling clubs, gentlemen betting on surviving her, taming her, whispers of a horrid nickname reaching her ears. If he thumbed his nose at Society, then this madness would stop. It must. No one would believe the earl foolish, or weak enough to be served up as another unfortunate victim of Poison Ivy. Maybe, in time, his friendship would ease the terrible guilt she suffered because of Timothy's death.

If he wished to form this bond, she must have faith he meant her no harm. She must become the butterfly and flutter close to danger.

"Ivy, I'm begging you to reconsider. Something dreadful will happen, I just feel it. If only you saw him at the Sheffield Ball after you escaped. His eyes were so cold, so cruel. Even Alan was furious with him."

Ignoring the dire warning, Ivy's mouth curved with a mischievous grin. "So, you and Bentley are on first name terms, are you? After only six months dancing about the issue? How scandalous, Lady Morgan!"

Sara flushed pink but she did not contradict the statement. "If we can stay on point...Alan expressed concern for your welfare."

Ivy waved a dismissive hand. "There is no cause to be troubled on my account. Truly. He means me no harm." A bit sheepishly, she confessed, "He called me a butterfly."

Sara regarded her with such a blank stare, Ivy had no choice but to relate the entire incident.

"Oh, no," Sara groaned in despair. "There's nothing for it, is there? You won't change your mind about this, will you?"

"There is nothing to worry about, Sara..."

"Have you forgotten what happened with Timothy?"

"This is nothing like that!" Ivy protested.

"You're right! It's worse! Much, much worse!"

The two girls regarded one another, each determined to have her way.

"I'm going with you. To the opera," Sara finally said. "You cannot go without someone to protect you. At least to provide the semblance of a chaperone."

"I will not require a chaperone, dearest. I'm Poison Ivy,

remember? Should anyone require protection, according to the gossips, it's Ravenswood." Admittedly, Ivy needed a chaperone yesterday. The light, sweeping caress of Sebastian's mouth was far more exciting than any advances tolerated over the past two seasons. Something about him sent sparks skittering along every nerve ending she possessed, his fingers burning like hot irons on her skin. She'd never felt this way before. She was not sure she liked it. It made her feel…not in control. And, *that* was something she definitely did not enjoy.

"I need time to benefit from Ravenswood's friendship, and I have two weeks in which to accomplish it. Surely, I can determine his sincerity before the opera. All will work out to my advantage, you will see."

"Ivy, *please.*"

"Not another word, Sara. If you should prove correct in your suspicions, I give you free rein to say so." Despite her nonchalance, Ivy could not entirely dismiss her friend's apprehension nor her own.

"I can't help but worry when you find it romantic to be compared to an insect."

"If he tries anything worse, I shall immediately hand him over to you and your dreadful temper."

"What has your father to say on this matter?" Sara sipped her tea, ignoring Ivy's comment regarding her fiery nature.

"Oh, blast his network of spies. It wasn't easy convincing Father only politeness forced me to accept Ravenswood's invitation. He's probably planning a grand wedding to take place next June."

"How will you deal with a dilemma of such magnitude?"

Ivy shrugged. "The usual strategy. A hasty escape to America, should he press the issue."

Both girls began to giggle until they collapsed against the settee.

"I believe you mean that! But, eventually, you *shall* marry. We both shall, if our parents have their say. It is expected of us, after all. And it's what we are meant to do, to wed, to be wives. To keep our husband's homes..."

"To birth the next heir." Ivy's sarcasm was soft and cutting. As young women born of wealth and breeding, they existed as valuable assets, cherished commodities in a man's world of dowries and alliances. Contracts and bloodlines, and above it all, marriage for gain and power.

Sara gasped in feigned horror. "How terrible if you should fall in love with someone your father *wants* you to marry! Then what shall you do?"

The gentle teasing stung. No one really knew how damaged Ivy was by the memory of her own dear mother and the desperate love Caroline carried for an indifferent husband. Ivy was determined to escape the bonds of marriage like that her parents endured. A love burning bright at its beautiful beginning only to die a slow painful death at the last breath of it, shriveled and pleading for scraps of attention was not what she wanted. Or in her mother's case, with armloads of suffocating, sweet smelling roses surrounding a lonely deathbed.

Ivy squelched a rare pang of jealousy at the straightforward nature of Sara and Alan's burgeoning romance. Theirs was a sweet and uncomplicated affair. If all went well, Lord Bentley would request Sara's hand in marriage. If her dear friend were fortunate, Alan's interest and his love would never stray nor fade.

Dismissing her melancholy, Ivy changed the subject to the Quinn Ball. It was simple to distract Sara by focusing on Alan's impending escort as it was the earl's first time doing so in that official capacity, and she was naturally thrilled beyond measure.

SEBASTIAN WAS EASILY LOCATED IN THE CRUSH OF PEOPLE. WITH his height, he towered above other men, the starkness of his formal apparel out of the ordinary in a society obsessed with bright, eye-catching colors. Like a predatory jungle cat, he stalked a ballroom bursting at the seams with preening peacocks.

His gaze landed on Ivy, his silver eyes traversed her body from head to toe in a manner very improper. The slow, wicked grin spreading across his features sent a hot tingle rushing through her, the blood sliding with a peculiar thickness through her veins. Never mind she was in the midst of a Scottish reel with Count Monvair, the earl sought her out. It was so exhilarating Ivy could scarcely concentrate on the intricate steps of the dance.

From beneath lowered lashes, she watched Sebastian prowl until he reached one of the many oversized pillared columns. Placing his back against it, arms crossed over his broad chest, he presented the very portrait of bored elegance until his brow furrowed into a slight vee.

"*Mon cher*...your slippers must hurt like Lucifer himself. Mine pain me as well." Phillipe Monvair leaned in, dragging Ivy's gaze from Sebastian. "Might we find a private spot? I could help you remove the devilish things. Rub your toes, *oui?* It would be my greatest pleasure."

"No, thank you." If Sebastian learned of the Frenchman's proposals, the results would not be pleasant. "My slippers are fine, as are my toes within them. But you may excuse yourself, should you wish."

"*Non! Non!* Only if you felt discomfort, *ma petite,* I would happily assist." Monvair glanced over his shoulder to where the Pack waited impatiently. "Come, we dance instead."

The sudden tornado of annoyance spinning through Ivy had little to do with Monvair and his improper suggestions and everything to do with Lady Veronica Wesley. Clad in a stunning silk gown of sapphire blue, she boldly sidled up to Sebastian and Ivy watched, gritting her teeth, as the earl bowed at the waist. He kissed the lady's offered hand while she tapped his forearm with an intricately carved wood and silk fan. It was rumored she shared his bed once again, although the same gossips gleefully crowed the

Earl of Ravenswood never chose the same woman twice once an affair ended.

Monvair grunted in protest when a spool-heeled slipper ground his toe.

"Oh, dear," Ivy muttered, her lack of attentiveness mortifying. "Forgive me, Count. I lost the step."

"No harm done, *mon cher.*" Monvair bounced on one foot to recapture the pace of the dance.

"I shan't do it again," she promised, giving him a smile that led men to do as she desired without murmur or complaint. The count's bearded face collapsed into an expression of such adoration, Ivy questioned he felt the pain of his crushed toe at all.

Risking a second glance during a sweeping turn, Ivy saw Lady Wesley frowning, hands fluttering with stylish grace while Sebastian regarded her, his features hard as flint. As the reel ended, he pushed off from the column almost violently, leaving Veronica to stare after him, bottom lip worried between her teeth.

When Sebastian located Ivy and Monvair on the opposite side of the room, his aggravation was unmistakable.

Unaware of the potential danger stalking in their direction, Monvair tugged Ivy to a shadowy alcove. There, he launched into a rambling breakdown of the outrageous cost of his new royal purple and butter yellow waistcoat. Held hostage to his inane chatter, Ivy nodded politely, waiting for Sebastian to come as the strains of the next dance, a lilting waltz, drifted into the nook, mingling with conversations and laughter and the clinking of glasses. She thought her heart, pounding with excitement, could be heard above it all.

"Lady Kinley promised me this dance," Sebastian announced without preamble, invading the close space like a giant forcing his way into a fairy's cottage.

"Are you sure, Lord Ravenswood?" Ivy's head tilted, some devil within her incited to tease him. Perhaps she did not care to dance at that moment? Perhaps she was content to debate the advantages of silk over velvet for waistcoats with Monvair.

"You don't remember? Lady Kinley? Shall I remind you of the moment you pledged it?" Sebastian's tight smile dared her to deny it, and before Ivy could form a suitable response, his arms wrapped around her waist. As Monvair sputtered and nearby guests twittered in amused shock, Sebastian nearly lifted her off her feet and whirled her away.

The way his eyes skimmed over her, hot, and possessive, was electrifying. The man was sinfully handsome. He was dangerous. And he smelled divine, a mouthwatering aroma of cinnamon and exotic spices, clean and honest. Not heavy cologne covering an unwashed body or male sweat. It was scandalous to think such thoughts, but Ivy wanted to strip the earl of his shirt, take it home, and sleep all night rolled up in it and that delicious scent.

Sebastian's lips curved in amusement as Ivy's gaze roamed his face. She could not stop staring at his mouth, which was as finely molded as the rest of him. What might he taste like? Would he taste of cinnamon too? When he kissed her before, it was all too brief, and she'd been too startled to make note of all those essential details. She would not make the same mistake the next time.

When his smile widened, as if able to read her mind, a warning tingle skipped down Ivy's spine. Flustered, she watched Monvair trundle with dull resignation back to the Pack. Sebastian followed the path of her attention.

"That was entertaining."

"It was the height of boorishness." Hoping to sound reproachful, her words came out in a breathless rush instead. Why could she could only think of Sebastian kissing her, his lips pressing hot against hers? Sleeping nude with his clothing whispering across her bare skin, chased by his warm fingers. What the devil was the matter with her?

His expression remained a study of unrepentant gratification. "I thought it rather brave of me."

"How so?"

"I saved his toes and sacrificed my own." Seeing the reluctant smile hovering on the corners of her lips, Sebastian ducked his head. "He survives to waltz another day." His breath fluttered hot in her ear. "However, were his intentions to get you alone, then he is *most* fortunate I intervened. He *lives* another day."

Had they not garnered everyone's attention when this brazen earl whisked her onto the floor, they were certainly the epicenter of attention now. "I confess I did step on his foot." Ivy did not dare mention Monvair's outrageous proposal.

"You weigh no more than a woodland sprite. Monvair will endure, and if not, others await anxiously to take his place."

Along the edges of the ballroom floor, the Pack paced back and forth on tenterhooks. Visibly horrified by Ivy's choice of a dance partner, they mumbled amongst themselves as if making plans to steal her back.

"You've upset the balance of things by stealing me from the count," she said.

Sebastian swept her a glance from beneath lowered lashes. "You do not belong to him. It is not stealing."

"I do not belong to anyone, Lord Ravenswood," she shot back but he only smiled at her heated statement, as though he knew secrets she did not.

It made her nervous, that smile of his. She was swimming in deep waters, and the earl had far more experienced at this little game they played.

"We have the attention of nearly every guest in attendance." Ivy nodded at the glittering crowd suspended along the edges of the marble floor. There was much whispering and passing of knowing glances. All concerning the two of them, no doubt. "You could not sneak a teaspoon out of here without someone's notice."

"Must I prove a point? I'm an expert in such things." His arm tightened at her waist, his eyes hungry and hot. "And in other matters. I could show you."

"I can't imagine what you would gain from such actions." From his slight frown, her bluntness shocked him.

"You cannot begin to fathom…" Sebastian took a deep breath. "I'm a selfish bastard so I assure you it would be well worth my effort." His eyes flared with the confession and he seemed unable to conceal the desire lurking in those grey depths. "Would it be considered bad form to point out I just stole the waltz I wanted?"

Ivy laughed despite herself. As they danced, he had maneuvered her to one of the French doors opening to an elevated terrace with an overview of the gardens. Before the tune ended, he tucked her hand into the crook of his arm, leading her out into the brisk night air.

Taking care for the pale coral silk of her ball gown, Ivy leaned against a waist high stone wall bordering the promenade. Along with the help of a full moon, bobbing Chinese lanterns gave a magical glow to the shadowy expanse of lawn. A giggling couple, unaware they were watched from above, strolled to the darkest of the garden paths winding through the estate and stood indecisively.

"Your actions embolden others," Ivy rebuked as the couple below suddenly disappeared from view, holding hands as they eased down the obscurity of the path.

"Meaning the Pack follows where others might lead?" Sebastian rested his forearms on the top edge of the stacked stone. The heat coming from his body was comforting. She should have been cold in the night air without a wrap on her shoulders, but it was difficult to feel chilled with him standing so close.

"They are very persistent, and pursuit is a game to them. Attempting to corner me alone is a singular objective." Ivy glanced at the earl's profile. "When one succeeds, others try to emulate. I am the one who suffers their efforts."

It was dangerous and exciting to be with Sebastian in the perfumed darkness. Ivy's heart pounded, which was unnerving and out of the ordinary. Her heart had never thudded with such confusing, wild exhilaration before.

"Demand they desist in their pursuit." His jaw clenched.

"Their ears hear only what they wish. So, I frequently ignore their foolishness. Sara says I'm so far away sometimes it's a wonder no one taps my head, searching for me," she smiled. "The Pack can be relentless, but I've no wish to hurt anyone or crush fragile egos by refusing..." Her words trailed away, the harsh memory of Timothy Garrett stinging her like a slap to the face. "What I mean is..."

Sebastian pushed off from the wall at the sudden distress in her voice. If his thoughts shifted to her role in the death of his cousin, he gave no indication. "I understand more than you realize. Marriage-minded mamas and a few fathers use to pitch their daughters at my feet with alarming frequency. My doorstep was quite littered and ignoring them was not an option."

Waiting for the earl to strike with cutting swiftness, Ivy wondered if perhaps he *was* sympathetic. The tenseness in her shoulders eased.

He had tangled his fingers with hers and staring at their merged hands, Ivy nearly forgot to breathe. His hand was huge, swallowing her palm. She felt tiny and fragile next to him. Was it possible Sebastian meant her no harm? Was she naïve to trust him? She shook away the doubts.

"I find I do not like the idea of you being hunted."

A faint confusion threaded Sebastian's words but Ivy had no time to contemplate it when he moved with a sudden purpose, pushing until her lower back was flush with the stonewall.

What was he doing? Would he kiss her? Here? Now? Ivy sucked in a breath, waiting. He crowded her, but she did not mind. Far from it. She quivered with longing, her gaze drifting to his mouth. *Cinnamon, he will taste of cinnamon.* Sebastian's head dipped and her lips parted with anticipation.

From the corner of her eye, she saw movement. Viscount Basford marched onto the terrace as if going off to war. From the depths of a deep tunnel, Ivy heard him inquire of a small group assembled near the open doors if anyone had the pleasure of seeing the Countess of Somerset or, perhaps, the Earl of Ravenswood passing through recently. A young lady giggled, pointing toward the darkened end of the terrace.

Sebastian stepped back. Her hand slipped from his.

Ivy stifled a moan of irritation.

"There you are, my dear," Brandon's tone held a proprietary timber as he strode toward them. "I had no idea you had wandered out here."

If it were possible to slap the viscount across his smug face at that moment, Ivy would have. Obviously, he'd been searching for her and now that he'd found her, she was his by prior rights.

The two men gave one another perfunctory bows, a cool frostiness chilling the air. It lingered as Brandon took Ivy's elbow, his grip tighter than necessary. He wished to demonstrate his favored position in the Pack. Most of all, he meant to remind Sebastian he was the outsider.

Sebastian's attention dropped to where the viscount's hand grasped Ivy. His eyes narrowed.

"The earl and I were enjoying a breath of air, Lord Basford," Ivy said. She hesitated to put the viscount in his place with Sebastian as a witness. The night of the Sheffield Ball sealed hostilities between the two men and inciting further animosity was unwise.

"I see," Brandon muttered, giving Sebastian a glare that said he did indeed "see," and he did not like what he saw. Tearing his gaze from his opponent, the viscount said to Ivy, "I hoped you might grant me the next waltz, my dear."

Sebastian assessed Brandon while Ivy wished he would say something. Lay claim to her for the next dance; beseech a walk in the garden. Carry her off into the night. Anything to keep her from leaving his side. When he remained silent, irritation swelled until Ivy remembered she was the one begging him to limit his contact with the Pack. He only did what she wished.

Internally, she screamed in protest. *What is wrong with you? Do you wish me to go?* Sebastian seemed uninterested as Brandon pulled her away. It was admirable how he ignored the viscount's hostile glares, one brow raised in bemusement as he was left behind on the moonlit terrace.

Much later Ivy shook free of Brandon's grip and the attention of the Pack to discreetly seek Sebastian out, but he had disappeared. She spent the remainder of the evening berating herself for the bitter disappointment she felt.

The following two weeks were thrilling and overwhelming as Sebastian laid an unexpected course of action. He monopolized her at every available chance. Every ball Ivy attended, he did as well, making a point of detaching her from the Pack to claim the waltzes. Every single one. If this were not vexing enough for the Pack, the earl managed to occupy the seat beside her at the midnight suppers for those balls. Many hostesses found themselves apologizing to other guests for the unfortunate confusion. No one could explain the mix-ups, which occurred only when Lord Ravenswood was in attendance.

He arrived at Kinley House daily for tea, much to Sara Morgan's consternation, the open irritation of Ivy's butler and her father's silent, glowing approval. At a piano recital given by one of Sara's gifted young cousins, the earl gained the seat beside Ivy for the performance and the dinner which followed. When Sara grumbled that the devious earl somehow managed to charm her own mother into granting him the favor, Ivy grinned like a madwoman. Lady Morgan, Sara's mother, did not believe in tit for tat favors.

One blustery afternoon, they shared an open carriage ride through Hyde Park, along with every other member of London society. That day, sitting quite close for the sake of sharing warmth, Sebastian proved very attentive, ensuring Ivy's cloak was buttoned securely, the carriage blanket tucked tight about her.

The earl was charming, witty, and disturbingly handsome with impeccable manners. He presented her with all manner of little gifts; a perfectly formed pear, a beautiful quill set with an intricately constructed inkwell in the shape of a long-legged crane; the bird's body contained the ink, the head dropping back for the quill to be dipped into it. On another visit, he brought her a small, bejeweled box containing tea from his Caribbean estate, Rosethorne.

Ivy insisted such gifts were highly improper; he should refrain from giving her any others. Sebastian only smiled and murmured, "I do as I please, Countess. Have you not discovered that yet?"

Again, he brought her roses; dark pink ones smelling of lemons, with petals soft as velvet.

She should have told him of her aversion to the blooms, but he disarmed her in the most devious of ways. Roses were a favorite of his mother's, Sebastian said. Their scent reminded him of her and the similarities, although for vastly different reasons, tugged at Ivy's heart. She lacked the strength of will to send the flowers to the church cemetery. That bouquet, like the first, was placed on her bedside table and Ivy often paused to inhale its essence. How strange they did not possess that sickly-sweet odor she hated. The wild roses had a different essence, one she found tolerable.

And Sebastian made her laugh. Doubled over with peals of delight, Ivy forgot the ugliness of the past year. Sometimes, she even forgot the earl was Timothy's cousin and possibly meant her harm.

The Pack seethed in powerless limbo as whispers of her involvement in Timothy's death receded. Sebastian's pet name for her was overheard at some point, and there were those who swooned over the romantic aspect of it. The gossips reported if the earl held no misgivings about Lady Ivy Kinley then maybe little validity existed in the horrid rumors she drove a young man to his death. Perhaps Lady Garrett overreacted from the depths of profound grief. After all, she re-entered Society after a rather short mourning period.

It was two weeks of whirlwind bliss but the night of the opera loomed, and questions regarding Sebastian's motives still plagued Ivy. What were his real intentions when it came to this odd courtship? Did she wish him to kiss her again? Yes. No. She wasn't sure. Other than the extraordinary incident at the Quinn Ball when he pressed her against the stonewall, Sebastian kept a respectful distance.

Sometimes, he watched her with the most peculiar expression. He would look away, realizing Ivy's gaze was upon him, and then reconnect his eyes with hers a moment later. Those fleeting instances chilled her, but he would say something to make her laugh, or his hand would catch hers, and her apprehensions would melt. She could not stem the anxious feeling that something momentous was on the verge of happening-something that could never be undone or forgotten. On the night of the opera, when the Ravenswood coach clattered into the Kinley House courtyard, her nerves were wound tighter than a child's toy top.

"Milady, he's here." Her maid drifted in, a vague smile on her ruddy face. Molly voiced her opinion many times over, comparing the earl to what she called 'the pitiful lot o' them.' Not a single gentleman in the Pack was worthy of her mistress, but Lord Ravenswood...oh, he was something special.

Grabbing up her cloak from the bed, Ivy regarding Molly in bemusement. The older girl simply smiled back before shaking the cobwebs from her head.

"So sorry, miss," Molly giggled, settling the midnight blue velvet over Ivy's shoulders. "I've got my heads in the clouds tonight, I do. 'Tis a fine evening you'll have with his lordship. Should I wait up for you?"

"There's no need. It will be quite late when I come home. I'll manage on my own."

Reaching the top of the grand staircase, Ivy felt like a sacrificial lamb led to slaughter. Sebastian waited for her descent, gazing up at her with those stormy eyes, his face impassive. He rested one arm on the curved newel post.

He just might be the Devil himself, his hair the color of midnight reflecting the gaslight of the enormous crystal chandelier, the angular planes of his face half in shadows. Sin and heat and power all coiled up and packaged in unembellished, ebony black evening clothes. Only a snowy white ascot and cravat relieved the starkness of his attire. With the power to bore straight to the center of Ivy's soul, his eyes prompted a shiver. The tiny smirk playing along the corners of his mouth signified he knew all of her jumbled thoughts.

Concentrating on placing one foot before the other in order not to trip and land in a clumsy heap at his feet, she continued down the stairs. Upon reaching the bottom step, his eyes swept her with such heated approval that Ivy actually took a half step back. Intent and desire existed in that look he gave her. Lust...

Taking her hand with a chuckle she suspected was meant to ease her anxiety, the flame in his eyes banked itself to a glow. His lips brushed the material layered over her fingers, his voice a low-slung rumble.

"Good evening, my beautiful little butterfly. Are you ready to depart?"

The heat of him drifted clear through to her backbone. "Yes." Ivy clenched her jaw tight. She thought her teeth might chatter out of her head.

"Shall we then?" Sebastian tucked her hand into the crook of his arm. His brow lifted in an inquisitive manner to the butler. The man stood gawking at Ivy as though she were a foreigner rather than the girl he'd adored and served since birth.

"Must I open the door myself?" Sebastian muttered aloud in an aggrieved fashion.

Recalling his post, Brody bounded forward to fling open the doors. His face stained a deep crimson, he offered Ivy her pier glasses and the earl his overcoat and hat.

Once they settled in the lustrous dark blue lacquered coach emblazoned with the Ravenswood crest, the coach door shut with a decisive click then jerked forward with a crack of the whip. In the gathering twilight, it clattered across the cobblestones of Mayfair's pretty streets before turning toward the theater district.

The surprisingly roomy interior of the vehicle shrank to one of disquieting intimacy. Sprawled like an opulent king against the dense squabs of the ivory leather opposite Ivy, Sebastian's long legs invaded the open space between the bench seats to brush against her skirts. "Comfortable?"

His wolfish smile was one Ivy had never seen before. She suddenly felt like a meal. His breakfast, supper and dinner, all in one, and the Earl of Ravenswood watched her as if he was starving.

"Yes, thank you." She licked suddenly dry lips. She was far from comfortable. He knew it.

"You're flushed. I hope you are not taking ill."

Could her cheeks get any hotter? Her heart thump a little slower? Over the course of two weeks, she'd laughed in amusement with this man, twirled in his arms, sipped champagne while debating legislation, Parliament, literature and the arts. She drank tea and performed numerous piano arrangements for him in her music room. There was little to be nervous about.

But you were never quite so... alone... with him all those times, were you?

Ivy slammed shut her internal dialogue.

"I'm fine." She touched the strand of pearls encircling her neck. Inside her gloves, her hands were clammy, her cloak far too warm for the closeness of the coach. The indigo velvet felt incredibly heavy upon her shoulders. How she wished to undo the frogs at her throat, to rip the garment away. The manner in which Sebastian scrutinized her stopped her. It was as if he *waited* for such actions. He quivered as if on the verge of pouncing, fingers curling and uncurling in anticipation for a bit of flesh to reveal itself.

Twin leaded crystal lanterns bracketed the benches, the low light casting the interior in a golden glow as the daylight eased away. The cushions were luxurious; the expensive vehicle well sprung. It floated over the irregular thoroughfare, and his coachman was an expert at controlling the horses. The evening was filled with the resonances of typical London traffic; the deafening clatter of wheels against rough cobblestones, the cries of coachmen for others to move aside, the snaps of whips, dogs barking and the whinnies and snorts of horses. Inside the vehicle, those noises were subdued, and the hush between Ivy and Sebastian swelled.

"You are very beautiful." The flash in Sebastian's eyes darkened to something mysterious.

The words, warm and disarming. curled around Ivy. She swallowed a nervous laugh. "Thank you." The anticipation strumming through the earl was magnified a hundred times over once it transferred to her. She felt coiled so tight, she might burst into a million shards of light if he dared touch her.

"I hope you've not reconsidered my escort." Crossing one leg over his knee, the motion moved him a few inches away.

Ivy exhaled in relief. It was difficult to think clearly with the earl so near, even if only his knee brushing her own caused her brain to dissolve into complete mush. "I thought you might reconsider the invitation."

"I confess," Sebastian's teeth flashed white. "I've anticipated this for days. Time moved with vexing sluggishness. Until now."

"Patience is not one of your virtues?"

"On the contrary." His reply was a measured drawl. "At times, I'm very patient. Lately, I've demonstrated ungodly amounts of it."

Ivy's head tilted. "What might cause a loss of tolerance?"

"You'll have to wait and see."

"You are teasing me," she laughed. "Someone surely told you I'm known for my rather impetuous manner. Patience is an admirable quality I'm afraid I possess not a fragment of."

"I've been forewarned. It will be pleasurable to postpone certain events when I deem it necessary." His smile was faint, a tense undercurrent flickering in his words.

"And your temper? Is it easily lost?" Ivy referred to the notorious duel with the Earl of Landon. Other than the fact it originated over a woman, the particulars still remained secret. Did he still long for her? Regret her loss?

Sebastian smiled again, tenderly but with enough cruelty to make Ivy regret posing such a reckless question. "Losing one's temper is for fools, hotheads, and children. At some point, I've been all three. Make no mistake, test my temper and you will find the penalties and punishment unpleasant, but I seldom, if ever, *lose* it. Or anything else for that matter."

A warning, perhaps? There was no explaining her increasing fascination with this man. Like swaying near a rampant fire on a winter's night; should she get too close, she might be incinerated by flames, but the urge to draw near the intoxicating heat was beyond her control.

"We shall cause a disturbance this evening," Ivy pointed out.

Sebastian's broad shoulders lifted in a nonchalant shrug. "I'm no stranger to gossip. It does not change, regardless of the city or country."

Sebastian's frame of mind was not considered when it came to the chatter they spawned together and the new storm to be stirred. It was one thing to whirl a few waltzes in the midst of hundreds, having Ravenswood's exclusive escort quite another. Guilt plucked at Ivy. Hiding behind him, taking asylum in his strength, and his ill-advised belief in her innocence, elevated her no higher than the Pack. Using him benefited her situation. The whole situation was wrong. So very wrong.

Dropping her gaze, she examined the material of the earl's trousers. It was a fine, dove-gray wool, an expensive fabric. Irish, if she didn't miss her guess. From the knees down, he sported jet-black boots much finer than the Hessians London's gentlemen currently favored. Italian leather, luxurious and buttery soft. Her reflection flickered in the glossy blackness of those boots, mirrored back in the reddish glow of the leaded lanterns. Caught in a flash of hysteria, Ivy giggled. Sucking in a proper breath of air was impossible but here she sat, contemplating the earl's exquisite taste in men's fashion.

"Sebastian...this is a mistake." Her heart punched with increasing bangs within her chest, a frantic drumbeat of warning. She did not lift her eyes from his boots. She felt him stiffen, his body remaining in its negligent position. No. It was not safe whirling close to this particular fire.

"Whatever do you mean, Countess?"

"I- I've done you a disservice. My intentions are not honorable." Somehow, she forced her gaze up to his.

"And mine are?" His smile was devastating.

"You're teasing me again," she whispered in anguish.

With one smooth movement, he was at her side. His hands, encased in the finest kid leather black gloves, clutched her arms through the velvet cloak. Rotating her toward him, he began stroking the material as if it were her flesh.

Ivy melted at the hypnotic rhythm. Heat spread through her veins with the molten smoothness of honeyed whiskey. Alarm bells rang with a frantic clamor in her ears. When she tried to speak, Sebastian pulled her to him, and she forgot what she wished to say. He had never held her so close before. Something wild sparked within her.

"Be quiet," his voice was rough. "I've no interest in your damn confession. It will not keep me from you, or save you from me. You cannot know how I've obsessed over this moment when we would be alone."

"But I-"

Sebastian slid his hands from her arms to her throat. As he cradled the sides of her neck, all coherent thought vanished. With the slightest effort, he could end her life with his bare hands. Once, she might have thought that to be a distinct probability, but not now. She did not believe he would hurt her.

His fingers laced at the back of her head while both thumbs coasted with nerve-wracking deliberateness, from a delicate spot on the underside of her chin to the hollow of her throat. Could he feel her pulse race through the leather of his gloves? The blood quickening below her skin? Ivy plummeted into a disorienting bog of instinct. It demanded she dissolve and thaw. Her head tipped back. Her eyes grew heavy. *Let the earl do what he will. Open to him; lift your mouth to his. Kiss him. Let him kiss you...*

His hands skated up until his palms cupped her face. Like silver fire, his eyes burned in the dimness of the coach. Different from the golden radiance of the lantern light, but warmer, some-how. A foreign tingle pulled from the pit of Ivy's stomach when his hands remained on either side of her jaw, holding her prisoner. Their eyes locked.

"I don't understand what is happening." She did not intend to whisper her confusion aloud, but the words incited Sebastian. Dark, primitive need flared in his gaze.

"Listen to me, Ivy. Be very quiet, very still and listen to me. Whatever you say, whatever you do, any attempt to stop me, will not work. I will take what I want and you will let me."

"I will?" What did he wish to take? Her soul? He could have it. Her body? That too. She was drowning in him, and God help her, she loved it. She wanted more. She could not tear herself away from him. She did not want to. "What...what do you want?"

"You. I want you. Ivy, you will crave it, these things I intend to do. You will beg, yes, beg me and I will do these things. To you. With you. For you. You will not stop me. Indeed, you will not *want* to stop me." His hands tightened on her jaw, keeping her steady, the leather suddenly hot against her skin. As if he were made of fire beneath the gloves. "Are you ready, Ivy? Because I must taste you before I go mad. Say yes. Say, *'yes, Sebastian, please taste me'*"

She stared at him, and as if in a dream, she repeated the words in a voice so husky, she did not recognize it as her own. "Yes, Sebastian. *Please*...taste me."

Sebastian's lips curved. His lashes dropped, hiding his eyes. "Good girl."

The kiss was like nothing Ivy imagined it would be. This kiss was so achingly sweet and so captivating, it sent her soul soaring. His mouth coaxed hers to open even more. *Cinnamon.* And the spicy sharpness of bourbon flooded her mouth. The two flavors created an intoxicating fusion. Everything inside her somersaulted. Melted. Burned. What was wrong was suddenly right, the forbidden instantly allowable. Long held boundaries erected by society, by the world, even her own self-imposed confines, were promptly reduced to cinders. The fluttering ashes of restraint drifted away on a moan.

Ivy was giddy with confusion, with the need to belong to him. No words existed to stop him, not when his hip pressed her leg, not with his mouth upon hers, not with his hands holding her so tight.

Sebastian traced the shape of her lips, and when she inhaled in delight, the kiss deepened to one darker, hungrier. His tongue delved in slow, deliberate sweeps before dancing away in a teasing manner. He was testing her, to see if she would follow.

Allowing the butterfly come to him.

She would. She did.

Her nerves sparked, liquid and hot. Blindly, Ivy sought Sebastian's mouth again and again. She let him kiss her until she was melting into the cushioned seat. Her hands fluttered across the broad expanse of his chest, his pulse thumping beneath the pads of her fingertips. In the haze of foreign sensations, there was a realization the earl's heart did not keep time with the pounding of hers. No, his heartbeat was slow, methodic. Controlled. How was that possible? Why was he unaffected by the turmoil of emotions cascading around them? How could the swirling chaos inside her soul not devastate him too?

Her face still cradled in the palm of his hands, Sebastian's fingers inched upward, threatening to entangle in the elegant upsweep of her coiffure. When she groaned her pleasure, he abruptly pulled away, removing his hands and allowing a bit of space between their bodies. He remained between her legs, but her skirts kept him from direct contact with her body. Wanting his heat and hardness to scorch her, she arched against him.

His head twisted, presenting his cheek. "Right here, if you please."

Ivy made no move, her eyes drowsy and full of wonder at the burning world he just inducted her to. Tendrils of desire tangled about her limbs. Why did he stop? Why was he talking instead of kissing her?

"You should slap me quite soundly for my actions." He waited for the palm of her hand to connect with his flesh. "Especially for what I made you say."

His statement seeped in, slowly making sense in a languid world.

Sebastian wished her to strike him.

With a resounding wallop, a proper young miss would remind Lord Ravenswood that such valuable liberties were hard pressed to be won. Her easy capitulation to his advances flashed in Ivy's frazzled mind. Would he think the worst of her for allowing such a kiss? Would he believe this to be a common occurrence? That she routinely granted such intimate favors to members of the Pack? Her cheeks burned, recalling the words she repeated at his command. *Taste me...*

No one ever dared kiss her in such a way. In such an all-consuming, possessive sort of way. She was far too eager for it to continue. The need for his mouth upon hers made it difficult to form coherent words and string them into complete sentences.

His dark brow rose. "I shall not offer again. Last chance and I must warn you, I do not play fair."

"All's fair in love and war," Ivy whispered. She was drunk on that kiss he gave her, shuddering, intoxicated by it.

"A sentiment usually touted by the victor, wouldn't you agree?" His eyes glittered.

Where might this dark path lead? Whatever ensued from this point on was as much in her control as it was his. Resisting him was useless. It would probably damn her soul to hell, but Ivy did not care. If he were dangerous, she would deal with the consequences later.

Her hand slid to his cheek, applying gentle pressure until he faced her. The distance placed between them was erased as the soft rocking of the coach invariably moved them to closer proximity. If he were to turn just so, move over her, pull her closer, just a little more, he'd be between her legs. What might happen once he was there?

"I *should* slap you." Her voice was shaky.

"But you won't, will you?" His lips curled into that wolf-like grin. They both knew complete surrender was at hand.

"Why is that?" Ivy's brow furrowed.

"Because I'm going to kiss you the way I wanted the moment I laid eyes on you. And you want me to do just that. I can see it in your eyes." The harshness of his tone indicated he held onto his desire by a mere thread. But still, he waited for her permission. *If she gave it...*

"Yes." Although her words were shy, she bravely met his gaze. "Yes, please kiss me."

Sebastian did so with a thrilling ferocity, his tongue thrusting to mate with hers. The banked fires within Ivy roared to blinding life. His roughness should have shocked her, but it did not. She did not understand the need to be closer; she only knew it must be so. Whatever he wanted, whatever he asked of her, she would gladly give him, everything if only he continued kissing her. *Dear God, she wanted more. Needed more...needed something...something only he could show her...*

Sebastian devoured. He claimed. He licked and teased until Ivy was faint with breathless excitement. Deep inside, where she hid from the world, sensations burst into full bloom, desire stamping out caution. There was no protection from his advances or the threat of inevitable misery. Her moans of pleasure silenced the last of the alarm bells.

At last, he seemed disconcerted by her. He felt the same madness after all, for an agonized groan escaped him; his hands moving from her upper arms, to her waist, then higher beneath the cloak until he cupped the underside of her breasts. Her shuddering pant of response caused them to swell near to overflowing the gown's midnight blue edge.

I want your mouth there, on my skin. If he stopped plundering her mouth, Ivy would utter the command aloud. But his kiss was too deep, too greedy, too ravenous and without mercy for any words to rise between them. One hand roughly weighed the fullness of her breast, his palm burning and hot through silk and leather while she wished not a scrap of cloth existed to bar the earl's touch. Arching into his palm, a mystifying urge to be petted and stroked drove her almost mindless. Whimpers of frustration escaped her, and Sebastian growled in complete male response, a conqueror ready to claim his prize. He jerked her closer, fingers curved in readiness to pull the bodice of her gown low so tender flesh would be bared to his mouth.

The coach came to a stop, jolting them to awareness, shaking them apart.

An awkward silence crept in, time dripping steady as raindrops as they stared at one another. Their breaths, heavy in the warmth of the coach, combined with the chill of a spring night in London to leave a foggy condensation on the leaded windows beyond the drawn curtains.

Sebastian, with a marked lack of haste, removed his hands from her body. Like a beautiful jungle cat, he unfolded until he no longer reclined against her, no longer between her thighs where Ivy wanted him so fiercely for reasons she could not begin to comprehend.

He gave her a rueful smile. "We've arrived, my dear."

Brushing aside her fumbling hands, he realigned the frogs of her cloak, holding her gaze with a hypnotic force. Her pearls were readjusted, stray curls tucked back into her coiffure, then, with exquisite tenderness, he trailed one finger across her cheek. It was the barest of touches, but it sang straight to Ivy's soul. Eyes fluttering shut, her head tilted back, lips parting to receive a kiss that never came.

Her eyes snapped open as the grinning footman swung open the door and the world intruded with a rude, bustling intensity into the charged, steaming interior of the coach.

Taking a deep breath, Sebastian stared at Ivy as though she were something quite dangerous and very rare. His words, so softly spoken, held a touch of regret.

"Never have I despised the opera as much as I do this very moment."

CHAPTER 6

*S*ebastian anticipated a curiosity regarding his escort of the countess. It was expected the first time he appeared in public with her officially upon his arm. People would whisper and point, speculating on their relationship and what it possibly meant when the Earl of Ravenswood spent every possible moment at Lady Ivy Kinley's side.

Reality was Society's fanatical need to witness it firsthand. The enveloping chaos as they descended from the coach was overwhelming. Snippets of conversation strung out in their wake in the struggle to gain the entrance of the opera house. One statement in particular, stood out from the rest.

"One must wonder, who will ruin whom?"

Ivy surely heard the taunts. Her tranquility amazed Sebastian. Perhaps it was why she surrounded herself with the Pack. They provided a dubious insulation from the daunting cruelty of the *ton's* larger predators.

"Introduce us, Ravenswood!"

To his great annoyance, while Ivy grinned, he found himself doing just that. A ridiculous undertaking, as most were already familiar with the countess. Sebastian ground his teeth at their little games. Many of his old friends were a dissolute bunch, with more than a fair portion of debauched exploits, some he initiated. Watching as she interacted with them left him a tangled mess, burning with an impotent desire to prove his possession of her.

It was difficult to say from where this violent strain of jealousy erupted. It inched along Sebastian's veins with insinuating stealth until he nearly strummed with it. He waited with clenched fists to witness the alleged exercise of Ivy's feminine wiles, but those artifices were missing here too, as they had been for the past two weeks.

It defied explanation, but a surprising edginess existed within the countess. He discovered the more enthusiastic a man's pursuit, the more remote Ivy's demeanor became, a faint air of unattainability swirling about her like an exotic perfume. That aloofness carried an enticing magnetism, her cool half smiles drawing male attention with a perplexing lack of effort. Every time she spun away in another's arms, men twisted in her wake, mute with longing. Did she know her casual indifference could drive a man mad with the need to tame her? Or did she not care?

Ivy laughed at a witty observation by Lord Whitmore while Sebastian felt every nerve and tendon within him tighten at the bright, rich sound of it. A crushing desire to have her smile at him, with him, because of him, for him, swamped him.

And there lay Ivy's true power.

Entering the Ravenswood private balcony, he saw Alan and Sara from across the loud, glittering space. From Bentley's private box, Sara's concern conveyed itself across the expansive theater. She was too far away to rescue Ivy. Not that Sebastian would allow it. He had no patience for such nonsense tonight.

Removing their cloaks, he helped Ivy into a brocade and gilt chair, noting with distinct male pleasure how her skin glowed in the softened gaslight. How would the flesh concealed beneath the modest bodice of her gown taste? Would it possess a different flavor than the delicate line of her neck?

Ivy's smile turned self-conscious. "Is something amiss, Ravenswood?"

"No." Masking his hunger, he settled into his seat. "And you are to call me 'Sebastian,' remember?"

Below the balcony's ornately carved plaster wall, he used the tip of his finger to stroke the underside of her arm, tracing an indiscernible pattern on the patch of skin exposed below the gown's capped sleeve. His gaze drifted to her lips.

It was foolish, succumbing to the need to taste her mouth inside the coach. Not once, but twice. He wanted to taste her again. It was damned difficult to steel his reactions. Once alone, he was afraid of his actions in the face of such temptation. Now that she had granted permission, all he could hear was her soft voice urging him on.

Moving so quickly was unwise. Before taking his full revenge, Sebastian wanted Ivy completely infatuated. Having sex was not enough. It would make him no different from her other lovers. No. She must be hopelessly, madly, in love with him and this meant wooing her.

His eyes shadowed, he said, "I was wondering…"

"Wondering…?" Ivy prodded.

"If your skin should taste of warm cream or fresh honey." His words, edgy with erotic tension, wrapped about her. Ivy sucked in a breath. "Both, I imagine. I look forward to discovering the answer and you will too. Shall I tell you my findings later?"

The lights went down for the first act. Her breath came in quick, shallow pants and biting back a small laugh, Sebastian decided it was unfair to use his expertise against her. Resting his arm on the top line of her chair, his fingers stroked the delicate curvature of her throat and collarbone. Disobedient curls at the nape of her neck twirled around his fingers with sly eagerness, as if impatient to be trapped within his hands. From that point on, he merely toyed with those curls.

Ivy seemed determined to follow the plot of the opera, but Sebastian's attention and that of the boisterous crowd made it difficult. Avid spectators seemed far more interested in the scene presented in the Ravenswood box. Several attendees peered through their opera glasses in the countess's direction only to hastily look elsewhere when the earl's stony visage manifested in their viewfinders instead.

By intermission, he had his fill of being gawked at by friends and strangers alike. Until Ivy shared her speculations as to what might happen during the next acts, he considered throwing her over his shoulder and carrying her out of there like a bloody caveman. Now, he dreaded spoiling her enjoyment of the play, and that irritated him too.

Resigned to another couple of hours in hell, Sebastian left her beside one of many pillared columns adorning the grand lobby. Formal waiters could not keep pace with the demands of the large crowd, and at Ivy's smiling request, he was off in search of refreshments. How quickly he fell into a servient pattern; one set by the Pack and sweetly governed by her whims.

Returning with two goblets of champagne, he paused to exchange brief pleasantries with an old friend of his father's.

"You do understand the lady cannot help it. We all had a part in making her the epicenter of attention."

The familiar drawl snapped Sebastian's head about.

Nicholas August Harris March, the Earl of Landon and imminent heir to the Duke of Richeforte, stood as part of a group of two other men and three women. With his darkly gold, tousled hair and glittering green gaze, he commanded attention. Two of the women applied themselves enthusiastically to the task. A flame-haired beauty dangled on one arm, a hopeful expression carved upon her face, while the other, a pretty brunette sipped champagne. Tristan Buchanan, Viscount of Longleigh, watched in bored amusement, his arm wrapped about the waist of an ebony-haired infamous actress.

"She's quite the challenge, if you don't mind that sharp tongue of hers," Lord Marcus Connell remarked.

Nicholas's eyes twinkled. "I happen to have quite a fondness for the female tongue. Sharp and otherwise."

"Really, Landon," the redhead pouted, ice blue eyes flashing. "If I did not know you better, I'd believe you are considering joining the Pack."

"Darling, you actually do not know me at all. I have reasons for keeping my distance from the lady, stunning though she is." Nicholas squeezed the pretty baroness while slanting a glance toward Sebastian. "You see, I should hate to lose your scintillating company. Not to mention the field around the countess is always a bit congested." A contemptuous smile lifted his beautiful mouth. "And recent participants do not play well with others when a lady's treacherous heart is concerned."

The two men locked gazes, Sebastian's stonily accusing, while the man he once called 'brother,' boosted a brandy snifter in a restrained salute.

Sebastian struggled to keep his attention on the prattling conversation of his father's friend, but old resentment rose to choke him. Excusing himself with a feeble excuse, he spun fully toward Nicholas.

Nick's eyebrow rose. Emerald eyes luminous with an almost cruel light, his voice vibrated with delight in recognition of his new audience.

"Of course, the worst of it is, the moment one turns his back, a fresh victim slips into the vacant spot," Nicholas chuckled softly. "How troublesome it must be to those so very dedicated in their pursuit! Everyone knows I'm not one to suffer fits of jealousy and I most certainly do not follow the Pack. After all, what a lady does, and with whom, when she's not entertaining me is none of my concern. As long as I find my pleasure, what do I care?"

The others laughed, excluding the baroness. Unamused, her fingernails dug into the muscles of the earl's forearm, and with the elusive grace of a seasoned bullfighter, Nicholas extricated himself until he stood a few paces away. To regain her grip, the baroness needed to reach out, making it obvious the distance was intentionally placed. A clever trick, designed to embarrass a lady with her own boldness.

Nicholas' glance found Sebastian's. For the space of a heartbeat, the two men shared a memory. As young men, with Alan's enthusiastic input, they perfected this move to avoid the clutches of overly eager females.

The flash of former friendship was brief.

Sebastian looked away in a haze of anger, Nick's words slowly registering. *"...the moment one turns his back, a fresh victim slips into the vacant spot."*

His eyes searched for the spot where he left Ivy. She was not there.

"So damn vague of you, Landon," Viscount Longleigh chuckled. "I thought you avoided the debutante set like the damned plague they are. Will you share details?"

"Come now, Longleigh. There are ladies present." Nicholas tipped the chin of the quiet brunette, earning her sultry smile. The flame-haired baroness silently fumed as attention was lavished on someone else. "In a private setting, I might divulge such information. As it is, we are all aware an affair is one thing, claiming a woman as your own is quite another. Rest assured, if I were ever inclined to stake a public assertion of sole possession, on the countess or any woman, she would not find herself left alone to fend off those who are, shall we say, a bit overzealous. Careless and loose my affections might be, a man would certainly face my wrath if caught trespassing upon my claim."

Sebastian stalked away, gritting his teeth as a roar of laughter accompanied Nick's next words, "But then again, our lovely countess probably objects to being staked and claimed. One must be extraordinarily careful, considering her reputation."

Beyond the last of the pillars, he found her. Relief flooded him, fighting for space with a tide of jealousy.

Ivy's back pressed against one of the last marble columns in the hall. Bleeding into the dark edges beyond the gas-lit brightness of the lobby, it was a perfect spot for lovers to steal a hasty kiss or two. Viscount Basford held her arm, the angle making it difficult to determine her reaction. Neither heard Sebastian's approach.

"Are you enjoying yourself?" Brandon's tone was peevish.

"Oh yes! The performance is quite incredible, don't you think?"

Brandon seemed poised to give her a rough shake. "You know that's not what I mean, Ivy. *Him.* Are you enjoying yourself with him?"

"Why wouldn't I?" Ivy's head tilted. "Ravenswood and I have many things in common. I enjoy his company very much."

"You have but one thing in *common...*" The viscount bit out.

Sebastian scowled. The damned fool had one thousand pounds riding at Brookes he would be the one to tame Ivy Kinley. Basford's hold was tenuous at best; the countess was slipping through his grasp as quickly as his recklessly wagered money.

"Be very careful, Ivy." Brandon's head dipped toward hers. "You have no idea what Ravenswood is about, although I confess a particular admiration for his methods. He ought to be ripping you to pieces for that business with his cousin. It's quite brilliant how he's managed to disguise his intentions thus far. Devious, actually. I've no wish to see you hurt."

"Basford," Ivy warned in a sharp voice, "you've no right to speak of Lord-"

"I'd much rather rip *you* to pieces," Sebastian interrupted.

The viscount dropped Ivy's arm as if forged of hot iron. Smoothing his cravat, he quickly recovering his bearings. "I only repeat the same observation others have made, Ravenswood." His shoulders lifted in a shrug, his gaze narrowing as Sebastian approached. "Am I in danger simply for extending greetings to Lady Kinley?"

"Not in present company." Sebastian's eyes gleamed with the yearning to exterminate Basford, on the spot. How inconvenient for the man to caution Ivy of his intentions. Were he not holding two goblets of champagne, he might actually punch the other man in the mouth.

But this called for a different tact, one excluding a brawl at the elegant opera house. With slow deliberateness, Sebastian remarked, "I imagine my behavior at the Sheffield Ball seemed odd, but I was in a peculiar mood that evening. In atonement for my dreadful conduct, I've placed myself in Ivy's service and shall accompany her to any social event she desires."

A smile of unapologetic blandness met Brandon's glare. Knowing the use of Ivy's given name would needle the viscount to the point of distraction, Sebastian's lashes dropped as he finished smoothly, "Of course, I should hate to be a nuisance, hounding her, if my devotion was not...wanted." The pointed pause left no doubt as to his opinion of the Pack.

"You would be bored to tears if you attended *all* social functions with me, Ravenswood." Ivy stepped between the two men circling one another with the bristling dislike of rival roosters. "Thank you for the champagne."

Handing over one goblet, Sebastian's gaze flickered around the lobby. Their darkened corner of the lobby was drawing quite the crowd. Nicholas stood at its back edge, grinning.

"You have no idea the number of gentlemen who favor our sweet countess," Brandon said tightly. "Lady Kinley is very dear to all of us. I'm afraid there may be no room for others in our midst."

"And I'm afraid I don't care, Basford." Sebastian's lips stretched with a lethal smile. "In fact, I'm certain of it."

Brandon's expression grew fierce with increased abhorrence, Sebastian's with aloof detachment. The cold silence turned uncomfortable, especially when Sebastian began examining his meticulously groomed fingernails. A flare of bright red infused the viscount's features at the blatant dismissal.

A flickering of lights accompanied the faint sounds of the orchestra tuning their instruments. Ivy exhaled in relief at the signal for patrons to resume their seats, thinking the veiled trading of insults could cease. "Please excuse us, Lord Basford. I should terribly hate to miss a moment of tonight's performance."

Nearly stomping his foot in frustration, the viscount had no choice but to kiss Ivy's offered hand and bow to his newly confirmed rival.

Unable to let the matter go without a warning, Sebastian propelled the countess forward with a firm hand to her lower back so she could not overhear. His advice was an icy growl. "I'm a selfish man, Basford. It would be wise to keep your distance."

Sebastian did not caress Ivy upon returning to their balcony seats. They watched the remaining acts of the opera in silence, and other than assisting her in donning her cloak and lightly holding her elbow as she stepped up into the coach, he did not touch her. A tightly coiled air wound between them during the return to Kinley House until Ivy turned to him, her confusion apparent.

"I've angered you in some way."

"It is of no matter." His hands fisted at his sides. Why had she stood on the darkened edge of the lobby with Basford? Why did she allow the viscount to hold her elbow? If she only knew how close he was to snatching her up and kissing the memory of every man from her wicked soul, she'd be too frightened to speak.

Ivy's lips tightened. Cold stillness stretched out like an endless deserted beach until the coach clattered to a stop.

Only when he was seconds from losing her, did Sebastian relent. He did not trust himself. The night was too dark, her eyes too mysterious as she gazed at him. He was too full of desire. Too full of unexpected jealousy with the realization he was only one of many in her damnable Pack. And he wanted to be the only one.

"Ivy...I'm not angry with you."

He wanted to kiss her. To touch her. To work these odd tangles out in the most dissipated way possible. The distance between them in the warm, shadowy confines of the coach ought to be enough to protect her. But it wasn't.

Which infuriated him. Shielding her from danger should not be his priority.

I am the danger.

"I know the viscount is vexing. He concerns himself unnecessarily for my welfare. Discounting him, I had a lovely time. Thank you, for…everything." When her cheeks flushed Sebastian knew she did not refer to the entertainment provided by the opera.

"I enjoyed myself as well." This was the problem. He was out of sorts, and he did enjoy himself. Too much. Until Nicholas March reminded him of a woman's treachery and Basford reminded him of all the others pursuing Ivy's affections.

Sebastian never doubted his self-restraint before. His ability to remain immune to any woman's charms always served him well. It fell to pieces with Ivy. Not only did he conduct himself with an embarrassing lack of control, he topped it by threatening a rival in an unprecedented display of jealousy. No, things were not going to plan and damned if he wasn't to blame for half of it.

When the footman tapped on the coach door, Sebastian swung it open, jumping out and brushing the servant away. He assisted Ivy down, her small hand enveloped in his causing a shimmer of protectiveness to coil inside him. These bedeviling emotions were unfamiliar; worse than a punch to the stomach.

Trailing her up the brick steps of the house, he watched the condescending butler swing open the door, and before he contemplated the madness of his actions, Sebastian followed Ivy inside.

Brody eyed him with ill-concealed suspicion, but Ivy gave him a smile of pleased acceptance. Then her eyes widened as Sebastian unfastened the frogs of her cloak. Sliding the garment from her shoulders, he handed it to her butler without a second glance at the man.

"Would you care for a brandy?" She politely offered once she found her voice. If possible, Brody stiffened even more. Still holding the cloak, he glared at Sebastian as if he were a snake slithering into sight and which now needed disposing of. Quickly. Without mercy.

"Not a good idea," Sebastian muttered, although he'd sacrifice his black soul for a bottle of the stuff. Or better yet, aged bourbon, if it might dull this strange edge. Yes, a whole case of the stuff, just to be sure. God, his fingers twitched with the need to touch her.

Ivy turned to the butler. "That will be all, Brody. Thank you."

"I'll see His Lordship to the door." Brody's alarm was apparent even in the dimmed light of the foyer.

Sebastian flicked him a warning glance. Damned if he'd be bullied by a servant. "I'll see myself to the door."

"Um, yes," Ivy nearly stuttered. "The earl is perfectly capable of seeing himself out."

"But milady! It is not proper!" Brody's face paled to a distinct shade of green as thoughts unexpectedly escaped into words.

Sebastian's mouth tightened into a constricted line of imperialistic disapproval. His glare at the insolent servant should have incinerated the man on the spot.

"It's quite alright." Ivy's laugh was smothered behind a gloved hand. "Brody, I'm fine. You may go."

Shoulders drooping with defeat, the man gave the two of them one last concerned glance, executed a crisp bow and quit the room.

"You should dismiss him," Sebastian said.

"I would not ever do such a thing. Brody has been with us since before I was born, having been my mother's butler at Somerset Hall before she married my father. He's a fine man, a loyal servant. I'm very fond of him."

"He doesn't care much for me." Why it mattered that the butler like him or not, Sebastian could not say.

"Oh, that's nonsense. But he is always rather gruff with gentlemen, and I suppose I've grown accustomed to it."

"Very well. Keep your beloved butler."

Sebastian removed his hat and gloves, tossing them onto a nearby table. He paced the perimeter of the foyer, boots clicking with measured treads on the marble floor. Coming to a halt, he leaned against one of the carved marble pillars defining the space.

Ivy pulled off her gloves as well, setting them carefully on the same table, along with her pier glasses.

"Are you sure you won't take a brandy?"

Something indefinable flickered in his eyes as he studied her profile. "I must be going."

"Yes, of course."

There was a slight tremble of her hands. When she bit her lower lip, he grinned. "Come here, Ivy."

"What if I don't wish to?" Her voice was hesitant resistance. Sebastian's smile was complete wickedness.

"You have no choice."

"Don't I?" Ivy traced the edge of the marble table with an index finger. "Everyone should have choices. Mine is to remain safely out of reach."

He chuckled at her naivety. "Oh, little butterfly... a minor point to be considered *before* inviting me to stay." Her eyes met his, bright with sudden alarm and Sebastian blew out a sigh of exaggerated patience. "Very well, I shall come to you."

Ivy attempted to keep a healthy distance but her retreat did not deter him. If anything, it increased his lethal determination, his eyes glowing with the excitement of the chase.

He finally cornered her against the far wall of the foyer, where the shadows were the deepest and most secret, where the low gaslight of the chandelier did not quite reach. Bracing his hands flat on the wall on either side of Ivy's head, Sebastian leaned in and then did not move at all. Closing his eyes, he breathed in her scent, that intriguing blend of oranges and lilies. That damned perfume had tied him in knots for the better part of two weeks. He wanted to devour her - just for that scent alone.

And although there was no logic to it, he was going to give her a chance to save herself.

His hands lightly curled into twin fists, a muscle pulsing in his jaw. Sucking in a deep breath, he released it and his words were a hoarse whisper.

"Call for your butler. Your maid. Better still...call for your father."

"What?"

He confused her. Understandable. How did one respond to being hunted in her own foyer then instructed to call for help?

"I dismissed Brody," she stuttered, "My maid has been abed for hours. As for my father, he's presently not even in London…I don't understand…"

Sebastian's eyes snapped open, hot pinpoints of desire flaring in their depths. The opportune moment to take yet another piece of her presented itself. And he possessed precious little self-control with her anyway. "It can't be said I denied you a chance to escape, Countess."

His mouth swooped down to claim hers, a torrent of heat and sexual frustration. The interlude in the carriage was tame compared to this assault. A greedy flame ignited within him. Ivy tasted so goddamn sweet, kissing her should be a crime. Thrusting his tongue deep, he gathered as much of her into his mouth as possible. There was a flash of a struggle before Ivy sighed. Her arms curled about his neck.

Although Sebastian trembled with the effort not to do so, he did not crush her to him. It was a simple defense mechanism. Without it, and he would likely take Ivy Kinley right there in the shadowy corner of her elegant foyer.

It was far too soon for that. She did not love him. *Yet.* It was not possible to crush her heart. *Yet.* But soon, judging by her enthusiastic responses, soon he'd have everything from her.

As her arms squeezed about him, he maintained the distance between them, her breasts barely brushing his chest as he ravaged her mouth. Holding her was embracing liquid fire. She filled his hands to overflowing, her curves somehow bending around him. Dear God, it was a bloody fight within his soul not to throw her against the wall and sink into her heat. As the kiss went on, his legendary resolve inevitably slipped. Would she stop him from whatever he wished to do?

One touch of her. One touch and no more. Slowly, Sebastian gathered handfuls of her skirts, his free hand wrapped firmly around her waist, keeping her in place. Pulling the frothy petticoats to one side, up past her knees, the bunched mass hung over his forearm. His hand swept beneath the drifts of fabric.

Ivy accepted his palm splayed across the upper part of her thigh. Having breached this forbidden land so easily, he dared to steal more. His fingers trailed higher, over the garter holding her stockings. Discovering the smoothness of bare skin above a circlet of soft lace was magical. His core jerked with lust when Ivy quivered. Her mouth melted into his. Sebastian pressed closer to the bewitchment of her body. Defenses be damned. He needed more of her.

Heat spiraled about them both.

His hips fit the space between her thighs perfectly, as though he were always meant to be there. The skin beneath his fingertips felt as fine as newly woven silk. He imagined the color to be of honey-tinged cream, the hidden curls at the apex of her thighs surely a soft, gilded chestnut. Sebastian's groan rumbled deep in his chest. He knew how she would taste on his tongue, buttery and sweet, like honeyed milk.

He scattered new kisses in different places. Delicate kisses to the faint freckles skating across her nose, shutting his eyes to the dazed light in hers. His lips grazed her chin, trailed down her throat before leisurely traveling up to nip her ear. He smiled with understanding as her breath came in desperate little gasps. Her breasts swelled against the limitations of her gown, and he considered dragging the bodice down to fully savor her. When her fingers slipped through the thick black waves of his hair, pressing his head harder against her, he decided he would do that too. *In a moment.*

"Stay still," he ordered when she swayed and dizzily clutched at his shoulders. And when his fingers swept into the heat between her thighs, Sebastian found he was the one suddenly motionless.

The feel of her on his fingertips drove him insane. She was soft and wet, those low, panting sighs of hers arousing him to a fever pitch. He wanted to push himself into her, as deep as possible...to bury himself in velvety warmth, cradled within her and with her heartbeat all around him. Somehow, he managed to remain still, waiting for her decision. Either come to him or stop him. She must be on the verge of stopping him. She had to be. She could not allow this to continue...

Ivy shifted. Her legs parted, allowing him greater access. Like a butterfly opening her wings. Inviting him to explore. To plunder and claim.

Revenge, the need to see her destroyed. Timothy's death. None of it mattered. The only thing he cared about, here, *now*, was how to possess her.

CHAPTER 7

*I*vy could not breathe. Could not rationalize, could not reason, nor fight. She could not form a clear thought in the muddle her brain had become. Finding the slit in her silky undergarments, his fingers speared through her tight curls, and how his hand came to be there, she did not know. Overwhelmed by pleasure, her legs fell open, wanting more. *More...please...more.*

Then a sudden panic gripped her. She shoved him but Sebastian dragged her closer, sensing the chaotic turmoil inside her.

"Be still," he whispered again into the curvature of her neck, his fingers motionless, just resting on her *there.* His touch stole all the air from her lungs until all focus centered on his hand. It felt so warm, so invasive between her thighs. The unfamiliarity carried a strange sensation of weightlessness, as though she were drowning in a hazy sea of pleasant breathlessness. His muscled forearm pressed against a sliver of exposed skin on her belly and the sharp pang of longing deep in her core carried all the heat of a lightning bolt.

For a long moment, Sebastian did nothing but allow her to become accustomed to the heavy heat of his palm, the bluntness of his fingers and the rough pads at the tips pressing against her. He was so still that Ivy's tense muscles began to ease. Why he wanted to place his hand there bewildered her, but he was not hurting her. It merely felt...odd.

In the faintest hint of a caress, his lips brushed her temple. "Easy...shhhh...have you any idea how much I want to touch you? Don't move, sweet, I won't hurt you..."

He did the most amazing thing.

His finger dipped into the moisture high between her legs, driving just deep enough to enter her. Collecting the dampness on his fingertips, he swirled it over and around sensitive skin she only now realized existed.

Ivy's knees buckled. Her head spun with maddening pleasure. She might collapse to the very floor if Sebastian did not hold her so tight, keeping her steady. His finger delved deeper, to the first knuckle, her flesh accepting it. Oh god, she should stop him. Put an end to this insanity. But she did not. Sebastian Cain was showing her heaven in the palm of his hand, and she could only tremble and moan.

"Sebastian..." Did she utter his name to stop him? Or to encourage him?

The silver depths of his eyes glittered. Answering her dilemma, his finger slid higher inside her.

"Sweet fires of hell, you're so goddamn tight...let me, Ivy, let me in...yes, yes, that's it..."

Gripping the muscles of his forearm through the cloth of his coat, Ivy swallowed hard. When Sebastian shifted so he was flush against the center of her body, she allowed it. When his finger sank to the hilt, his palm cupping the mound of soft curls, she willingly bent to him.

Beneath the solid pressure of his chest, her light corset and chemise rubbed in torturous slides against the sensitive peaks of her nipples. Inside her, his finger felt so thick and foreign, explosions of sweet intensity throwing Ivy into a new universe. She wanted him, regardless of the danger. Wanted to wrap around him, pull his mouth down to hers. Wanted his hands on her, around her, in her, anywhere he cared to place them. She wanted everything that was him.

If you let him in, he will destroy you. The whispered warning came from somewhere deep inside, an internal primal fortress desperately screaming to save herself. She ignored it, urging Sebastian's head down until his lips closed over hers.

It was a slow, wicked tandem of drawing, thrusting, his mouth and fingers working in harmony. Filling and emptying, withdrawing and circling, he stroked and played her until Ivy quivered. Inside her, something beautiful fluttered with the delicate shyness of an exotic butterfly. It was terrifyingly splendid. Every part of her soul was being torn apart, lost during some manner of necessary transformation.

Nipping her ear, his whispered words were a fiery command she could not disobey.

"Place your arms around my neck."

Ivy marveled at the heat of his skin. He was fire come to life, clad in an expensive suit. If he were naked, he would likely burn her flesh and she would welcome it.

Sebastian's breathing turned harsher as if desperate to retain his self-control. "Surrender to me, Countess…and …do…not… make…a sound…." With each syllable, his finger plunged, pacing word to action, punctuating one with the other as he deliberately unraveled her.

His mouth fastened on a sensitive area where her neck met the curve of her shoulder. Even without the muttered order, Ivy was incapable of speech. His teeth held her in place, and she could only shudder. His thumb nestled into her folds, pushing against a hidden point of flesh so sensitive it seemed to be aflame and Ivy saw stars. Waves bore her upward, tilting madly before cresting unexpectedly. Dragged under, she felt herself plummeting, drowning and just as suddenly soaring, flying high above the earth and the heavens.

Despite the warning to remain silent, a choked sob of stunned pleasure escaped the walls of her lungs. In great defiance, it skittered about the foyer, the cry of fairy princess released from a dungeon, bouncing noisily off the gleaming stone floors and tall marble columns.

Sebastian swallowed the musical sound, crushing her mouth while the inner channel of her body pulsated and clenched his fingertip. With hard hands, he held her aloft when she sagged, his kiss one of restrained brutality. As seconds passed, as sensations throbbed over and through her in glorious waves, he abruptly shoved her against the wall. There was the vague realization of his free hand going to the buttons of his breeches. Ivy waited complacently, making no attempt to move away. She welcomed his ravaging kiss, meeting his tongue in innocent mimicry.

There was more Sebastian could do. He could join his body with hers; push into her until he filled her. If the silken steel rod confined by the Irish wool barrier of his trousers were to somehow come inside her, all sensations currently flooding her would be magnified a hundredfold. How she knew this, Ivy did not know, but she was acutely conscious of things as never before, her eyes suddenly opened. Whatever Sebastian wanted to do to her, she welcomed it. Whatever he wanted from her, she would give it. She ached for him…for it, whatever *it* was.

At the opposite end of the oval foyer, an elaborately gilded clock began to chime the hour. The melodious peals fired a volley of two cannonballs into the dark stillness. A death knell to a magical interlude.

Sebastian tore his mouth away. With the same hand used to intimately invade her flesh, her skirts were jerked back into place. A desolate moan at the sudden abandonment escaped before Ivy could swallow it back.

Knees wobbling with newfound awareness, her fog of lethargy disappeared as the cool air of the foyer invaded the warmth created by the closeness of their bodies. The earl…oh God, he had come dangerously close to making love to her. In her own front hall. And she would not have stopped him.

His lips brushed over hers. It was a gentle kiss redolent of regret and frustration, with nothing remaining of the heated passion moments ago.

Ivy hated herself for it, but she wanted the other, the wild, burning kiss that made her forget who she was. Clinging to Sebastian, she tried to find it while he disentangled himself, dragging her arms from around his neck.

"Good evening, Countess."

Before she could jerk the scattered pieces of herself back together, before the delicious spasms within the deepest part of her had even subsided, Ravenswood departed in a swirl of black, the front door clicking with subtle finality.

Ivy slumped against the wall, fingers drifted up to her bruised lips. A sob escaped as she traced their tenderness.

Dear God. She would deny him nothing.

CHAPTER 8

*T*he night he left Ivy standing in her foyer, soft and boneless from a rocketing climax, his neck warm from her breath, his fingers warmer still from her heat, Sebastian knew what he must do.

Distance. He needed to distance himself. At least temporarily. The taste of her mouth, the feel of Ivy in his arms, none of it was conducive to his plans of ruining her. Somehow, during their time together, during waltzes and suppers, and afternoon teas, he began regarding her in a different fashion. Not as prey, but as an incredibly desirable young woman he was developing an increasing fascination for.

The roads to Kent were in good condition and bore no reason for his delay this afternoon. Three broken harness straps on his matched gray geldings. *Three.* It was foolish to ignore his coachman earlier when the man protested pushing the beasts to greater speeds. Once the leather snapped, forcing them to limp to a nearby inn, the older man looked at Sebastian and simply shook his head in exasperation, as if to say, 'I told you so.'

Sebastian did not elaborate on the reason for the breakneck

speed he demanded. Instead, he barked orders to repair the damn harness quickly so they could continue on to Bentley Park.

Two weeks had passed since seeing Ivy, and his hunger was sharp. Time could not dull the memory of her smile, or the sparkle of her eyes when amused. Distance did not explain his inability to concentrate on estate matters. Or why the purchase of five race-horses paled in comparison to her lips and their sweet taste of oranges and honey. Even when he worked to the point of exhaus-tion, images of her silky flesh filling his hands crept into his dreams every night, denying him the black oblivion of sleep. His thoughts overflowed with her and Sebastian hated that fact almost as much as he knew he should hate her.

"Remember Timothy." The mantra was often repeated. Revenge was a messy, ugly business. Glowing eyes and sweet, sweet lips should not sway him.

Two hours idle waiting on repairs ought to have provided addi-tional time to steel his resolve. It only allowed his emotions to simmer. Reaching Bentley Park, Sebastian's temper seethed just below a deceptively calm surface.

It mounted by degrees when Ivy was unseen among the sixty guests gathered at the estate. Hot, dusty, impatient, Sebastian strad-dled a razor's edge to see her. The irritation experienced when she was not immediately available to soothe his senses was vastly disturbing.

Inquiries revealed her location on the west lawn where several guests gathered to try their hands at archery. Sebastian nearly sprinted down the oak-shaded lane toward the range until, with a muttered curse, he forced himself to a more dignified stroll.

Gathered in the slope of a small valley, a group of brightly dressed gentlemen and ladies mingled. Ivy and Sara stood at a marked chalk line, holding bows notched with arrows. A young man, slightly pudgy and earnest of face, hovered at Ivy's side. She listened intently to him, brow furrowed in concentration.

Alan, watching the girls with a slight frown marring his brow, caught sight of Sebastian. Waving a hand in greeting, he excused himself from a cluster of men observing the proceedings with unusual interest.

Ivy glanced over her shoulder at Sebastian's approach, but there was no smile of welcome. The line of her mouth tightened, her attention flicking back to Lord Kessler as he repositioned her fingers upon the string.

There was no ignoring the twist of excitement in his stomach, even with her obvious dismissal. It was damned difficult to tear his eyes away from her. Why did he stay away for so long? Whatever the reason, it was a mistake.

"Glad you could make it, Seb." The two men shared a brotherly embrace. "I was beginning to think we might not see you at all."

"Broke three harness straps. I stopped at the Red Lion for repairs."

"Racing the Devil himself...that's not like you," Alan said before adding with a faint scowl, "now that you've arrived, you can assist in an important matter. I've not had a blasted moment alone with Lady Sara since her arrival yesterday."

"You require my help in this, of all things?" Sebastian's brow lifted. "You're lord and master here. Arrange a rendezvous in the library or a drawing room. You've never had difficulties before coercing women into darkened corners."

Alan's gaze fixed on Sara while they strolled some distance away to discuss matters in a more practical manner. "Her oldest cousin accompanied the girls to act as chaperone. But where Lady Burkestone proves lax in her duties, Lady Ivy takes up the reins. And there's a damn maid capable of snapping out of a dead sleep the instant I come within twenty steps. Between them all, there's not been a single opportunity to make so much as an inappropriate suggestion. You will be a welcome distraction, for one of them at least."

"I'm of no help with a bothersome maid." Sebastian's eyes snapped to Ivy when she laughed at something Kessler said. "And I cannot promise a miracle with Ivy."

Alan shot him a questioning look. "She's not once mentioned your name. Where the hell have you been? I heard you went to Scotland."

"After four years abroad, my attention was required at my estates. And yes, I was in Scotland. Those racers I purchased were at Hawick and I went to retrieve them." Sebastian nearly growled his response.

Bentley snorted in disbelief. "I'm glad you could forgo your responsibilities. For this weekend, at least." Nodding toward Ivy and Kessler, he said, "She's charmed everyone. Away from the Pack, out of London, and she's a different person. Relaxed, and with a devilishly engaging sense of humor. Half the men here are mad for her. I don't believe her fortune even factors into their affections, and there's been no mention of that rather scandalous wager. Do you find that odd?"

"I don't care if they are all hopelessly in love with her," Sebastian's expression was sullen. What had he lost during his absence? "I am pursuing her."

The two girls both readied their aim and let loose the arrows. Sara's landed close to the bullseye while Ivy's arrow hit the outside rings. Several guests clapped. Kessler gave a hoot of admiration for Sara's aim. In quick fashion, they notched a second round of arrows, and again, the young lord stepped behind Ivy, this time fitting his body to hers. Guiding the bow to a better position, he gripped her elbow, situating it slightly higher. When she drew back on the weapon, her wrist located next to her ear, Kessler's mouth hovered there as he imparted advice.

When his hand drifted to casually rest on the swell of Ivy's hip, holding her flush alongside him, fingers flexing tight enough to leave indentations on her silk skirt, Sebastian's shaky temper reached a flashpoint.

"Bloody hell." The curse whistled out before he could bite it back.

"Careful, Ravenswood," Bentley laughed as Sebastian stalked away. "She is armed, after all."

~

EVEN BEFORE SEBASTIAN APPEARED ON THE HILLCREST, WITH THAT fierce expression on his stern face, Ivy knew he had arrived. Maybe it was a change in the wind or the way the back of her neck prickled, the hair standing on end. An electric charge, like that the air carried just before a summer thunderstorm, rolled through her and she just knew.

He's here.

Conflicting emotions swelled in her heart as Sebastian stalked down the hill, the breeze playfully tossing his raven-dark hair about. She wanted to run to him. Throw herself into his arms and beg him to never let her go. She wanted him to kiss her. Hear him say he missed her. And she wanted to strike him until his handsome face turned red from the heat of her palms. He should know he meant nothing to her and she did not care if she ever saw him again.

She did none of these things. When she threw Sara a helpless glance, she mouthed back a clear directive, *"Ignore him!"*

Swallowing her heart, which was for some reason lodged in her throat, Ivy did just that. She allowed Kessler to position her fingers on the bowstring, his instructions a meaningless drone in her ears. She could not even see the target. It blurred in her vision as all senses tuned to Sebastian. Alan greeted him, the two men walking some distance away for a low, murmured conversation. When Lord Kessler situated her for the second shot, she became vaguely aware of his hand applying a light but steady pressure just above the curvature of her hip.

Sebastian is coming. The air positively vibrated with waves of possession. Ivy fumed. Did he think he could reappear and his absence be forgiven? There wasn't even a note explaining where he'd gone. It was only because of a conversation overheard between two women, former mistresses no doubt, that she learned he'd gone to visit a number of his estates before traveling to Scotland, of all places. *Scotland.*

121

The earl's low growl held the power to freeze a lion in mid-pounce.

"Step away, Kessler."

Scotland. I was forgotten in favor of the desolate barrenness of Scotland. Ivy swung about, the arrow leveled at Sebastian's heart.

Kessler, a red flush staining the round cheeks up to the tips of his ears, scrambled a good ten feet away from her backside as a collective gasp swept the crowd. With a litany of choked curses, two gentlemen landed flat on the ground. Others simply knelt low enough to stay beneath the arrow's range.

"Your assistance is not required, Lord Ravenswood." She held Sebastian squarely in the bow's sights.

An agonizingly long moment passed. Realizing their souls were safe, the two men hoisted themselves from the lawn. Sweeping bits of grass and dirt from their breeches with brisk slaps, they ignored ladies tittering behind upraised hands and tilted parasols.

"For God's sake, woman," Sebastian hissed, immobilized by Ivy's unblinking gaze and steady aim. "Must I be sacrificed as a demonstration of your inexperience?"

Pinning him with a steely glare for a brief second, Ivy suddenly whirled, prompting another flinching wave to ripple through the crowd. The same two gentlemen, plus three more, dropped like stones.

With the barest of consideration, the arrow flew.

No one saw Ivy's satisfied smile when the weapon hit dead center of the distant target with a satisfying thump. Sara's muffled snort of amusement filled the astounded silence.

"I say," Kessler said hesitantly. "I'm a far better tutor than I thought!"

Ivy lowered the bow. Everyone commenced to chattering all at once. The five men, rising to their feet, sheepishly chuckled amongst themselves. Alan, with an exasperated glance at Sebastian, brushed past to take Sara's bow.

"Lady Sara, would you accompany me for a stroll around the

lake? I'm sure your delicate hands need a respite and I, for one, would enjoy the exercise." His joviality sounded forced when he turned to Ivy and Sebastian, now glaring at one another with enough heat to set the surrounding trees ablaze. "Lady Ivy? Will you join us? For propriety's sake, of course."

"An excellent idea!" Kessler exclaimed as Ivy silently ripped off the gloves protecting her fingertips. "I'm happy to escort you, Lady Kinley-"

"Like hell you will," Sebastian snarled. Shoving past the man, he reached Ivy in two strides, yanking bow and gloves from her to toss them aside. She gasped at his rudeness while Kessler shot back as though scalded by hot water. Ravenswood's open hostility froze the young man with uncertainty.

Not averse to digging heels into the gravel should her protection be required, Sara gave Ivy a wink and cheerfully stated, "It's a foolish man that underestimates Lady Ivy Kinley, Lord Ravenswood. She's full of surprises. Why, just last year…"

Sebastian and Alan exchanged glances, a subtle, mutual nod passing between them. Then Alan tugged Sara toward the distant lake, cutting off whatever else she might have said.

Three young women surrounded Kessler, insisting on gathering up the discarded items for him. Their conversation quickly turned to requests for tutorage in archery. Watching for a second, Ivy went to join them but found her arm within Sebastian's unyielding grasp. When she tried to struggle free, he gave her an invisible, warning jerk and turned her toward the path.

Sara threw a distressed glance over her shoulder while Alan inexorably marched her at a quick clip until they were several paces ahead. In contrast, Sebastian walked slower than a snail as they followed behind. Not one of the guests seemed inclined to rescue either girl. Even Lady Burkestone, after a considering frown, turned back to the cakes and lemonade table set up in the shade of a huge oak tree. The banter of those at the archery targets faded as the gravel walkway bent and thick trees concealed them from view. Alan and Sara moved so far ahead it was assured all conversations would remain private.

"You had no need of Kessler's tutelage." Sebastian sounded abnormally calm.

Ivy shrugged. "I've had instruction since the age of five."

He looked as if he might grind his teeth to dust. "Why the charade? Do you enjoy tempting him?"

She frowned. "What, pray tell, is tempting about archery? I had no wish to embarrass Lord Kessler with my level of expertise."

He snorted. "Why should you give a shilling about that?"

Jerking her arm from his grasp, Ivy's pace increased until he gripped her elbow again. He pulled her to a stop while Ivy folded her arms to stare straight ahead. She would not look at him...not while he was being so damnably unkind.

"I asked you a question. Why should you care? About embarrassing him? He means nothing to you."

It is obviously beyond your comprehension." Ivy bit out.

"Try me. Although I find I am more curious why Kessler thought he could touch you. His hands were all over you..."

"Why do you care where he places his hands?" She hurled the words at him. "I mean nothing to you."

"Do not play games with me, Ivy."

Ivy wanted to throw her hands in the air in exasperation but she stood her ground. A strange spark flickered in Sebastian's gaze as he stared down at her. He was turning her words over to find a chink in the armor he obviously did not expect. Did all his female conquests welcome him with open arms when he disappeared from their lives for weeks on end, without a word of explanation? If so, they were weak, foolish chits with jelly for backbones. She felt sorry for the faceless women, suddenly afraid to be counted among their numbers.

"Some of the guests were discussing Lord Kessler's lack of attributes when it came to outdoor pursuits. Lord Bentley mentioned the archery range, and I noted Kessler's enthusiasm. I requested his assistance to bolster his confidence. And it worked, before you so rudely yanked me away. Three of those same ladies begged his assistance." Her tone was acid sweet. "Whatever is the matter, Ravenswood? Jealous if you are not the center of all female attention? Are you that cruel to begrudge poor Kessler just a tiny bit of adoration from the fairer sex? You've more than a fair share of it, you pompous ass."

∽

IVY'S EXPLANATION OF THINGS SEEMED REASONABLE, EVEN admirable. Bloody hell, Sebastian felt a shade guilty, being so heavy handed. Did she tell the truth or was she simply a good liar when put on the spot? Her contempt for his display of jealousy stung more than he cared to admit.

Allowing her to ease away, Sebastian retained the hold of her elbow as they resumed walking. His head tilted to the couple ahead of them on the path. "They seem to deal well together." When Ivy failed to respond, his shoulder nudged hers. "My temper, butterfly. Watching Kessler handle you disturbed me greatly, I'm afraid."

"Your temper?" Ivy's brow arched. "The one you never lose?"

"The same."

"I don't understand you, Lord Ravenswood," she confessed.

"You are hardly alone in that, my dear, and are we back to formal titles? Although I confess, 'Lord Ravenswood' has a much nicer ring than 'pompous ass.'" He grinned. "Come now. Let us find more pleasant matters to discuss. Tell me your opinion of Bentley and Lady Morgan's budding romance."

Again, Sebastian knew Ivy's innermost thoughts from the expressive light in her eyes. She did not trust his motives and was still angry, but she would permit the argument to die.

"Sara enjoys the earl's company a great deal." Her reply was cautious.

"You adore her, don't you?"

"She's been my dearest friend since we met at finishing school. Have you and Lord Bentley been friends for long?"

"Since childhood. Fortunately, Alan has always believed in me or should I say, the *good* in me," Sebastian said with a dry laugh, linking their arms together. Ivy briefly resisted before surrendering like a lamb led to slaughter. "Would you be happy if they married?"

"It is what Sara desires. The earl is quite handsome, and he would provide well. Most importantly, he's very kind and seems to worship her."

Watching the couple duck out of sight and behind a tree, Sebastian chuckled. "I imagine Alan is stealing a kiss right now."

A reluctant smile broke across Ivy's face. "Lord Bentley has managed to sneak more than one past my surveillance. I'm afraid I'm a dreadful chaperone."

"It would be awful for us to impede the course of true love." Sebastian led Ivy off the path, disregarding her gasp of shock. "It suffers terribly without the numerous obstacles constantly tossed in its way." Leaning against the rough bark of a sheltering elm, he dragged her against him, one arm wrapped tight around her waist, holding her immobile. "I missed you."

Ivy's chin tilted at the pressure of his forefinger tracing the curve of her jaw. "Did you?" She tried sounding cool and detached, but her breath hitched the slightest bit.

"Yes." His dark eyes delved into her soul. "I did. I *do*. Far more than what is rational, unfortunately."

Ivy was silent before blurting out, "You forgot about me."

"Never." Sebastian's finger drifted down the arch of her neck. "How can I ever forget you? Or how you moaned my name when I touched you?"

Ivy shivered, her aqua blue eyes clashing with his. "Where were you, Sebastian?" The question was a whisper. "Where-"

"Does it matter?" he murmured. "I'm here now."

Sebastian could not explain this growing obsession. And reconciling that obsession with revenge was becoming a difficult task. He wanted her. With every loose thread of his soul, he *craved* her.

This hunger, it was disturbing. Ivy's smile entranced him.

Those huge eyes of hers, the color of the sea on a summer day, made for drowning in. Some mornings he awoke with fingers tingling from dreams of stroking the petal softness of her cheek. Dammit, even her perfume intoxicated him. That curious mix of oranges and lilies possessed the power to tangle him into curious knots, leaving his mouth dry with lust. He thought about it at the oddest times.

Bringing both hands up to cradle her face, he used his tongue to trace the seam of her lips, waiting for them to part. When they did, he slid inside, gently exploring her mouth with long, slow sweeps until she gripped his forearms for support. She tasted of wildflower honey and lemonade. When he finally raised his head, the golden flecks in the depths of her eyes shimmered up at him like flashes of sunlight on the ocean. Intriguing how he could make her storm clouds dissipate with just a few simple kisses. It was knowledge he would use to full advantage.

He loved how her pulse pounded against the tips of his fingers. Like a tiny sparrow beating its wings, hopelessly captured in the cage of his palms. "You shouldn't look at me like that."

Breathless, Ivy leaned into him, hands braced against his chest, her face tilted to his. "Like what?" Chestnut curls tumbled to the indentation of her waist, and should he wrap his arms completely around her, those soft ringlets would tickle his hands.

"As if you wish to finish what we began that night..." The pulse at the base of Ivy's throat leaped at the whispered suggestion and Sebastian smiled as he abruptly pulled her back into the sunlight.

Sara and Alan had returned to the path as well, laughing with one another. Not once did they glance back at their trailing chaperones.

Sebastian took Ivy's hand, their fingers twining loosely. She blinked several times to regain her senses, stunned at being kissed in shady seclusion one moment to walking sedately in the sunshine the next. Small quivers revealed themselves in her fingers when his lips brushed across her knuckles in the softest of caresses.

Sebastian did not bother to hide a wolfish grin of satisfaction.

~

IVY DID NOT EXPECT TO FIND SEBASTIAN'S CIRCLE OF FRIENDS TO be so kind and gracious, although a handful appeared genuinely confused by her attendance at Lord Bentley's country party. It amazed her that all followed Sebastian's lead without question. The subtle display of his powerful influence was proving every bit as advantageous as she hoped.

Following dinner, a spirited game of whist ensued, with gentlemen pitted against the ladies. Partnered with Sara, Ivy suspected Sebastian and Alan of throwing their hands more than once. She wished to seize his cards and reveal the truth, but that would be bad form.

Sebastian glanced up from his bourbon as if sensing her thoughts. "You are by far the better player, Lady Ivy."

"If you believed that, you would play to win." Ivy gestured at the cards. "It is beyond fantastical we bested you and Lord Bentley in the last five hands. You will not hurt our feelings by winning a hand or two."

"Perhaps I am only lulling you into a false sense of security with a display of my incompetence before I take all."

Sebastian's eyes shone bright with something unknown. For a brief moment, Ivy wondered if she were being pacified into compliance in other matters. Her fingers tightened on the cards she still held.

"No need to mollycoddle us, Lord Ravenswood," Sara said with an arched brow.

Ivy laid the cards down before she bent them beyond repair. "We could win, even if you play your best."

"Is that so?" A grin of pure devilment crossed Sebastian's features, his gaze never leaving hers. "I propose a wager to settle the matter."

Laughter rippled in the wake of his comment, ears pricking at the mention of 'wager." The two smiling so pleasantly across the card table were players in the most well-known stakes in all of London.

Lady Burkestone piped in, conflicted if she was expected to stop something potentially scandalous. "I say, might this be a bit improper?"

Sebastian shot the woman a quelling glance. "Probably. By the way, Lady Burkestone, are you aware Lord Bentley's chef concocts the most wondrous strawberry tarts this side of Paris? They really are a marvel. I understand they are on the menu for tomorrow and he always begins their preparation the night before. Something about the strawberries having to set properly…"

"You don't say? How interesting." Lady Burkestone rose from her chair, unable to resist the lure of the decadent treat. "I think I'll run to the kitchens and have a peek. Our own cook has an absolute talent for ruining strawberry tarts. It's quite awful, really. There must be a trick to the process I can make note of."

When she was gone, Ivy shook her head at Sebastian. "Do you think this is wise? After all, you have no real knowledge of my skill at whist."

"And you've no knowledge of my skill at winning wagers."

"My lord, you are either very brave or very foolish. Perhaps both. So, tell me, what is your bet? It must be agreed to before it can be properly done."

"A little thing to most, but I claim a kiss as my prize," Sebastian's smile was serene. Murmurs rumbled amongst the men while several ladies leaned forward to impart their most sincere advice on how to best lose the game.

Ivy had no intention of losing. Holding up a hand to halt any further words of encouragement to that end, she considered the earl. "A kiss *and* my ruined reputation? It is far too steep for a simple game of whist. When I win, what prize shall I claim?"

"Why, naturally, a kiss. Would any of you consider less?" Addressing the ladies, Sebastian garnered a round of emphatic headshakes and vows to the contrary.

Ivy laughed in amused disbelief at his audacious statement. "No matter who wins, you emerge the victor while I'm left with a reputation in tatters."

"That is the crux of the issue I face, my dear." He winked at her. "Should I lose to win, or play to lose? Either way, I will delight in the outcome."

Ivy's complaint was half-hearted. Her reputation already hovered on the verge of ruin. She would not think about that now, not with Sebastian grinning at her like that. The prospect of winning or losing the wager was quite titillating. Oh, her reputation be damned! The gauntlet flung at her feet caused a surge of excitement to tilt her stomach. How enjoyable it would be to beat him at *something*. It wasn't fair the handsome devil should find victory in everything.

To be honest, the abandonment over the past two weeks still nipped her. Despite the unspoken acceptance of his unorthodox apology, she wanted to beat him. If only for the momentary satisfaction it provided. Sebastian found it easy to overlook her existence and she wished to prove, if only to herself, she wasn't one of the many spineless women he surrounded himself with.

Sebastian shuffled the cards. "Is it a play or no? Mind you, this will not be a quick, impersonal peck. I shall accept nothing less than a full minute of your...undivided attention."

Ivy's heart skipped as his voice curled around her. He clearly referred to the night of the opera. Arching a brow, it was just as clear he wanted her to remember. But which part? The kisses in the coach? Or the moment he showed her paradise on the tips of his fingers? The slow grin spreading across his handsome face told her. His fingers thrusting between her legs, hot and insistent, demanding she succumb to bliss...

"I would be a fool to agree to those terms." Her face felt hot enough to burst into flames. If anyone guessed her thoughts...

"I would never mistake you for a fool, Countess, but a kiss is what I wish for my forfeit." He knew she was remembering the moment she climaxed, pressed against the wall of her foyer.

The others watched with curious half smiles. Sara wore a perplexed frown, trying to determine what had just occurred.

"I agree with that portion of your terms only," Ivy said in a voice as shaky as her knees. Sebastian Cain was far too gorgeous and far too bloody sure of himself. Was it possible to bring the arrogant devil down a notch or two? Because it wasn't right to remind her of tender kisses and burning caresses and then give her that cocky grin when he knew full well she wanted more. "For my own wager, you shall serve as my groom during the picnic and the ride tomorrow. A humbled earl is the prize." The ladies murmured at the cleverness of the terms while several gentlemen grinned at her naiveté behind raised tumblers of brandy and port.

Something dark and mysterious flitted in Sebastian's eyes. Agreeing without hesitation, he kissed her hand over the whist table to seal the bargain, and Ivy experienced a moment of unease.

"I do hope to prevail. My wager would be the more pleasant undertaking." Sebastian motioned for Alan and Sara to pull their chairs closer.

"The idea of you chastened is quite pleasing, my lord," Ivy purred. "I shall employ all my skills to ensure success."

While watching the battle over terms, Alan smiled in appreciation for what he considered harmless fun. Sara grimaced with concern. Any attempt to intercede, he interrupted, warning her with a murmured, "Let them be." Now, they both frowned, realizing their mistake as Sebastian dealt the cards.

"I do expect you to act the part in every way, including mucking out stalls." Ivy flashed him another impudent smile.

"I fail to see the necessity of manual labor." Sebastian paused in mid-deal, his brow furrowed.

"Afraid of the consequences when you lose?"

"I'll have that kiss, my lady."

Ivy nodded as the game began in earnest. "We shall see."

An hour later, the final card flipped, and Ivy gave an unladylike hoot of triumph. Her reputation would remain in its only slightly tattered state for the time being. Sara breathed a sigh of relief, squeezing Ivy's hand beneath the table while Sebastian and Alan each executed gallant bows. They retreated as others gathered around to offer congratulations.

"Here! Here!" Lord Bancroft, an old friend from Oxford days, raised his glass in a tipsy salute. "To Ravenswood! He emerges the victor after all!" A chorus of boos and cries met his words.

"Are you mad, Bancroft? The earl must play the groom after all," Lady Ansley giggled, giving Ivy a wink. "You should have Ravenswood perform all manners of beastly, disagreeable things, Lady Kinley. It's not often you have an earl at your beck and call!"

Bancroft snorted, wrapping his arms around his stomach to contain his merriment. Port spilled, creating a scarlet stain on his peach hued silk waistcoat. "Nothing requested by the countess could be deemed disagreeable. If it is a beast she needs, I imagine that will be seen to as well. Ravenswood, do not hesitate to call upon me should you need help. Indeed, the three of us could have a jolly time." The handsome young lord swayed, turning a leering, alcoholic-fueled smirk to Ivy.

"Make your apologies, Bancroft. Now. Or would a private meeting at dawn be preferable?"

Sebastian's voice was a sudden plunge through the fragile ice of a pond in the dead of winter. Instant. Immersive. Freezing. Dark winds swirled through the room, sucking the conversation and all warm joviality into a vacuum of silence. All eyes turned to the earl; a rigid statute by the fireplace with eyes of scorching black.

Ivy shivered. This was Sebastian on the night of the Sheffield Ball, the night he hunted her with icy intent, ready to destroy and rip *her* to shreds. A glacier existed inside his soul, the ability to hurt another. That ice threatened to encase her only a month ago, but she'd forgotten the danger while basking in the warm summer of his smile. Yes, she'd seen this man before, and he terrified her.

Bancroft blinked stupidly. He stared at Sebastian for several seconds, the appropriate words rattling around before they managed to roll off his tongue. "Sorry, old chap. Didn't mean to offend-"

"Not me, you drunken buffoon." With lethal calm, Sebastian slowly tilted his head in Ivy's direction.

Bancroft was intoxicated, his words meaningless and offensive in a manner Ivy did not completely understand. But Sebastian did. His gaze bore into the other man with cold intensity.

Bancroft swung toward her. A belated sense of self-preservation seemed to filter through his befuddled haze. A private meeting at dawn meant one thing only. "My apologies, Lady Kinley." Bowing in her general direction, he nearly toppled over a table before catching himself on the edge of it. "I fear I'm not fit for civilized company this evening. Again, my apologies."

Ivy nodded, her eyes locking with Sebastian's as Bancroft's entreaty, punctuated by several hiccups, echoed in the awkward silence. The man made his exit, knocking over an ornate tea table in the process as Sebastian accepted a tumbler of whiskey from a somber servant. The atmosphere of the room quickly returned to its former gaiety.

∾

"SMARTLY DONE," ALAN MURMURED.

"Do you imply I lost on purpose?" Sebastian's lips quirked.

"You know damn well what I'm talking about. Although, I should have seen *that* coming. Bancroft has not lost the tendency to get deep in his cups. I hope this will not put a damper on the remainder of the weekend."

"It won't. He can sleep off his stupidity, and you can be glad I do not have to kill him. That would have surely ruined the party."

Alan's smile widened. "There's little doubt you've staked your claim now. First, the incident at the archery range, now this. And, I hope you appreciate my efforts on your behalf. Good God, I've never played at whist so terribly in my life."

"Nor have I. However, I had complete confidence in my ability, and yours, to lose gracefully without arousing suspicion." Sebastian played very hard to lose. As Ivy's groom, there was the opportunity to touch her quite often. Hell, he'd muck out a stall or two if the possibility existed of stealing a kiss, or more, from her. She could not know what she wagered. Or did she?

"I should have made a similar bet with Sara," Alan mused in regret.

"You've no need for such underhanded methods, Alan. Lady Morgan gives you no cause to devise such elaborate schemes. I must press any advantage to overcome Lady Kinley's suspicions."

"Should she suspect your motives, Seb? I cannot allow any harm to come to her. She is quite dear to Sara and Sara is dear to me, so naturally, I have an interest in their mutual contentment."

At the disapproving undercurrent in Alan's tone, Sebastian shuttered his eyes. "Considering our circumstances, is it any wonder the countess harbors some degree of suspicion? I hold her in the highest esteem, and she intrigues me. She appears to enjoy my company. I delight in hers. What is wrong with a bit of contrivance if it accomplishes the chance to spend the afternoon close to her?"

"Do not hurt her, Seb."

"I've no intention of doing so."

Giving Sebastian a silent, thorough consideration, Alan wordlessly clinked his glass to his and returned to Sara's side.

Bentley was becoming quite fond of Ivy. He would not stand by and allow her destruction. He would be heartbroken to discover the truth later. Sebastian felt a twinge of apprehension to realize he might lose another close friend because of a woman. A strange wistfulness abruptly overcame him as Nicholas March, the absent piece to the former trio of the friendship, rose to mind.

The three of them became men together, experiencing adventures and surviving the various scrapes young gentlemen of leisure were wont to find themselves in. Sebastian foolishly believed nothing could destroy that bond. Then, Marilee twitched her tail, pitting friend against friend. Nicholas attempted to explain his betrayal only once; the dreadful night Sebastian discovered his fiancée's unfaithfulness. He cut Nicholas' excuses short in a fierce rage. While Alan struggled to pull them apart, they brawled like commoners on the steps of Nick's London townhouse.

Two days later, they met on a misty field in Regent Park. Sebastian had Alan and Timothy for seconds, but Nick stood resolute and alone. He refused to name seconds, remarking with a rueful smile only two men were worthy enough to serve at his side, and unfortunately, they stood on the field opposite him. Alan, pale and visibly shaken that morning, lamented the loss of their friendship while Timothy spewed curses and insults, threatening to shoot Landon himself if Sebastian did not.

To his credit, Nick ignored the brash young man, and seemed strangely *willing* to die in Sebastian's quest for satisfaction. True, he fired his weapon first, but into the air and not at his target, while Sebastian missed his aim at the last second, the bullet skimming the outer edge of Landon's upper thigh.

Afterward, Sebastian wondered why Nicholas never corrected the gossip or laid the blame for the duel at his feet. Nick merely smiled whenever the three of them encountered one another, those dark, green eyes of his glittering with something oddly resembling pity. His manner, considered cold by those outside their tight circle, evolved into something cruel and mocking. Six months after the duel, he set sail in his private yacht to various ports for the next two years. The departure, without a word of explanation, nearly drove the Duke of Richeforte, into an apoplectic fit of rage. It put the old man abed for close to a week and from all accounts, *that* pleased young Nicholas immensely when he learned of it.

Maybe it was due to the incident with Bancroft, or maybe it stemmed from seeing Nick the night of the opera, but Sebastian could not ignore the bizarre spasm of nostalgia for his deceitful friend. The walls of his chest clenched, an uncomfortable, hot tightness rattling his bones. He dismissed it to seek out the countess, finding it far easier to forget old betrayals and the disloyalty of those once trusted in the sunshine warmth of Ivy's smile.

CHAPTER 9

*D*uring a restless night of tossing and turning, Ivy reached a conclusion. Sebastian playing at groom was an awful idea; he would inevitably turn the situation to his advantage. Before she was hopelessly muddled in a tangled mess, before he mucked one stall, or bridled a single horse to use as leverage, she must forego the bet. At three in the morning, her concession speech, complete with an appropriate level of sarcasm and humor, was concocted and rehearsed until it sounded perfectly believable.

Ivy intended to grab a scone and a gulp of tea in the dining room on her way to the stables, but a few guests, uninterested in the ride planned for the day, lingered around the table. She politely avoided questions regarding the activities planned for the earl, vastly relieved when no one ventured to make an inappropriate remark. Lord Bancroft stumbled in, sullen and bleary-eyed, to sit at one end of the huge table, studiously ignoring her.

A small crowd milled about the stables when Ivy arrived. They called out encouragement to someone inside. More people trickled into the courtyard as she weaved her way through and coming to a stop outside the double doors, she groaned. She was too late.

"I say, you missed a spot," the Earl of Granger remarked. "Right *there*, Ravenswood."

"Oh. Many thanks, Granger." With a quick scoop of the muck rake, the offending bit of matter flew out of the stall and onto the polished boots of the stocky blonde earl. There were howls of amusement, echoed by the chuckles of a few stable boys gathered in the aisle ways. Fascinated to see a member of the nobility undertaking their task, each secretly hoped Ravenswood might undertake the mucking of all fifty-five stalls.

"Damnation, Ravenswood, you got me with that one!"

"Hmm," Sebastian murmured. "That was the point."

It was impossible to see all of Sebastian through the iron bars. Only the top of his head and those broad shoulders were visible as he labored within the box stall. While Ivy debated what to do, one woman detached herself from the group to walk toward her.

Touching Ivy's arm, the lady grinned. "Who knew Ravenswood might stoop to such efforts to gain a woman's favor?" Lady Caroline Robertson was a lovely woman with dark brown hair and even darker brown eyes. A young, wealthy widow, she was popular and well thought of, and discreet in her affairs, enjoying a favorable reputation among interested gentlemen. Ivy believed the widow's estate bordered Beaumont, Sebastian's country estate, but she wasn't certain. A tiny flame of resentment licked her with the thought.

"How lucky you are, my dear, to have the earl attending you today." Caroline's warm eyes touched on the stall where Sebastian worked so diligently then drifted back to meet Ivy's.

"I intended on releasing him from the wager." Ivy grimaced when another toss of the rake garnered more laughter.

"That wouldn't do at all, my dear. If you believe he will allow you to forgive a debt, you've much to learn. The man always pays what he owes. And collects what is due." The lady's smile turned unconsciously sultry.

What remained of Ivy's self-confidence disappeared like a puff of smoke. A romantic connection once existed between the earl and this old friend. Perhaps it still did. Strange how such matters held a great clarity now. Was it possible others could see what lurked beneath the surface when she and Sebastian were together? It was a disquieting thought.

"Have you known the earl for long, Lady Robertson?" The devil prodded her to ask the question.

Caroline's laugh was far from malicious. Waving to a gentleman arriving at the stables, she admitted, "Long enough to know the man is an awful tyrant! Now, there's Lord Daven, the handsome thing. He's to be my companion today. Try not to tweak Ravenswood's nose too much." Then, with a sly wink, she added, "Unless you are interested in his ideas of retribution."

Excusing herself, Caroline nearly sprinted across the courtyard, calling out to Lord Daven. Ivy stared after her in confusion as Sara came up to link arms with her.

"It would be for the best if you released him from the wager."

Nodded at the group standing precariously close to where Sebastian worked, Ivy said, "I'm afraid to get any closer to tell him. Besides, I've just been advised Ravenswood will not allow it."

"I should stay close to you today." Sara smoothed away a few scone crumbs from the sleeve of Ivy's riding habit. "It's not safe, darling."

"If I go through with it, I intend to keep him busy with plenty of demeaning tasks. He'll not have time to attempt, nor think of improper things. And should he find a spare moment, the man will be so irritated, seduction will be the last thing on his mind."

"It's not safe," Sara repeated when Sebastian lifted his head, scanning the faces of those gathered around. Like a tiger on the hunt for the lone gazelle left on the plains, he found Ivy in the crowd.

Ivy's heart swelled. The man was worldly and handsome and oh, so dangerous. Her previous trepidation concerning his pursuit suddenly seemed to be a moot point. After all, he was no different from other members of the pack…regardless of the anticipation tingling in her veins every time those grey eyes of his slid her way.

Sara groaned in exasperation as Ivy returned Sebastian's heated stare with an answering smile. The air between the two of them fairly crackled with electricity and people were whispering of it. "If you are not careful, you will find yourself truly ruined before this weekend is over. You are already being referred to as Ravenswood's Lady Butterfly by some here."

"It is much better than Poison Ivy," Ivy replied with firm practicality. "Sara, you worry overmuch. In the midst of all these people, I am perfectly safe with the earl. As safe as you are with yours."

Had Ivy bothered to notice, she would not have missed the guilty tremor in Sara's voice, nor the flush in her cheeks when her friend breathed, "Safety in numbers, my dear, is vastly overrated. Certain men have little problem overcoming even that dubious handicap."

SEBASTIAN FEIGNED CONCENTRATION ON THE MUCK SHOVEL gripped tight in his hand. Was Sara reminding Ivy to have a care for her reputation? Warning her away from him? Considering the challenge thrown at Bancroft last night, it would not be farfetched to think so. His interest in her was clear enough; upon their return to London, it would become blatantly obvious.

Ivy would ignore Sara's warnings. She was close to succumbing, ready to drop into his lap like a bit of ripe fruit. The Revenge Situation, as he now referred to it, was moving along very well indeed.

After wiping his hands on a hot towel a stable lad offered him, he made his way to where the horses waited. On the other side of the courtyard, Ivy hugged Sara and began walking toward him. Hiding a smile, he whistled a light tune as he tightened the sidesad-

dle's girth and adjusted the single stirrup on the mare assigned
to her.

"I did attempt to catch you before it was too late. How could I
know you were so eager to muck stalls?" Ivy stroked the dark bay
mare nuzzling into her palm. "Hello, Lilly. Oh, you are a beauty,
aren't you?"

"Merely fulfilling my part of the wager." Sebastian's bow was
mocking. "As your slave, I'm yours to command."

"You are not to be my slave." Her grin held no artifice. "Just a
groom."

"Let us not quibble over the designation." Removing the halter,
Sebastian dropped a bridle over the mare's head, slipping in the bit
with practiced ease.

"I do hope you have been given a steed befitting your new
status. A cart horse, or a mule perhaps?"

Sebastian gathered up the reins to lead her horse from the railing. "I brought my own." His nod indicated a dark gray stallion
standing apart from the others. Occasionally, the beast flung out a
massive rear hoof, followed with an inquisitive look from liquid
dark eyes to observe the victim. When a boy carrying a grain
bucket jogged by, the stallion bared his teeth and gave a low
whinny. Recoiling in surprise, the lad dropped the tin container,
spilling half the oats. The horse nickered in satisfaction, dipping
his head to the limits of the reins tethering him to the post and
lipping up the feed in record time while the youngster collected
himself and the empty bucket. Shaking an angry fist, he hurried on
before the stable master learned of the mishap and boxed his ears.

"Dear Lord," Ivy breathed. "He is most certainly not a
servant's mount."

Sebastian chuckled, wagging a finger at her in mock disappointment. "Like his owner, he is quite capable of behaving when
necessary."

The gray calmed with a quiet word from Sebastian, and as the
bay mare came alongside him, nickered softly and lowered
his head.

"There is nothing to be afraid of," Sebastian said to Ivy. "Raven has certain ideas how he should be greeted. Keep your hands level and approach from the side, so he may see you better. I'm unsure how he formed these opinions, but it's easier to humor this small vice than to try and change him."

"I'm not afraid," Ivy retorted. "But I'll blame you should I come away with half an arm missing." She stroked Raven's neck, wary enough not to get too close, but the horse stepped toward her, bumped his finely sculpted head into her chest and promptly dozed off in contentment.

Sebastian leaned in. "See? Nothing to be frightened of. In fact, I daresay he likes you." Holding Ivy's gaze across the expanse of Raven's broad head, he smiled. "Your touch soothes him."

"Do you think so? He seems half wild and not to be trusted."

His laugh was soft. "Some things are better left wild. Like the roses I sent you. Their scent lingered far longer than ordinary hothouse roses, I vow."

"That's true although I despise roses…" Ivy bit her lip at the confession.

Sebastian cocked his head as her voice trailed away without an explanation for such a puzzling admission. Didn't all women enjoy flowers, regardless of the variety, especially if a man thought to give them? Was this why she never kept the floral arrangements sent to her? He assumed she rejected the gifts simply because she relished toying with the men who gave them.

Ivy caressed Raven's smooth forelock, her mouth tight against any further insights to the cogs of her mind. Sebastian allowed the moment to slip by and decided to focus instead on luring her to him.

"Are you ready to ride, Countess?" Dark with subtle meaning, the words curled around Ivy. When she swayed, he lowered his head to hers. He was so close to those sweet lips he longed to taste again. Unable to erase the flavor of her from his mind, he relived the night of the opera many times. How she came undone on his fingertips, as though she never experienced a climax before. How she clung to him when the wave overtook her. It was so bewitching, the way she reacted to his touch. He longed to slip his hands between her legs again, to elicit the same response again and again until she was limp with pleasure and begging for more.

Raven's eyes snapped open as the grip upon the leather reins tightened

One quick kiss. No one watched them. He could steal a kiss. Just to sustain him until they were alone. The spark of panic in Ivy's turquoise eyes told him she realized his intent.

"Come along, you two!" Alan's voice was booming, tight with frustration. "If you insist on making calf eyes at each other all day, we can't be blamed when you are left behind."

Everyone was mounted and ready to depart, staring with ill-concealed amusement and curiosity. Sara, her blue eyes wide with alarm, seemed on the verge of wringing her hands.

Ivy moved until Raven's sleekly muscled form was between them.

"Coward," Sebastian whispered, his lips curved in a grin. "No kiss for your groom?"

She blinked. "I hardly think it proper to go about kissing grooms here at Bentley Park, but I shall consider it." Pulling Lilly's reins from his loose grip, she stepped to a nearby block to mount the mare on her own. No doubt overhearing her words, a young groom nearly broke his neck jumping to assist her.

Sebastian did not trust himself to reply, and while she swiftly regained her composure, he stood gawking like a simpleton.

Giving the groom a smile of thanks, Ivy settled into the saddle. "Well, maybe not a groom," she clarified, gazing down from her lofty height, "but perhaps a gentleman who offers his assistance without expecting something in return?"

It was that enigmatic half smile, the flash of challenge in her eyes driving Sebastian's insatiable need to conquer her. His hands tightened on Raven's reins until the stallion stomped a hoof, tail swishing in irritation.

"It's unwise to play games with me, Ivy," he warned in a low voice, swinging up onto Raven's back. "You won't care to pay the price."

Her reaction was a cool shrug. "You've yet to fulfill the wager you lost. Perhaps you are not as lucky as you believe."

"We'll see who emerges the true victor." He nodded at the group trotting away from them. "Shall we join them or stay behind and devise a new wager?"

"You can be quite insufferable," Ivy said with admirable calmness. "In fact, you recently were referred to as a tyrant."

Sebastian's gaze roamed over her. She was so damned beautiful, perched atop the dark mare, wearing an amethyst riding habit and those eyes flashing blue green fire at him. As a tyrant, he could snatch her down from that horse and have his way with her, do things that would have her pleading for more. "We can explore that, if you wish."

In reply, Ivy nudged her mount forward, quickly trotting after the others while Sebastian chuckled at her avoidance of him and his suggestion.

The outing was enjoyable, although Sebastian insisted on stopping often for varied reasons. To check the bit on Ivy's mare, to ensure the girth was tight enough, to alter a strap here, a strap there, adjust the stirrup on her saddle. Soon, others gleefully joined in to suggest items requiring his scrutiny.

Each time an inspection was undertaken, he demanded she dismount. Hands encircling her waist, he would swing her from the back of the horse, permitting her to find her footing only after an excruciating long glide down his body. Keeping his back to the others shielded his actions from curious eyes.

The party stopped beside a small, curving stream to allow the horses a bit of water and Sebastian stood at her knee, ready to tug her down once more.

"I insist you put a stop to this," Ivy stared down at him, gripping the reins.

"What do you mean?" She'd been subjected to the journey down his body seven times thus far, and although immensely pleasurable, Sebastian neglected to consider the pure torture of it. By sheer willpower alone, he suppressed the erection lurking inside him, but it twitched to life each time she shimmied down his length.

"You know exactly what I mean!" Ivy hissed.

The first time Sebastian helped her dismount, she should have slapped him senseless instead of tolerating his actions. He knew she enjoyed his attentions even if she struggled to maintain an air of outraged modesty. Bloody hell...she played this innocent act with practiced flair, her dedication to the performance admirable. If he didn't know any better, he might have fallen for it.

Slanting Ivy a wicked grin, he seized her about the waist. "Why, Countess, I have no idea what you're talking about."

She gripped the reins even tighter, eyes flashing with determination she would not be plucked from the mare's back. "You-you are running out of excuses to justify your despicable actions." When his hands lowered, her sigh of relief was audible.

How amusing she underestimated the depths of his resolve to be alone with her.

With a quick flick of his wrist, the single stirrup of the sidesaddle was unfastened. Ivy's heel slid free as the iron separated from the leather. Her mouth dropped open in horror.

"Go on ahead," Sebastian called to the others, his eyes raised and locked with hers. He grabbed her ankle, preventing her from furiously kicking him in the chest. "This damnable stirrup has come completely apart. It will take more than a minute or two to repair it."

Sara watched them in tight-lipped disbelief and for a moment, Sebastian believed she would gallop straightaway to attach herself to Ivy. But Alan quickly reached to take the lady's mare by the bit, murmuring something before letting her go. With one last worried glance over her shoulder, Sara wheeled her horse around.

Sebastian flashed Alan a grin of thanks as the others reluctantly moved away from the spring. When the last of them disappeared through the meadow and into the thick of the woods, he turned to Ivy.

"Now that they're gone..." Swinging her down in a flurry of skirts, he ignored her gasp of frustration, enjoying how she squirmed with the energy of an angry kitten. He did not release her even when her toes finally touched firm earth. Keeping her molded against him, one arm encircling her waist, his thighs pressed hard to hers.

While she was off-balance and struggling, he tipped her chin with the palm of his hand to claim her mouth with a voracious hunger. Ivy's attempts to push him away continued unabated, and Sebastian allowed her to twist and writhe. When she finally stilled in defeat, he bit her lower lip, swollen pink from his kisses.

"Arms around my neck, Countess."

Ivy scowled but did as directed.

Immediately the kiss melted to something soft and fluttering, rewarding her acquiescence to his stern command. Under the urging of his fingers, her riding jacket opened, the proper ascot coming unwrapped with alarming ease. The tiny pearl buttons of her lawn shirt slipped one by one from their moorings as though commanded by unseen forces. As the cool morning breeze drifted over them, he backed her into the concealing shadows of the grove until she was caught between the sturdiness of an elm tree and the warm hardness of his body. A low growl rumbled through him.

Time for the countess to surrender another piece of herself.

Sebastian's hands skimmed past rows of petite ruffles lining her chemise, playing, testing, tugging at the silk ribbons holding it all together. The edge of the garment eased down, slowly, before Ivy even realized what was happening to stop him. His lips closed with unerring purpose over a rose petal nipple. God, never had he had tasted anything so sweet, so fine, as her soft flesh.

Ivy choked in surprise as his tongue swirled and licked her. Her gloved hands moved to his head, sliding through his hair. She may have thought about yanking him away. Her hands clenched in the soft waves with a sudden ferocity just as Sebastian, with a wickedness long ago perfected, raked his teeth over the hardening bud of her flesh.

It wasn't fair. He knew that. She would forget to struggle, to protest. To breathe. As expected, Ivy drew him close. He held her nipple, caught fast between his teeth, and flicked his tongue back and forth over the contracted tip with a merciless intensity. With a moaning shudder, she pulled him even closer still.

It was heaven. Or, maybe it was hell. There was no guarantee such pleasure could continue forever. Ivy Kinley tasted of oranges and the freshness of spring. Damn, he couldn't get enough and he feasted until her head tilted against the rough bark of the elm and she began arching into his mouth. Trailing his tongue over the valley between her breasts, Sebastian began anew with the other peak, savoring every nuance of her. When he pulled back, her eyes snapped shut with the sharpness of abandonment, and a sob of protest rang out in the little glade.

"Ivy." Sebastian's voice was hoarse. She was boneless in his arms, as if she was melting into him. If he must sell his soul to the Devil, he would do it, just to have her. "Look at me. Open your eyes and *look* at me."

She focused on him, her eyes heavy, now more green than blue, the thick eyelashes sweeping across the upper curves of her cheeks. The sprinkle of freckles across her nose beckoned him to kiss each golden one. "Sweet, sweet Ivy," he breathed, catching her bottom lip between his teeth. "Christ, you are destroying me."

Pulling off her riding gloves, Sebastian flung them to the side along with his own. He shrugged out of his coat and removed hers as well, tossing the garments carelessly to the ground. Taking her hands, he placed them on his midriff, silently telling her what he wanted her to do.

Ivy faltered, then slowly pulled his shirt free of the confines of his breeches, unfastening buttons until the hot flesh of his stomach was exposed. Drifting with purpose, her fingers smoothed the fabric aside. When she finally touched bare flesh, Sebastian's groan vibrated through them both.

The dips and elevations of the muscles lining his abdomen seemed to fascinate her. She explored his ribs, the slabs of muscling constructing his back and bunching along the line of his broad shoulders. Her hands skimmed over his flat, dark nipples, a wordless murmur escaping her when they contracted to hardened points and stabbed at her palms. When she traced the swirl of dark hair below his navel with a fingertip, Sebastian's teeth clenched so hard he thought they might crack. She was a witch. Driving him to the brink of utter madness.

He captured her wrist when she fumbled with the top button of the breeches. Filled with confusion and desire, her eyes lifted to his.

"*Don't,*" Sebastian growled. "I won't be able to stop if you continue..."

A light flared in Ivy's eyes, a flash of understanding. "But you are so beautiful." Her whisper was bemused wonder, her free hand gliding along the washboard of his stomach. "I want to touch you..."

A strangled laugh choked Sebastian. Making love in this unguarded, open environment was truly insanity. He needed privacy, the seclusion of a locked room to strip her bare and fill himself with her scent. Fill his mouth with the taste of her. Over and over until he was saturated in her.

With a reluctant sigh, he drew the chemise back into place. With her breasts covered, his thoughts became more rational. "Men aren't beautiful."

"You are." Ivy did not question why he covered her nudity. "I've never known anyone like you. I want to know why I tremble when your fingers are on my skin, why I cannot stop thinking of you, day or night. I cannot stop thinking of the last time we were together. I want so desperately to be angry with you, but I have missed you too much. Everything about this feels both dangerous and incredible. Sebastian, help me. Help me understand." Standing on tiptoe, her mouth pressed to his neck, where the pulse beat so strong in the hollow of his throat. Almost hesitantly, she bit him softly, and then kissed where her teeth marked him.

It undid him, that sweetly wicked bit of a kiss. It ruined him, those heated words of a temptress and the teeth of a tigress. Groaning in surrender, he hauled her against him. Why waste words on the unexplainable? He would *show* her instead. Even if it was dangerous to do so.

He kissed her repeatedly until she was panting and frantic with need, clutching him, her body trembling. When he lowered her to the ground, cushioned by discarded riding coats and soft green grass, she went willingly. Her chemise was jerked down a second time, her breasts exposed to the cool air only to be consumed in the fiery heat of his mouth. Shoving the skirts of her riding habit high, his hands slid with unrelenting purpose between her thighs. For a sliver of a heartbeat, as on the night of the opera, she clenched against his touch.

Sebastian waited, as he did before, his breath still, his hands still, his heart still. He thought he might explode, waiting, wanting, hating himself. Hating her for his vulnerability to this dangerous obsession.

Ivy relaxed, softening, melting, giving herself over to him. Her stomach quivered as his fingertips coasted through the soft curls at the juncture of her long legs. When his touch dipped to trace the center of her being, she exhaled a sigh of sweet welcome, shaking Sebastian to his core. He could not move, overcome with gratitude. This beautiful, enchanting creature belonged to him, if only for this moment.

Time stood unmoving, only dust motes dancing restlessly in and out of the broken sunshine. The muted trickle of water flowing in the shallow stream and their breathing filled the innumerable seconds, the chirping from a robin's nest hidden among the elm's branches creating a cadence backdrop.

"Do you want this, Ivy?" His hand collected her need, giving it back in slow, sweet glides that left her soft and damp. "If this continues, we will never go back to what we were before. Do you understand? Do you understand what I want from you?" If she told him to stop, he was unsure what his reaction might be.

Ivy arched into his hand in response. "Yes, Sebastian. *Yes.* Show me, tell me how to please you."

Sebastian's eyes flamed hot. Shifting his body, he braced himself up on one elbow to unfasten his breeches. He grasped her wrist, dragging her hand to the space between his thighs and although she appeared mystified, he did not let go until her fingers closed upon his solid length. The thrill of it threatened to unman him as he filled her palm, his flesh straining.

"Here, sweet, touch me here, *like this.*" Words filled his throat, choking him. The pleasure was excruciating. Soft and hesitant, her touch was an exquisite fire, her fingers quickly learning the shape and size of him.

This sweet innocence was a gift from an impressive arsenal. The façade was appealing, a welcome change from any other woman in his orbit. It made the game of pursuit and capture infinitely more stimulating. Ivy enjoyed it too. What else explained the flashing grin she threw him sometimes, the one that said, "Oh! Isn't this fun?" whenever he won a kiss from her? What a treasure she was. Tailoring responses to a man's enjoyment. Having never seduced a virgin before, he liked the illusion too much to destroy it. For now, he would play her games. Even if it were all a facade, unreal, it was still incredibly arousing.

When her touch became bolder, Sebastian's hand drifted to the core of her body to resume his measured assault with clever fingers.

Ivy knew just how to squeeze him, when to stroke faster, and softer, all of it interspersed with a butterfly touch as she gently explored his straining erection. She possessed the delicate artistry of a skilled courtesan, but Sebastian feared he lost the conquest of the moment. She tied him into knots with her magical fingertips. He could not allow this. He must shatter her first. Her heart won by the conquering of the flesh under his hand.

The tempo of his fingers increased, swirling over and into her soft wetness as she mirrored the actions upon his body. He had no idea how close she was to climaxing until a muffled cry escaped her. The knowledge she flew apart on the tips of his fingers flung him over the edge as well. Groaning with satisfaction, he fused their mouths in a blistering kiss as the universe splintered apart in a kaleidoscope of sensation. Pleasure wound tight about them, stitching two imperfect halves together to form one unbroken piece.

An eternity passed before they drifted back to the cove of elm trees where a carpet of deep, fragrant grass cushioned their bodies and a lazy, winding stream sang so sweet.

CHAPTER 10

olly settled a ball gown of deep green emerald silk over Ivy's head. Cut square across, the harsh lines of the bodice dipped low before narrowing at the waist and flaring into wide, graceful skirts. Ivy ignored the matching satin gloves, hoping Sebastian would forgo the formal items as well. When he took her in his arms, she wished to feel his hands on her, skin to skin.

Swallowing past the catch in her throat, she wondered if it were possible no one saw the effects of the miraculous events of this afternoon. Was she not visibly branded in some way by Sebastian's touch? She should be, after the liberties she allowed him. Only his discretion kept matters from progressing any further in the secret cove of trees today. He could have tossed her skirts and made love to her several times over. Beneath the onslaught of caresses, the burning, rough silk of his fingers, she practically begged him to do so. She wanted him to touch her, wanted his hands on her, around her, his fingers *inside* her.

Ivy shifted, an inarticulate sound of agitation earning a questioning glance from Molly as she placed matching slippers on her feet. How could she forget his choked groan of release and her own shattering response? She could not, for it seared into her brain. Somehow, that sleek, heavy part of him was supposed to fit inside her, the fluid expelled into her palm meant to be *inside* her. None of which seemed remotely possible. Sebastian's finger barely fit, stretching her almost painfully, before a delicious sense of yielding overcame the discomfort when he stroked her. Something even larger burrowing into her body was unimaginable.

The discovery he had hair down there too, only much coarser and more abundant, amazed her. Ivy wondered what he looked like completely unclothed. Blast it, the entire interlude left Ivy with a litany of unanswered questions. If only her explorations could have continued. *If only Sebastian had not seemed to tremble on the very narrow edge of his self-control.* Perhaps, it was for the best things ended as they did.

That morning, after leaving her side and returning with his silk handkerchief cold and damp from the icy waters of the brook, she did not understand. Suffused with embarrassment, she allowed him to clean away the evidence of his passions from her palm. With gentle fingers, he refastened the buttons of her blouse and helped her to stand, tugging her skirts back to a decent state. His hand held her steady at the elbow when her knees wobbled. Retrieving their coats from the ground, he shook them out; muttering under his breath to discover the mud stains on his and the wrinkles on hers. Assisting her into the fashionable jacket, his palms smoothed out the creases with impassive firmness, over her shoulders, down her chest and her back while Ivy sucked in quick breaths of heated joy.

When he swung her onto the mare's back, Sebastian had yet to utter a word directly to her, but his eyes, when Ivy stole a glance at him, glowed with the tiniest bit of victory.

This cursed infatuation left her achingly vulnerable, in danger of becoming one of his many conquests. Her calm prudence fled with distressing ease when she was with him, for he intoxicated her. The lateness of the hour nor too many glasses of champagne could not excuse her wantonness. Not this time. The admiring whispers of the women pursuing him, scrabbling for any crumb of affection tossed their way all made perfect sense. The realization should be chilling, now that she was one of their number.

But it did not. And probably would not. It would surely bring heartache, but she was in love with Sebastian.

A devastating diagnosis. If Sara's glum prediction evolved, Ivy knew her ruination was imminent, and if his reputation proved true, the earl would quickly lose interest in her.

She had two options. Maintain a measure of distance from him, resulting in a state of absolute misery, or, revel in Sebastian's attention and glory in the dizzying pleasure while it lasted.

Ivy sighed. Either way, when things came to their sad, inevitable end, she was doomed.

SEBASTIAN SMOOTHED HIS EBONY-HUED EVENING JACKET, CURSING softly under his breath. The failure to exploit Ivy's flagrant invitation that morning had his nerves stretched taut as piano wires. He possessed the devil's own temper since returning from the ride, snarling and snapping, earning curious glances and muttered whispers from others. His new valet, William, hired during his last trip to Scotland, was already accustomed to his employer's turns of ill mood. The elderly man sidled out of the way as Sebastian debated the wearing of formal gloves, only to toss the things aside with a muttered curse.

Why? Why did he not take Ivy? He ought to have parted her pale, creamy thighs, unbuttoned his breeches and slid deep inside her. At the very least, part of his revenge would be fulfilled. Ivy would be his. He could have had her, quenched his thirst for her. When he overcame her half-hearted resistance, she proved quite willing, damned near driving him crazy with that flirtatious exploration of his body.

The interlude by the stream was all too brief. Sebastian's teeth clenched, remembering how he erupted within her silky grasp, every bit of it orchestrated with the finesse of a seasoned courtesan. It was damned difficult not to take her right there on the ground in a flurry of heated need and impatient lust. She knew he would not succumb to such temptation, but it certainly did not stop her from trying to manipulate him.

Soon, his moment would come to claim her. It would be at *his* leisure, with no threat of interruption and not on the hard, cold forest floor. In the privacy of a bedchamber, he would take Ivy Kinley as many times as needed; slake his thirst until she no longer fascinated him, taste her as often as he liked, over and over until she was out of his blood. He planned to make love to her until they were both wrung dry, sweat dripping from their bodies in mingled rivulets of passion. He would fall asleep to her sighs of contentment ringing in his ears. Then, he would roll atop her, kiss her awake and begin anew. She would be unable to escape. He would make damn sure she did not want to.

∼

THE SMILE IVY GAVE SEBASTIAN FROM ACROSS THE ROOM WAS SO radiant, it pierced him like an arrow. Unlocking her arm from Sara's, she waited patiently for him to come to her.

Alan stood closer to the two girls, claiming Sara quickly, lifting her off her feet in his enthusiasm. She laughed in delight as he twirled her before pulling her into a remote corner where they proceed to laugh and whisper to one another. Sebastian was further away, in conversation with Lady Caroline, but he abruptly excused himself as the lady shook her head in bemusement.

"Goddamn it," he muttered, forced to the sidelines by couples taking their places for the next dance. Another laid claim to the countess before he could reach her, sweeping her away to the tune of a lively Scottish reel. Shooting Sebastian an apologetic smile, Ivy turned her attention to the gentleman holding her hand.

Is it necessary for Darington to hold her so damn close? Sebastian swirled his bourbon in distraction, eyes glued to Ivy laughing in delight, her feet flying through the pattern. She was never this carefree with the crowd in London. In Town, she was polite and distant and Sebastian was glad. This display of genuine pleasure was simply too overwhelming. Those sparkling, laughing eyes of hers made a man desperate to gain her attention, to prove himself worthy of that attention. It suddenly was not foolish at all to consider writing a sonnet or two, or twenty, all dedicated to Ivy Kinley's beauty. Maybe he should buy her a caravan of precious jewels. Or paint her portrait. Or simply sit in worship at her feet.

Whether laughing or aloof, there was no shortage of men eager to adore Ivy. Should she shun society because men found her irresistible?

Making excuses for her left him irrationally angry. With himself.

Even with the dubious aid of three more bourbons, his mood did not improve.

Ivy curtsied deeply to Lord Darington at the end of the dance and Sebastian nearly cracked the crystal tumbler he held. She must know how enticing she was. Her breasts strained against the confines of the square neckline, nearly spilling over, the emeralds at her neck twinkling as if to beckon every man to enjoy a closer look. He squirmed, conflicted, unsure if he wished to rush over and yank the bodice higher or relax and admire the lovely view.

Her gloves, worn to conceal the pale pink stripe of a scar, were missing. Somehow, their absence left her more exposed than the low-cut nature of her gown. Without knowing why, Sebastian interpreted it as a sign, one last barrier eliminated between them.

Ivy waved off the invitation to another dance with a laugh. Darington, the fool, stared after her while she drifted away, his disappointment obvious to anyone watching. Another heart captured and crushed by Poison Ivy.

Something dangerous glinted within Sebastian as she approached, something cruel and hard in direct contrast to her softness. He hated it, but it was necessary. It was the only way to withstand what boiled inside him. *Tonight, I'll have her.* He would not yield to her intoxicating softness, but he would wait no longer to claim her body. When he took her, it would not be with sweetness and endearments. It could not be, not if he did this for Timothy's sake.

"Good evening, Sebastian."

He straightened from leaning a shoulder against the jamb of the terrace door to brush a cool kiss across her bare knuckles. "Countess. You are enchanting, as usual. Are you enjoying the ball?"

Ivy took a discreet step away from the simmering heat in his gaze. "Very much so. Lord Bentley is a wonderful host, although you probably believe this all terribly provincial. Considering your travels abroad, I would think you might find country life a bit sedate."

Sebastian's eyes narrowed. Few dared mention his sojourn from England. It was a dangerous subject. "Before leaving for the Continent, I treasured time spent at my estates. I love being in the country." Giving her a sideways glance, he smiled. "I am particularly fond of stolen moments by winding streams and elm trees. To discover we share the same affection pleases me. In the near future, I would enjoy showing you a similar locale at my ancestral home. It's quite lovely."

Ivy's face flushed pink, but she did not retreat, her eyes holding a spark of challenge. "I cannot imagine when such an occasion might present itself again, my lord."

The corners of Sebastian's mouth lifted. "A small matter and one easily remedied. I shall arrange a visit to Beaumont for you."

"Perhaps." It was a noncommittal reply, designed to drive him wild with longing, but Ivy's eyes were deep, guileless pools of aquamarine. "Will you remain in London for the rest of the Season or return to France?" Her question was unexpected. She half turned from him, watching the couples swirl around the ballroom floor.

Sebastian frowned. What lay behind her desire to determine his plans? Were things becoming too complicated? Perhaps she did not want him as her next lover. If so, that was most unfortunate. His intentions were for the event to take place that very night. And he intended to enjoy himself very much.

"My plans have not been fully put into place." His stomach tightened when she lightly touched his arm.

"I do hope you stay." Bringing his attention to Alan and Sara, dreamily smiling at one another as they whirled around the ballroom floor, Ivy continued, "I am sure you will want to be here for the wedding."

Sebastian's eyebrow shot up. Last evening, Alan confided his plan to ask for Sara's hand but other than Sara's parents, no one else knew of the impending engagement. "Are you so confident of a match?" Why his friend's plans to marry bothered him, Sebastian could not say…but it was not jealousy.

Watching Sara giggle as Alan whispered in her ear, Ivy sighed. "Lord Bentley will not be able to resist Sara much longer…she hopes she has captured his heart as he has captured hers." Glancing up, a small frown marked her brow. "You shall not repeat this, will you, Sebastian? Sara would be devastated to know I divulged the depths of her feelings, even though I did not mean to do so."

With a grim smile, he leaned to whisper in her ear, "Do not worry. Your secret is safe. I will be here for the wedding."

Her gaze grew tender. "Then I am happy. Not only for their sake." The tiny squeeze she gave his arm shot straight to his groin. "I would miss you terribly if you went away again. Or, if you decided England was no longer to your liking."

Yes. Tonight. It must be tonight before I'm hauled off to Bedlam. Prepare yourself, Countess. I'm coming for you.

ONLY IVY NOTICED ALAN PULLING SARA OUT ONTO THE TERRACE and away from the cheerful chaos of the ball. She made no move to follow or stop them. Neither Lady Burkestone, in deep conversation with another lady regarding her new French seamstress, nor Posie, Sara's ancient maid, asleep in a chair in a distant corner, seemed to take note. To ensure no one disturbed the couple, Ivy positioned herself before those terrace doors, refusing numerous offers to dance.

When the lovers returned half an hour later, Ivy grudgingly allowed the Marquis of Berkshire to pull her into a waltz. She was so very curious as to what was said on that terrace. Sara glowed and Alan wore such a pleased smile, his face appeared in danger of splitting in two. From over the Marquis's shoulder, she watched them find a darkened corner to share a glass of champagne. For the rest of the waltz, they remained there, laughing and whispering until Alan pulled Sara up onto the musician's platform.

"Friends." Alan slid his arm about Sara's waist, smiling with indulgent patience when she blushed a pretty pink. People murmured with excitement, shuffling closer. Ivy's heart contracted with a painful tightness while the Marquis gave her a puzzled shrug.

"Something wonderful and quite amazing has just occurred. My deplorable state of bachelor misery will soon end. Lady Sara Morgan has granted me the greatest honor by agreeing to become my wife."

The room erupted into cheers, men letting loose with whoops of approval while women squealed in glee. A loud din of voices erupted as well-wishers converged on the happy couple. Alan found himself repeatedly slapped on the back in congratulations while several ladies tugged Sara to their midst. The heirloom Bentley diamond and ruby ring, passed down from countess to countess for generations, glittered on Sara's finger, admired with much thoroughfare. When the Marquis rushed to join the throng, Ivy was abandoned. Her failure to go congratulate the new couple was incomprehensible but her feet felt glued to the floor.

She was not alone in withholding her well-wishes.

Sebastian stepped through the entrance leading from the attached conservatory, three men pushing past him to investigate the commotion. He leaned against the doorjamb, arms lightly crossed while observing the festive celebration. Unaware of her perusal, his face was a blank canvas giving little insight into his private thoughts.

Suddenly, Ivy believed Sebastian to be the loneliest person in the entire world. An overwhelming sadness flooded her, an irresistible urge to go to him, to envelope him in her arms. He might shove her aside, snarling at the slightest hint of pity, but she felt drawn to him in a manner hard to explain.

She'd taken only a few steps when Sara burst through the horde to wrap her in a fierce embrace.

"Can you believe it?" she exclaimed, laughing and crying at the same time. "Oh, Ivy. It's a dream come true, a fairytale. Look, I may bruise from pinching myself so many times!"

"I am so happy for you, dearest. So very happy. I knew this would happen." Ivy hugged her tight, searching out Sebastian over her friend's shoulder. "Bentley had no choice but to fall in love with you."

Sebastian's attention finally shifted to them, those slate colored eyes of his remaining unreadable. A jolting undercurrent passed between them and Ivy shivered. He appeared almost a stranger. When she gave him a tremulous smile, wiping tears from her cheeks while Sara embraced her again, he merely bowed his head, an odd expression crossing his face.

For the next few moments, Ivy was caught up with a group of other women in admiring the engagement ring. Not until Alan pulled Sara away was she able to look for the earl. By then, however, Sebastian was gone.

Where he went, and why he did not return for the remainder of the evening, dominated Ivy's thoughts. Later that night, as Molly packed away various items into their traveling trunks for the return to London the following afternoon, worry for Sebastian drove away any thought of sleep Ivy possessed.

Clad in a puff of a nightgown, constructed of delicate white lawn and lace with numerous ribbons and full flowing sleeves, Ivy sat at a walnut wood vanity, pulling an ivory backed brush through her hair. She found it difficult to erase the image of Sebastian's expression as everyone congratulated Alan and Sara. For just an instant, when he looked at her, there was a mix of both wistful and guilty jealousy in his features...

"Such a lovely time you've had here, milady," Molly remarked cheerfully.

"Yes, it's been wonderful." With the exception of the last two hours, everything was almost perfect. But the dark air Sebastian wore about him tonight tied her into anxious knots. It was a startling departure from the playful earl who kissed her into submission that very morning.

"Now that Lady Morgan got herself engaged to the earl, you're sure to visit this place often. All seem right pleased with the match." The maid finished with her tasks, taking the brush from Ivy's hands to pull the curls into a loose braid.

"I'm so very happy for her." A twinge of something stirred within Ivy. Elation for Sara, yes, but a tiny sliver of her heart wished...

"Ooh, and Lord Bentley, he's a handsome cove, that he is," Molly sighed, then with a sly grin, she added, "but not as handsome as what your earl is. I must say, I've yet to see his match if you don't mind my boldness in sayin' so."

"Molly," Ivy admonished as the maid chuckled.

"Maybe your earl will have the itch and propose too, milady."

Before Ivy could comment on such an unlikely scenario, there was a soft tapping at the door.

"It must be Sara," Ivy murmured. Now that everyone had retired, Sara probably wished to share her joy. It was a scenario reminiscent of their days as schoolgirls, when they would spend hours flung across their narrow beds, sharing secrets and dreams until the wee hours of the morning. Throwing on a robe, Ivy stood behind Molly as she cracked the door open.

Both women gaped in horrified shock. One massive shoulder propped against the doorframe, Sebastian's grin was cocky, his eyebrow lifting in a slight arc upon seeing Ivy in her flimsy nightclothes. His own shirt lay unbuttoned to the top of his dark breeches, the open edges revealing his naked chest. In the low light cast by the hall scones, his exposed skin gleamed and Ivy's eyes glued to the burnished expanse before jerking her fascinated gaze away.

"Obviously, I was not expected," he drawled. A blood red rose dangled from his hand. It was mesmerizing, the way he spun it back and forth in his blunt, elegant fingers.

Molly reacted first. Sputtering in outrage, she drew herself up to the full height of five feet and one inch.

From the relative safety behind Molly's shoulder, Ivy's voice shook. "I thought you were Sara. This - this is disgraceful, Ravenswood. You must leave at once!"

He only smirked at that, his height giving him an unfair advantage. "Not an option, Ivy. Shall I tell you why?"

He intends to enter my room! Just as Ivy realized it, Molly attempted to slam the door in a flurry of evasive actions.

Sebastian's toe blocked the effort. His boot wedged against the frame with the firmness of a boulder and even Molly did not possess the courage required to shove the door on a blooming earl's toe. It was the only thing keeping the door from crashing shut. Not his shoulder, nor his leg; not even an arm. Just his toe. The power one earl's toe held was rather astonishing.

With an awful deliberateness, he warned, "We've unfinished business, you and I. Now, let me in. Before things get messy."

He could not possibly mean to force the issue. Not tonight. He was obviously hanging onto civility by a mere thread and that confused Ivy. Sebastian exercised restraint on the banks of that stream today. He gave pleasure when he could have taken everything without a whimper of protest from her. Would he *really* take by force what she denied him now?

He had been drinking. Why? Was he not happy for Alan and Sara? Was he angry with her for some reason? Did he regret their actions that morning? Or was he sorry for not taking more? Was that why he stood at her door now? Impatient and hungry?

Ivy swallowed, gripping the edges of her robe with tight

fingers. The faint odor of bourbon and expensive cigars wafted from Sebastian. Mingling with the crisp sweetness of cinnamon and the powdery fragrance of roses, it created an intoxicating blend. Another indefinable air also clung to him, one concocted of sin and pleasure. He was so handsome, shrouded in the darkened doorway, with eyes glittering and mysterious, the rose dangling from his fingertips. Those hands of his caused her to lose all reason. Perhaps he *could* come in...

"Your services are no longer needed," Sebastian snapped at Molly. The weakness he sensed in Ivy was as powerful as fresh blood to a wolf.

The maid's loyalty was too deeply ensconced to abandon her mistress. "Beggin' pardon, milord. You're a frightful sight, roaming about, half-dressed. It is indecent for you to call upon milady at this hour. With her feeling poorly, she's bid me stay close." Her fiercest frown accompanied a half curtsy just before her heels burrowed into the carpet. "I'll not be going anywhere without her say-so."

Sebastian scowled at the unanticipated obstacle to his intentions. Ivy's shoulders lifted in a weak apology when his glare shifted to her.

"She is right, you know. You are half-dressed," Ivy's reply was a fragile rebuke. "And frightful."

Thank God for Molly. Her bristling, crimson-faced presence served as the sole deterrent to an otherwise incredibly foolhardy and irreversible decision. Pulling her robe closer, Ivy waited to see what Sebastian would do.

HE DID NOT EXPECT THIS. DID NOT EXPECT A DAMN MAID TO BE guarding the sanctuary of Ivy's bedchamber like a demon of the underworld. No, he imagined sweet-talking his way in, overcoming objections with kisses. He envisioned caresses and whispers of everything he would do to her until the countess surrendered with a willing sigh.

A thorn bit into his thumb. He gripped the rose so violently, its stem was crushed. A vision of slowly tracing that rose down Ivy's lovely and very naked body, from forehead to the tips of her toes, plagued him from the moment he pulled it from a floral arrangement in the upper hall. He possessed every intention of kissing the path forged by the softness of those petals.

The vivid schemes his brain created drove him to distraction. The sweetness of the interlude beneath the elm trees only inflamed his appetite and damn it to hell, he tired of playing these games. He was half-mad with need. Need he hardly understood.

He wanted her. Tonight. He would have her. Tonight.

"Dismiss her." His command was a growl, frustration and alcohol blending into a dangerous combination. How loud would Molly scream if he shouldered his way into the room? Would anyone investigate if the redheaded fiend landed on her arse in the hall? "Dismiss her now."

Ivy took a deep breath, her gaze unwavering. "I will not do that, Sebastian. You know I cannot let you in."

Was that a glint of triumph in those lovely turquoise eyes? Or panic? Everything was upside down. Sebastian was not sure of anything anymore. *Damn you! Do you enjoy seeing me groveling at your door? Dancing to the merry tune you play?* His hands clenched and for an instant, lunacy threatened to overtake him.

Reason tried desperately to gain his attention. Once again sharp thorns bit into his palm.

"Ivy, so help me, I will break this door down. Let me in...."

Once he disposed of Molly, he would lock the damn door. He'd have Ivy all to himself. Even if the maid shouted her head off in the hallway, he could slake his thirst before anyone stopped him. And should Ivy scream, well, there were ways to prevent that. His kisses would easily transform her screams to moans and pleas for more...

He was stunned when Ivy pushed Molly out of the way. Standing in the narrow opening, her hands gripping the edge of the door, Ivy was within his grasp if he only reached out to seize her. The odd sorrow flaring in her gaze immobilized him. Suddenly reconciling his overwhelming desire with the cold, hard plans for revenge was impossible.

Against all reasoning, scheming and design, he simply wished to hold her, his arms wrapped tight about her. He wanted to wake the next morning, warm and sleepy, with his butterfly countess smiling into his eyes. Her fragrance swirled about him, mingling with the aroma of the rose to tickle his nose. Like powerful witchcraft it sapped his strength. Leaving him vulnerable to whatever *she* desired.

"I beg of you, Sebastian, do not do this. Not tonight, when the two people we hold most dear have declared their love for one another. Do not ruin the perfection of *their* moment. Please say goodnight to me." Rising on tiptoes, she kissed him softly on the mouth. "*Please.*"

Sebastian shuddered. Violent need and the want for something more coursed through him.

He wanted to snatch her to him. He wanted to carry her off to his quarters as though he were a bloody pirate flush with hard-won treasure, or a Viking warrior enjoying the spoils of war. She was so damned beautiful and glowing and that braid her unruly hair was twisted into practically screamed for his hands to untangle it, to spread across the pillows in all its glory. He wanted to kiss every golden freckle scattered across that pert nose of hers. He wanted to explore the softness of the flesh behind her knees, the thinness of the skin covering the veins of her wrists. Everything that made her Ivy, he wanted to discover. He wanted to learn all her secrets and make her his forever.

"I want you," he breathed, dizzy with all his wants. "And I will have you..."

She smiled, nodding in understanding. Soft, sad, sympathetic. "Yes. But not this night."

While he stood there, thinking of all the things he *wanted* to do, she gently closed the door, her eyes holding his until the golden light from her room disappeared. Before Sebastian knew what happened, he was alone in the shadowy corridor.

Ivy had tamed him, for the moment. A tangled confusion replaced the coldness in his heart, ripping fissures into his cruel resolve. The rose gripped tight between his fingers bore smears of blood across almost every petal. *His* blood, much darker than the blossom's hue. With deliberate savagery, he crushed the flower until petals rained to the floor, a scattering of scarlet reminders the countess won this skirmish.

"Please," she had said even while turning him away.

Much later, the memory of her lips brushing his was a burning reminder of his own dark desires as he tossed and turned in his solitary bed. Sleep finally came close to dawn and dreams mocked his failure to take what he wanted. Dreams where Ivy writhed as he brought her to climax after climax. She wrapped about him, whispering her need and in his damned dreams, Sebastian willingly did everything she asked and more.

"Please," Ivy said. In the darkest corners of Sebastian's imagination she opened her arms, begging him to claim her. *To love her...*

It burned like the coals of hell to admit she possessed a piece of him.

CHAPTER 11

Gossip regarding a peculiar incident outside Lady Kinley's bedroom door on the last night of the Earl of Bentley's country party circulated for days. Following an apparent misunderstanding, the Earl of Ravenswood, half-undressed and magnificently foxed, located his own bedchamber. It was then, the unnamed source gleefully reported, the earl slammed the door shut in a fit of such bruising ferocity, every portal in that wing of the house shook.

Naturally, once details emerged of Sebastian's attentive nature during that weekend, it was assumed he committed himself to an exclusive pursuit of the countess. But, many whispered, something was not quite right.

Upon return to the city they attended one ball and a play together, the atmosphere between them best described as cold and strained. Indeed, Sebastian declined to dance with the countess at the ball. To Ivy's surprise, he did not even kiss her hand at the end of those two evenings. He deposited her on Kinley House's doorstep as though eager to be rid of her.

Her rejection of his advances at Bentley Park must have stung his pride enough to freeze the ardent pursuit. Or had he simply

tired of her? A man with his appetites would find such inexperi-
enced prey not worth the effort. After all, women tumbled headfirst
in his bed with no demands or expectations on his person. The earl
was accustomed to such behavior. Could he understand she was
not like those women and never would be? She wanted more. She
would have all of Sebastian. Or none of him.

It seemed logical to cut ties. To end this madness and accept
defeat. Ivy's soul wept at the thought, finding it impossible to
commit to the idea. She could not let him go, could not imagine his
lips never touching hers again. But she also could not continue this
way, held hostage to the mercurial swing of the earl's moods. This
hopeful, agonizing limbo, her heart teetering in the balance, was
causing untold pain.

After that first week Sebastian did not call on her, although he
remained in London. With the evident chill in their relationship the
Pack happily filled the void. Ivy hid her turmoil beneath smiles of
indifference as whispers trailed in her wake.

Her resolve to end the relationship grew apace with the aching
in her heart and one week stretched into two. Ivy decided if she
heard from the heartless cad again she would tell him to go straight
to the devil.

On a bright morning bursting with all the warm freshness of
late spring, a simple request arrived from the Earl of Ravenswood.
Would Ivy accompany him on a turn-around Hyde Park that
afternoon?

"You wish to change again?" Molly's tone verged on incredulous. "That's four times, milady."

Ivy ignored the maid's pursed lips of disapproval. "I can count,
Molly. Yes, again. I believe the yellow this time."

Once moonstruck over the earl's striking good looks, Molly
had decided Lord Ravenswood was not so grand a prize after all.
She grumbled of the earl's lack of manners all the way back from
Kent. The man was a blackguard she complained to Brody the first
chance she got, even after Ivy scolded her.

A damned scoundrel, Sara pointed out the day before during

tea. "I told you so," she had mumbled, patting her friend's shoulder while Ivy wept into her hands.

"This will do," Ivy smoothed the sunny yellow silk with the palm of her hand. The fabric might add some much-needed color to her wan features.

"It'll have to...'is lordship will be here any second," Molly huffed, shoving a matching parasol into her hands.

Molly's disgruntled mutterings, paired with Brody's baleful glares, formed a depressing backdrop as Ivy descended the stairs to wait in the music room. At promptly one thirty, an open carriage pulled into the small courtyard and soon after that, the doorbell rang with the cheerfulness of funeral bells.

Following an exchange of aloof pleasantries, Sebastian handed Ivy up into the carriage. As the driver guided the vehicle down the crowded thoroughfare, the earl deliberately settled on the opposite side, his arm stretched across the back of the leather seat. His long legs brushed her skirts. Blast it. Her heart clenched with injured misery when he did not sit beside her.

The next fifteen minutes was a study in wretchedness. The carriage rattled along Mayfair's quiet streets, giving way to busier thoroughfares before easing into the pleasant, forest like roadway to Hyde Park.

"I do hope this beautiful weather lasts." Her remark elicited the extent of what Sebastian offered during the entire drive, a stilted procession of mumbles and inaudible responses. Ivy grit her teeth. "I hate when it rains."

Sebastian regarded her as if she were daft. "It would not be England if it did not rain."

It took a moment for Ivy's anguish to melt. Not into a placid pond of cool water but a storm of hurt fury, boiling inside her, steaming and clawing to escape. Sebastian toyed with her as if he were a sleek jungle cat and she the meekest little field mouse.

But even mice possessed teeth. Sharp ones.

The gates of Hyde Park loomed ahead. Ivy nearly choked on the words. "This is the last time you will call on me." Her breath caught in a slight hitch. Digging fingernails into her palms through the silk gloves, she steeled herself. "Your affections have obviously cooled, and I no longer wish to see you."

~

SEBASTIAN WAS SHOCKED.

Ivy had reached her breaking point. For some reason, he never considered the possibility *she* would be the one to declare this war at its end. He controlled this game of passionate hostilities. Not her.

She is done with you...

Alarm surged throughout his soul, sickening and unfamiliar. She wore some kind of fanciful hat, framing her face to perfection, shading the flecks of gold dust sprinkled across her nose, her eyes enormous and beautiful beneath the wide brim. Smudges of fatigue darkened her eyes, her cheeks paler than ivory roses. But a cold resoluteness glinted in her gaze before the lacy parasol tilted to shield her face from his hot stare.

Just as well, Sebastian thought. *I can't face you.* Didn't dare look her in the eye now. Because she would know the awful truth. That he desperately wanted what Alan had with Sara. And he wanted it with Ivy.

Whatever it entailed, however it must be accomplished, Sebastian craved the happiness he saw illuminating Alan's features the night of the engagement. He wanted the same joy shining on Ivy's face that he witnessed glowing from Sara's. He could not admit he was envious of their friends, but damn it, he was. He would marry Ivy if necessary to obtain that giddy euphoria. To have her.

Even if it meant betraying his own blood. And abandoning any hope for revenge.

Sebastian slowly shook his head. "My affections have not cooled by any measure. Ivy, you don't know what you are saying..."

Don't let her go, don't let her go, don't let her go...

169

Animosity rolled from her, thickened the air, buffeting him. An urge to swat at the heaviness of it nearly lifted his hand.

"I know *exactly* what I am saying," Ivy whispered, gripping the parasol so tight, Sebastian recognized the silent yearning to crash the frilly thing over his head.

Locking his hands behind his head, his legs stretched to invade the space next to her knees. An arrogant smirk played across his face but churning inside him was a dazed panic. It made his words reckless ones. "And what shall you do, Ivy? Choose someone new? Let him caress you and hold you as I have? Shall you kiss him and pretend it is me? You'll find no other man to give you the pleasure I have, and little butterfly, there's still so much more to experience. We've only just begun to explore."

Ivy sucked in a breath of outrage. The parasol tilted just enough to reveal her face. "There shall be no need to pretend. You shall be replaced. Indeed, I will erase you. Quite easily, I assure you."

Reclining against the squabs of the cream leather seat, Sebastian presented the very image of nonchalant elegance, but jealousy sliced and twisted him with her words, leaving his insides a violent mess.

"Bloody hell. What more do you want from me, Ivy?" His voice turned raspy with restrained vehemence. "I've quoted poetry, sent flowers, danced and courted you. I let you beat me at whist, I cleaned fucking stalls, fetched countless glasses of damn champagne." His eyes traveled down her body with slow, salacious meaning. "And I played your personal servant for an entertaining morning."

"Three. Three glasses of champagne, if memory serves correct," she whispered with biting softness, ignoring the profanities and the reminder of liberties he had taken. Sebastian knew every blistering moment replayed in her mind as heat flushed her face. "And how dare you allow me the win at whist. I might have known your motives were mercenary."

"I can't let you go. Not yet. I won't let you go."

"I don't particularly care, Sebastian." Her gaze skittered away to focus on the horizon. "What you desire has no bearing on my decision. This is a necessity. For my own sanity."

Silence stretched between them while Sebastian willed his emotions to a more manageable state. A new strategy formed. While it might paint him as a monster, he took full advantage of Ivy's vulnerability for what they shared.

Reaching for her hands, he quickly stripped her gloves away. When she tried jerking from his grasp, he held tight, thumbs grazing her palms, tracing the scar marring her left hand.

"Ivy, I do not say 'please' nor do the words 'forgive me,' regularly cross my lips, but I say them now." His husky murmur was an act of sacrifice for the Revenge Situation. For Timothy's sake. *For my own sake... maybe it is possible to have both. Ivy and my revenge.* "Please, do not do this."

"Let me go."

He refused the command, holding her hands even tighter. "Tell me what I can do."

Ivy glared at him, all heartache from the past two weeks visible in the shimmering depths of her eyes. "You can go away and never come back. Plummet from the face of this earth. Die a thousand horrible deaths... have your heart ripped out as mine-" She bit her lip as Sebastian stared in dumbfounded silence at her.

Each wrestled with inner thoughts until an ordinary bumblebee forced the issue.

It darted past on an exploratory mission. Drawn by the intriguing yellow tulip shade of Ivy's gown, the determined insect whirred in again for a more thorough examination. Yanking her hand from his grasp, Ivy brushed the bee away. It floated next to her shoulder, buzzed around the sleeve of her dress as if considering the fluttering petals of an exotic flower before zipping up to investigate the confectionary-like flowers contained on the bill of her hat.

"Your perfume may have something to do with its persistence." Sebastian's lips quirked with a hint of a smile. He could not fight the lure of her fragrance. Was it surprising a mere bumblebee found it difficult to resist?

Ivy batted forcefully at the insect, squealing in alarm as it plunged close to her ear. Shifting her parasol to block the creature made it more resolute and angry. Their argument forgotten for the moment, she sat helpless while it hovered as though she were a rare flower requiring immediate pollination. Finally, with a little bark of laughter, Sebastian knocked the bee away with a firm swipe of his hand.

Five seconds later...

The creature doubled back, diving alternatively at their heads. A stream of colorful oaths and a flurry of arm movements were Sebastian's only defense.

The parasol landed on his head with a solid thump.

He turned a stunned glare on Ivy.

"So sorry," she said flatly, her expression revealing her satisfaction.

"Have you lost your damned mind?"

"I was not aiming for you," Ivy insisted.

"Give me..." The depth of fury contained in those two words alone was astounding, *"the damn parasol..."*

A particularly vile curse exploded from Sebastian as he snatched the parasol from her without permission. Remaining seated, he began to swing the frilly weapon at the invader, causing the lightly built carriage to shift and sway. The dramatic maneuvers did not deter the stubborn insect.

Ivy ducked as the parasol whizzed by her head. Straightening her hat, now tilted in a rakish manner and covering most of one eye, she scowled. "Is it your intent to kill me? Or the bee? Either way, your aim needs improvement."

Sebastian clenched his teeth, mustering up every bit of patience he could find. "Perhaps, you should not have worn a yellow gown along with that blasted lily and oranges perfume."

The smile she gave him was sickly sweet as Christmas candy. The bee encircled them, its droning buzz almost loud enough to drown out her words. "Perhaps this bee is attracted to asses masquerading as gentlemen."

He frowned. "That's not funny."

"I beg to differ." Ivy calmly met his glare. "I find this all vastly amusing."

With another grunt, Sebastian refocused his attention, feinting and parrying the tenacious insect like a buccaneer battling another pirate on the high seas. Two additional bumblebees appeared, the devil take them. The blasted winged demons appeared capable of calling in reinforcements, and banding together; they attacked with the fierceness of an uncivilized army. Were it not for the alarm in Ivy's eyes, Sebastian suspected she possessed magical powers in the world of bees, the ability to summon hordes of the insects to do her bidding.

Standing to fight the damned things, his movements became further exaggerated by the precarious position. Carriages along the park's gravel drive slowed. People on horseback stopped to watch the Earl of Ravenswood fight a battle against nearly invisible foes. To his great annoyance, Sebastian overheard many less than complimentary comments while the carriage rolled along at a sedate pace. Others could not be blamed for their curiosity. The scene bore all the exciting thrill of a bizarre, mobile play as it rolled by at a sedate pace.

"What the blazes is he doing?" One lord on a bay gelding inquired of a Marquis taking the air with his new wife in their new phaeton. The three watched as the distinctive dark blue carriage trundled past, the earl standing at full height, swinging the frilly parasol. Occasionally, he ducked his upper body from side to side, scowling and cursing.

"He appears quite possessed," the marquis commented.

"Lady Kinley does not seem unduly distressed." His new wife assessed the situation. "I do believe she is laughing."

To be fair, it began as a giggle, smothered behind Ivy's hand. As the battle against the bees became increasingly agitated, her giggles blossomed into choked gasps until she struggled to catch her breath. By the time Sebastian bellowed, "For God's sake, man! Can't the damn horses move any damned faster?" to poor, hapless Bowden, who doggedly continued along at the dignified pace a member of the realm needed to maintain in the middle of Hyde Park at two o'clock in the afternoon with the rest of Polite Society, Ivy was roaring with unrestrained peals of laughter.

Bowden responded to the harsh command with a click of his tongue and a snap of the whip. The horses leapt forward, eager to be away from whatever made the entire carriage shake and roll like a demon possessed vehicle from hell.

Sebastian lost his balance as the carriage lurched forward. Had they not rounded a curve on the gravel drive, he might have succeeded in regaining his stance or even landed backward onto the leather seat. He may have slid to the floor. Instead, he teetered, on the verge of tumbling over as Ivy let out a muffled scream. Snorting in alarm, the horses surged again as she managed to grasp a handful of his coat.

Sebastian did not remain in the carriage.

With instinctive reflexes, he tucked into a loose ball. A less than perfect rolling motion was executed upon hitting the ground, and he tumbled off the gravel path as the carriage rattled on without one of its passengers.

Puffed white clouds drifted across the deep blue expanse, the silhouettes of two birds darting to and fro far above him. Staring up at the sky, Sebastian struggled to breathe. Was it safe to unfurl his body? It didn't feel like it. Hopefully this shortness of breath was simply the result of having the wind knocked from him and not from any broken ribs.

Shouts echoed in the distance, various gentlemen inquiring to his welfare. If he did not get to his feet soon, he'd find himself surrounded by those curious to learn what forces demolished the fearsome Earl of Ravenswood. He possessed a ready answer for that. Ivy Kinley. Should anyone be stupid enough to question him, it was Ivy Kinley who had laid him low.

Sebastian rose stiffly, brushing his legs off. *Damn.* His coat ripped after all. While Ivy's cry sounded desperate when she grabbed for him, he now questioned its sincerity. She probably enjoyed watching him tumble from the carriage. Maybe she nudged him a little on his way over.

Waving away two lords approaching on horseback, Sebastian began the walk to where the carriage waited for him. Those fifty or so yards seemed more like fifty miles. Every living creature in Hyde Park surely watched his progress as he limped along, raking a hand through dust-powdered hair to shake out a few small pebbles caught in the waves. Spying the parasol in the gravel, he retrieved it, although it was a twisted mess of lace, boning and unfortunate silk blooms. He found a perverse pleasure in its destruction. *I must have landed on it.*

Ivy silently watched his approach from the backside of the carriage, eyes wide as he slapped the parasol with angry thumps against his leg, a delicate substitute for a riding crop.

Seeing the dangerous glitter in Sebastian's eyes, she wisely uttered not a word, a slight twitch of her upper lip the only indication of her amusement. Bowden stared straight ahead, respectfully resisting any urge to turn and view his employer's scuffed state. Even the horses knew better than to fidget or stamp with impatience as Sebastian placed both forearms on the carriage doorframe. Leaning heavily against it, his eyes closed for a brief moment. His sorely tried temper needed taming before he could contemplate speaking to her, much less sit in the same vehicle with her.

With a muttered curse, he flung the parasol with such force it bounced off the cream-colored leather seat to land at Ivy's feet. Biting her lip, she picked it up.

"I tried to save you." Her voice lilted with barely suppressed satisfaction as she examined the once pretty accessory. "I did not think you would go over the edge."

"An unfortunate hazard, it seems." Lifting his head, Sebastian watched a brightly colored butterfly flit up and over the carriage. It hovered about Ivy for second or two before continuing on its way.

"Oh? Do you fall from carriages on a regular basis?"

"I consistently find myself on the verge of some manner of edge around you. The edge of insanity, the edge of my temper." He nearly ground his teeth to powder. "The edge of lust."

Ivy swallowed hard. "I'm at a loss on how to remedy your problem."

"I have several ideas. None you would like."

Her head tilted in consideration. "How do you know that?"

"Trust me. Especially as you have no idea which emotion I may indulge."

She met his scowl with a slow grin of acid sweetness. "I'll require a new parasol to deal with your ill humors, my lord. Another rap on the head would be to your benefit, I think."

A CHOKED, STRANGLED SOUND BUBBLED FROM SEBASTIAN'S throat. Ivy tightened her grip on the parasol. Would she need it to defend herself? Should the earl turn violent, would Bowden rouse the horses to carry her away if need be? She should mind her tongue when he was so angry...

A chuckle escaped him, followed by bellowing laughter.

Despite the frustration with the inability to tame the earl and her heartache with the decision she would never see him again, Ivy's soul melted in a puddle of longing. Sebastian laughed, as she'd never heard before. Oh, he had chuckled in the time since she met him, grinning as they shared amusements, and she witnessed him enjoy humorous moments with Lord Bentley and other friends. This was different. This was genuine and real, twisting her heart in a way pretty words and passionate kisses would never achieve. She stared at him as he flung himself into the seat beside her, gaping while he swiped tears of merriment from his cheeks.

Had he ever laughed like this? Surely, he must have. Only, it must have been years and years, maybe even since before his parents died. This came from somewhere deep within him, a place where sunlight did not dare venture. Ivy wished to crawl up into Sebastian's lap and kiss him for that beautiful, golden sound. It liquefied and burnt to a cinder every intention she possessed of erasing him from her life. She could not bear to let him go.

The carriage proceeded from Rotten Row to a more secluded section of the park, and the laughter faded, the lighthearted moment replaced by a shaky truce.

Sebastian regarded her solemnly. "Will you forgive me?"

Ivy's heart thumped. If she accepted, things would go on as before. If she rejected the apology, Sebastian would deliver her to Kinley House, deposit her on the doorstep and that would be the end of matters. This business of forgiving him was becoming too familiar. And far too easy.

Her throat tight, Ivy nodded her consent as she examined the parasol. "The poor thing. You've ruined it." *And me. I'm at your mercy, fool that I am.*

"It served its purpose well as Slayer of Bumblebees. I shall purchase you another, although I believe the cost is offset by the damage my coat suffered." After showing her the rip in the garment, he took the parasol from her, tossing it to the opposite seat. "A rather flimsy weapon, but necessary for your protection."

"My protection!" She gave him a mock frown. "You were only interested in saving yourself. It is a shame about your coat, although you might have avoided the mishap by not standing up in a moving carriage."

"I'm convinced you assisted with my tumble." The accusation was half-hearted even as he gave her that lazy grin which never failed to set her heart to racing.

"Perhaps I could have held tighter to you." A giggle escaped Ivy at the thought of the earl waving the parasol around his head. "Oh, what do you suppose others thought? Our exploits shall keep the scandal sheets quite busy this week."

"The gossipmongers can hang." Sebastian reached for her, gathering her into his arms, tilting Ivy's face so her pretty hat was not in his way. "Ah, Ivy…damn it all to hell. I might possess the willpower to resist you if your lips did not taste like the finest of wines." His lips brushed against hers, laughter evident in the sweetness of the gesture. "And if I did not have every intention of becoming intoxicated." For a long moment, he kissed her, making up for the time missed over the past few weeks.

On the return to Kinley House, Ivy did the unthinkable, the rash, the absolute scandalous. She invited him to the monthly dinner.

"If you are otherwise engaged, it is understandable," she assured him, the words hovering on her lips to remind him of the dinner's intent. But surely, he knew. It was no secret this took place once a month. Sebastian was absent from London during the last one, but he must know.

Earlier, he had captured her hand, his fingers tangled with hers and every so often, he lifted it to his lips, his mouth skimming her knuckles. He did this now, lingering to taste her skin, sliding her palm to cup his clenched jaw. He held it there, the force of his hand covering hers and Ivy stayed, a willing prisoner.

"Of course, I shall come." His gaze darkened. "I see no reason why this should not be a nightly occurrence."

"Every night?" Ivy's heart beat so erratically it was difficult to form words. The faint stubble of his chin scratched her palm, the heat of his skin warming hers. She dared not hope too much, but he could only intend one thing with a statement of this nature.

This would be the last night of the Pack's monthly dinners. As each devotee requested her hand in marriage, Ivy would refuse in customary fashion until the last one. That request would be the one she wished for her entire life. When Sebastian proposed, she would say *yes*. *Yes,* with her heart unlocked, her soul open to his. A thousand *yes's*.

Sebastian loved her. The spark in his eyes, how his breathing hitched whenever their gazes collided, it all told her the truth. A fire ignited between them when their flesh happened to touch, whether fingertips, or lips, or other, more intimate places. They belonged together. She belonged to him. She would say yes. To anything and everything he wanted. She would be his wife. *His.*

Ivy curbed her soaring exhilaration. "Eight o'clock, then."

Sebastian waved Bowden's help away as he exited the carriage. Gathering up her gloves and the ruined parasol, he handed them to a Kinley footman before gripping Ivy about the waist to swing her down. Pedestrians on Mayfair stared at the sight of the Earl of Ravenswood with his arms wrapped about the Countess of Somerset as though they were a married couple.

Setting her on the sidewalk, his embrace lasted longer than was proper. Finally, with a frustrated sigh, Sebastian tilted her chin with a forefinger, his gaze inscrutable. "I shall count the seconds until I see you again."

CHAPTER 12

"*A*re you sure?" Alan shook his head with a bemused smile.

The two men lounged in Sebastian's library. Having gone over a report on a mining operation considered for investment, the invitation to the countess's dinner was mentioned in casual passing.

"Of course. She did invite me, after all."

Alan choked on a laugh, taking a swallow of his brandy. "I doubt you shall fit in very well with the usual company."

"What the hell are you talking about?" Alan's amusement exasperated Sebastian. What was so comical about dinner? It simply existed as a prelude to the real purpose behind the evening's agenda. The countess would be his and he was imagining the ways he would have her. Her reluctant admission of a broken heart was the key to unlocking the last door to her surrender. And he grabbed it to force his way inside.

"You honestly don't know?"

"Enlighten me."

"It's the Pack's monthly dinner." Alan's grin was unabashed. "They arrive at Kinley House at the same time, on the same day, once every month during the season. A great to-do since Lady

Kinley's coming out. You missed the grand affair last month when you took off for Scotland to purchase those new racers, but everyone knows- I thought you did as well."

"You mean, she..." A terrible, dawning fury washed over Sebastian. He'd been deceived. The game, this game of blood and revenge, was hers all along.

When he got his hands on her, it would not be a pretty sight.

"Marriage proposals are tolerated only on this one day. Poor bastards, she refuses them, but they can ask. And the Pack gets it out of their system for a time, at least until the following month. It certainly does the trick. Sara tried doing the same last season until her parents realized it." Alan refilled Sebastian's glass with bourbon. "Here, you need something stiffer than brandy. You see, each man awaits his turn and their golden opportunity, then pops the question and makes his case. Which drives her father quite mad. All those eligible bachelors under his roof and not a chance in hell one will be accepted. You realize, as the forerunner this season, you'll have the first crack at her. Unless you wait at the end of the line. Who knows? By the time Lady Kinley gets to you, she may accept a proposal out of sheer exhaustion."

Alan laughed, not fully appreciating the fury swirling within Sebastian. "I suppose the *ton* was so caught up gossiping about the two of you, it forgot the familiar scandal of the dinner. How she accomplishes it, I don't know, but it seems not one man is ever discouraged enough to fail to appear the following month, ready to bedevil her anew. Of course, the procedure is not without flaws. Her butler broke up a few scuffles last year. The scandal sheets adored it. Unusually devoted man, her butler," he mused, examining the contents of his glass before casting a suspicious eye at Sebastian. "You're not ribbing me, are you, Seb? You truly didn't know?"

Sebastian was silent. He was so stupid. When had she determined his true intentions? The only person with any inkling of his plan was his aunt, and she'd never betray him.

Ivy played the injured victim so well. How fortuitous to see her today, the exact day of the monthly dinner. She could not have planned it any better. She knew him well enough now, knew how he enjoyed the pursuit, the excitement of it. Only *he* decided when and if this relationship would end, but her threat today had him panting at her heels. Holy hell, if she sweetly requested he swim across the Atlantic Ocean and back again, today of all days, he would have done so without question.

Was there a better way to foil his plans of revenge, to prove her mastery, than to have the Earl of Ravenswood show up on bended knee alongside the other fools? Her manipulations and tactical schemes were worthy of a seasoned warlord. It was quite brilliant, and now he hovered on a razor's edge of becoming the laughing-stock of London, the very latest of Poison Ivy victims.

He underestimated her, those innocent smiles and breathless gasps of passion playing him straight to a hangman's noose. A deafening roar filled his head. They laughed over bumblebees and parasols and it felt damned good to let his guard down, to lower the heavy burden of his icy exterior. He'd not laughed like that since before Marilee. Good God, since before his father died...

Alan stared at him. Was it because of the anger shining from his eyes like twin candle flames? Or because the ache of devastation tumbling across his heart could not be concealed?

"Sebastian." Alan chose his words with care. "Timothy attended those dinners. Undoubtedly, he put forth his share of marriage proposals. It's said Lady Kinley is gentle in her refusals. I don't know what happened between your cousin and the countess, I don't know what circumstances led to his death, but whatever occurred, I do believe she was always kind to him."

Sebastian swirled the bourbon in his glass, staring into its amber depths. He did not trust himself to utter words.

"Eventually, she must heed her father's admonishments to select a husband," Alan said hesitantly. "You obviously care for her. Do you think...?" The half-formed suggestion trailed away when Sebastian's lips curved into a faint sneer.

"I will indeed have a proposal for the countess." Eyes flashing dark and unapologetic, he leaned forward, clinking his glass with Alan's in a hollow salute.

I'll have her heels in the air and her heart bleeding in my pocket by the end of the evening.

∼

As Sebastian descended from the Ravenswood coach, Count Phillipe Monvair advanced on the sidewalk to shake his hand with vigor. It appeared the count was of a forgiving nature, willing to pardon every instance Sebastian stole Ivy from him.

"Monsieur, so you come to try your luck with our beautiful countess, *non*?"

"Luck has little to do with it," Sebastian replied in great irritation.

The dark-haired Frenchman grinned. Garbed in an unfortunate combination of scarlet and emerald green satin, his chest puffed out, Monvair resembled a scrawny Christmas tree, lacking only a candle in both hands to complete the image. "So true, *mon ami,* so true. But then, one never knows when our lady may find herself at odds and accept a proposal, *oui*? I have asked many, many times and always the refusal. But, *se la vie.* I ask once more."

"And is this your last?" God help him, or damn him, for his curiosity. "Time asking, that is."

"*Mon Dieu, non*! I will ask until she accepts or no longer allows our determined requests."

Shaking his head in disbelief, Sebastian took the steps into the house two at a time as Monvair followed, chattering in a cheerful mix of French and English.

Subjecting Sebastian to a thoroughly condescending smile, Brody took their hats and gloves before showing them to the conservatory terrace where twenty or so men waited. The scene reeked of male tension and anticipation.

Accepting a brandy from a passing servant, Sebastian considered the gathering. Jealousy flooded him, leaving him damp with the strength of it. Damned if he understood the Pack's dogged pursuit of Ivy. If she had yet to accept a proposal, what led any of them to believe she ever would? This farce was nothing but a way of keeping fools under her spell.

God help him, the fact he had become one of these oblivious men nauseated him. Tossing back the brandy, Sebastian grabbed a second from the tray of the same impassive servant. An irritating voice within warned he was drinking too much, too quickly and he ruthlessly stifled it.

Scattered about the conservatory, men rehearsed proposals, their faces earnest as words were recited in their proper order. There was a sad humor in the scene. However, the thought of Timothy practicing, scraping together his courage, made Sebastian's blood boil in a cold, dark rage.

"Good evening, Lord Ravenswood."

The gilded blonde man addressing him was the one who took a tumble, champagne tray and all, the night of the Sheffield Ball. What the devil was his name? Ah, yes. Andry...Lord Christopher Andry. Although suffering a minor case of tongue-tied nerves around Ivy, he proved no less diligent in his pursuit. Sebastian had seen him many times, hopping about her with the devotion of an eager puppy, prattling of damned butterflies or dragonflies or some manner of bug, for god's sake.

"If I may comment, sir, you appear quite miserable." Christopher took a quick gulp of his brandy.

Snagging yet another drink from the same scowling servant, Sebastian gave Christopher his fiercest glare. He would like nothing better than to slice this young lord, and every other man here, into thin, bloody ribbons. Tossing back the liquor, he realized he had swallowed, in short order, three tumblers to Christopher's one.

"Whatever gave you that idea?" Sebastian drawled, leaning back against the cold plaster wall. Seeing Christopher's hands tremble the slightest bit, he discovered a tiny shimmer of satisfaction in frightening the young man. These damned fools...it would serve the little witch right if she came in and no one was there to pay court. Yes, he should do exactly that. Terrify them until they all departed. The alcohol seeping through his veins brought a slow, steady surge of hot rashness with it. No one would challenge him. Nor dare stop him.

"You are scowling quite fiercely, my lord." Christopher was hesitant as he added, "and you do not seem the type to put forth a proposal in this manner."

"What might that type be?" While noting Christopher's slight stutter was absent, Sebastian took inventory of the group assembled, measuring each man. Seeing the Viscount of Basford, his rage spiked to even further heights. The man deliberately disregarded the warning to keep his distance.

"Well, my sort, actually. You do not fit in, precisely. I wonder why you are even here. You see, I don't expect Lady Kinley to accept my proposal, but I never miss the chance to ask her. None of us do," Christopher admitted with great candor. "But, why should you allow her the opportunity to refuse you?"

"Are you so sure Ivy will refuse me? And, if you know she will reject you, why subject yourself to the humiliation?" His bluntness was offensive, but he didn't care.

After a moment, Christopher answered, and Sebastian had the distinct impression this young man pitied him. "Surely you know the answer to that, Ravenswood."

Sebastian knew...he knew exactly why every man was here. The same reason he was here. The chance to possess lightning, to win the game.

To capture and tame a butterfly.

"Rejection is not as crushing as you might believe," Christopher finally said with a smile. "Lady Kinley is always kind in her refusals. Even I, with my clumsiness and my cursed shyness, am the bigger man for having asked her. She accepts me as she does the others, no more, no less. As an equal. She never fails to treat me as such." The younger man leaned forward, an eager glint in his brown eyes. "You might not understand, but my status as one of her suitors has greatly impressed a young lady my family has deemed acceptable. There are hopes of making a successful match in the very near future, which my mother believes is due to Lady Kinley. Having been allowed to practice courtship, Mother says we owe Lady Kinley an enormous debt."

"Practice?" Sebastian scowled. "What the devil are you babbling about, Andry?"

Christopher waved his hand in a dismissive gesture. "Ah, come now, Ravenswood. We both know Lady Kinley would never wed a man like me. Her advice has been most helpful on how to best to present myself. My father has remarked on more than one occasion that if I possess the courage to pursue the countess, then I should have little trouble courting a mortal woman. And he was quite right."

Good God. Were other men using Ivy in the same manner? For even worse reasons? Damn. He should have instructed Gabriel to investigate every member of the Pack rather than focusing solely on evidence of her affairs. He had no idea what manner of men pursued Ivy, let alone their secret agendas. Was she even aware of being used?

Sebastian thought of Lord Kessler and Ivy's assistance to the earnest young lord with hidden archery skills. One of the ladies from Bentley's country party was now thoroughly enamored of Kessler. They were quite the item, thanks to Lady Ivy Kinley and her subterfuge.

Acquiring another brandy, he nodded toward an older man. "What of Viscount Batten? Does he require the countess's assistance in courting women?"

Relaxing at Sebastian's more amiable tone, Christopher shook his head. "Batten courts Lady Kinley out of loneliness. He lost his dear wife and their infant during childbirth two years ago. Perhaps heartache led him here, an opportunity for companionship with no attachment."

Sebastian mulled this over then pointed out Count Monvair.

"Impoverished royalty." Christopher's brow furrowed with

quick disapproval. "As part of the Pack, he enjoys greater accessibility to other heiresses. Of course, if she accepted his proposal, he would be overjoyed to spend her fortune. She is far too intelligent for that old trick, but he is witty and charming and amuses her."

"Viscount Basford?"

"Thus far, he is the only one capable of winning her hand. Excluding you, of course." Christopher amended with an apologetic smile. "Basford has convinced himself, and others, Lady Kinley will marry him. I admit I suspect him responsible for keeping that terrible rumor circulating, the one regarding your cousin and, forgive me for repeating it... Poison Ivy."

Sebastian grimaced at the reminder of Ivy's notorious nickname. "Is there evidence to back your allegations?"

"No," Christopher sighed. "Only a feeling. But, oddly enough, every time the rumors reach a peak, the viscount becomes the favorite. At least until you entered the race. I cannot discount the happenstance of it all. Such a shame. I never believed Lady Kinley to be the catalyst for...." his words trailed off, unsure how to speak his opinion on the matter.

"Pray, continue," Sebastian drawled, taking a sip from his glass.

Christopher took his own healthy gulp of brandy. "She is always thoughtful. Even when angry or ignoring us, she remains kind. I cannot believe she would intentionally harm someone." Giving Basford a disapproving glare, he murmured, "I pray the viscount will not ever win her hand. He would not be good to her. There are rumors of his cruelty, of certain unsavory interests, despite his excellent name and courteous nature. He would not have her best interests at heart. No...he would not be good for her."

Ivy entered the room, eliciting a flurry of activity. Men rose like a flock of multicolored ravens but she seemed not to notice, staring through them, searching the conservatory until she located Sebastian leaning against the far wall. He could not bring himself to return her warm smile.

Tomorrow it would be all over London he had attended one of these notorious dinners, presumably to ask for her hand. Beside him, Christopher smoothed his black evening coat with a nervous hand, standing straighter, narrow shoulders squaring as Ivy glided toward them.

What a piece of work Countess Ivy Kinley was. No one could be that kind and good. So innocent and sweet of nature. There wasn't a woman alive capable of being the angel Andry depicted. Yes, she might help the Pack find wives, but only so a new victim could fill the vacant spot left behind. Her deeds came from boredom, not benevolence. It was an opportunity to play men so she possessed a never-ending supply of fools, lined up in worship for as long she liked.

They all deserved each other, Sebastian thought. Fury rose in a choking wave until he had to swallow past it.

Every man present had his own ulterior motive, but no one was there to destroy her as he intended.

"Lord Andry," Ivy addressed Christopher first and he lit up with adoration. "Is it true you've discovered a new species of butterfly? How fascinating. I'm looking forward to a discussion on the subject."

His chest puffed with pride. "I've recently had that specimen mounted and readied for viewing, should you care to see it. But tell me. Is it your opinion I should share it with Lady Lindsey?"

Ivy reached to squeeze his forearm. "You must! She'll be astounded you found such a remarkable creature. And you must tell me her thoughts on the subject."

"It will be my pleasure." Christopher turned to Sebastian with an explanation, "Lady Anne Lindsey and I have much in common, for which I can thank the countess."

"I cannot take too much credit, Lord Andry. You two would have discovered your similar interests eventually. But I would ask you a question. Might you have any information regarding bumblebees and their habits?" Flashing Sebastian a conspiratorial grin, Ivy missed the dangerous gleam in his iron-grey eyes while Christopher cocked his head, stuttering some scientific fact to which no one paid the slightest heed.

The sight of her captivated every man in attendance, her skin glowing with the richness of fresh cream when contrasted to the warm apricot hue of her gown. With a bodice low enough to fuel the imagination, the silk fabric skimmed her body before flowing out in a graceful circle. Sebastian glanced at his hands. They itched with the need to pull her to him. Lust, anger, brandy and jealousy whipped within him to create a poisonous, boiling stew.

She believed he had come to beg for her hand on bended knee.

Bended knee? She'd get his knee alright...she'd find herself thrown over his, her curvaceous bottom punished for daring to make a fool of him. He'd spank her to within an inch of her life and relish watching her prettily apologize with tears and soft kisses before he took from her flesh what was his by right of revenge.

Swallowing the rest of his brandy, he handed the glass to a servant before he cracked it.

She tricked him, tangling him with these worshiping fools. But now, with witnesses to her downfall and to her heartache, the time had come to destroy her. It was time to take the final payment.

"My lady, you are ravishing as usual." Taking her hands into his much larger ones, Sebastian raised them to his lips. She wore elbow length silk gloves. Remembering the scar on her left hand, he again pondered which of these men might be responsible. And why Ivy protected his identity.

Flushing with uncertainty at the coolness of his tone, Ivy's gaze skittered away. When she attempted to tug free, he did not release her. The others grumbled but Sebastian did not care.

"I must have a word with you. It is a private matter."

"Later, after..." Her smile was suddenly wide and warm. As if she knew, knew what he wanted to do and found it agreeable.

"Indulge me."

"Ravenswood, if you would only-"

Taking her by the elbow, he propelled her through the crowd, ignoring comments he'd best wait his turn. With great difficulty, he held the urge to punch the nearest belligerent face daring to voice an objection. The only thing restraining his fists was the reluctance to become one of the numerous scuffles Alan previously described. That pompous butler Ivy employed would appreciate any reason to toss him into the street.

Entering the oval foyer, Sebastian placed a firm hand on the small of Ivy's back and guided her down the hall. Furthest from the conservatory was her father's private study.

Jonathan Kinley was in Ireland and would not be present to save his only daughter. Which was most fortunate. Sebastian did not intend to allow anyone or anything to stay him from the course set two months prior. Shutting the door, he turned the key. The soft click of the lock tumbling into place echoed in the room.

Ivy backed away until her father's desk bumped her hip, bringing her up short. The spark of abrupt panic in her eyes gave Sebastian a small twinge of enjoyment.

"Surely *you* are not afraid of me, Ivy," he murmured, and her chin jerked up at the unexpected taunt. Advancing until any chance of escape was blocked, he eventually caged her against the desk. "I'm curious why you invited me tonight?"

"I wanted to see you." As if searching for something deep within him, her gaze probed his. "This afternoon you gave all indications you wanted to see me. I don't understand why you are angry. I'm sorry..." Puzzlement mingled with radiant hope in her sea green eyes. Of course, she was confused. She was accustomed to men blindly pledging their devotion, not questioning her tactics.

"*Sorry.*" He mocked her words so she winced to hear them on his lips. "Are you *sorry* you've tied me to those other fools dancing a merry jig to the tune you play?"

His hands rested on either side of her hips, bracing against the desk. Leaning into her, his breath blended with hers. He was so close the golden freckles sprinkled across the bridge of her nose could be counted. But he had no wish to count them. Damn it, he wanted to kiss them. Each one.

"What are you talking about, Sebastian? I don't understand."

Baffled by the accusation, her brow knitted. Trying to determine the thread of the conversation, she supplied in tentative explanation, "It's the monthly dinner…"

Although his voice retained a level of admirable control, Sebastian clutched the edge of the desk, his nails digging into the oak. He did not trust himself to touch her. "The goddamn monthly dinner. Damn you, I'll not play your games, Ivy."

Seeing his knuckles turn white, she slumped in abrupt understanding.

"Oh, Sebastian," she said in a strangled whisper. "Do you believe I would toy with you in such a manner? There are those placing wagers on who shall emerge the victor in this battle. But this is not a game. Not to me. Never to me."

"Isn't it, Ivy?" he said flatly, leaning forward to brush her lips with his own, the flick of his tongue teasing the sensitive corner of her mouth. It was the only part of her he allowed himself to touch, and even that left him reeling with desire. "This is all a matter of battle lines, after all. You schemed and plotted and planned, haven't you? Now, you think you have me, a prisoner of war, like every other bastard out there. I nearly gave you what you wanted most. Me. On my knees. Another victim for your damned collection."

"No, no, that's not what I wanted," she cried out, eyes wide with the ugliness of his words. "I only want *you*. You, Sebastian. I want to be with you the moment I wake in the morning, and I miss you when I finally fall asleep at night. Nothing else matters, nothing other than you and me."

"Oh, butterfly. Can't you tell me the truth?" Sebastian nibbled her lips. When she gave a little sob of pleasure, he did it again, hating himself for enjoying it as much as she did. If she possessed a single ounce of self-preservation, she would be terrified. But Ivy was captive to the emotions he aroused within her, still willing to let him in, still hoping he meant her no harm. "There is so much more than desire between us, isn't there? History and secrets." He referred to Timothy, but she failed to make the immediate connection. "Tell me, Ivy. There is something you want from me, isn't there? Come on now, tell me the truth."

"I am telling the truth, I swear it! Only, I thought-"

"What?" When she hesitated, he nipped her ear, demanding, "What did you think? What do you want? The same you require from the others? Complete and utter devotion until I die? Or just until you tire of me?" The words were a hiss of condemnation.

"I thought you cared for me," Ivy whispered, her arms winding about his neck. "I-I wanted you to keep the Pack at bay, so they would lose interest in me. When we formed a relationship, I hoped it would be understood I'm not a threat. Or a challenge to be won. I know it was wrong to use you like that...I tried to tell you, the night of the opera. Do you remember? But you said, you said you did not care. You said nothing would keep you from me." Her words caught on themselves, unsteady and high pitched with desperation. "Oh, Sebastian, you do care for me. You must... after everything..."

The words, *"after everything I let you do,"* went unspoken but Sebastian heard them as loudly as a scream.

His hand ran up the outside of her leg to her hip, skimming along the silk of her skirts to come to rest in the small of her back. The partial confession infuriated him even as the night of the opera haunted him. *My intentions are not entirely honorable...* she told him then. He ignored that warning.

She tricked him, but he allowed it, blinded by his craving for her. She thought she won the game. Fury drummed in his veins. With a sudden dizziness, Sebastian realized he was capable of physically hurting her.

"Were you expecting a proposal? Don't lie to me, damn you." The kisses he pressed along the edge of her voluptuous mouth were deceptive in their gentleness.

"N...no," she choked out.

She was a liar. She lied straight to his face. She expected the Earl of Ravenswood on his knees. Her victory stung with the pain of a thousand nails driven into his flesh all at once.

"Liar. You don't wish for me to propose?"

"No...yes. I don't-Sebastian, *please*."

His lips stretched into a thin line of cruelty. "I *do* have an offer for you, sweetheart."

Her breath escaping in a shaky puff of relief, Ivy immediately relaxed in his grip. He bit back a laugh at her astounding vanity. She still believed he meant to ask for her hand. Instead, she delivered the instrument of her downfall.

He liked the way her breath came in soft gasps. He loved her hands sliding through his hair, how she pressed against his chest in thankful submission. It would be so easy to toss her skirts, to take her right there. He had carried this lust for an eternity. It was part of his soul; this incessant want and desire part of the fabric twining the two of them together. To rip everything to shreds, he needed only to claim her.

This, this would be *his* victory, the moment he snatched triumph from her, made her pay his price. His path lay clear and open, waiting for him to seize it without mercy.

With one hand, Sebastian swept the neat and orderly desk clear of items. This was what he'd dreamed of, what he desired and craved from the moment he clapped eyes on this deceitful, cunning, bewitching little countess. Every delectable inch of her would finally belong to him.

He lifted her, depositing her on the edge of the desk while hiking her skirts at the same time. Pushing apart her knees with rough hands, he positioned himself between her legs. She did not fight, did not cry out in horror or even seem frightened by his sense of urgency. The mere mention of a proposal untwisted doubts and melted any resistance. She unbent and opened as Sebastian pressed his arousal against her. Cupping the back of her neck, she was a willing prisoner while his mouth crashed upon hers in a seething flurry of dark desire.

Devouring the sweetness of her lips was not enough. He needed more.

Her skirts were twisted higher. Brushing past the flimsy barrier of her drawers, he eased a finger inside her intoxicating heat. Swallowing her startled sigh, he caressed the point of her womanhood with the pad of his thumb until she grew damp and restless. Forcing her to the edge of the cliff, he made sure she was trembling and ravenous before letting her plunge over. Erratic but steady, her climax pulsed against the palm of his hand and Sebastian greedily wanted every tiny shuddering beat to belong to him.

He wanted to move over her, replace his finger with his body. He wanted to thrust his way into her softness until she cried out his name in pleasure. Unbuttoning his breeches, pushing at her, rubbing against her sex, not quite entering her, he allowed his shaft to become slick with her moisture. Her climax left her hungry. She was desperate for his caress, mindless for it, almost incoherent from pleasure, and although his touch was rough, his grip harsher than any time in the past, Ivy was beyond caring. Caught in the whirlwind, she could not distinguish his wrath from passion. Sebastian knew it. He took full advantage of it.

"Yes, Sebastian, please, *please*." She tried pressing her lips to his and he evaded her.

Because he could not bring himself to kiss her when she was like this. He would willingly drown in her, losing sight of his ultimate goal if he gave in. To keep his wits about him, he must drag her to the brink of insanity before giving into her.

Yanking at the bodice of her gown, he pushed at the light corset until she was fully exposed. Crudely cupping one breast with his palm, he raised it to meet his voracious mouth, groaning at the taste of her sweetness. He clasped the rounded swell of her bottom, jerking her closer to the edge of the desk. His fingers dug painfully into the flesh of her buttocks as his erection quivered at her body's entrance.

Her low moan was a siren's call, her hips lifting in an ancient invitation. Rolling her nipple around in the wet heat of his mouth, his teeth raked it until it hardened into a tight little rosebud. Then he bit her, a sharpness that made her jerk and press closer to him.

Between her legs, she grew even wetter, the damp flesh against the tip of his shaft nearly unmanning him.

"Are you mine, Ivy?" His whisper demanded truthfulness. "Are you? Answer me, damn you, answer me."

"Yes, Sebastian, I love you, I love you. You- only you. Please, oh God, Sebastian, I don't know what to do. I need you.... inside me...*inside...please. Don't stop.*"

Hearing the words, tumbling from her beautiful lips in needy gasps, drove Sebastian to the depths of a gruesome brutality. The very last piece of her fell into his hands.

Her body was his. Her heart, her wicked soul. All his.

With no warning, he thrust, impaling her with one quick stroke. His head reeled with such unbearable sensations he barely comprehended that her cry sounded different from before.

Pain or pleasure?

Did it matter? Pinpricks of heaven, glittering and terrible, bombarded him. Sliced without mercy into his brandy-fueled, revenge induced haze. He melted into her.

Ivy was hot.

Slick.

Glorious.

Tight.

A beautiful creature he had no right to possess.

Tangling a hand in her hair, Sebastian forced her head back while keeping the other clasped on her rear. Ivy shifted, adjusted to the pressure. When he surged forward, she did not push him away. Instead, with a strangled whimper, she pulled him closer, her fingernails biting through his coat and shirt. A strange rigidity within her gave way to his invasion and torrents of pleasure flooded his veins as she opened to him. He glided into silken depths he never wanted to escape.

Goddamn you, Ivy-how, how will I live without you? How? How did this happen? That my soul entwined with yours?

Soft flesh encompassed his, holding him a tight hostage, pulsating and hot. All around him, her heartbeat fluttered with the delicate energy of hummingbird wings in slow motion. Sebastian buried deeper, then deeper still, until he was within her to the hilt and could go no further.

"You are mine at last, the devil take us both," he muttered against her pretty shell of an ear.

"Yes, yes."

Mine...mine.

Mine forever.

Again, and again, he thrust, stealing her muffled pants and gasps with quick, ruthless kisses. Grinding, slow at first, then almost frantically, unable to understand how incredible, and how horrible, it felt to make this a reality.

Ivy's fingers laced through his hair. Offering everything to him, her head lolled, her back arching.

"My god," she breathed in awe. "I didn't know it could be... yes, Sebastian, *yes, yes*. I'm yours, *yours...*"

An out of control wildfire, she burned him, her lushness coiling about him, squeezing tight as a vise. She hovered on the verge of peaking again; if he kept his pace, kissed her thoroughly with gentle, persuasive lips, she would discover ecstasy once more. And Sebastian knew he could not withstand her if this happened while inside her. His very soul would be lost.

If revenge was unnecessary, he would kiss her instead of breaking her...

Paradise this magnificent was not promised. The task hung over him, as heavy a burden as iron chains. Maybe it was a sign of his inner weakness or something born of shame, but when he finally spoke, his voice quivered. Whatever it was, he shoved it aside. His words, the actions, his body- they were all instruments of his vengeance.

"I want you every night." With each heated whisper of a word, he bit the flesh of her throat, thrilling to her moans of agreement. "Every goddamn night." His thrusts slowed. The giddy combination of heat, soft perfume and the brandy consumed earlier was making his head swim. Possessing Ivy was akin to drowning in an opium den, the sensations overwhelming and disorienting, the room swirling as her sweet softness drugged him.

"I want you available when I have need of you. In my bed, on my desk, in my coach, my library, my goddamn dining room table if I have the notion to fuck you there…I want to bury myself in you whenever and wherever I want." His sharp teeth nipped her ear. "Do you understand me, Ivy?"

"Yes, Sebastian, yes." Her murmur came apart when he ground harder against her. Slick with arousal, oblivious to his brutal words, willing to accept anything he did, she tried to answer him. "Anything…as your wife, I will do anything…tell me, show me. I love you so much…"

"*Wife?*" The harsh laugh was punishing. "You misunderstand me, butterfly. Goddamn. No, not my wife. Never that. I want you as my mistress. Don't you understand? My mistress. My own lovely, little whore to be used when and where and however I like."

Had Ivy heard him? Maybe she could not comprehend his meaning. Gliding in and out of her heat, Sebastian's brain vaguely registered every explosion of rapture while waiting for the words to penetrate. Another minute and he would forgive her, take her with tenderness. He would kiss her and care for her pleasure. Beg her forgiveness.

That could not happen. Sebastian focused on revenge. *Revenge. Remember, this is for Timothy. Remember, she is heartless…she caused his death…remember, you don't love her. You can't love her. You… cannot.*

A heartbeat passed. A second. A lifetime. An eternity.

In one huge gasp, Ivy sucked in her breath. She locked up in his arms.

There was a roaring within Sebastian to stop, but it was impossible. This business of destroying her would certainly kill him too; the tidal wave, once it overflowed, rushed forth to extinguish everything in its path.

"Your mistress? Your…whore." Stumbling on the words, her

hands, encased in pristine white silk, braced against the wall of his chest. "Sebastian? I don't understand. I don't...you- you don't want to marry me? You don't want...?" She stared uncomprehendingly as Sebastian methodically ripped apart her soul with everything brutal inside his own.

She said she loves you.

"What man wouldn't want you?" Pressing tiny kisses to the outermost corners of her lips, his body continued its seductive assault, punctuating words with unending thrusts of his hips. Ivy's eyes were unfocused, as if she could not understand what was being said; as though his words were a foreign language she had yet to learn. "Heartless little butterfly. Did you actually believe I would take you as my wife? Marriage isn't quite the thing for a woman like you. Not with your reputation. Not with your black, empty soul."

He was unprepared for the stinging slap across his face, but he half expected it. Like a heated sword slicing through flesh, it cut through his woozy pleasure.

"How dare you!" Ivy choked. "You- you bastard."

She shoved him, but with Sebastian between her thighs and her feet dangling above the floor, it was impossible to move more than a few inches. When she managed to wiggle so a heartbeat of a space opened between them, he grabbed her upper arms, giving her a rough shake. The fact their bodies were still joined heightened the barbarity.

"*How dare I?*" His fury was both hushed and terrifying. "Don't you realize I won the game?" The buttons of his evening coat bit into the bare flesh of her breasts, the gold metal branding full moon patterns on her white skin. How bizarre he had not removed a stitch of clothing. Destroying her required only the unbuttoning of his breeches.

"Ah, little, treacherous Ivy...breaking you, taming you, is why these men gather here. And it is just a game, because no matter how many come and go, we *all* want the same thing. To tame you. Each one of us wants to claim the victory, the opportunity to smear it in the face of the others." His voice dropped to a scornful snarl. "You drove Timothy to his death. He adored you, worshiped you, and you ground that devotion to dust beneath your heel. He took his life because of you. He chose to die because you, with your petty, selfish actions, rejected him. Does it excite you? Knowing that men take the risk of courting you, placing their bets they will *survive y*ou? Does it? Well, now there are wagers to pay, by God. Scores to settle. And it is my right to collect first."

Ivy whimpered at the mention of Timothy and the stakes placed on her head, but Sebastian ignored her distress, savage as a winter storm in his march across her heart.

"As for you and I, you've teased, tempted and enticed me. Truly, you led me on a merry chase, but this has been my game from the very start. There is not a man alive in London, in all of England for that matter, who can deny I've successfully tamed the sweet, deceitful, Poison Ivy. It shall be on everyone's lips come morning... *Ravenswood survived the Countess!* To your credit, my sweet, it's been a most entertaining ride." His hips rotated crudely, a stark reminder he had not finished mauling her pride and her soul.

A strangled moan of anguish escaped Ivy with the use of that vile moniker, a reminder of the *ton's* viciousness. The sound was almost animal like, the level of torment so deep Sebastian wavered. Even as whispering demons whipped him on, demanding he finish her, shame stabbed his gut at his own maliciousness.

"Breaking you has been pleasurable for us both and I don't intend for it to end. I still want you, deceitful, wanton whore that you are," he muttered roughly. "And you want me too. Your body cannot hide that from me."

Choking back another helpless whimper at the ugly words, Ivy renewed her struggles. Sebastian closed his eyes, silent, immobile as a wall of granite, allowing it until she finally hung limp with exhaustion in his punishing embrace.

Gulping for air, damp with perspiration, Ivy shivered against his chest. Locks of hair tumbled from her coiffure to cling to his neck and chin with the tenacity of a delicate spider web. Releasing the grip on her arms, Sebastian spanned his palms on either side of her hips, breathing heavily. Now that she was still, a dawning consciousness speared him with jabs deep enough to draw blood. The room spun with the crazed velocity of a kaleidoscope. He wanted desperately to shake his head, to clear the fog of lust and anger and brandy, to be able to think clearly.

The magnitude of his actions, the monstrosity of it all, seeped in. Slumped in defeat, Ivy wept quietly, wounded angel tears soaking through his shirt to cool the blistering heat of his skin.

Several things battered his intoxicated vengeance...the tight resistance to his invasion, the phantom sensation of a flimsy barrier giving way in the path of conquest. That haunting cry shadowed by the convulsive clenching of her legs as she held him tighter, her fingernails biting painfully through cloth and into the flesh of his shoulders while her body sucked him in deeper. Her reaction to his possession was baffling, but the trickle of comprehension clawing at his brain screamed for attention. Bloody hell, it was not possible.

You goddamn fool. You goddamn, heartless, stupid bastard. She's an innocent. A virgin...she's a virgin.

She couldn't be. She'd fucked half the men waiting in her conservatory with their pathetic rehearsed proposals. Hadn't she?

Sebastian rocked away, grabbing Ivy by the nape of her neck to stare down into her face. The golden cartwheel of freckles glowed in stark relief against the ivory paleness of tear-streaked skin. Darkened to the shaded dimness of a stormy sea, she gazed back with eyes wide and hazy. Truth was a harsh master, lashing him with every breath. It was not possible. It could not be. She could not be...

Pure.

Virgin...

Bitter regret washed away the scarlet mist of fury, turning him abruptly cold and instantly sober. What had he done? He hurt her. This...this was the act of a madman. An evil that could not be undone. This might be worse than rape. He tricked her into offering a precious gift then ripped it from her hands. *Oh, God. What kind of monster am I?*

"Ivy..." His hands dropped as if she were a lit flame burning his palms. "Sweet Jesus, what the hell have I done?"

Ivy's fist slammed his jaw with such uncanny precision and force that his teeth clicked together with a loud snap. Sebastian reared back, the salty tang of blood in his mouth. He'd bitten his own tongue. As he processed that, a tiny foot struck him, the wooden heel of her shoe finding his groin as if she'd practiced the defensive maneuver for years. Sebastian's body exploded in excruciating pain. *"Goddamn..."* Grasping the vicinity of his manhood, he stumbled away.

The space between them was just enough for Ivy to slide off the edge of the desk and regain her footing. Snatching her dress up to her shoulders, she darted to the side while Sebastian doubled at the waist, his hands braced on his thighs. He sucked in deep breaths, fighting the alcohol when it rose in his throat, a thick and obstructive tidal wave of nausea battering for release. Eventually, the pain eased to a point so it was possible to stand without retching. Ivy's sobs echoed throughout the room, a swirling cacophony pounding at his head, leaving him a bit wobbly on his feet. There was a flurry of rustling silk behind him, the sounds of metal against metal. She struggled to unlock the door, her fingers clumsy with blind panic.

Sebastian fumbled with the buttons of his breeches, gazing dumbly at his hands when they came away slick with fresh blood. The red smears confused him. Were the heels of her shoes that damned sharp? Had she cut him somehow?

Do you honestly believe that is your blood? An internal voice mocked his stupidity. *It's hers, you bastard. Her blood. Ivy's blood.*

Virgin blood. Sacrificed for his cousin's life.

The click as the key turned was loud as a thunderbolt. She was fleeing him, as though he were a demented beast, a twisted evil from the depths of hell. He reached to grab her, but even he was unsure of his motives. "Ivy. Holy hell."

Was it possible to beg forgiveness for the unforgivable?

With a nimbleness born of terror, Ivy evaded him. When she bolted into the hall, Sebastian stumbled after her, falling against a table. A priceless vase teetered, crashing to the floor in an ear-shattering explosion of porcelain. The sound would undoubtedly draw all guests to the foyer. But he must stop her. He must explain, catch her, even if there was little hope of undoing the damage.

A fleeting glimpse of apricot silk flying up the stairs was the last he saw of Ivy Kinley and his pursuit ended at the bottom of the polished marble steps. Not even he, the Earl of Ravenswood, who dared almost anything, risked following her up those stairs, not here in her father's house and with witnesses no less.

She loves you.

Struggling to compose himself, Sebastian gripped his chest. Overwhelming pain throbbed in relentless thumps. Such a strange feeling it was, to have one's heart shredded while it still beat steadily. Silent and sick, the horror of his actions washed over him anew to see his hands marked in startling red.

Slowly, he pulled a handkerchief from an inner pocket on his suit coat, using it to wipe the blood away, blotting at the miniscule stains on his coat where he'd touched his chest. Forcing the most arrogant expression imaginable to his features, stamped there by sheer willpower alone, Sebastian faced the men steadily gathering. Confused expressions exposed their thoughts: *What happened to our darling countess? What in God's name did you do to her? Why does the sound of her weeping linger in this hall?*

Sebastian did not think he would ever feel anything again. He became the cold, collected earl once more, the numbness a welcomed blessing.

Christopher Andry scowled, as if Sebastian were the Devil himself inexplicably landing in their midst, with great black wings beating the air. The other men mumbled, shuffling about, wondering what should be done to the creature before them.

How he stood, when his very knees threatened to buckle beneath him, was mystifying. To hide the weakness, Sebastian placed a casual hand on the balustrade of the stairs, sliding it up to grasp the finial of the newel post. The delicately carved wood miraculously supported his weight.

With the goal accomplished, the actual horror of what he'd done was slicing him to ribbons. Ivy was ruined. At the cost of destroying his soul. And hers. He carefully selected his words to inflict the most damage. And pain.

"The countess has taken issue with the ending of our association."

CHAPTER 13

*S*he was broken. Shattered into so many tiny pieces it did not seem possible she would ever be whole again. A burning hurt screamed within her heart, Sebastian's betrayal diminishing her into a creature she did not recognize. But even as she wept, something grew, something hard, something sharp and black. Razors replaced the softly feathered wings of innocence.

Ivy pressed the heels of her palms against her eyes. They stung from incessant weeping and the frost encasing her heart. All the fractured, scattered splinters were slowly contracting together, mending to create a glittering shell of a girl, capable of functioning without care or feeling. What had once melted so easily in the warmth of Sebastian's arms began to freeze again, and she did not care to stop it from taking place.

She would become something none of them expected, least of all the Earl of Ravenswood.

A butterfly metamorphosing into a wolf. Her ice-covered soul would make so.

"IF I AM TO HELP YOU, TELL ME WHAT HAS HAPPENED, IVY."
Jonathan Kinley's brow furrowed. He'd not taken the time to clean
up from his travels, arriving at Somerset Hall within days of his
daughter fleeing the city. His arrival was unexpected, having only
recently returned from Ireland. Shocked to see him standing in
their country estate's library, Ivy foolishly wanted to weep in her
father's arms instead of the anger she should have felt at his
intrusion.

"Do not concern yourself, Father. It is of little importance."

Jonathan's lips tightened. He pulled a chair to the divan she sat
curled upon.

The light in the library was soft and shadowy. Dusk would fall
soon. The servants would ignite the chandeliers and sconces inside
the oak paneled room. Huddling further into a cream-colored blanket, Ivy turned from her father's penetrating stare.

"It's all over London. Regardless what you may think of me,
my dear, I'm no fool. Now, tell me. Will he marry you? Or must he
be forced to it?" Jonathan reached for her hand bearing the faint
scar. Holding it gently while she sat stiff with distrust, he said, "I
cannot allow this to be the second time someone from that family
has attempted to ruin you."

Ivy's cheeks flushed. "I don't know what you mean, Father."

His eyes bored into hers. "I know full well the story behind this
injury and Timothy Garrett's part in it. Make no mistake. Because I
did not force the issue then does not mean I shall not force it now. I
do not know the circumstances behind this rift with the earl, but it
is something significant. I've heard he has broken your heart. That
your chances for a successful marriage are destroyed. I'll not allow
this to happen, to stand idle while you are ruined in such a fashion.
Ravenswood will marry you, if what is being bandied about holds
any truth."

Ivy tugged her hand from her father's warm grasp. Why did he
have to sound so reasonable, so...*fatherly?* Despite fierce promises
she would no longer cry over *him*, that heartless scoundrel, tears

sprang to her eyes. The subject of Sebastian and his betrayal must be avoided at all costs. It was too painful to address. "What of Timothy Garrett? If you knew of his actions, why did you not demand we wed? It was the perfect opportunity. I would not have been able to live the scandal down."

Her father regarded her sadly. "Did you think I would force you? I promised your mother you would marry for love and you would not have found happiness with Lord Garrett for a husband. All I've ever wanted was for you to be happy."

"You tossed every bachelor in London at me," Ivy accused in quiet disbelief. "You've harassed me to distraction, to make a choice, to wed. Forgive me if I do not believe you only desired my happiness."

"I was mistaken," Jonathan shrugged his shoulders. "You needed choices, eligible men you might not have considered otherwise. But, and this I swear upon your mother's grave, I never meant to force a marriage you did not want. Your mother wanted you to make your own decision, and I vowed I would abide by her wishes." He recaptured her hands. "I loved your mother. I still do, God rest her soul. Not a day passes when I do not wish I'd done things differently. You probably are not aware, for you were only a child, but we hovered on the verge of losing everything. How foolish I was then to believe I was only losing land and possessions. I made some appalling business decisions, lost a great deal of money and overcoming my mistakes, replenishing your mother's estates so you would have her inheritance as well as mine, was difficult. My intent was to secure our future so we would never face that threat again but in doing so, I lost two of the dearest people in the world to me- your mother and you. I do not expect you to forgive me. I only beg for it and hope someday you understand."

He smiled ruefully. "You are a smart girl, Ivy. I trust you to decide your own path, but do not think I lack the power and the means to force Sebastian Cain to the altar. With one word, he has no choice. If you want him, tell me and I shall make it so."

Despite herself, despite the effort to be brave, to remain resolute and unwavering, Ivy began to sob. She thought there was nothing left within her, no tears left to cry, but her father's support, when she least expected it, his explanation of the events detaching him from their family, overwhelmed her. Without warning, she flung herself into his arms, grateful for his embrace wrapped tight about her.

"Mother loved you so much, and I do too. How you must have suffered when things were desperate and money was the only thing you believed would save us. You did what you thought best, I only wish you had told me sooner. It is in the past...let us move forward from it." Stifled by his overcoat, her breath escaped in a shuddering gasp as she admitted, "As for Ravenswood, he will not marry me. He despises me, blames me for Timothy's Garrett's death. I'd rather go into exile and never again show my face in society than face a lifetime with a man who hates me as he does."

"There must be consequences for his actions." Smoothing her mass of hair, Jonathan stroked the curls as though she were still a child. "And you must give the impression the gossip means nothing to you. You've always been a strong one. God knows you have shown me your stubborn side for years. They cannot see your weakness now."

Ivy remembered the fierce promise made the night of Sebastian's betrayal. She disintegrated into a million pieces that night, those pieces scattered about. The blood on her thighs, the ache between her legs, her virginity stolen by a man whose chief objective was to destroy her, she had wept until she was ill. No one must know. Especially her father.

No, she corrected bitterly. *Sebastian did not steal it, my innocence. Nor my heart. I gave everything to him, wrapped in ribbons. A gift. Of love.*

Sebastian once boasted of his patience, and to have his revenge he needed only to bide his time. She recalled the analogy Sebastian gave her, of waiting for a butterfly to land before casting the net, of hunting beauty by remaining still and waiting until it ventured close, close enough to be easily captured. How skilled he'd proven himself at the task. How easily he ripped apart her wings.

~

SEBASTIAN WAS SURE OF IT. HE WAS A MONSTER. FACED WITH THE cold proof of his barbarity, there was little doubt of the evil inside his heart.

Thank God, Ivy ended the assault before he climaxed inside her, although even now he ached with a yearning it seemed impossible to survive. How had he missed all signs of her innocence? Why had he failed to recognize the purity of her kisses, the awestruck wonder in her eyes every time he brought her to the peak of satisfaction? Bloody hell, when she melted on his fingertips, it was because he was the first man to touch her so intimately.

I'm a fool. A blind, arrogant fool...

She would never forgive him. How could she? His plan to ruin her was successful. He could not forget the terrible hatred in her eyes. There was no satisfaction in taming Poison Ivy and revenge, once the sweetest of goals, left a sour taste in his mouth. No amount of alcohol could wash it away.

Sebastian departed the city the following day, stopping at Beaumont before traveling to his far-flung estate on the Scottish border. Unable to erase the self-loathing, he promptly buried himself in the cold, drafty castle rising up out of the moors.

A month slipped by before he could consider returning to London. Remaining at Kleychord Keep posed the very real possibility he might drink himself into oblivion. Or become lost in the mists for all eternity as he indulged in hours of aimless wandering of the desolate, barren heaths stretching to the east of the castle. The servants, superstitious and fearful for their master's wellbeing, whispered of the earl's despondency, his tendency to roam both day and night. It would leave him a victim of one of the brackish, ebony lakes dotting the land. The dark bodies of water often took man and beast unawares, swallowed whole and never seen again.

"If it 'appens," the housekeeper said, with a hastily signaled sign of the cross, to the cook, who also crossed herself with a shudder, "His Lordship 'ill be nae but a ghost 'o the moors, 'auntin' Kleychord Keep for all eternity in search 'o peace.

Sebastian did not scoff the prediction. It held far too much truth to disregard. He already felt like a ghost, and peace was damnably elusive. It could not be found on the moors nor at Beaumont, or any of his lesser estates. It was elusive in sleep, in his waking moments and he'd searched for it at the bottom of countless bottles of bourbon. Ivy's pale face, as he cut her with words and destroyed her with actions, haunted him at every turn. Never had he forced his attentions on a woman before. How badly had he hurt her? How much did she hate him? How could he live without her?

Because he could not stay away from her.

He would encounter Ivy in their social circles, unless he left England as he'd done before. But he wouldn't. He couldn't. She was as essential to his survival as air, but it was pathetic that the prospect of a confrontation with her was both dreaded and anticipated.

Filled with trepidation, Sebastian arrived in London, accompanied by his silently suffering valet. William found employment with the Earl of Ravenswood to be an exercise in patience. However, the elderly man dealt with his lord's moody fits with a tolerant smile and a quick and ready wit. The nights Sebastian drank himself into a stupor, his expensive clothes hopelessly wrinkled and often torn during attempts to undress, William met with aplomb and murmured assurances everything would be put to rights.

Ensconced in his study at Ravenswood Court, a bottle of bourbon on the desk between them, Sebastian motioned for Gabriel Rose to begin. It was his first day back in London and the city buzzed with news of his return and Ivy's possible reaction. It made him weary.

"Do you want the news sober or after a few?" Gabriel asked calmly, eyebrow raised.

"Is it as bad as all that?" Sebastian scowled when the other man tilted his head. "A couple of drinks then, if you don't mind the wait."

"If it's not to excess again." His friend grinned. "It's only a month past that I met you at Beaumont before you left for Scotland. You were drunk out of your mind, if you do not recall my visit. You stayed foxed for the better part of a week. Bloody hell, one night you dropped your breeches and proceeded to piss on the fire in the drawing room. Another, well, I *know* you don't recall, but you shot the eyes out of nearly every mounted game in the billiards room before I managed to take those damned pistols away from you. You insisted the beasts were accusing you of -"

Sebastian winced, holding up a hand. Leave it to Gabriel to bluntly remind him how spectacularly smashed he was. "There were other factors in play."

"Ah, yes." Gabriel nodded. "I gathered that from the scolding Lord Bentley gave you. I had such hopes you would come to your senses, but the moment he left, you decided I must continue my watch over the girl you claimed to care nothing for. That same night, sometime after midnight if memory serves correct, you decreed in a drunken fit of rage that I should repack and return to London at once. There was no arguing the journey could wait until morning. Just so you would think I had departed, I was forced to sleep in the stables."

It was neither particularly surprising nor outrageous that the man spoke with such blistering candor. Although Gabriel was not recognized as being of nobility, despite being the bastard son of an unknown lord, the two of them had become close as brothers during their travels. He was an equal, a close friend and confidante, and free to speak his mind with Sebastian.

"I apologize for my abhorrent behavior. What did you discover during my absence, my curious, insolent friend?" Sebastian muttered.

"Two sets of opinions, mind you. The first being you ruined a countess. The second, that a countess ruined you. Of course, when you initially set me to the task three months ago, I placed my own wagers and won quite handily." Gabriel's smile was serene. "Tell me. Did you anticipate it being so painful?"

Sebastian stiffened. "You overstep your bounds, Rose. I'll not discuss a private matter between myself and Lady Kinley -"

Gabriel laughed out loud. "Good god, man! What do you take me for? I meant *you!* Did you imagine *your* ruination to be this agonizing torture? The amount of money I won indicates it was."

"You placed bets. Against me. Why, may I ask? I accomplished my goal. I destroyed her. Without hardly trying, I might add."

"Ravenswood, I've known you for nearly four years and never have I seen you destroyed. I've never seen you besotted by a woman, worry about her, worry *for* her. Drink to oblivion because of her. She haunts you. Ruined you, no matter the lies you tell yourself." Gabriel shuffled his papers and took a sip of his bourbon. "Now that I've diagnosed you, finish that drink and I'll fetch another bottle. You're going to need it, although there is a bright side to the information I'm about to share."

"And that is?" Sebastian growled, tossing back the liquor. Then ignoring the civility of a glass, he grabbed the nearly empty bottle to drink the last of its contents straight from the rim.

Gabriel shook his head in bemused resignation. "As before, there is no evidence Lady Kinley has taken any lovers. Her choice of companions, however? Troublesome, to say the least." Leaning forward, his brown eyes flashed with ill-concealed sympathy. "Settle in…and do try to control that unfortunate temper of yours."

Sebastian's presence at Whites triggered a comical flurry of activity. In the main salon, various gentlemen either tripped over themselves to greet him or studiously avoided his gaze. It was difficult deciding which was worse, as he suffered claps on the back and congratulations on his victory. Destroying Ivy resulted in quite a few tidy sums collected, but some losses were suffered simply because of bets placed against members of the Pack. A glance at the wager books was impossible; to view the list of winners and losers would rip apart whatever heart Sebastian thought he still possessed.

Everyone carried a tale or two of the countess's exploits. He almost wished Gabriel had not related everything, his blood racing to learn of the activities Ivy was indulging in. Dangerous things. In dangerous places. With dangerous men.

Slipping inside one of the numerous card rooms, his presence went mercifully unnoticed. Men huddled over tables cluttered with a varied collection of glasses and cigars, a lively discussion holding their rapt attention.

"I tell you, it was Lady Kinley at Gentleman Jim's two nights past. I would recognize those lips anywhere. And she wore roses in her hair. White roses with one red, mind you." A young rake vowed over a forgotten game of hazard. Several gentlemen snorted in disbelief.

Sebastian froze. That first afternoon he called upon Ivy to set his revenge into motion flashed in his mind. The Thomas Carew poem...

"*Read in these roses the sad story, of my hard fate and your own glory. In the white, you may discover, the paleness of a fainting lover; In the red, flames still feeding, on my heart with fresh wounds bleeding.*"

He was so goddamn arrogant reciting it to her, so confident in predicting her downfall. Now, she mocked him with it. She hated roses...

No. She *hated* him. Enough to wear the flowers as a reminder of treachery.

"Every damned woman in London is wearing roses in her hair, you fool. And you've not been close enough to Poison Ivy's lips to tell them apart from your own blooming mother's."

A round of uproarious laughter swept the room as the first man scowled in rebuttal. "We danced the waltz last week. I can assure you, I know her lips. Venturing into the gardens, I had the chance to taste their sweetness as well. If my stupid, meddlesome brother had not intervened with three other friends to drag her away for a bloody game of Queen of Sheba, dear gentlemen, I could relate much more."

"Yes, yes and you would have been discovered the very next morning in those same gardens. A solid block of ice. The countess has real snow in her veins now, that she does. She was merely toying with you, Blackton," Baron Millerson said, a gentleness underlying his gruff nature. "Now that the Pack's done for, she's learning a new craft, running with Clayton and Danbury's set. Discovered how amusing it can be to play with her victims, especially the naïve ones. Don't be a fool, man."

"That's not true," Blackton stated heatedly, staring at the cards in his hands, remembering the moment shared with Lady Kinley. "I'm hardly innocent and the countess, she was kind and sweet. And so fragile, like the butterfly Ravenswood called her..."

"As fragile as when you saw her cheering on two men pounding one another to bloody bits in the ring?" Someone piped up to even more laughter.

"Best to stay away from the Butterfly Countess, Blackton. Save for one purpose only, if you understand my meaning. Unless you wish to end up as Ravenswood haunting the empty moors like some damned dark ghost." Tossing down his bet, Millerson nudged the man beside him to do the same.

"Or ten toes up like Timothy Garrett." Tristan Buchanan, the Viscount of Longleigh, offered from the back of the room. Murmurs of agreement echoed his dry comment.

Hearing these men speak of Ivy in such familiar tones made Sebastian's heart contort with guilt and ugly jealousy. How quickly the tables turned. It seemed he was one of her victims after all. People whispered of *him,* how she brought him to his knees, while in the same breath they marveled how he tamed her. Their mutual downfall and triumph was beautifully twisted together in the most grotesque fashion.

Backing away in haste he nearly bowled over a barmaid delivering the next round of drinks.

"Pardon, milord," she exclaimed as two glasses jostled, sloshing over the tray to create a puddle on the lush carpet. "I thought to slip behind you."

All eyes turned Sebastian's way, a hushed, awkward silence falling over the smoky room. Men nudged one another, murmuring low while Blackton flushed scarlet. Solemn, pitying glances passed from man to man, and before Sebastian knew what was happening, they surrounded him, hands clasping his shoulders, his ears filled with apologies and supplicating words meant to appease him. One phrase uttered by a faceless bastard echoed repeatedly in his brain.

She deserved it, she did.

Only Longleigh, calmly sipping his brandy, did not rise to join the others.

It was too much. Shoving his way through Sebastian could not escape the club quickly enough. *She deserved it...* Deserved his cruelty ripping her apart? Did she deserve the same wrenching pain he suffered? Ivy's suffering was surely a hundred times more brutal...and at his own hand.

Stumbling out into the moist foggy air of a London late spring night, Sebastian did not stop until he reached his waiting coach. Gripping the back wheel for support, head hanging low near the gutter, he became violently ill.

~

"I DON'T UNDERSTAND YOUR MELANCHOLY," RACHEL REMARKED IN the unsettling silence of the vast dining room.

Sebastian stared at his plate of untouched food. He agreed to dinner as a necessary illusion of normalcy, necessary to hide the fact his perfectly planned world was falling to pieces around him, his legendary control reduced to rubble. Broaching this particular subject was unexpected on his aunt's part. Madness, actually. Could she not see he was on the verge of becoming unhinged?

"Leave it be." His voice was dangerously soft.

"If you should feel the slightest pity for her, do not bother. Like a wicked little cat, she lands on her feet." Rachel tipped back the remnants of her wine, an unsteady gleam in her eyes.

Shifting in his chair, the unnatural level of animosity his aunt leveled toward Ivy struck Sebastian. Something sizzled in his brain, a flash of mystery. For the first time ever, he pondered a novel question. Why did Ivy cut Timothy from the Pack?

What did Timothy do to *her?*

"Did you not hear me, madam?" The brandy was going down much too smoothly. It was damned difficult not to drink so much, and Sebastian was trying so hard not to. He wanted to drown himself in the numbing shroud of it and forget everything he'd done. Forget everything, forget *her* while he drowned in misery.

Rachel sneered. "Do you believe she's suffered? She has attended every ball and soiree held this past month. A new escort each night and never the same twice. She even has a new title." The laugh was ugly. "The Unbroken. They are all calling her that, although some refer to her as the Ravenswood's Curse, now that you've become a victim. And God knows, the *ton* does love a victim. Especially when it runs in families." Slamming her empty goblet down, she motioned to the footman. With an apologetic glance at Sebastian, the servant refilled it. "You didn't ruin her, Sebastian, you emboldened her. The chit had the impudence to give me the cut direct, laughing at me while Danbury and Clayton urged her on-"

"Enough," Sebastian growled, standing so abruptly his chair crashed to the floor. His head pounded with guilt, jealousy and a whole host of other emotions too unbearable to confront. Eventually another man would have her in his bed, but Sebastian knew he held no say in her actions. That right was lost the moment he broke her heart and crushed her soul on her father's desk.

Rachel's words followed him as he stalked from the room.

"She won, Sebastian. A century ago, she would have burned at the stake, for she is a sorceress sent to bedevil men. Witless puppets dancing to her every whim, all of you. You did not make her pay as you said you would. Now all of London knows the truth. She beat *you* at your own game."

CHAPTER 14

*M*olly stepped back and with a sigh of contentment gave the shining curls one last pat. "You look like a princess in a fairytale, that you do!"

"Do you not think the diamonds are overmuch?"

"Oh no, milady! You look right beautiful." The servant winked. "A gent might go blind just lookin' at you."

"Molly!" Ivy adjusted the three-tiered diamond necklace gracing the swell of her breasts before tucking in one of the roses woven through her hair a bit tighter.

The ball gown, a silver hued silk shot with glittery satin strands, twinkled with shimmery iridescent lights every time she moved. The dressmaker said it would appear she wore a gown spun from fairy wings and no truer statement was made. Ivy wanted the magical confection the moment she saw it, although it was only half constructed at the time. The silk was the exact color of Sebastian's eyes when he kissed her the first time in her music room. Long before he broke her heart.

Madam Jocelyn was very convincing in arguing the cut of the gown should be a bit more daring. Such a unique piece of fabric, she insisted, simply cried out for an adventurous style. Admittedly, the petite French seamstress was correct, but the gown now skated on the verge of scandalous. It dipped lower than anything else Ivy owned. She felt the need to keep tugging the edges of it upward. Trimmed in delicate vines of pale shimmery green, an ivory corset pushed her breasts up into twin mounds of creamy flesh. One deep breath and she might actually overflow its confines. But it was the design of the gown's back where Madam Jocelyn earned her outrageous fees.

From tiny cap sleeves barely skimming the tops of her shoulders, the dress curved in a dangerous dance along the edges of her shoulder blades, leaving Ivy's entire back naked to the waist. This vast expanse of skin was most concerning. By necessity a dance partner would place a hand upon the bare flesh of her lower back to guide her. Such intimacy bordered on the outrageous.

Molly had threaded several roses throughout the loose braids of hair grazing the top of Ivy's shoulders. All snowy pristine white save for one, the roses existed as a silent stab at *him*, intended to prove his existence meant nothing to her all along. Each bloom began as a bud. As the night wore on, the petals unfurled in the warmth of the ballrooms and the late spring air until all became lush and full. The flowers were now a signature; worn to every social event. At the end of the evening, as Ivy departed, each was tugged free, tossed to whoever cared to catch one. There never seemed to be a shortage of men scrambling and frantic to catch a favor from The Unbroken.

One rose was never white. Always placed above her left ear, the side of her body where her frozen heart thumped, that rose was red. Bloody, scarlet, brazen red.

It received special treatment. Petal by petal, Ivy would destroy the perfect bloom to the crowd's delight. Oftentimes the petals showered her last dance partner. Sometimes the recipient was her escort or a lucky fool chosen at random. The most anticipated nights were those when, in a subtle erotic gesture captivating any man fortunate enough to witness it, Ivy kissed each petal before releasing it so it drifted in her wake. Many heads shook in scandalized disapproval, but she did not care. Every red rose ruined was the earl's treacherous heart, ripped to pieces in her bare hands.

Ravenswood had returned to London and was rumored to be attending the Faringdon's Ball tonight. Ivy hoped it was true. He would see men waiting to dance with her, plying her with champagne and begging to accompany her along garden paths in the moonlight. Her broken heart wanted nothing less than Sebastian Cain to see others pursuing the woman he had so callously discarded.

Most of all she wanted him watching as she destroyed her roses, the blossoms ground to dust beneath her heel. Wanted him to know they meant nothing to her. That he meant nothing to her at all.

But, then again, it would be wise to tread cautiously. Ivy intentionally sought the company of society's rakehells, knowing the outrageous exploits would reach Sebastian's ears. Her choices were dangerous, although she discovered a perverse pleasure in navigating this narrow tightrope. These particular wolves toyed with her, biding their time for the right moment to pounce, but Ivy enjoyed outmaneuvering them.

She whirled through the nights alone even when she had an escort. Sara pleaded with her in vain, distancing herself when Ivy ignored her. Her father, frozen with indecision as she spiraled away, came to realize any attempt to pull his daughter from the cliff's ragged edge was futile. Their newly mended relationship was too fragile to keep Ivy from drifting alone in her sea of heartache.

And so Ivy spun. She danced. She teased and kissed. She allowed embraces filling her to the brim with freezing rain and still...

There was no escaping Sebastian.

"It's not fair," she muttered, forced to compare new caresses and kisses to those he gave her. It wasn't fair that in the midst of dancing and socials and operas and clandestine boxing matches, her thoughts filled with him. When a man smiled or laughed, or took her hand to press a kiss, Ivy automatically compared him to Sebastian. Tonight, his memory and his kisses would hold her hostage no longer. She would break free of him somehow. She would erase him from her mind.

With a grim smile of determination, Ivy caressed the scarlet rosebud with gentle fingers. She could erase him from her heart. Even if the required price was that of her own soul.

∽

IVY LAUGHED AND FLIRTED. SHE DANCED UNTIL HER FEET SURELY ached. The goblets of champagne consumed were too numerous to count. She teetered with charming sweetness, leaning against one man or another and those surrounding her perked up like predatory beasts trailing a wounded doe.

Icy anger settled over Sebastian. He watched from a shadowy alcove near the garden entrance, miraculously hidden by numerous plants. Lurking like a nefarious criminal. It was disheartening, the depths he had sunk. He literally hid behind potted palms in an attempt to spy on her. *Potted palms, for Christ's sake.*

The Earl of Clayton pressed another glass of champagne into Ivy's hand. Notoriously dissolute, Clayton held a decided taste for virgins. The man's dark eyes roamed with insolent enjoyment over Ivy, touching with appreciation on the twinkle of diamonds framing her magnificent breasts, breasts which threatened to over-flow the confines of the ball gown. If she took a deep enough breath, they would. And those damned roses sprinkled like fairy dust in her hair…they taunted Sebastian. A reminder of all he lost when she slipped through his fingers.

Damn her. Did Ivy have any idea of the danger she was in?

Is the risk from these other men? Or from myself?

When she turned to thank Clayton for the champagne, Sebastian almost choked.

Bloody hell!

Ivy's naked back gleamed like warm silk, the gown swirling

around the lovely curve of her hips. With impotent fury Sebastian watched Clayton's hand drift to rest in the shadowy hollow of her lower back. Those blunt fingers of his lightly stroked the indentation of her bare spine as if he already owned her. Clayton obviously discovered a recent preference for fallen countesses. He boldly staked a claim but his possessive efforts did little in warning others off. Some old members of the Pack were already edging in, including Basford who appeared apoplectic with the need to rescue Ivy.

Sebastian's gaze dropped to his hands. They shook. Hoping to calm the murderous blood racing through his veins, he sucked in a deep breath.

Lord Danbury leaned close, his mouth beside Ivy's cheek while she laughed at his whispered comment. The melodious sound echoed, high and brittle to Sebastian's ears. Ivy Kinley was a glittering, dazzling creation. Almost too stunning to gaze upon, an air of mystery shimmering about her. Enticing, bewitching and unattainable. Before he ruined her, that innocence lured men; now an elusive wickedness tempted and teased. This was not the Ivy he knew. This…this was a creature fashioned from his own cruelty.

She smiled too brightly, hands resting much too casually on the gentlemen's arms congregating about her. Each glass of champagne pressed upon her swallowed with astonishing quickness. She was well on her way to being thoroughly intoxicated if she was not already. When she swayed again on unsteady feet, Danbury flashed a triumphant grin. Knowing glances flew between the five men huddled in the dimly lit corner.

A dark fire lit Sebastian's eyes.

Nicholas March, the Earl of Landon, sauntered up to the outskirts of the group, his golden head tilted in contemplation. He seemed to debate joining the men gathered around the countess or remain on the fringes as an observer. However, he did not intercede.

Crossing his arms because his hands now twitched with a lethal anger, Sebastian watched the men - *no…not men* - *jackals* -

circling her. They gathered for the kill after playing with her for so many weeks. Beasts, all of them, and he was the pack leader who'd set them on her trail. Word of his return to London must have reached her by now and consummate predators, these men picked up on Ivy's weakness, her heightened propensity for recklessness. They hunted her. Tonight, she would be their entertainment. And it would be too late to save her. Hell, she probably had no wish to be rescued. According to all rumors, she was quite content to be their prey.

Clayton brushed a soft kiss to the top of her shoulder. Ivy acknowledged the intimate caress with a confused half-smile and Sebastian's tightly held temper reached combustion levels. A red haze of anger blinded him with such thoroughness he did not see Nick shouldering through the small group.

Nicholas's hand closed with a proprietary firmness on Ivy's elbow, an unreadable expression crossing his features. The man's aloofness possessed a legendary status, so his intentions were a curious puzzle. Unless it was to his personal benefit, one should not expect his assistance. With a tendency to utilize tactics delicately subtle in nature, his brazen approach was shocking.

Should the countess accept his aid...well, Nicholas' methods of repayment would prove much higher than she could afford.

"Some breathing room for the lady, gentlemen." Nick's words carried over the lilting sounds of the orchestra. By his tone he knew his order would be obeyed without question.

The men bristled, sensing their prey slipping through their fingers and into the hands of the soon to be titled Duke of Richeforte. Was it worth a challenge if he tried claiming the countess? He had never showed any interest in her before, other than a polite regard. Everyone knew he shunned the debutantes and virginal set as if all were afflicted with the French clap. But now, Ivy was damaged goods. Now, his jaded tastes found her worthy of attention and if Landon wanted her, none of them stood a chance in hell.

Nicholas's lips quirked when Ivy half stumbled, half fell

against him. The twin dimples flitting in both his cheeks apparently hypnotized her. She stared unblinkingly at the man. Nudging her upright, he kept the grip on her elbow. "Would you care for a turn around the terrace, Lady Kinley? For a bit of, ah, fresh air?" Without waiting for consent, he propelled her forward, detaching her from the group with expert precision. Claiming her for himself.

Sebastian's vision clouded red, hands clenched even tighter, ready to smash, to destroy.

To kill.

Only to find he was saved from murder by the most unlikely of saviors.

"My dear Lady Kinley! My goodness, Lady Kinley! I've been searching for you everywhere. Have you ever seen so many people? It's an absolute crush!"

Lady Veronica Wesley, a vision in lavender silk, her mouth stretched into a broad smile, jaw tilted in grim understanding, barreled into the group. Taking Ivy's arm, she practically wrenched her from Nicholas's grasp.

He relinquished Ivy without a single word. A familiar expression of bored amusement slipped over his fallen angel features, the glittering emerald eyes unreadable. It was something Sebastian always envied about his former friend...the uncanny ability to keep his emotions from being used as arsenal.

Ivy twisted, unable to focus on who tugged her away from the center of male attention. Squinting, her face pulled into a perplexed scowl. "Lady Wesley?"

"Yes, my dear! I had to discover who made this lovely gown for you. It's quite stunning! The way the silk flows, these shiny strands. You simply must give me your dressmaker's direction. Are the shoes made to match? And what a gorgeous display of diamonds! I vow they are fit for the queen. Were they a gift? Or, perhaps your mother's? Now, she was a beautiful woman, wasn't she...it's said you resemble her a great deal."

With a stream of distracting questions, Veronica maneuvered Ivy toward a set of doors leading to one of the many garden terraces. The jackals muttered in dissent. Their prey was in danger of being whisked out of reach. By a mere woman, no less. As a group, they trailed the two ladies, unwilling to allow Ivy to escape so easily.

Nicholas strolled in silence behind the clutch of men. Sebastian did not know what thoughts turned behind those cold eyes of his, but thank God, he no longer had Ivy in his grasp.

Every muscle in his body constricted and even Nick scowled with faint disgust when Clayton snagged Ivy's arm in a vise-like grip. Veronica's eyes widened before she burst into peals of laughter. She retained her hold, a tug of war looming, with the countess as the prize.

"Gentlemen, please. Lady Kinley and I only mean to step outside to discuss a few things. One can hardly carry on a private conversation in this din!" Veronica flashed a carefree smile at the grumbling men. It was a reminder how accommodating she could be if the terms were suitable. Years ago, she directed the same smile at Sebastian prior to the onset of several debauched nights. That was the night her bed proved too small to hold them and the two additional ladies she laughingly presented as a birthday gift. It was shortly after that he purchased the massive bed Lady Veronica Wesley enjoyed to this day.

"Will one of you be a dear and fetch some champagne? And when we return, we shall all continue our chat in a more private setting. Won't that be nicer than this crowded ballroom?" Veronica's suggestion was a sweet purr, the insinuated nuance of something so wicked and divine it left the men spellbound. The possibilities of such a tryst were incentive enough for Clayton to drop Ivy's arm. He gave Veronica a sharp nod of compliance.

Nicholas March's golden head tilted. Ivy and Veronica were each subjected to his cold calculation.

Sebastian's guts tightened in horror. Every last one of these men would die if they dared...

There was only one reason to venture outside and this was to escape the crowd inside. Ivy had no particular interest in escaping. In vain, she attempted to pull free from Veronica's tight grip.

"Why'dchu hold myarm?" Her words slurred. "You don' 'ven like me...call Poison 'vee. I know you... 'eard *you*!"

Shocked twitters of laughter rippled through a growing crowd of fascinated spectators. Sebastian grimaced. Blood roared in his veins. The urge to destroy all of them, including Nicholas March, bloody hell, *especially* Nicholas March, almost overwhelmed him.

The face of each man staring after Veronica as she dragged the countess away was committed to memory. Only until he turned to slip out the terrace doors did he realize Nicholas was almost upon him.

Their eyes locked, with neither man moving for a long moment. Then, a slow smile of mockery hovering on his lips, Nick bowed. A dark golden brow lifted, silently daring Sebastian to emerge from the shadowy alcove.

Sebastian's hands tightened. Damn it, his teeth hurt from clenching them so hard. He wanted to storm over and knock that insulting grin from Nick's face. Knowing if he stayed a second longer he would do something regrettable, he abruptly turned his back and stalked away.

LAUGHTER AND LOUD CONVERSATIONS ECHOED BEHIND THEM AS Veronica propelled Ivy to the closest set of garden doors. As they drew away from the stimulating confines of the ballroom, Ivy's pace slowed.

"Wait," she moaned, swallowing hard and closing her eyes. "Moving...too fast...I'm going to be sick."

"A few more steps, Lady Kinley. You'll feel so much better on the terrace. The fresh air will do wonders," Veronica urged before mumbling under her breath, "and a pot of strong French coffee would do even better."

They reached the terrace without incident but as the door

closed behind them, Ivy stumbled. Momentum carried them along, nearly tumbling both to the stone floor.

With one arm, Sebastian put Veronica to rights while scooping Ivy up into the curve of the other.

"I've got her," he growled, the timber of his voice revealing nothing would change that fact. Yes. He had her. And she was not sliding through his fingers ever again.

CHAPTER 15

*S*ebastian carried the countess to the edge of the terrace. With barely restrained patience he deposited his burden none too gently on a bench in an alcove sheltered from the sharp breeze. Letting out a heavy, inarticulate moan, Ivy leaned against the rough wall as though appreciative for the cold brick pressed against her cheek.

Veronica twisted her hands at the stony glance Sebastian threw over his shoulder. "You frightened me. How-how much did you see? Or hear?"

Assured Ivy would remain propped against the wall, he took Veronica by the elbow. She swayed toward him with a quickened breath.

"Enough to know you saved a few lives tonight, Ronnie." A slight smile flitted across his lips when her eyes widened. "I had no idea you held the countess in such high esteem. You have my thanks for coming to her aid."

Veronica's gaze flickered to Ivy. Her beautiful shimmering gown shot sparks in the pale moonlight. "I could not stand by while they…" She swallowed her words when the grip on her arm tightened. "Whatever shall we do with her? My plan was to get her out as quickly as possible. I dare not go back through the ballroom."

While they watched, Ivy began to slide from the bench in a fluid heap of silk and tangled limbs. In two strides Sebastian was at her side. He jerked her to her feet, one arm snaking about her waist.

She blinked at him in meek confusion. "Are we there yet?"

Moving closer, Veronica instinctively reached to steady Ivy when her knees buckled again. Reluctant concern was evident in the lady's features and seeing it, Sebastian cursed beneath his breath. His arm hooked tighter about Ivy's waist.

"I shall take her home and you should depart as well," he instructed. "Take care no one sees you- use the north gate to the gardens. I will leave through the south."

"You are quite obsessed with her." Veronica subjected him to a shrewd consideration. "I'm not sure you are even aware of how much."

Sebastian scowled at her observation. "Don't be ridiculous, Ronnie. Those men do not give a farthing if she is willing or not. In fact, they prefer the later and you know that is the truth. I have no desire to see her so brutalized. For what it is worth, I'm sure Ivy will be grateful for your assistance."

"Oh? I may benefit from this impulsive act of kindness? How intriguing." Veronica's gaze darted to the terrace doors. "But a discussion for a later time, as someone may come searching for us at any moment."

Which would be a complete disaster. Sebastian was hungry for blood...anyone's would do. It was a test of his restraint that he did not storm into the ballroom, to beat those jackals to hell and back. Did he dare contemplate it?

"Get your damned hands off me."

The precisely enunciated words were barely audible, but Veronica's eyes widened at the hatred they contained.

"You...you *vile,* heartless bastard. Let go... let go. *Let me go."*

Ivy squirmed, swaying with an unsteady grace. When Sebastian tightened his hold, it was as if an icy bucket of sobriety doused her. Striking out with relentless ferocity, she pummeled his chest, kicking his shins when she could get her feet untangled from themselves. Even dampened by the debilitating effects of alcohol, she fought like an off-kilter whirlwind as a torrent of curse words poured from her lips. Were he not so angry, Sebastian might have been amused. Where had she learned to swear with such brilliant fluency? No doubt Clayton and his fellow reprobates. He scooped her off her feet, turning her so she was pinned against his chest and the blows could no longer strike his face.

"Be still!" His breath hissed in her ear and unable to stomach the swift change in body position, Ivy capitulated at once with a nauseated moan.

Veronica could not conceal her horrified fascination. This fierceness between the earl and Ivy, the possessive glitter in his eyes, it was a recipe for disaster. Jealous, furious men did things usually regretted much later when tempers cooled. And Sebastian was livid, his patience having snapped at last. "Seb," she ventured quietly, "perhaps I *should* see her home after all…"

"No."

"For her own safety…"

The glare Sebastian threw Veronica was nothing less than violent. Before she could manage an apology, he was gone in a swirl of black, Ivy's glowing silver gown melting into the ebony darkness of the garden as he carried her away.

Left alone in the cool spring air, Lady Wesley hugged herself. She could not help but compare the countess to a fairy queen in a tragic fable, an innocent stolen by a devil from the starless side of moonlight.

SEBASTIAN'S INTENTION WAS TO TAKE IVY STRAIGHT AWAY TO Kinley House. At least at first. Inside the confines of his coach, she rallied in drunken protest, cursing and kicking until he pinned her against the leather seat with the weight of his own body. Although it calmed her, the sudden lethargy was more an overabundance of champagne than any comfort found in his arms. With a rap to the coach's roof, Sebastian instructed Bowden to continue to Ravenswood Court. Silence soon filled the interior of the vehicle. Ivy's mumbled curses died away as exhaustion overtook her.

In the dark solitude of the ride, cradling her against him, Sebastian did not dare examine the reasons for his actions. Veronica was right. He courted disaster. Ivy was in jeopardy with him. It would be so easy to slip inside her rooms, to leave her untouched and tucked under the covers of her own bed. No one would ever know he ventured inside the walls of Kinley House. This was madness. What he felt for her was madness. When it came to her, it was impossible to follow the path of reason.

In the end, he quite simply could not force himself to let her go.

SEBASTIAN UNROLLED THE COACH BLANKET, ROUGHLY DEPOSITING Ivy onto his bed. Against the darkness of her hair and the dark blue coverlet, white roses glowed with the brilliance of snowflakes, clinging with determination to the silky strands of her coiffure. One red rose lay entangled in a gleaming lock of hair. It coiled low over her heart, bright as an accusing splotch of blood.

What the hell was he doing?

Sebastian tossed his evening coat away before disposing of his shirt and silk cravat. He poured a stiff tumbler of brandy.

Too late for second thoughts. Now. What to do about her.

CHAPTER 16

*I*vy braced the upper half of her body upright on stiff arms. Her hair was a disaster, crushed roses and curls streaming in a waterfall over her shoulders. A lamp on a table beside the bed, along with a low fire in the massive fireplace, provided barely enough light to illuminate the room.

The heavy masculinity of the space was confusing, although the silver and midnight blue colors of the bed clothing and drapes seemed familiar in their pairing. *Where am I?*

Her gaze landed on him. Sucking in a breath of absolute horror, a dazed consciousness slammed through the fuzziness enveloping Ivy. Sebastian stood by the fireplace, half-undressed. His chest was bare, the broad expanse of muscles stacked like molten iron.

"What have you done?" Sloppy with panic and champagne, her words slurred together. "Have you gone mad?"

"Most certainly." The corners of his mouth lifted in a slight smile as he sipped from the glass he held.

The slabs of his abdomen rippled with his movements, gleaming gold in the light of the fire. Although she shouldn't, Ivy stared as if hypnotized.

She forced herself to stand then just as quickly sank back down. The room actually tilted side to side, a rudderless schooner in a hurricane. At its far end Sebastian was a lost cork in an endless ocean, bobbing with relentless energy. Watching him was both fascinating and nausea inducing.

A bedpost would provide a sturdy anchor. Moving carefully, Ivy scooted to the end of the bed to wrap her arms around one of the massive supports.

"You monster. I d-demand you return me to the Faringdon's ball at once. You've no right to bring me here...no right!" To her ears, the words jumbled together in an incoherent mess. Leaning her forehead against the cool wood of the post, she squeezed her eyes tight, determined to regain control by sheer willpower alone.

When she dared to reopen them, everything seemed to have changed course. The room now spun in slow, ever narrowing circles and in the middle of these spinning circles, she sat. A target.

Sebastian did not move. Leaning a shoulder against the corner of the mantle, the glow from the flames illuminated only half his face. Shadows danced across his cheekbones and lips and he... he...Ivy swallowed hard, nearly moaning aloud. God help her, he was as dangerously dark and exquisitely handsome as ever.

Seeing him was more devastating than she imagined it would be, her heart shattering into a million tiny pieces, the splinters painful and stabbing every raw nerve. Bloody hell, she could not tear her eyes away from him. Because he looked thinner, his features a tiny bit haggard. Was it just the dark stubble of a beard making it seem so? Grazing his chin, shadowing his cheeks, giving him the air of a pirate. She hated that his dusky eyes gave no inkling as to his thoughts.

"Do you know what those bastards planned for you tonight, sweetness?" His brow arched high. "Do you? You would not have enjoyed it. And were you fortunate, you would not have remembered it. I've seen the damage done to their playthings before. They do not play nice at all. They would have torn you apart.

Although with Lady Wesley to rein them in, they might have shown restraint, just to have their fun again in the future." Jealousy colored his words, turning them ugly and hurtful.

Ivy's tongue was thick in her mouth. "I've no idea what you are talking about." Licking her lips, she wished for something, anything to drink.

When he stalked toward her, she shrank back, but he only handed her a tumbler then resumed his stance by the fireplace. The distance appeared necessary as his hands clenched into fists.

"My dear, they could hardly resist your charms." The words slapped her - a cold, hard drawl. "You were making it so damnably easy for them. Hell, each one of those jackals would have cocked up between your lovely legs tonight." His gaze was contemplative and cruel. "Or, maybe you hoped Landon would claim you. He wanted to. He tried to. He had you in his hands for a moment. Did you like him touching you? Have you a taste for dukes now? He's soon to come into his title. God knows he suffered no qualms in the past when stealing what is mine. Tell me, Ivy. Would you have let him fuck you?"

Befuddled by his calm demeanor, Ivy swallowed every drop in the glass he gave her.

The brandy scorched its way down her throat until her eyes watered. Then she choked and sputtered, the horrible ugliness of his words sinking in. Sebastian believed she wanted another man? After what he had done? Disgust washed through her, thick, hot, heavy. Without thinking of the consequences Ivy hurled the tumbler at him.

Ducking the hopeless aim, his brutal laughter rang out as the crystal crashed behind his head. Shards of glass tinkled musically to the floor in a harmless waterfall.

Fueled by something so black and searing it was unrecognizable, Ivy lurched from the bed. In a clumsy attack, she swung fists at his cruel grin, but Sebastian captured her wrists with one large hand, holding them with appalling ease in the small of her back.

"You bastard," she gasped. "You've no right to question me. You do not own me and you never will. I will bed every single one of them if I wish! Every single one! It's what's expected of me, isn't it? *A woman like me?*"

Sebastian's eyes turned darker than the night around them as she flung his words at him. His gaze pinned her, drinking her in. Like early moonlight frost, the gown swirled, illuminating Ivy's features. "Shut up, damn you." He gave her a rough shake. "You think my hunger for you is satisfied? That my desire is quenched? Far from it, little hellion and I'll be damned if another tries to take what is mine."

"I'm not yours!" Ivy cried out. "I'm not! I don't belong to anyone! I-I hate you." Her struggles were already fading as brandy coursed through sluggish veins to blend with champagne. Waves of dizziness rose and fell. She could not allow him to be stronger than her now. Please, not now. *"I hate you!"*

"No, you only wish you did. And it wouldn't matter anyway. I can't keep myself from you and you can't keep yourself from me," he snarled. His hand tangled in her hair, pulling until Ivy had no choice but to look into his eyes. A white rose crumpled in his fist, crushed petals falling to the floor. "How many of them have you slept with, Ivy? And who? Tell me. Now."

"I cannot count the number." Let him decipher the meaning of that, if he could. If he dared.

"Who was it?" The question was a roar. "If one of those bastards hurt you…"

"Not a single one took me by force," Ivy sneered. "That distinction is yours alone. The only man to go so far. The only one who had to."

Pinpoints of unholy fire flared in Sebastian's eyes as he realized she twisted what had happened between them and molded it the situation now.

"Goddamn it," he breathed. "You're playing a dangerous game, Countess."

Were it not for the tight grip he held on her hair, Ivy would have tossed her head, beyond caring for her safety. "A game I am winning. Shall we place it on the books? We will lay our wagers and I'll have you mucking a hundred stalls when it's all over…"

Sebastian gave a strangled curse, a muscle ticking in his jaw as her taunt hit home. Lust and anger drove him now, all traces of civility melting away.

Hooking his fingers into the top tier of the diamond necklace, Sebastian used it to jerk her closer until their faces were mere inches apart, the scent of crushed roses swirling between them. Where his knuckles rested flush with the hollow of her throat, Ivy's pulse beat with frantic thumps. He controlled her as a master would an unruly pet. "Careful, love. I am a very poor loser."

"You told me once you rarely *lose* anything," she retorted just before her teeth sank into his bare shoulder.

He flung her off with a grunt of surprised pain. Ivy staggered away. With the newfound freedom, she slipped off her shoes, using them as weapons to hurl at his head. While not quick enough to outpace him in such an inebriated state, she nevertheless turned toward the bedroom door.

Dodging the missiles, Sebastian caught her about the waist. He flung her with unceremonious disregard onto the bed, pinning her to the mattress before she could bounce up. One of his hands anchored hers high above her head while she bucked like a wild mare to dislodge the crushing weight of his body.

"Bloodthirsty little bitch." His eyes blazed with silver fire. "Holy hell, I *will* tame you…I will get my fill of you. If it kills me, if it is the *last* goddamn thing I do…"

A stream of colorful oaths poured from Ivy in response. When Sebastian abruptly rolled half off her, she stared in open-mouth surprise, silenced by the success of her efforts.

The relief was short-lived. His hand snaked between them to disengage the concealed hooks in the bodice of her gown. Ivy flailed and cursed but the bodice parted into two halves. In a matter of seconds only the grace of the corset covered her.

Sebastian's eyes narrowed in appreciation. Her breasts swelled to the top of the undergarment; the exquisite lace and ivy trimmings quivering with her anger and gulps for air, the diamond necklace glittering like drops of ice on her warm skin. With an impatient movement and a quick twisting of her arms, the entire gown was swept away. Ivy cried out in horrified distress, left only in stockings and roses, diamonds and that damned corset which would have given a monk plenty of reasons to question celibacy.

Ivy was far from vain but hoping her appearance would not inflame a man's passions was foolish. Red-hot rage flowed like a river, over and through her. Sebastian had no right to see her like this...*no right!* But there was no stopping his gaze from devouring her, burning her, from memorizing every detail of her body. She could only tremble and endure it.

Sebastian seemed almost dazed when his eyes finally rose to clash with hers. "Goddamnit, Ivy. You would tempt a saint."

"You are hurting me," was her hissed response.

"Am I?" Sebastian blinked, his words softly chilling. And gentle. "Maybe I want to hurt you. Maybe this is the only way to handle you and what lies between us. Or perhaps this is some horrible form of self-torture, something I deserve..."

A flash of pain stabbed Ivy. Memories of teasing one another during a game of whist, laughing over bumblebees, and soft, hot, soul-searching kisses by a babbling stream bombarded her. Waltzes by moonlight, playing piano for him. The sweet gifts he gave her, the thoughtful gestures no one else probably noticed. She recalled every instance he held her hand tight. The occasions he steadied her on the steps into Kinley House because a sheet of ice lay over them. She remembered when he tugged her to him, her head resting against his shoulder in sleepy contentment coming back from seeing a play. The quirk in his lips whenever he called her "little butterfly." And she relived each and every kiss they'd shared, starting with the first disastrous one in her music room.

A hysterical sob caught in Ivy's throat. She tried turning her head but he would not allow it, would not let her escape so easily.

"You are driving me to goddamn madness. Do you realize

that?" Sebastian's voice lowered, became softer. "I've said things that I should never...done terrible things. Dear God, what are you doing to me? What have I done to you?"

Frustrated regret shaded his words, regret Ivy did not have time to dwell on as his mouth closed over hers in familiar, searing possessiveness. Panicked, she kicked at him, but he simply threw one muscled leg across both of hers. For a long time, with exquisite, beautiful roughness, he simply kissed her.

Only when she stilled beneath him, limbs quivering, did his approach become gentle. Nibbling at her lips, sucking her mouth into the heated vortex of his own, his tongue delved in and out, stroking persuasively. The grip on her wrists loosened, not enough to release her, but enough so he would not bruise her.

Ivy struggled to hold herself from him, to hold tight to her anger, her fury. She tried, oh how she tried, to ignore the shivers vibrating through her, to ignore the awful trembling in the pit of her stomach, the thrill when his tongue coaxed hers to mate with his. Each time Sebastian lifted his mouth from hers, she turned her head, determined he would not kiss her again. But he was stubborn and relentless and she was drunk and tired, heartbroken. He wore her defenses down, and she had missed him too much to remain frozen forever in his embrace.

Nuzzling behind her ear, his teeth raked a sensitive spot where the line of her neck met the curve of her collarbone. She inhaled sharply, hating him when her pulse jumped in instant response. When his mouth drifted to her breasts, her low moan could not be contained. The last bit of flimsy protection the corset provided drifted away, magically disposed of. How he accomplished it she did not know, but with the exception of stockings, the last of the roses tangled in her hair and the diamond necklace, she was bare.

"Shhh..." Sebastian's lips burned everywhere they pressed, his words a litany of desperate hunger sucking her in. "Quiet now. Easy...easy. Sweetness, my beautiful little butterfly. Let me touch you, Ivy, yes, yes, that's it. Let me have you...let me love you. This is madness, what is between us...a fire that cannot be extinguished. A thirst I can't seem to quench. Somehow, you've destroyed me and I cannot bear it. God, I've missed you so terribly."

One hand roamed her body, gliding, touching wherever he desired. Easing the weight of his leg away, he traced an intricate pattern on the soft skin of her knees, trailing his fingers up between her thighs and Ivy helplessly, hopelessly, opened to him.

It was a losing battle to the warmth of the room, the heat of his kisses, the beguiling scent of lush blooms. A sly lassitude stole her will to fight him, easing Sebastian's path. She floated, weightless and dizzy. She was supposed to be angry. She must attempt to free herself, but she found it difficult to muster the required fury when sapped of all her strength.

As his mouth closed over the peach perfection of one breast, Ivy twisted against his grip in one last act born of desperation, moaning in despair at her own weakness.

Sebastian growled against the honey softness of her flesh, applying the same attention to the other breast until she was breathless and straining against him. Unable to fight him any longer, she returned his kiss when he claimed her mouth again. His fingers danced lightly over the flesh between her thighs, finding her wet and velvety. When he slid one devilish finger into her depths, her stomach clenched. The sensation was almost unbearable. He stretched and filled her, pushing deep to slide against a secret part of her. His mouth remained locked on hers, mimicking the drawing and stroking motion of his finger until Ivy dissolved in knife-sharp pleasure.

There was no need to hold her prisoner now. Melting against Sebastian in a tangle of legs and arms, warm, adrift, every bone in her body disintegrated, her climax shattering her with its intensity. She was nothing more than a pliable doll, to be toyed with as he wished.

He rose from the bed to tug her stockings off, tossing them aside so they fluttered to the Turkish carpet like ivory feathers. Rustling noises drifted to her ears as if from far away and when

Sebastian's nude body covered hers, Ivy was not shocked. He fisted one large hand in her hair, pulling her face to his. Kissing her with a restrained roughness, he slid between her legs, and she tasted the sweet bitterness of brandy on his lips.

He branded her, flames of fire licking her flesh everywhere their skin touched. The muscled length of his legs parting hers was strange and thrilling, the coarse hair of his thighs slightly abrasive against her smooth skin. Dreading the pain felt the first time, her knees instinctively bent as he fit against her. She tensed, waiting for him to thrust inside her.

Sebastian immediately stilled. He removed the red rose from the tangles of her hair with careful fingers. His eyes never leaving hers, he deliberately tore the blossom apart, cascading the fragrant petals over her breasts and stomach.

Ivy's heart jerked, stopped, then found its beat. Her ritual with the roses. He knew why she did it, understood the unspoken message directed only to him. She wanted to sob. She wanted to scream. To laugh.

She wanted him to never let her go.

Splaying her fingers against the hard plane of his chest, she neither pulled him close nor pushed him away. She simply waited, covered in rose petals. A log in the fire cracked apart, the shower of sparks highlighting the depths of his eyes. His hips tilted to the entrance of her body and Ivy swallowed convulsively. His shaft felt impossibly large and hard against her tense softness. *How did that ever fit inside me?*

"I hurt you before," he whispered. "My poor darling girl. Forgive me."

Ivy's eyes fluttered shut. Did he speak of when he took her virginity and broke her heart? Or earlier tonight, when his cruel words lashed her and striped her soul? Then she could not think at all as he slid with excruciating deliberateness, with heart-stopping finality, full length into her. Once sheathed to the hilt, Sebastian paused, a shudder of a breath escaping him. His arms trembled slightly.

When he took her on her father's desk, the act hurt so terribly. But even then, that terrible night, a confusing compulsion to keep him inside her, to have him slide deeper, made the possession feel strangely beautiful. That same bewildering urge overcame Ivy now as Sebastian's body stretched hers. The stinging pain she felt was not as sharp as she remembered, not as painful as before; in fact, the discomfort was short-lived, quickly melting to become something else. Something wicked and dazzling and just beyond her reach. The rich fullness of him inside her ignited every nerve ending she possessed and ones she never knew existed. Invasion drove all coherent thought from her brain. Unexpected ripples of ecstasy cascaded throughout her limbs. Shameful how easily she succumbed to his caresses. Later, when she was sober, she would hate herself for it, but right now, pleasure swamped her until she was drowning in it.

Seconds ticked away as he waited. And waited. Until Ivy realized he waited for her.

A twinge pulled at her, tugging at the depths of her stomach, the very depths of her soul. Whether it was the alcohol or his touch, or both, her senses reeled in a kaleidoscope of intense delight. A tiny portion of her brain still howled in protest but the last bit of willpower to resist evaporated. She would not stop him.

She shifted, her hips lifting in a tentative gesture. Sebastian's sigh was almost imperceptible. His dark head dipped to her breast. Easing one nipple into the moist heat of his mouth, he rolled his tongue over the peak, biting down, gently at first, then with increasing pressure. And Ivy was lost.

Clutching at his broad shoulders, her palms smoothed over the rippling muscles. His body joined with hers felt so different from the other times when he brought her to a shattering peak with his fingers. This, this possession felt more intense, more powerful. More everything.

"Sebastian." Her moan was soft. *"Yes..."*

Sebastian's dark head lifted, a flame of triumph glittering in the depths of his eyes. Ivy didn't care.

"You are mine, Ivy, although you may believe otherwise." His words curled around her. "I won't let you go now. You *belong* to me. Damn you...damn us both...damn this crazy world and everyone in it, but you belong to me. Do you understand? You've always been mine. You always will be. *Mine*.

CHAPTER 17

*T*he night he so brutally snatched her innocence from her, Sebastian did not fully appreciate the rare, fleeting beauty the Heavens gave him.

He meant to hurt her then, to abuse the trust she placed in him, to punish her. But now, he wanted Ivy with a desperation never experienced before. He wanted to possess her until she moaned his name with every thrust of his hips. He needed to see the flush of passion on her skin as he brushed it with his lips, to taste her arousal and drink her in like the finest of wines. He ached to give her such soaring pleasure, every painful memory beginning with him would be forever erased.

Come morning, Ivy would hate him again, if she remembered this seduction, if intoxication did not blot it from her memory. Sebastian knew he would remember this night for the rest of his life. He experienced a fleeting pang of remorse. He wanted her to remember it too, without anger or the ugly cloud of revenge shadowing the memory.

Ivy squirmed, her long slender legs wrapping loosely around him, and Sebastian paled, sweat beading on his brow. The rose petals he scattered across her stomach rubbed softly against his skin. It took all his strength to keep from surging into her.

Christ, she had no inkling of the power she held over him. Her lush tightness, all of her inner channel muscles, were clenched against his intrusion. Despite his bitter accusations and her own words to the contrary, Sebastian knew he was Ivy's only lover. He could not mistake the signs of flesh well acquainted with pleasure, not after the number of women he had enjoyed over the years. Her body was taut around him, almost unbearably so, her arms and legs awkwardly wrapped about him in innocent desire. No, Ivy was still his. Despite the pain and heartache suffered at his hand, she was his alone.

With the flurry of a trapped hummingbird, her heartbeat thumped, working its way to the inside of his veins, in his head, around his shaft. She reached to ruffle her fingers through the thick waves of his hair, brushing back a lock from his brow, and Sebastian closed his eyes in torment.

Jaw clenched, he finally met her questioning gaze and said, "Bloody hell, you aren't making it easy for me to do this slowly." He nudged forward a little more.

"I don't understand." Ivy's ragged whisper was half gasp and half moan. "Would you rather move quickly?"

Sebastian choked back a laugh, his forehead touching hers. His blood thickened to the consistency of lava. "Ivy, slow or fast, it won't matter. I've no control with you. Holy hell, you have no idea what you are doing to me."

Sliding his lips along the side of her neck, he nibbled at the slim column until he reached one of her earlobes. With a tiny bite, he won a gasp. When he chased it with a sweep of his tongue to ease the sting, she gave him a melting sigh. His hips prodded hers, and with a maddening rhythm, began to slide in, then out, stretching her, filling her. The blood whirred around his head in a self-contained tornado, exploding into his veins, rushing to the extremities of his body.

The silk of her skin, the warmth of her, her scent. That damned orange and lily perfume combined with the aroma of crushed roses; it all surrounded him. He rocked against her, the tempo slow then quicker, harder. Containing his impatience made him quiver. Sliding a hand to the outside of her thigh, he hitched her leg higher. Maybe he could ease back to a rhythm that would not send him catapulting into a climax.

"Damnit..." Gliding into her slick heat was far too easy in this position. With a silent groan of anguish, he gave a compulsive, deep plunge and suddenly, everything within Ivy tightened around him.

It was the strangest sensation. Even with his vast experience, Sebastian never felt its like before. He tried to withdraw, to slow himself, to slow her, but it all rushed so recklessly, too quickly, too frantically. Ivy would not allow his retreat. Clutching him, she arched with a high, keening cry of pleasure.

A portion of his consciousness shouted at him, to withdraw before it was too late, but he could not resist. With a strangled curse, he thrust into her just one degree more. Taking her, branding her, marking her as his possession. The need to find release was excruciating.

"God, Ivy...I can't stop."

Her orgasm sent beautiful shivering waves reverberating throughout his entire body. She trembled beneath him. Catching her hips in an almost violent grip, he tried holding her immobile.

"Don't stop." Was her broken response. *"Oh, please...Sebastian...please."*

He plummeted with her incoherent command, spilling inside her with a hoarse, muffled shout of male conquest, a forceful culmination of pent up desire and the need to possess. He barely heard Ivy crying out her pleasure. The throbbing satisfaction inside him was almost painful, the world fading to black as he gave himself to her. His heart, his very soul exploded from him, rocketing around the world before slamming back into his body with the fury of a lightning strike.

When sanity returned, Sebastian discovered the pieces of

himself, the fragments missing for so very long, were right there before him. This girl, this exasperating, headstrong, mysterious girl, held them all along.

Such frightening sensations, he mused, these quivers of protectiveness unfurling in his heart for the girl lying damp and breathless beneath him. So foreign and yet, nothing ever felt more magnificent than holding her, feeling the quivering of her body. Slipping his arms under her shoulders, he folded Ivy closer to him, savoring the odd, fragile emotions, promising himself he would not be so selfish again in their lovemaking. Something extraordinary had happened to him, although it was all too terrifying to contemplate in its entirety.

As his heartbeat slowed, finding its normal cadence, he felt the slightest change sweep over her. Sebastian frowned, puzzled by the new, soft ripples.

She was weeping.

Rolling to his side, he positioned Ivy until she lay cradled against him, her head pillowed on his shoulder. Tears splashed his skin, her breath moist where it feathered his neck. With soothing murmurs, he stroked her hair, brushing kisses against her forehead, but she did not acknowledge his caresses as a tangle of emotions escaped.

She cried for a long time, until only ragged breaths of exhaustion remained and she drifted into a restless slumber. Sebastian rose and threw on a silk robe, crossing the room to lean a forearm against the marble mantle.

There were so many things to consider, things lurking below the surface of his controlled veneer. Something far more lethal than revenge and punishment had wrapped itself around his heart. Rubbing his chest, he stared into the flames of the banked fire. It was harder than he imagined, scouring away the guilt plaguing him since that night in her father's study.

A stark realization illuminated his entire being; twisting sensations evolving from the moment he laid eyes on Ivy at the Sheffield Ball. Emerging from the darkened corner of Kinley

House's entry hall and in the shadowy interior of his own coach. Unfurling in dazzling beauty on ballroom floors as he whirled Ivy to the lilting strains of waltzes. Feathering coyly during walks in the moonlight. Without warning, these emotions bloomed in the shade of a cove of elm trees and flourished while duels were fought with persistent bumblebees. But tonight- tonight everything burst forth in full conquering glory. Like a butterfly born in spring.

He needed Ivy. He wanted her. He longed for her smile, her touch, her scent.

I love her.

Loved her beyond all reason. Loved her fire, her sweetness, her soul. Her body. Her mind. All of her.

Tonight changed everything. Sebastian glanced at the bed, where the source of his confusion and the threat to his sanity slept in a tangled heap of white silk sheets and red rose petals. He wanted to crawl back beside her, gather her close and shield her from men who would hurt her, men like himself.

Gingerly, he touched his shoulder. Ivy was not completely helpless. Her teeth left their mark, and drunk or not, she fought like a true hellion. With the frustrated awareness of a man who planned for everything, who held purpose and reason for every action, Sebastian was suddenly unsure of his next steps. He made love to her…and it would never be enough. This obsession would never end. He wanted her for eternity.

How he would gain her consent, he had no idea, but on the morrow, he would obtain a special marriage license. Convincing Ivy Kinney to become his wife was a problem in need of a solution. But his wife she would be.

CHAPTER 18

The room tilted when Ivy sat up. After an endless, hovering, moment, it righted, but slowly and awkwardly, like a broken toy boat set adrift in a rough pond. Burning waves of nausea rose in her throat. Choking it down with determined swallows, she collapsed against the pillows with a tormented groan.

The silver ballgown lay draped over the back of a chair near the foot of her bed. Her undergarments sat folded and stacked in the brocade seat, her shoes lined up in orderly fashion beneath the chair, as though she had just slipped them off. She ventured a peek beneath the coverlet.

A peach colored nightgown. One she did not recall donning. Nor did she remember removing any clothing to put the flimsy garment on. Mangled white roses lay scattered everywhere; on the vanity table along with the diamond necklace, on the floor, in the bed. The red one was missing, but that was not out of the ordinary.

Pushing her tangled hair back, Ivy probed her temples. Her head throbbed as if a hundred tiny devils beat it with mallets. Wearily, she managed to pull herself higher onto the pillows, and in reward, unrelenting details of the night splashed across her mind.

Ivy swallowed back a sob of misery. She remembered arriving at the ball, men quickly gathering around her. Clayton, Danbury. Brandon Madsen watched with grave concern from the edges. The Earl of Landon held her arm, wishing to take her somewhere. Lady Wesley stopped him.

Lady Wesley? The lady in question had never been complimentary; there was no explanation for her involvement. Pressing her temples even harder, Ivy struggled to dredge forth more. She leaned against a wall, the cold brick soothing to her heated face. There were moments of sickness, dizziness and cursing and Lady Wesley babbling nonsense about French coffee.

Oh, God help me.

Had Sebastian truly carried her, tossing her like so much unwanted baggage into a luxurious coach with cream-hued leather seats?

That particular memory ended in a vague recollection of fighting him in his bedchamber. Thrown onto a huge bed while he loomed over her like a beast guarding a new kill. She remembered tasting blood in her mouth. *Did I bite him? It's all such a blur...*

She threw her shoes at him and perhaps a brandy snifter. Or did she? Everything tangled in her mind, knotted in half bursts and blinding flares.

They made love.

Ivy moaned, praying it was a hallucination, a vivid dream brought on by vast quantities of alcohol. Or perhaps a nightmare, if one did not care to place too fine a point on it.

Sebastian's scent clung to her, an intriguing combination of soap and cinnamon and spice, and something else, something foreign, the smell of sex. The junction of her thighs was too tender, her breasts still tingling from his greediness for any of this to be a fragment of her imagination. Touching her mouth with trembling fingers, she remembered pulling his head down to hers, demanding he kiss her.

"Oh, no." Erotic fragments of the tattered evening flashed like lightning in her mind. *"No, no, no."* She pressed her palms to her eyes. If she rubbed hard enough, maybe she could somehow block it all out. The dark, possessive kisses, whisper-soft caresses. The slide of his body entering hers as she surrendered.

Soft pillows muffled her cries. "What have I done? *What have I done?*"

She had clutched him to her when she thought he would withdraw, her hips meeting his thrusts with wanton eagerness. Reaching the pinnacle of satisfaction, she moaned his name, once at the tips of his fingers and twice more as he plunged so deep into her very core. For some distressing reason, these particular memories were crystal clear. She could not escape their clarity; they burned like raining hellfire.

Ivy took a shaky breath to calm herself, her eyes slowly adjusting to the morning light. It was then she saw the envelope on the bedside table. A single, wild red rose in full bloom lay atop it. Where, and how, did he obtain a wild rose? The whole of London was bankrupt when it came to red and white roses, courtesy of her awful ritual. With trembling hands, she ripped the envelope open.

Lady Veronica Wesley provided your escort home.

The note drifted to her lap. Ivy possessed no recollection of the time after they made love. Exactly how Sebastian managed to spirit her away from his bed and into her own, with no one seeing or hearing a thing, was miraculous. She ought to be grateful for the alibi, should anyone question her.

Sebastian made love to me, and I loved it...

All of it. Every heart-stopping, terrible, beautiful moment of it...

He covered me in red rose petals and made love to me...

One hand slid to her stomach, fingers wobbly coasting from navel to the curve of her lower belly. Sebastian made love to her. What if...*what if*...

What if she became pregnant?

Disturbing visions flooded Ivy's mind. The earl, standing like stone beside his massive bed, while she writhed in silent agony giving birth to his bastard.

Tumbling from the bed, she staggered to the watercloset. She made it just in time.

Her stomach expelled the evils of the previous night into the porcelain washbowl, purging the horror of her own thoughts. When the spell was over, she collapsed against the wood panel wall of the small room. To combat the undulating waves of sickness, she pulled her knees to her chest, arms wrapped about them as she drew in deep breaths. Tears pricked behind her eyelids but she fought them back.

Her heart, fragile and torn, thumped slow and steady while the scattered pieces were scraped together. She did not know what to do. She could only wait for Sebastian to make the next move.

CHAPTER 19

ive. Five sleepless nights spent tossing and turning, waiting for Sebastian. Ivy drove herself mad during those nights.

On the sixth day, she listlessly accepted Brandon's persistent invitation to an afternoon play. Members of the disbanded Pack seemed so innocent now when compared to her latest group of debauched admirers.

Brandon appeared genuinely concerned as he carefully handed Ivy up into the coach. Solicitous and calm, he inquired of her health, remarking how pale she was, before launching into a monologue of his activities since their last bit of time together. The steady monotony of his words lulled her. Soon, her thoughts bogged her down. She wondered why Sebastian had not come to her. And she might have convinced herself it was all a bad dream, if not for the rose accompanying the alibi note. And the tiny bite marks he left on her skin.

Ivy was so emotionally bruised she failed to notice the coach's detour until it was too late. They had traveled past the outskirts of London, heading north at an alarming rate of speed when Brandon's intentions became clear.

"This is not the route to the Lyceum."

"Change of plans, my dear," The viscount admitted gently.

"These new plans include abduction?"

His gaze roamed her features. "Merely a ride through the countryside, darling. Relax. You might enjoy a change of scenery."

"I've no desire to see the countryside. Please turn the coach around and take me home."

"My dear, that's not possible. Now, do not be difficult. We have business in Gretna Green, you see, and our attendance is mandatory for these matters to work." Brandon's tension visibly increased as he spoke. "Your infatuation with Ravenswood ran its course, and I've grown weary waiting for you to accept my proposal."

"I don't wish to marry you." Ivy's face flushed with anger. Would she go through life constantly abducted at one point or another?

"This is a necessity, Ivy. I want you for my wife, and you are in desperate need of a husband."

"I'm in desperate need to be left alone by selfish men." The viscount was subjected to her cold stare. "And I was not infatuated with Ravenswood. Like you, he was little more than another suitor, bedeviling my steps. The gossips read far too much into his courtship." The lie tasted bitter on Ivy's tongue. No other man on earth was like Sebastian Cain.

Brandon smiled, his tone dispassionate. "Of course, I must ignore the favors you granted him if I am to take you for my wife. A sacrifice I'm willing to make." He flicked a speck of imaginary dust from his coat. "Your intimacy with that man angers me, although there is a bright side. The punishments I will mete out for the loss of your virginity will do much to appease me."

Ivy's blood chilled at the mention of punishments. What the devil did he mean? Why was his smile so frightening? So...*different?* "I did not grant him favors."

The viscount cocked his head. "Didn't you?"

Why did she not see this coming? Brandon believed himself

the leader for her hand, although with no encouragement on her part. Fear left her mouth dry as Timothy came to mind. She survived that particular abduction. She would survive this too. But as she traced the scar hidden beneath her glove, she wanted to scream with helpless fury.

Brandon's smile turned cruel with her silence. "I lost a great deal of money wagering I would be the one to break you. On our return to London, all will be put to right, and with your fortune, my losses will be covered quite handily. Although, I don't wish you to think I only married you for your considerable wealth, darling."

"This will be annulled," Ivy said.

"Do you take me for a fool, Ivy?" Brandon might as well be a stranger; none of his previous courtly mannerisms in evidence. "I will have you. Best to resign yourself to it."

"You will not be able to keep me." Her head tilted with a sudden thought. "Have you considered I might be with child?"

He frowned. "Ravenswood broke off with you over a month ago. If you were breeding, you'd know by now."

"But, are *you* certain?" Ivy asked. "Five nights ago, I was in the earl's bed. I could be carrying his babe now. You would claim his bastard as your own? Take that risk?"

"I don't believe you." His hand waved in dismissal, but a fraction of doubt quivered in Brandon's voice.

"Oh, it's quite true. He came for me at the Faringdon Ball. You probably saw Lady Wesley escort me to the gardens; she helped him, to take me away. My disappearance created much gossip but it was Ravenswood's doing, of course. He cannot stay away from me. I do believe the man is quite obsessed. Something in the family bloodlines, no doubt. You know his cousin suffered the same affliction..." Ivy shook her head as if in remembrance. "That very night, Sebastian took me to Ravenswood Court. Stripped me bare, laid me out on his bed. Then he..."

Brandon shook with impotent fury. "Shut up, damn you, shut up! Even if true, it changes nothing! We will wed, and if you are with child, there are ways to rid you of it. One never knows with first pregnancies. They can be so tenuous, so very fragile. Accidents are such a worry. We would start anew, and none would question the brat you carry is mine. I'll make damn sure of it, even if it means keeping you under lock and key."

The horror of his suggestion was sickening. Whatever Ivy hoped to accomplish by revealing Sebastian's actions, Brandon smashed to bits with brutality. Despite her intent to be strong, tears welled in her eyes.

Leaning forward, he cupped her chin with merciless fingers. "Get some rest, my dear. When we stop to change horses, I suspect I'll need to restrain you."

"You are despicable," Ivy choked, jerking away to press against the far wall of the coach.

"And you keep adding to the punishments, darling. Addressing me in such a manner is worthy of something quite painful."

They continued through the afternoon and as darkness approached, a heavy rain erupted. The two horses labored in the thickening muck. In some parts of the road, the mire quickly became fetlock deep. Rain beat mercilessly against the glass of the coach windows while a harsh wind buffeted the vehicle until it became difficult to remain seated. Brilliant flashes of lightening illuminated the murky black skies with growing frequency. As the storm grew, leaves and debris scuttled across the road and the horses whinnied loudly in protest as the coachman drove them onward with increasingly sharper cracks of the whip.

At one point, the coach skated sideways on a patchy sheet of mud, and Ivy's heart lurched at the unsettling feel. The horses were slowed to a walk and she wondered if she dared an attempt at escaping. The coach moved so slowly, she might not be injured if she jumped. Would she reach the woods quickly enough to hide in the cover of darkness?

She would not be a helpless victim again, not as she had been with Timothy. She must fight until there was no strength left in her body. Sensing her intentions, Brandon moved to the seat beside her. Ivy reacted with the panic of a cornered fox. He gripped her upper arms and she bit at his hands, surprising him with her fierceness.

Brandon stared on the blood on his wrist then his hand lashed out, causing Ivy to crumple with a dazed sob, her hand to her jaw. "Save the hysterics, Ivy." With a punishing grip, he held her hands in one of his, leaving bruises on the pale skin of her wrists. His other hand clutched her face, fingers biting into the tenderness of her cheeks. "It will be so much better if you don't struggle."

"I'll fight you with all I have." Ivy's response was a dizzy moan of pain.

He swooped in, kissing her so hard, his teeth ground against her own, his tongue whiplashing hers until she gagged. Ivy tasted blood; his or hers, she was unsure.

When Brandon finally released her, he laughed, licking his lips as if relishing the flavor of her, blood and all.

"Oh, very well. Fight, if you must. I'll find pleasure in it too, that much is certain."

SEBASTIAN DID NOT VENTURE OUT, UNSURE OF HIS COMPOSURE IF he should happen to encounter Ivy at any one of the social functions taking place around London. No illusions existed as to the sudden influx of invitations garnered upon his return from the wilds of Scotland. Hostesses and society matrons speculated if the two most notorious members of the *ton* appeared at the same place, fireworks would forthwith commence.

Of course, no one knew fireworks *had* already commenced. Sebastian hated himself for taking advantage of Ivy's inebriated state, but an inner voice mocked the faint sense of chivalry. He'd do it all over again if the opportunity presented itself. He tasted her kiss even now…

There was still the matter of regaining Ivy's trust. Winning her love again. He encountered no trouble when it came to obtaining the special marriage license; his level of power ensured its relative ease of procurement. But it did take longer than anticipated. The magistrate owing him a favor had only just returned from Paris two days before, the license arriving at Ravenswood Court that very afternoon. Now, the difficulty lay in convincing the bride to marry him, a bride who hated the very sight of him.

"Only yourself to blame, Ravenswood," Sebastian muttered, flopping into an overstuffed leather chair. It was pouring rain and the steady drum of raindrops combined with his mood to make for a bleak, miserable evening.

Tomorrow would be better. It must be. Because tomorrow he would claim her. Tomorrow, he began the journey of regaining her trust and her love. Tomorrow could not come quickly enough.

Sebastian barely noted the melodious chimes of the doorbell down the long hall. Even the sounds of a scuffle and raised voices in the foyer failed to intrude on his melancholy. Only when the door to his study flew open, crashing against the opposite wall, did he acknowledge the intrusion.

Soaking wet, furious, Lady Sara Morgan stood in the doorway. Aunt Rachel hovered behind her, face pinched in outrage at the young lady shoving her way into their home in the midst of a thunderstorm. Sebastian regarded his friend's fiancé with a puzzled frown. What the devil was she doing?

"*Get up,*" Sara snapped.

Sebastian smiled then realized her seriousness. The girl's coiffure was a saturated mess; a blonde curl drooping over one eye, the rest hanging in a tangled mass down her back. Her dark rose silk evening gown was hopelessly rain-soaked and most certainly ruined; the matching slippers splattered with mud and sopping wet. She'd catch her death of cold if she didn't get out of those garments and into something warm and dry.

"She barged in, demanding to see you. Jackson informed her we were not receiving guests, but she pushed her way through." Rachel sputtered with rage while Sara, sweet, gentle Sara, wore the countenance of an avenging angel. Or a rampaging murderess. Either possibility was terrifying. Neither boded well.

Other than to lift a sardonic eyebrow at her soft-spoken, steely command, Sebastian did not move.

Sara swung toward Rachel with clenched fists. "I won't repeat myself, Lady Garrett. Be silent."

The older woman's thin lips clamped shut.

"As for you, my lord," Sara snarled, advancing on Sebastian with deadly intent. "I told you to get up."

"To what do I owe this little visit?" Ignoring the directive, Sebastian extracted a cigar from the ornate humidor on his desk. Lighting it with an unhurried air, he reclined in his chair, drawing deep then exhaling so the smoke swirled high overhead.

Just beyond Sara, Gabriel Rose appeared in the doorway, huge and menacing. His brows raised in silent query. Should he remove the girl or allow her to stay?

Sebastian gave a subtle shake of his head. He had no desire to see his friend's fiancée manhandled from his home.

"Ivy…" A shimmer of fear flitted in Lady Morgan's gaze. She glanced at Rachel then focused on Sebastian, her voice stronger. "It's Ivy."

One would never know by looking at him, but every nerve in his body drew up tight as a bowstring at the mention of Ivy's name. For a moment, he believed Sara had come to exact vengeance, either for his most recent seduction, or that terrible night in Lord Kinley's study. He certainly deserved punishment for both. Indeed, there were many things he was guilty of, things he would most likely burn in hell for.

Did Ivy tell Sara of his misdeeds? That others might learn of his brutal treatment caused a moment of concern before calmer reasoning prevailed. No, she would not share those private matters, those intimate details and heartbreaking moments. She would keep their secrets. God help him, Sara came for something far worse, something very frightening. It must be if she was desperate enough to beg his assistance.

"Yes?" Sebastian drawled, a portrait of casual indifference. "Pray continue?"

"I don't know what else to do, where to go. She's been taken." A widening puddle of raindrops formed at Sara's feet. An expensive rug hung in a state of imminent ruination. Her shoulder's slumped in despair. "Lord Ravenswood, she's been abducted."

Sebastian felt as though someone kicked him in the stomach. Exhibiting an aura of calm he did not feel, he knocked ashes from the cigar into a heavy cut crystal dish, his gaze meeting Gabriel's above Sara's head. The man immediately departed to begin gathering necessary items.

"Are you sure Lady Kinley is not with Edwardson? I hear she discovered a new appreciation for boxing and he recently obliged her. Or, perhaps she's taking part of the gambling at Madam Cheverly's with Lord Grantville." The acid in Sebastian's tone was harsh enough to etch stone and directed inward. *My God, Ivy...is it true? Have you already turned away from me? Perhaps you flew from me of your own choice. To escape my cruelty.* "There appears to be a great number of gentlemen providing the countess with an escort lately. Perhaps "abducted" is too a strong word."

"That's not Ivy!" Sara cried out. "That pale, hollow, glittering creature is not Ivy!" Rushing around the corner of the desk, she grabbed Sebastian's arm, frantically seeking an answer in the slate-hued gaze regarding her so calmly. "That girl staring through me with those brittle eyes is not the sister of my heart. That vacant girl walking about as though dead inside is not my dearest friend. Can't you understand? She's not been the same since that night of the Pack's last dinner. Whatever you did to her, whatever you said, whatever happened between the two of you, *you* destroyed her. I don't know if she will ever come back, if she will ever be the same. Or if she *can* come back, but do not dare pretend to be indifferent, Ravenswood. I *know* you care. Dear God in heaven, you *must* care."

Rachel's laugh sounded shrill and oddly cold in the cozy warmth of the finely appointed study. "What interest could he have in that trollop? What a twisted plot you devised together, now that the earl tossed her to the side. She's always been one to seek attention."

Sara released Sebastian's arm, turning to the older woman. "You don't know anything about Ivy. You have only your hate of her, but you are wrong. Wrong! You think Timothy was so blameless, so innocent? You have no idea what he did to her...no idea at all."

"I know she drove him to his death!" Rachel sneered. "She teased and tormented him until he took his own life!" Latching onto Sara's arm with a cruel hand, fingers biting into the soft flesh, she tried yanking the younger woman toward the door.

Sebastian stood to intervene.

"Let go, madam!" Sara pushed with enough force to send the woman stumbling. Rachel landed on her backside, her head knocking against the mahogany wall with a hard thud. Too stunned to react immediately, she moved with slow, careful movements, rising from the floor on unsteady feet to stare at Sara with newfound respect.

"I'm not leaving until I've had my say and you both shall listen to every word," the girl vowed through gritted teeth, tiny fists clenched as if ready to strike anyone who attempted to leave the study. "Do you hear me? Every word."

"Sebastian! Call for the bobbies!" Rachel probed at the lump rising on the back of her head. "Where's in God's name is Gabriel? Surely your damned man can handle removing this chit-"

"He kidnapped her," Sara interrupted quietly, her eyes glittering blue ice as the awful truth was exposed.

Lady Garrett and Sebastian both stared at her.

She continued with relentless intensity. "Timothy Garrett abducted her. Attempted to carry her to Gretna Green. When she fought him, he struck her. Only Ivy would not give up. She attempted to jump from the coach and when she managed to get the door opened, Timothy slammed it shut. Somehow, Ivy's hand was sliced open on a bit of metal. It must have terrified him. With all the blood, he probably thought she was dying."

Sara wiped tears from her eyes. "He had the coach turn back, carried her back to Kinley House. Lady Garrett, believe what you will, but I saw Ivy's face, the bruises, the scrapes; the wound she suffered attempting to escape. And, I've known her pain, her heartache when your damaged son took his life. Simply because he could not possess her when he thought she belonged to him."

Her voice dropped to a whisper. "I swore a vow. I swore never to say a word. Never, not when she was vilified for refusing to see Timothy and not when she was blamed for his death. She trusted him, cared for him. She was his friend when he least deserved it and he abused that trust so horribly. When he died, Ivy wept so many tears. She felt responsible, although there was nothing she could have done to save him or to heal the madness inside him."

Sara's eyes bore holes into Sebastian. Was precious time wasted coming here? Attempting to sway the man who delighted in breaking her friend's heart? "I told her Timothy was unnaturally obsessed, that he'd changed from last season. The medication he took for his headaches, it turned him into someone possessive, bitter and ugly, in words and actions. It made him a monster that we no longer recognized.

Ivy's heart is so tender beneath that icy veneer she presents to the world. She believed she could help him, that her friendship was enough. You've seen the scar, Ravenswood. Have you not wondered about it? How it came to be there? Brody stitched it, with the late countess' own sewing kit. Ivy never told anyone the truth; she even hid it from her father." Sara's words caught on a heart-wrenching sob as her emotions finally overflowed. "*She would never have told a soul.*"

A dreadful silence filled the room, with the exception of Lady Morgan's soft weeping. Sebastian was so overcome with regret and shame, it was difficult to draw a proper breath of air. His chest tightened until he could only rub it, hoping to ease the unrelenting pain. Tossing the cigar into the fireplace, he unlocked one of the drawers of the desk, drawing out the marriage license and Timothy's well-worn last letter.

*What have I done to her? What has my family done to her?
Forgive me, Ivy. My love, my very heartbeat, forgive me.*

Rachel's eyes widened. "Sebastian, you can't believe this
farce! My Timothy would never do such a thing…they fabricated
this tale to make him the villain. He cannot defend himself against
these lies!"

"Ivy could not defend herself when Timothy tried to take what
would never belong to him." Sebastian gathered up the documents
and stalked to the door.

"You are not going after her. I forbid it." Rachel threw herself
in his path. "She is a disease and it is good riddance, I say. Good
riddance!"

He stared at the woman. How she could blame Ivy for Timothy's death was inexplicable. "Of course, I'm going after her. How
can I not? I highly suggest staying out of my way, madam."

Brushing past her, he took Sara by the arm and pulled her into
the hall with him. Their ancient butler, Jackson, held his overcoat
and assisted in tucking the papers into a deep, inner pocket for
safekeeping. The foyer was a mass of activity, servants running to
and fro. Gabriel trotted down the stairs, carrying a box containing a
brace of pistols. He handed it to Sebastian along with two leather
pouches full of gold coins. "Raven will be ready momentarily. I
would like to accompany you, but what are your wishes on the
matter?"

"Ride ahead to Beaumont. Tell the staff to prepare themselves
for my arrival and the countess. I'll send word to you when I've
secured her." Sebastian drew up short…he neglected to inquire
who dared to kidnapped her. Christ, if Nicholas March was
involved in any way, he might actually rip the man apart with his
bare hands.

"Who has her?" he snapped at Sara.

He was forced to repeat his demand before Sara, staring at
Gabriel Rose with wide-eyed curiosity, answered.

"Viscount Basford. He came for her this afternoon under the
pretense of taking her to an afternoon play at the Lyceum. Ivy's

butler sent for me when she did not return, and an inquiry at the viscount's house revealed his immediate departure for business in Scotland. I've no doubt they are headed to Gretna Greene. I was four houses from here at the Waring musicale, which Ivy was to attend as well. It's how Brody knew where to find me. You must understand, I had no one else to ask assistance of, Ravenswood. Alan is at Bentley Park; it would have taken far too long to send word to him."

Sara's gaze drifted to Gabriel. She'd never seen a man with so many bulging muscles and such kind eyes before. And such a fearsome scar as the one slicing his face. "Lord Kinley is unaware of these developments, but should Basford make it to Scotland, there will be no choice. The marriage will stand." Forcing her attention back to Sebastian, she added softly, "Although I despise you for trying to destroy her, I pray I'm not wrong in believing you care for her...even if only a little. If you do not, Ivy does not deserve your contempt. She's been in such pain these past few weeks. She's not been...herself."

Sebastian's blood was little more than raging ice in his veins, but a curious sense of relief flooded him. Thank God, Nicholas's name did not spill from Sara's lips. Or Clayton or Danbury. Those men pursued women for sport and cruel pleasure. Basford on the other hand... goddamn Basford. The viscount was obsessed with claiming Ivy for his wife, eager to claim her fortune. Those facts made him a man easily dealt with. Hopefully he would not harm her until she was firmly and legally under his control, but what then? His sexual tastes would destroy Ivy.

Sebastian pulled Sara into a quick, unexpected embrace. "Forgive me, for what I put her through, for hurting her. I mean that with all sincerity. Do not worry. I *will* retrieve her." Pleased to see her nod, her eyes shiny with fresh tears of relief, he said, "Stay here as my guest and repair yourself. Word will be sent to your family, and fresh clothing obtained for you. Bentley will have my head if I fail to see to your safekeeping. I beg a favor, if you'll indulge me. I shall leave it to you to inform Ivy's father of the situation. Indeed, the next time he sees his daughter, she will be the new Countess of Ravenswood."

Sara gripped his arm, her jaw dropping with astonishment.

"Do not swoon. I only received the special license today and was gathering my courage to beg her hand in marriage." Sebastian felt immeasurable relief saying the words aloud. Even with the task at hand of rescuing his love, he was lighter, calmer than he felt in months. "I've made a bloody mess of things but, I cannot, and will not, live without her. If need be, I'll spend the rest of my life proving it to her."

Cocking her head, Sara considered the dark, moody earl who hurt Ivy so terribly. "I fear you'll have the Devil's own time convincing her."

Sebastian grinned. "The Devil and I are well acquainted, but for this, I ask for divine intervention. Since my standing with the Lord is a bit shaky, Lady Sara, will you say a prayer for the both of us?"

CHAPTER 20

*B*asford held a three-hour lead on Sebastian and while the rain finally slowed the roads were a sloppy muck. With Raven's ground-eating gallop, it was possible to catch the viscount's coach before it made the Lancashire border.

This was his blame, this danger Ivy was in. Had he not been so eager to believe the worst, he could have defended her, provided a shield against those wishing to exploit her. Even if he was unaware of Timothy's conduct, actions could have been taken to safeguard her from the hateful and destructive gossip following his cousin's death. He should have offered protection upon his return to England. Had he utilized his spies to uncover the truth, his part in causing Ivy pain would have been avoided.

The suffering at Timothy's hands paled in comparison to what Ivy endured at his own. Sebastian now understood when she said a friendship would benefit them both. She not only wanted to keep her wolves at bay; she was using the alliance to absolve guilt in Timothy's death.

Shame gnawed him. He forced Raven to greater speeds. He must find her before it was too late. He *would* find her.

Cantering up the lane of the Red Bell Inn, Sebastian recognized the Basford coach. Pulled into a far corner of the courtyard, the horses already changed out, the coachman stood at the head of a new team. Checking the harnesses, the man's attention was not on approaching travelers on such a dreary night. Now and again, he glanced from his task to the brick and timber building a few steps away.

Even close to midnight, the inn was lively, fiddle music pouring from half-shuttered windows. A stream of raucous laughter and raised voices tumbled into the muddied yard. The coachman probably hoped to grab a tankard of ale and a bit of warmth before continuing on the journey but he would find no such comfort this evening.

Sebastian dismounted at the edge of the cobblestones. It was unlikely Basford was with Ivy inside the inn. He would not risk the chance of an attempted escape, nor her appealing for a stranger's assistance. Possibly, he allowed her to use the facilities, but more likely, she remained inside the coach, and he with her. Or, he had restrained her while he ventured into the inn. The coachman would need dispatching, but that was of little concern. If the man proved a loyal employee, his elimination would be instant.

A harsh voice barked from inside the coach, followed by a choked sob. That one desolate cry sealed Basford's fate.

A bloodlust to protect his own swelled inside Sebastian. The urge was so strong, so overwhelming, he swayed with the force of it, lightheaded. He never experienced anything like it. Nothing on earth, in the heavens above, nor hell below, would stop him from reaching Ivy. *Nothing.*

Hearing the feminine sound, the coachman shook his head in disgust. It was then, by the faint light cast by a rain-shaded moon, he caught sight of the dark figure standing at the edge of the mist filled courtyard. Dressed in stark black, materializing like smoke from swirling, drifting shadows of light and the murky fog, with an ash-grey, steam-breathing stallion clip-clopping delicately at his heels, Sebastian must have appeared as an avenging devil of death.

"Attempt to stop me and you won't draw another breath."

The coachman swallowed hard at the softly spoken threat, nodding his wholehearted cooperation. Securing the horses to the hitching post with unseemly haste, he disappeared into the stables just as the coach rocked on its springs with lopsided violence.

"Don't. Please…oh, please, stop…"

Sebastian froze…his eyes closing in brief agony.

That was *his* Ivy's quivering voice. His Ivy. *Begging.* Her pleas echoed, crystal clear above the racket spewing from the inn. He heard the sharp crack of a heavy hand striking flesh and then…a tormented moan.

Bile, sharp and bitter, choked Sebastian. His vision clouded red, pinpointing the coach until it was the single object within his line of sight. Vaulting up the steps, he jerked the door open with hands trembling from rage.

At first, he saw only Basford's broad back. Not until a handful of the man's coat was in his grasp and the viscount physically wrenched to the side was Ivy finally visible.

She was a tiny heap of blue satin pinned against the far interior wall, legs sprawled open. Her skirts were shoved up past her knees, the gown's shoulder hanging to her elbow in a flounce of torn lace. Broken glass from a rosebud sconce glittered like moondust, sprinkled across her skirts, on the seats and the floor. Dazed, she stared at Sebastian from over Basford's shoulder.

If not for his concern for her welfare, Sebastian might have murdered the viscount right on that very spot, using the coach seats as a butcher's board. Snatching the man up by one arm, Sebastian's roar of fury was one commanded from the depths of Hell itself.

"What the hell-?" A horrible cracking sound interrupted Basford's indignant shout. Gaping in speechless shock at his arm, now dangling at an unnatural angle, the viscount did not struggle when yanked from the coach. He flew through the air, hurled nearly ten feet to land in a heap against a pile of crates. His high-pitched shriek of pain abruptly died away on a groan as he crumpled.

Sebastian intended, at that precise moment, to march over and break the other arm as well. And his legs. And ribs. The bones in his face. Every goddamn bone in the man's body.

"You goddamn, bloody bastard. How I'm going to enjoy ripping you limb from limb." Landing soundlessly on the cobblestones, Sebastian advanced on his prey. Single-minded in his purpose, he anticipated the crack of bones beneath his fists, the viscount's gasps of pain. His pleas for mercy...

Ivy's low moan swung his full attention back to the coach.

Not one soul ventured forth to investigate Basford's strange scream, a credit to the drunken energy of the inn. Only the burly coachman was curious enough, or perhaps foolish, to do so. Poking his head from the stable entrance, he squinted in alarm at the sight of his employer sprawled in a comatose slump. With a nod of respect to the earl, he stood apprehensively, unsure what action to take in this potentially dangerous situation.

"I require a moment to calm my lady," Sebastian growled. Without waiting for the servant's approval, he vaulted back into the coach, slamming the door in his wake.

Ivy huddled against the coach's wall panel, trembling uncontrollably. She whimpered when he reached for her and the sound shattered Sebastian's heart.

"Shhhh, my love. Shhhh...." His hand smoothed over her hair with exquisite tenderness. "It's me, little butterfly. It's Sebastian. I'm here now. I'm here and you're safe. Hush now."

He had reached her in time. She was alive, relatively unharmed, still whole. And while he doubted he held the Good Lord's ear after all the wickedness in his life, Sebastian sent a prayer heavenward anyway.

Thank you, God. Thank you.

Ivy shook violently. Brushing away the broken glass, he located her cloak, drawing it over her shoulders. Her skin was like ice, teeth chattering with the discordant rattle of tin cups. Having long ago worked free of its pins, her hair hung in a messy tangle. Sebastian removed his gloves to smooth the curly waves back from her face.

He passed a gentle thumb over her swollen lip. Faint red marks discolored one pale cheek; in the dim light, he saw bruises on her wrists, dark smudges in the shapes of fingers marring her upper arms. The muscles of his stomach tightened. He would beat the viscount until nothing remained but a pool of blood and broken bones. Hopefully the bastard would survive that, because Sebastian then planned on killing him. Very slowly.

"Sebastian?" Her face pale as ivory, Ivy's eyes held a misty, haunted air. She stared right through him.

"Yes, love. I'm here. Will you do something for me? Will you lay down? Close your eyes for a moment? I must have a word with the coachman, and then I'm taking you someplace safe. Yes, that's it, lie down, sweetness." Recognizing the effects of shock, Sebastian helped her curl up on the seat. He settled his own coat and a hastily discovered coach blanket over her, tucking everything in tight. God, he ached to soothe her, to hold her close, to ensure no one ever harmed her again...including himself.

He swept a soft kiss across her frozen lips when she suddenly gripped his hand tight. "I won't let anything happen to you, Ivy. I shall be just outside the coach. Close your eyes. That's a good girl."

The coachman stood over Basford's crumpled, unconscious body. He glanced up as Sebastian approached.

"I'm sure there is no need to impress upon you the necessity for discretion. Word of this misadventure goes no further than the courtyard of this godforsaken inn. What is your name?" Withdrawing one of the small bags of gold from the inner pocket of his coat, Sebastian tossed it so the servant caught it mid-air. "For your troubles then, George Quick, and for the duties you will undertake on the lady's behalf. We will continue on to Bentley Park. Do you know of it? I shall ride behind you. My stallion would highly object if I tied him to the back of this vehicle. Should the viscount regain his senses and possess any notion of following, which I doubt, I will handle matters. Now, in the near future, I imagine you shall find yourself without a post. A problem easily remedied as you will seek out the stablemaster at Ravenswood Court, or should you find country life more to your liking, present yourself at Beaumont in Kent. In either case, your services shall be engaged immediately."

"Right, sir. Thank you, sir." George grinned, his decision already made to become a coachman at Ravenswood Court. The Earl of Ravenswood possessed an excellent reputation as a fair and just employer; his servants among the most envied of London. "Who will I say sent me, sir? I have no letters, sir, that is…"

"I am Ravenswood." Sebastian allowed himself a slight smile at the man's surprise while tugging his riding gloves back on. "There might be a question of thievery when it comes to the viscount's coach. I'll assure the innkeeper of its return tomorrow, and we shall be on our way."

"Right, sir. And sir, I do wish your lady good health. It didn't sit well with me, what milord Basford done."

"I'm glad to hear it, George. As you are now in my employ, I'll trust you to inform the viscount to expect a visit from my seconds. When you return the bastard's coach, of course."

Bentley Park was not far from the inn. Although they quarreled at their last meeting, Sebastian knew Alan would never deny him aid, especially if it were for Ivy's sake. During that last encounter, Alan openly berated him, cursing his stupidity. Quite foxed at the time, Sebastian stubbornly refused to answer for his actions. Before long, Alan threw up his hands in utter disgust, leaving his friend to find the bottom of a bottle of bourbon. That was more than a month ago and they had not spoken since.

The clock chimed three in the morning as Sebastian appeared on Bentley Park's doorstep with Ivy in his arms. A majority of the staff was immediately roused to tend to the countess. She slept through the journey, remaining in a deep slumber even when carried upstairs and placed on the soft down coverlet of a guest bed.

Alan murmured instructions to his housekeeper then laid a hand on Sebastian's shoulder. "I've sent for the physician. You probably remember Dr. Moseby. An ancient cuss but damned efficient."

"I believe she is only in shock, but it's best she is checked over." Giving an abbreviated version of the transpired events, Sebastian said, with a slight raising of an eyebrow, "That Sara of yours is terrifying. Marry her, Alan, as soon as possible, so the only earl she may order about is you."

Alan laughed softly. "She loves the countess as if they are indeed sisters. You cannot hope to escape her wrath if you continue to harm Ivy."

"She'll demand my head on a platter if I don't send word of Ivy's safety. Will you attend to it? And send word to Lord Kinley as well. I'm sure his concern is tempered with delight he'll soon have an earl for a son-in-law." Sebastian's lips quirked at Alan's surprise. "I can't imagine why you are shocked. You know I am insanely in love with her. There's no other explanation for my stupidity or my abhorrent behavior."

"I am damn glad to hear it, Seb. But please, allow Martha to watch over the lady until the doctor arrives. She'll take excellent care of her- Lord knows she nursed our cuts and scrapes often enough when we were lads."

"I must refuse your offer, Alan." Sebastian smiled as the elderly housekeeper bustled into the room, setting down a basin full of hot water. Another maid followed her, carrying a stack of clean towels. "Martha, if you've some type of gown I can put Her Ladyship in, it would be much appreciated."

Alan frowned. "It isn't proper for you to be here, Seb. Think of her reputation."

"We will be married once she regains her health, so reputations be damned. I will be the only one caring for her."

When the necessary items were at his disposal, and the room cleared, Sebastian stripped Ivy from the torn clothes. He kissed the bruises on the inside of her wrists, washed her face and brushed out her hair, smoothing the tangles until they lay in some semblance of order. Martha had procured a fresh cotton gown and he maneuvered Ivy into it. She sagged, limp in his arms as he situated her in the bed, the pillows propped at a comfortable angle. Once she was as clean and warm as he could make her without benefit of a full bath, Sebastian held her hand, watching over her until the doctor's arrival near dawn.

He breathed easier in light of the sleepy physician's assessment. There were no visible injuries other than scrapes and bruises, Ivy's nearly comatose state attributed to the body's natural mechanism of handling trauma. The countess would be fine upon waking, the elderly man assured him, although he administered a dose of laudanum to ease any pain.

Settling in beside her, Sebastian renewed his vow to be the first person her eyes touched on when she woke. He would somehow make amends for every terrible thing he had done.

$\mathcal{T}$he room was unfamiliar and the bed, although comfortable, not her own. Evening approached; the afternoon shadows growing long and purple on the walls, the lighting darkly gold. Someone held her hand in an almost painful grip; Ivy wiggled her fingers against it. A man's dark, disheveled head rested on the coverlet and when she disengaged her hand to slide a palm over and through the thick hair of her sleeping guardian, it did not disturb him. Such beautiful waves, so glossy and black, sifting through her fingers like soft feathers.

Sebastian raised his head, pinning her with confused eyes, and Ivy's heart soared in a response so joyous she choked on an indrawn breath. The earl slumped in a chair beside her bed, but why? As she watched, he straightened, arching his back with a groan, then froze.

"What happened?" Ivy whispered when he quickly reclaimed her hand. He did not answer; instead, his fingers tangled with hers. Bringing them to his lips, he pressed warm kisses to her knuckles, his eyes closed as if in prayer or, perhaps even stranger, gratitude. The chair scraped closer, the sound impatient and startling in the room's stillness. The relief that seemed to swamp him, the way he looked at her, as if it were an eternity since he laid eyes on her, was all so mystifying.

"I don't understand." Her gaze flitted about the room, finding some aspects of it familiar now, before drifting back to him.

Dark stubble shadowed Sebastian's chin. Even darker circles ringed his eyes. Disheveled, looking as if on a bender for a week, his shirt fluttered open, rumpled and half-tucked. The buttons strained, mismatched to the opposite holes. It was so unlike him, the cool, elegantly collected Earl of Ravenswood, that Ivy felt unreasonable fear squeeze her chest. Something horrible must have occurred.

"You must remember." His murmur was so soft; it was almost difficult to hear. "Please try, Ivy."

Her brow furrowed. Remember what? Where was she? What catastrophe transpired to bring Sebastian to her side? When he cautiously brought a hand up to brush a curl from her temple, she shied away, baffled by her own immediate response to his gentleness.

Memories brushed her mind. Suspicion spiked within her, a thousand spears, hot and pointed digging into her flesh. He couldn't be trusted; he'd break her heart again. She could not trust anyone. Not even someone she once loved...or those claiming to be friends.

When it rushed in, she crumpled. Buckling under the weight of it, she helplessly sought the warm strength of his arms.

"It's all right, love, it's all right." Sebastian climbed onto the bed. Gathering her into his arms, he embraced her as a torrent of horrific images engulfed her.

"He wouldn't let me go. I begged and cried, but he wouldn't let..." Tears saturated the material of his shirt. She still did not understand how or why he was there, but she clung to him. In the midst of a desolate sea, he was a huge, solid rock, a lifeline she could not surrender. How she had missed him, the awful magnitude of it repressed inside her soul until this moment. Beneath her cheek, his shoulder was warm, his breathing deep and easy, large hands soothing as though she were a child startled awake by dreadful nightmares. Ivy wanted to crawl into his lap and never leave it.

"I'm here now. I'm here and the Devil himself would need to strike me dead before I let anyone harm you." Cradling her face, he kissed away the tears staining her cheeks.

"Where are we?" Her question emerged in a choked whisper. *Why, why is he suddenly assuming the role as my protector? It makes no sense.*

"Bentley Park."

Ivy swallowed, trying to regain control of her wildly careening emotions. She foolishly fell in love with this man at Bentley Park. Suddenly, it felt like wolves, not memories, ravaged her heart.

"Oh. My head hurts," she said woodenly.

Concern flitted across his haggard features. Sebastian rolled from the bed but soon returned with a small brown bottle and a spoon. "It's laudanum," he explained. Ivy swallowed the bitter liquid without question. She hoped the drug would overtake her quickly, the pain of seeing him easing into a cloud of dark oblivion. It would be easier to forget his treachery there.

"Is the viscount dead?" Much of what occurred inside the coach was a blank space. Ivy remembered bits and pieces of Brandon's cruelty and more vaguely, the moment Sebastian appeared to pull her tormentor off her. But nothing beyond that, or how they came to be at Bentley Park.

"God, I hope not. When I left him, he was very much alive." Sebastian sank into the chair, watching her carefully, as if anticipating something unpleasant. "He's very lucky in that regard. Considering."

"Why did you come after me, Sebastian?" Her hands, which previously clutched his shoulders as she wept, now clenched handfuls of the coverlet.

"Your butler is a highly suspicious man. I'm not the only gentleman he dislikes." He ignored the crux of her question. "He sent for Lady Morgan when you did not return and she, in turn, came to me. Demanding I rescue you."

"Did her anger shock you?" Few people had actually witnessed Sara Morgan's anger. She hid the emotion well behind a pretty veneer of blue eyes and soft blonde hair. It was a frightening sight when set loose, but Ivy adored her for it. China dolls were not known for tempers, and Sara's made her very real.

"Surprised more than shocked. She was less than with enchanted with me. I was informed, in no uncertain terms, what she expected me to do." Sebastian smiled while pouring a glass of water from the pitcher on the bedside table. "And I found myself following her orders." He handed her the glass.

Sipping the water slowly, Ivy tried understanding him. Why did this man, once so intent on destroying her, rush to her rescue? Why, after shattering her with his treachery, did this man give two shillings for her wellbeing? Her head spun, trying to fathom Sebastian's motives, to second guess his intentions. Forming defenses to his attacks exhausted her. Her fingers fluttered at her temple, probing a bruise there, before dropping back to her lap.

"I regret you were put to such trouble. I had no idea Basford would attempt something so reprehensible." Ivy's gaze flitted away from his penetrating one. "It was… unexpected." Had Sara blackmailed him in some way? Used Bentley's friendship against him? Threatened him with some manner of dire consequences? What might possibly bend the Earl of Ravenswood to do another's bidding?

"Timothy's attempt at abduction was unexpected."

Their gazes collided. Ivy's breath escaped in a panicked whoosh. "What?" *Oh no. No, no, no. Oh God, Sara...what have you done? You promised me.*

"Ivy, tell me what happened. Sara related some of the details, but I want to know-I *need* to know. What did my cousin do to you?"

Physically, she moved not a muscle, but Ivy retreated from him. "You wish to compare our versions."

Sebastian exploded from the chair. "So that I know how the bastard hurt you! So that no one ever hurts you again!" Agonized fury rolled from him in waves.

Ivy trembled. "No one ever wounded me as you have, Sebastian." The softness of her words could cut stone. "It broke my soul, trusting you. Ruined me. All the while, you knew just what you were doing. That hurt the most. You *knew* you were breaking my heart. And you enjoyed watching me fall to pieces, didn't you? Can't you understand I suffered more at your hands?" Chin tilted, her gaze clear and steady, it was a stark contrast to the weeping Ivy he held in his arms only moments ago. "None of it matters now. There is no need to revisit the past. No need for empty gestures of atonement on Timothy Garrett's behalf, and please, put aside any misguided beliefs the viscount must be punished for his actions. You cannot change what either man did. Or what you did."

Sebastian's eyes turned so haunted and dark it was staggering to see. "I ask again." Sinking back into the chair, his low voice quivered. His hands raked through his hair. "Tell me. All of it."

Ivy's temper flared at the subtle hint of intimidation. Relating Timothy's actions filled her with dread. It would provide Sebastian more reason to despise her, further justification for his hatred. But the opportunity to pour it all out, to tell her side specifically to this man, burned every barrier previously erected. *Will he believe me?*

"Timothy kidnapped me." The words clung like icicles in her throat. She swallowed, fighting the urge to say more. *He won't understand...*

"Go on, love." Sebastian's hand gripped hers. He seemed to tamp down an inner rage, but looking down at her, both his tone and his eyes softened. "I want every detail, Ivy. Do you understand?"

Ivy nodded, took a deep breath. She gave in.

"He was to take me to Regent Park that day. For a picnic on a lovely afternoon. I told Sara of our plans, although Timothy specifically asked that I not. He said she was jealous of our time together. You see, she became insistent on knowing these things, where we would be, what days we had plans. Even for harmless, silly activities like picnics or museum visits. She did not trust him, tried to warn me, but I did not believe her. I was so foolish. So naïve. I thought maybe Timothy was right, that maybe Sara was a bit envious of our friendship. But for some reason, I always told her what she wanted to know. I suppose something inside me knew Sara was right all along."

Ivy's voice turned softer, eyes brimming with unshed tears. "Your cousin did not take me to the park that day. He arrived in a hired hack, said his carriage threw a wheel and he was too rushed to have another readied. Once I was in that dilapidated coach, once we were on the outskirts of the city, he told me we were going to Gretna Green. He kissed me, put his hands under my skirts- touching me where there was nothing to bar his way. Claiming he loved me, and I was his. I could not get away. I fought so hard, and he seemed to enjoy that until I bit him. He struck me, and that seemed to excite him more. He…he tore my dress from my shoulders, forced me down against the seat…"

Her eyes became hazy, the words dropping to a whisper. Sebastian squeezed her hand tight, caught in a silent pit of his own violent anger.

"I realized my only hope…to keep him from violating me, was to leap from the coach. Can you imagine? I probably would have broken my neck, but it was preferable to what Timothy wished to do. I managed to shove him away enough to open the door, and almost tumbled out before he slammed the door shut. My hand was in the opening…a bit of metal sliced my palm open."

Ivy smiled ruefully. "I thought it cut my hand off. I screamed and screamed, it hurt so terribly. It must have scared the wits out of Timothy, and all the blood certainly didn't help. The driver pulled the coach to the side of the road, calling out to my welfare. Timothy awoke as if from a delusion. He wrapped his cravat around my hand, sobbing, begging my forgiveness. Then he got out, explaining to the driver there'd been an accident and we needed to return to London. They argued over the price. When

Timothy got back into the coach, he made me drink from a little bottle hidden in his waistcoat. I suppose it was the medicine for his headaches. It made me very woozy and the next thing I knew, I was at Kinley House and Brody was stitching my hand." Tugging away from Sebastian's grip, she examined the neat white scar slashing across her palm.

"The wound was easy to conceal if I wore gloves. The bruises and my swollen face proved more difficult. I left for Somerset Hall and remained there almost a month. Sara concocted a tale that I'd been thrown from my mare and cut my hand on a rock." Ivy frowned, lightly tracing the wound with a fingernail. "Shortly after, Timothy began sending the letters. He would personally bring them to Somerset but I refused to see him, so he left them with the butler. I was so afraid, I hid in my room, hoping, praying he would just go away. Disappear. Something desperate existed within him, something so terrible it was incomprehensible. Sara said he was obsessed. I knew he would harm me if I were ever alone with him again, but how was I to avoid him in public? I could not hide at Somerset forever. When I returned to London, he came to Kinley House every day, always with his letters."

Sebastian handed a bit of paper to her. When Ivy finished reading, it drifted to her lap.

"This was on Timothy's desk when he was discovered? I received fifty-eight similar letters. All within a month's time. Sometimes, I received two a day. They were all the same, begging, demanding, threatening. He wanted to see me, to continue our relationship..." Ivy's guilt trembled in her words. "I think maybe, I should have seen him. I had no idea he would hurt himself. He was so sweet and so kind when we were introduced last year, so charming. I liked him very much. Being his friend was a great joy, but when he needed my friendship the most, I selfishly turned away from him." She searched Sebastian's features for signs of recrimination, tears streaming down her cheeks. "Can you forgive me? I never meant to..."

Sebastian enveloped her. "Don't dare apologize for Timothy.

Knowing how you suffered at his hands, I am ashamed to claim him as a blood relative." Cupping Ivy's face in his warm hands, he stared intently at her. "You are not to blame for his death. Even if an accident, it was by his hand. And God help me, were he not dead already, I would kill him myself."

"But, I should have…"

Sebastian interrupted her. "*Stop*. It doesn't matter anymore."

"It matters to some, your aunt for one. She'll never forgive me. Do you think you might speak to her?" There was no keeping the hope from her voice. She could not explain why it mattered Rachel Garrett absolve her of guilt, but it did. It mattered a great deal, actually.

"She is well aware of what her son did. She heard everything Sara related to me and while she does not believe it to be true, she will do as I say when we return. If she cannot accept matters, I will have her removed to one of my other estates."

When we return. There was much inferred from his simple statement. Did he mean the two of them together? Why should it be necessary to remove his aunt from his home? Sebastian assumed *they* would face the problem together. It abruptly dawned on Ivy the earl was in her room, without the benefit of a chaperone, and she only clad in a nightgown. After so many instances of shared intimacy, his boldness should hardly shock her, but it did. "Sebastian, who has taken care of me?"

He frowned, as though her question was inane after everything she just went through. "I have, of course."

"Do not joke with me." Ivy clutched a handful of the coverlet to her chest, slumping in the bed at the same time. Others must know he was in her room now, so brazenly casual, regardless of her state of undress.

"Your health is a serious matter, Ivy, and I do not jest. Since arriving last night, I've been the only one to care for you." He brushed a lock of her hair out of her eyes. "I intend to continue doing so as your husband."

"My husband!" she inhaled. "You've lost your mind. I'm not marrying you."

Sebastian's eyes narrowed. "The hell if you aren't."

"I cannot marry you." Agony suffused her whisper. Yes, he absolved her of Timothy's death, placing blame entirely on his cousin. However, the earl did not seem overly concerned with making amends for the torment he caused her. "I can't."

"The hell you can't. And you will."

"I won't."

"I've already informed your father you are," Sebastian said smoothly.

"How did you manage that before you even asked me? When? When did you tell my father this?"

"Before leaving London, I tasked Sara with relaying the news to him." Ignoring her distress, Sebastian calmly fluffed a pillow behind her head.

"Am I to understand you planned on marrying me before you even found me?"

"I did. I obtained the special license early yesterday morning as a matter of fact." His smile was determined.

"Before Basford abducted me?" Ivy twisted the coverlet into knots.

"Yes, love. And regardless of your views on the subject, I will kill that man."

Ivy covered her eyes with her hands. "You cannot. I won't allow it."

His brow rose. "*You* won't allow it. He abducts my fiancée and I'm not to hold him accountable?"

"I was not your fiancée then just as I am not now. You've no right to take over any aspect of my life -" Her words trailed away because, with eyes dark and hard, Sebastian leaned over her. Possessiveness was stamped on his face.

"Oh, I have the right," he growled. "Basford will experience the consequences of his actions. *You. Are. Mine.* You've been mine since I laid eyes on you at the Sheffield Ball surrounded by the damned Pack. The first time I kissed you, that afternoon in your music room, I bound you to me. When I showed you the universe in the palm of my hand the night of the opera, you bound yourself to me. As we lay beside that stream here at Bentley Park, I became yours as well. The night of the Faringdon Ball only sealed our mutual fates. You *are* mine. If you require a moment to adjust to the idea, I understand. But, make no mistake, Ivy. You will become my wife as soon as a minister is procured." Sebastian withdrew another document from a pocket on the coat draped across the back of his chair. He waved it at her. "Do you know what this is?"

"I don't care to know." Leaning against the pillows, Ivy closed her eyes. It was not pretense on her part. The laudanum was making her lightheaded and giddy. Besides, she was too exhausted to battle with Sebastian. Fighting him required all her strength.

"It's the marriage license I obtained after the Faringdon Ball." Dropping an octave, his voice became husky with emotion. "When I knew I could not live without you." He laid it atop Timothy's last desperate letter. Ivy knew an absurd desire to tear both in half. A lot of good it would do. Such childish endeavors would not deter Sebastian.

Fighting back a yawn, she said, "You don't understand, do you, Sebastian? How could I ever trust you? How do I know you aren't waiting to carve me up with your own particular brand of cruelty? I will not marry someone I cannot trust...no, I'm not marrying you."

The laudanum worked its magic, dragging her deep into the downy depths of the pillows. Sebastian's rugged face melted into a hazy mirage as a silky, warm lassitude slipped over her. Too drowsy to do much else, she frowned in disagreement while his words drifted like snowflakes around her.

His threat contained a gentle finality.

"How shall you explain your refusal, Ivy? Because I will tell everyone, anyone who will listen, that we are madly in love, that I have compromised you most thoroughly, and you are possibly carrying my child. You *will* be my wife. I want you. I will have you. One way or another."

CHAPTER 22

A giggling maid set up a simple dinner for Ivy. Following that, a full bath was in order and although the effort was surprisingly draining, it was well worth it. An opportunity to wash away the memory of Brandon's touch from her skin.

Ivy managed a smile when Alan poked his head inside her room. It seemed Sebastian was not coming to visit her and the disappointment annoyed her. From what she derived from the talkative maid, he had retired to clean up a bit and get some well-deserved sleep.

"He'd demand my head if he knew I was intruding," Alan said, giving Ivy a wide grin. "I merely wanted to be sure you have everything you need."

"I cannot thank you enough for your kindness, Lord Bentley. There is no better care than what you've provided."

"We shall practically be brother and sister when you and Sebastian are wed, doubly so when Sara and I exchange our vows. As family, we must look after one another. But, your gratitude is misplaced. Sebastian has hardly allowed anyone else to come near you." He winked conspiratorially at her. "It's quite remarkable to see a man of his character so out of sorts. I thought

I may need to knock him senseless just to have the physician examine you."

"I would like to observe Sebastian being knocked senseless," Ivy murmured.

"Well, don't worry. There is something about you…it regularly puts him out of sorts. Plenty of opportunities abound to knock him silly. Your father, Sara, and Lord and Lady Morgan arrive tomorrow afternoon. You must be pleased they are bringing a few personal items for you." Cocking his head, he remarked, "I know this is all moving terribly fast, my dear, but Sebastian, once his mind is set…I'm afraid he is not to be swayed."

Ivy knew the earl's flaws. Unfortunately, her father's pending arrival only complicated matters. Jonathan would not understand her refusal to marry Sebastian, especially when he wanted her so desperately and she once wanted him with equal urgency. The possibility of a pregnancy further muddied the issue, to the point that screaming with frustration seemed a wonderful idea.

"I'll say good night then." Alan's expression was sympathetic. "Do not fret, Lady Ivy. All will be well, you'll see. Sebastian is one of the finest men I know, if you look past his unfortunate arrogance."

Ivy nodded, throat tight with sudden, unshed tears. Alan closed the door behind him and the maid puttered about the room for a few minutes more, turning the lamps low before she exited the room as well. There was no dismissing the depths of loneliness swamping her at that moment, fear assailing her for what the following days might bring. Lying on her side, she watched the light from the fire cast gold, red and black shadows.

The chatty maid said the whole house was atwitter with the earl's romantic actions. The girl oohed and aahed, relating how tenderly he took care of her, the concern he showed, the look of fear upon his features as the physician explained the effects of both physical and mental trauma, and how Ivy suffered both.

Ivy wanted to shriek with frustration and reveal everything Sebastian had done. The man was untrustworthy, his actions simply for show. Like images reflected in the still waters of a shallow pond, there was no substance to any of it, his words and actions meaningless and empty.

There was no escape from this impossible mess. Unless she bolted, as she threatened so many times in the past. To France. America. Anywhere other than England where marriage could be forced upon her. Even as the prospect of running flashed in her mind, it was somberly dismissed. Sebastian *would* follow her. He would never let her go now that he'd made up his mind to have her. There was no eluding him. Intense anger sizzled through her with that reality. It wasn't fair. Once, she willingly gave him her heart. He carelessly trampled it. He did not deserve it a second time.

With the special marriage license, there was no need to elope to Gretna Green. Bentley Park possessed a lovely chapel and the wedding would take place in two days' time. Her father was on his way. Her dearest friend and Sara's parents would also be there, sharing what should be a joyous day. Their host was a gracious, kind man, deeply in love with the sister of her heart. And Sebastian vowed it impossible to live without her. *It could be the loveliest, sweetest wedding imaginable, if you allow yourself to be part of it.*

Ivy hated the insinuating weakness slyly suggesting she give into Sebastian's seductive trap. It was so much easier than fighting him.

WITH THE FIRE'S GLOW AND THE HELP OF A TURNED DOWN LAMP, there existed just enough light to make out the curves of Ivy's face. She lay curled on her side, one hand tucked beneath her cheek, the other folded beneath an elbow. Like little fans feathering cream, long, dark sable eyelashes brushed the tops of her cheeks. Her hair streamed across the pillow like chestnut hued banners in the wind. That mouth of hers, lips flushed pink, haunted Sebastian's sleep. He was restless, pacing his room with the intensity of a caged animal. Driven from his bed to her side, he found it no use fighting what pulled him there.

Her slumber was peaceful and sweet, and raw emotion rose unexpectedly in his throat to choke him. When he slid onto the mattress, Ivy did not stir as it shifted to accommodate his weight. Slipping a hand through the hair at her temple, he smoothed stray curls back from her face.

She did not wish to marry him. That reluctance to place her life in his hands was understandable. After all, he'd done precious little to gain her trust but provided countless reasons to hate him. It was impossible to go back in time, to erase all the hurtful things, but he would make her understand he could not live without her. Life without her would destroy him. It would be a mere existence and nothing more.

Sebastian knew the instant Ivy came awake, although she gave no indication of consciousness until her eyes slowly lifted to his. In silent question, she regarded him. Taking her hand, he folded her fingers within his own. They were warm from her breath. All tension left his body with a simple realization.

She's alive. I'm alive. And I love her.

"I did not love Marilee Godwin." He pressed kisses to her knuckles. Her skin smelled of soap and lilies. "I've never loved another soul as I love you."

He traced the lines of her slender fingers. "I was infatuated, but not in love. I pursued her for a year before she finally agreed to marry me. We were engaged precisely one month when she suddenly decided our wedding could not wait. Nor our intimate relationship, which up to that moment, consisted of nothing more than kisses. Of course, I reacted in typical fashion. Shocked and suspicious." His smile was crooked, reliving the memories. "A terrible argument ensued over my refusal to do what she wanted, which inevitably led to a revelation. She was nearly four months pregnant, and quite inconveniently, I was not the father."

"Who was it?" Ivy whispered. "Did she say?"

Sebastian sighed heavily. "She screamed it at me loudly

enough. Lord Nicholas Harris March, Earl of Landon, heir to the Richforte dukedom. My closest friend, and Alan's as well. Since Marilee's greatest aspiration was to become a duchess, I saw no reason not to believe her. Nick had refused to marry her however, which was the only reason she accepted my offer. It seemed even he was unsure who the child's father could be, which left Marilee only one option. To deceive me into going through with a hasty wedding and pray I was stupid enough to accept a premature infant as my own.

"Thank God, I never slept with her. I wanted her, but I had the foolish notion of saving that for our wedding night. Nicholas often questioned my infatuation with her, if I truly loved her. I thought he was ensuring my happiness, but after Marilee's confession, I suppose he was merely playing his damned games with us both."

Sebastian's hand tightened over Ivy's, the lines around his mouth turning deep and harsh. "The man was my friend! I know his secrets...things endured, things he suffered, things no man should be forced to bear. I entrusted him with my life and would have given mine for his. We were as close as brothers, but I wanted to kill him when his betrayal came to light." His laugh turned mocking. "Yet, I could not. In a strange way, I was more enraged over his disloyalty to me than by the fact he slept with her. If only he came to me, told me he loved her, perhaps I could have accepted it, lived with it. I would have hated him, but I would have respected the fact he loved her. But not this...not this treachery and Marilee's deception too."

He rubbed his eyes with his free hand. "That morning, I aimed for Nick's leg, to wound him before he killed me. God, how quickly he could have dispatched me. I've never known his equal in swordplay or pistols, then or since. But the fool spun about at the last second. His shot went straight up into the air. He never aimed at me, and I have never been able to reason why. In all the confusion, Marilee received word Nicholas died on the field. She hung herself in her father's library. Damnit, despite it all, I actually pitied Nick. Although it was said I broke the engagement for no reason and he championed Marilee because of my cruelty. I was sorry because it was his child- although I suppose he never knew for certain - and an innocent child did not deserve to die."

A long stretch of silence filled the space between them, each contemplating the sad tale and its effects on their lives now. How the actions of one woman could touch so many with such devastating results.

"Marilee took her secrets to the grave and Nick kept his silence, although I always wondered why he betrayed me for such a faithless creature. If she deceived me, she would have betrayed him too. Sooner or later."

Ivy squeezed Sebastian's hand, her eyes wet with tears. "Thank you," she said. "For telling me."

Sebastian's eyes dropped to their clasped hands. "Ivy, I am no more to blame for Marilee's death than you for Timothy's. What they did, they did to themselves."

"I've grown accustomed to holding myself responsible for it," she replied simply.

"I wanted so badly to punish you," he slowly admitted. "I wanted to punish you for Timothy. And for Marilee too. I wanted to hurt you for making me feel things I never wanted to feel. I believed you cut from the same cloth as her, using men to get what you wanted. I was wrong. You are not like her...how I ever thought that...I cannot..."

"You don't have to explain -"

"You don't understand, Ivy." Lifting his gaze to hers, Sebastian's eyes were tortured flames. "I was wrong and how I've suffered for my belief in your guilt. You deserve so much more than a mere apology. You should have my heart on a platter. My head in your hands, my blood at your disposal. What I've done to you is destroying me. I can apologize for how my aunt treated you, and for Timothy's actions, but what I accomplished is far, far worse. You hate me. I do not blame you. But Ivy, I'm begging you...you must forgive me. For the night I took your innocence, for the evening of the Faringdon Ball. Every time I was crazed with jealousy and rage and used words to slice you. For each time I hurt you..."

Taking a deep breath, Sebastian brought her hand to his lips, kissing it over and over, a man begging for alms. "I'm probably not making much sense, but I love you. Do you understand, Ivy? I love you, I can't live without you. Hell, I cannot *breathe* without you and I've no wish to. I can't sleep. I can't eat. I cannot tell you how many nights I drank myself into oblivion, but even that was not enough to erase your memory. You haunt my every waking moment, you invade my dreams, my nightmares, and when I wake, I want you in my arms. Ivy, Ivy, damn it to hell, I'm in absolute misery without you."

He leaned forward, breathing against her pale lips. "Please. Marry me....so I may spend the rest of my life taking care of you, spoiling you, cherishing you. Worshiping you. Adoring you. I want to make love to you. Have you angry with me, and then smile at me in forgiveness. I want to wake beside you so I can kiss you every morning." A desperate kiss pressed to her mouth. He licked her bottom lip, soothing the cut Basford inflicted in his cruelty. "Marry me before I lose my mind. Before I go insane. Goddamn it, marry me because *I love you,* because somewhere, hidden deep down inside your soul, you still love me too. Marry me because the next time the world crashes down around us, I might be too late to save you and that would utterly destroy me."

Ivy did not fall into his arms and confess her love in return. Tears streamed down her cheeks. A thin, brittle shell of ice encased her. His determined gentle tapping was hardly enough to shatter the frosty exterior.

"Dear God, don't cry," Sebastian whispered brokenly. "Don't cry because of me, little butterfly. I cannot bear it."

"Sebastian, do not ask this of me. Can't you understand? Don't you see? Someday, you will discover this is a mistake. Then, you will hate me for being your wife..." Ivy's voice cracked. "What you feel right now, it's not *real*. It's not real. We both know you will change your mind." She stiffened as his arms wrapped around her. He would not allow her to retreat behind a fortress of icy indifference. He trailed tiny, soft kisses to her forehead, her cheeks, and her chin until Ivy squirmed in silent protest.

"I will spend the rest of my life proving how precious you are to me. You do not have to love me right now; it's enough that I love you. In time, you will trust me again." Cupping her jaw, tipping it until her distrustful gaze collided with his, his thumb rubbed the delicate curve of her cheek. "Say yes, Ivy. Let me protect you and take care of you."

Ivy sighed, her eyes fluttering shut as his words entranced her. She wanted to give in. She wanted to so very badly. Sebastian kissed her again, and she moaned, a weakness within her that she must hate beyond all reason. She could not resist him forever. The opium laced laudanum made everything so much easier as he pushed his will upon her.

"I told you once I am a patient man and I'll prove it to you, if you say yes," Sebastian murmured, folding Ivy close so all she could hear was his heartbeat. He wanted her lulled into a warm cocoon of security she could not bear to give up. "I can wait for you to trust me. I can wait for you to love me again. Forever, if I must."

CHAPTER 23

The dark blue topaz, the size of a bluebird's egg, surrounded by a halo of diamonds and accented by a separate thin gold band weighed Ivy's hand down. The Ravenswood heirlooms. Delivered from London on his orders and arriving by special courier just the day before.

The ceremony was brief but memorable, mostly for the sense of entrapment gripping her when Sebastian slid both rings onto her finger. His voice was steady when repeating his vows, hers trembling and weak – especially when she vowed to obey her new husband. Those words nearly stuck in her throat. When the minister declared them married, instructing the earl to kiss the bride, Ivy was faint from the contradictory flood of emotions bombarding her.

Ivy expected a quick peck on the lips, a perfunctory nod to tradition. Nothing prepared her for the searing possession of Sebastian's mouth. His new status as husband evidently pleased him. His arms snaked around her waist, crushing her to him in full view of God and everyone. She endured it, breathing deep to steady her nerves when the kiss ended.

"Sorry, butterfly. I could not resist." His amused murmur tickled her ear when he finally allowed her to glide away.

In the tiny vestibule, Jonathan Kinley pulled his daughter into his arms. With cheeks suspiciously wet, he said, "You are so beautiful, sweetheart. You look so much like your mother today." Ivy held onto her father as long as she dared, until he stepped away, complimenting her gown. For a wedding dress, she wore her coming out ball gown from last season. The virginal white flattered her, but she could not help think how hypocritical it was to wear it. How far from virginal she truly was...

Sara flew at Ivy, embracing her fiercely, so overcome she both laughed and cried with happiness. Ivy gave her the small bouquet of red roses and sweet pea she carried while Lord and Lady Morgan offered their congratulations, politely hiding their curiosity for the full story behind this hasty wedding.

"You won the race to the altar after all, Ravenswood," Bentley joked, placing a resounding kiss to Ivy's flushed cheek. "With such a beautiful bride, who's to blame you?"

"You are closing in right behind me, with your own lovely treasure." Sebastian winked at Sara. "And you'll be damned lucky to have her running your life."

Just outside the chapel, Brody and Molly waited to greet the new couple, along with William, Sebastian's rather somber valet. It surprised her Sebastian invited the two trusted servants, as well as his valet, to attend the private ceremony. As much as she hated to admit, it almost endeared her new husband to her. Brody, in particular, seemed befuddled by the earl's invitation.

Accepting congratulations from the men, as well as Molly's curtsy and quick embrace, Ivy was astonished by Brody's announcement.

"We will be situated at Ravenswood Court, milady, before your return to London. Molly and I are grateful for the opportunity to continue to serve you." A familiar, audacious wink accompanied the formal words.

Ivy turned an unconsciously tender gaze to Sebastian when he slipped an arm about her waist. "Is this true?"

"Yes, my dear. Jackson, our own butler, has hinted for years he's ready for retirement. Your father had no objections to my stealing Brody away, and I believe no one better qualified to safeguard the front door of our home. You require a maid, so I obviously extended the offer to Molly."

He knew it would please her to see two familiar faces in his household. To put forth such confidence in Brody when he exhibited such cheekiness was an admirable gesture.

Molly, never one to bottle her thoughts, piped up with a brash grin. "Right smart of milord, too. He's doubled our wages! We're happy to be comin' with you, milady!"

Sebastian threw Molly an exasperated scowl, then taking Ivy by the arm he hustled her out into the morning sunlight.

Following the wedding breakfast, Sebastian and Ivy would depart for Beaumont. They would spend the next three weeks there before returning to London for the remainder of the season. Trepidation stabbed Ivy. She was married to the man striding silently beside her. *His wife, his wife.* The words repeated themselves in her mind. No need to be concerned for propriety's sake, no need for chaperones or doors shut between them. Soon, she would be alone with him, with nothing to stop him from claiming what legally belonged to him.

"Having them at Ravenswood Court means a great deal to me," she said.

"I did not bribe them. They were surprisingly willing to be at my mercy." Sebastian grinned, tucking her hand into the crook of his arm. "They would have come if I only paid wages in the form of apples and walnuts. They are devoted to you. Your father was especially agreeable to the idea of Brody serving in our household. Once we came to terms on salary and benefits, Molly followed suit."

"It was a lovely gesture." Emboldened by his good mood, Ivy considered the best way to approach the subject plaguing her the past three days. She tossed and turned into the wee hours of the morning, the faint circles under her eyes now its direct result. "May I speak with you? Privately?" She slowed until he came to a halt on the pathway.

"Of course." Calling to the others, Sebastian waved his hand. "My bride requires a moment of my time and her slightest wish is my command." His gaze lingered on Ivy's lips and she knew he was thinking of later, much later, when they would be alone without bothersome interruptions and he could indulge *his* every wish.

Cursing the hot blush spreading across her cheeks, Ivy let him pull her to a white iron bench. In the shade of a young oak, there was barely enough room for two on the seat. The length of his thigh pressed to hers. She desperately inched away as much as possible. They sat quietly while she fretted over the matter until it finally blurted out.

"Bentley went to the Viscount Basford's estate. You are looking for him, to set terms for this blasted duel."

"Yes. I told you this would happen." Sebastian's response was affable, even as he gave her a glance glittering with a frightening darkness. "They've had a devil of a time tracking him down. Basford has decided avoidance to be the best defense."

Ivy swallowed, meeting his cool silver eyes without blinking. "Please. Do not do this. Can't we forget that night occurred? Do you wish all of London gossiping why you challenged the viscount following our hasty marriage? Call it a wedding gift if you must. For me, for us. Only, do not go through with it."

She did not realize she held her breath until he smiled. Kissing her hand, Sebastian's warm breath sent unwelcome shivers quivering through her. That was simple. Too simple. Her heart thumped with relief as he regarded her for a long moment, as though deciding how best to respond.

"No."

Ivy snatched her hand away. "It is beyond ridiculous. There's no need for a duel." *What if you are injured... or worse?* "Will you enjoy the gossips ripping us to pieces?"

"We should be used to it, but ours is a wildly romantic tale. We shall start a new trend, don't you think? Elopements with friends and family sharing in the festivities. And whispers we were secretly engaged have already reached my ears."

"You mock me," she said stiffly because although the wedding was lovely and sweet and Sebastian seemed sincere repeating his vows, he forced this wedding upon her. To insinuate they were in love, after she endured weeks filled with such heartache, was more than Ivy could bear. Launching herself from the bench, she walked blindly in the direction of the house.

With a muttered curse, Sebastian rose, trailing a few paces behind. Hands clasped behind his back, he followed while she stomped like a furious Clydesdale. When she tripped on some loose gravel, he reached her in two strides to steady her.

Catching her chin between thumb and forefinger, Sebastian tilted her head, forcing her to look at him when she would have jerked away. "I'm not mocking you, but it must be done. Nothing you say, or do, will sway me from it."

Ivy's teeth clenched. "Ah! There's the earl I know...in all his arrogant, heavy-handed glory!"

Sebastian, to his credit, only smiled benignly. "Compliments will certainly not change my mind. Now, shall we try and have a pleasant breakfast with our friends and family? They all wait for us, and I prefer to reach Beaumont before nightfall. Husbandly rights and all that taken into consideration."

THEIR TRUNKS WERE SECURED IN A SECOND COACH. GOODBYES were now being exchanged. Sebastian feared his new wife might possibly change her mind when it came time to leave with him. She was pale as she and Sara embraced, sharing quiet words no one else could overhear.

"I would have found a way to destroy you," Jonathan said, coming to stand beside him.

"I know."

Jonathan would not have found success in bringing about justice for his daughter, but Sebastian would not have faulted his new father-in-law for trying. He married Ivy because he wanted to - not because he had to. Nothing anyone could have said or done would have forced him to it, had he not wanted her so badly for his wife.

"I hope I've done the right thing, not allowing her to refuse you. Considering the circumstances, there was little choice. She's been so damnably miserable of late." Jonathan hesitated before placing a fatherly hand on Sebastian's shoulder. "You will make her happy, won't you?"

"I will. She doesn't believe me, understandably so, but I do love her."

Recognizing the sincerity of Sebastian's somber declaration, Jonathan chuckled. "Your father and I once discussed the possibility of you two making a match. Your mother and Ivy's dashed that idea rather quickly. Said their children should make their own choices in love. I like to believe they secretly hoped you would find one another."

Sebastian smiled. There was satisfaction in learning his father would have approved of Ivy as his countess.

"Patience, Ravenswood." Jonathan watched his daughter accept a fond embrace from Alan. "She's a headstrong, determined creature. It is damned difficult to puncture that wall of indifference when she puts it up, as I well know. If you love her enough, and are patient enough, when that wall comes down, it will be worth it."

Sebastian's gaze slid over Ivy making her way toward them, a tiny grin lifting his lips. Neither she nor her father had any inkling of the incredible depths of his own determination and strength of will. "Don't worry, Kinley. I love her enough. More than enough."

Four hours alone with his bride, in the privacy of the coach stretched before them. A tantalizing situation. Once settled into the vehicle, Sebastian extended his legs to the confines of the space. Ivy's lips tightened as she accepted his presence. It was obvious she wished he would sit on the opposite seat; however, those days were in the past. He would get as close as possible and he would push past whatever barrier she put up. No doubt, it would create a scandal, and it was unlikely he would be able to keep his hands off her, even in the presence of polite society, but he did not care.

Summer was almost upon them, the days already beginning a slow slide into the perfumed idyllic span of warm hours when those born to leisure turned to outdoor pursuits. The London Season would end and Society would retreat to their rural estates, escaping the oppressive heat of the city for refreshing green woods and sprawling fields. It was imperative their reappearance in London go smoothly. The rampant curiosity regarding their hasty elopement would either thrill or tweak the tongue wagglers, and any gossip would surely follow them to the countryside. Sebastian would not stand for Ivy to suffer any backlash. It was his responsibility to protect her.

Sebastian watched Ivy avoid his scrutiny, staring out the window as emerald green pastures gave way to thick forests. She was bone weary, exhausted mentally and physically, the events of the past few days weighing heavily on her, but determined and unyielding, she sat ramrod straight. Until the coach would hit a rut or hole in the road, dislodging her position on the leather seat. Each time she was thrown alongside him and righted herself, every time she emitted a small cry of dismay, Sebastian hid a smile.

Hitting yet another bump, the coach lurched sideways. Ivy jostled, her hand landing high on the inside of his upper thigh. Cheeks flushing pink with mortification, she tried to jerk away.

He ensnared her wrist. "No need to scurry away, love. I won't bite." Amusement colored Sebastian's voice as he kept her pinned tight. "You are exhausted. Why not rest a while?"

Ivy's glare dropped to her trapped palm pressed against his thigh. "I'll not place my head *there*."

His brow quirked. "I meant only for you to lay your head against my shoulder." Giving her a sly grin, his gaze was warm and liquid when it rested briefly on her mouth. "Although, your idea has merit and would prove far more fascinating." Ivy scowled until he relented with a sigh. "My shoulder, then. Should you change your mind, my lap is always available. And I shall remain the perfect gentleman. On my honor."

She briefly resisted then with an abrupt exhale of defeat, slumped against him. All her energy seemed to drain away, sapped by the day's events, the emotional strain of the wedding, and the previous ordeal with Basford.

Placing his back flush with the silk paneled sidewall of the coach, Sebastian stretched vertically along the length of the seat, moving Ivy until she sat between his legs, her back to his. His arm draped lightly across her shoulder and with rhythmic strokes, he rubbed her upper arm. A moment later, both hands moved to her shoulders; the stroking morphed into massaging caresses.

Ivy melted against him with a tiny moan of contentment, lulled by the magic of his hands. He rested his chin atop her head and angling his cheek against her hair, he breathed deep of its clean scent.

"Mmmm, you always smell so delicious. Like sunshine and spring."

Ivy stayed perfectly still. Soothed by the warmth of the coach, the cadenced sway of it and her own fatigue, Sebastian realized she was drifting asleep. He moved until she was shifted onto her side, her cheek flush against his heart, his soul in danger of bursting with the tenderness his prickly bride evoked in him.

CHAPTER 24

*S*truggling to retain the pleasant state of drifting dreaminess with the jostle and sway of the coach soon became too much to ignore. Or maybe something else woke her.

Lifting her head, Ivy recognized the fire in the depths of Sebastian's gaze.

"Did you sleep well?" he asked, his voice wrapping about her, stroking her, it seemed, from the inside out.

She realized, with dawning awareness, the horrific position she was in. Sprawled in lethargic abandonment, ensconced in a circle crafted of his arms, breasts pressed flat against his chest, her hips were flush with his. Ivy braced her hands on his broad torso, frowning.

"I already know the answer." Sebastian laughed at her silent dismay. "How I enjoy it when you snuggle up to me. Anytime you feel so compelled, my arms are always open."

Ivy's backbone fairly cracked from rearing back so quickly, although his loose embrace preventing her from going very far. "I am *not* snuggling."

Sebastian countered with a grin of devious pleasure. "Oh, one could hardly call it anything else."

"You are a cad," Ivy retorted.

"No," he rebuked calmly. "I'm a man in love."

The urge to slap him literally caused her fingers to twitch. "Tell me, Sebastian." She could not help herself, her words dripping with bitterness. "Was this great love discovered before, or after you decided I was not a whore?"

Chilly silence invaded the coach. In an imperceptible motion, Sebastian's arms constricted. "Careful, my love." His warm, teasing manner vanished. "A sharp tongue can cut one's throat."

Ivy swallowed hard. She shouldn't push him too far, not when she was at his mercy. "Let me go."

"Never." The distance between them narrowed then disappeared. "We both know I'd have to slice myself open to remove you from my blood."

It would be easier to resist if he took what he wanted in anger, but his mouth was gently searching upon hers. *The devil.* He knew just how to kiss her, with varying degrees of pressure and softness, his tongue sweeping then probing, swirling and teasing in alternating assaults. Ivy wanted to struggle, and maybe she would have if Sebastian did not end the kiss. He released her just as she gathered her outrage.

When she did not immediately move away, his brow arched. "We are almost to Beaumont. It's unwise to ravish me now, my eager little wife. I fear there is no time to finish matters. Tonight, however, I shall see to things properly."

Ivy choked on an indrawn breath, scrambling away in a flurry of skirts and red cheeks to the opposite seat. "You are despicable!"

He laughed and raking a hand through his hair, his eyes held a twinge of regret. "So you keep telling me."

Constructed of warm, pale gray stone, Beaumont rose from the lush countryside, both imposing and welcoming at the same time. A gracefully curving gravel driveway lined with English yews stretched to the cobblestone-paved courtyard fronting the huge five- story building. An enormous stone terrace was anchored by massive stacked stone walls arching away from the main house like a pair of burly arms.

Two dozen stone steps spanned nearly the entire width of the mansion. In Ivy's mind, they led like the hangman's steps to a pair of double, English oak doors stained a rich walnut color. A grand, white marble and oak portico shaded those doors while smooth stone columns traversed the length of the grand terrace. From the main rectangle of the house, twin wings flared out and away. The wings were additions, but so well integrated one hardly realized they were not original to the footprint. Sebastian casually mentioned they contained the fifty-two bedrooms for the manor, with his personal suite of rooms taking up much of the south wing.

Occupying the focal point of the curved circular driveway, a grand, triple-tiered stone fountain filled the air with the lyrical sound of trickling water. An assortment of spring blooms surrounded it, softening all the gravel and stone and hard surfaces with a bright cheerfulness. A late afternoon sun bathed everything in a pinkish, golden light and the vast expanse of emerald green lawn dotted with yews and oaks gave Beaumont a lavish verdant appeal.

Servants poured from the house as the coach approached the base of the terrace steps. They busily lined up in order of house-hold rank. Stableboys and grooms trotted almost in unison from the direction of the stables. With the exception of the grounds staff, all wore the distinctive Ravenswood colors of dark blue and silver.

Ivy passed a hand over her hair, smoothing loose curls into place. She chose not to don her gloves when departing Bentley Park, so she pulled them on now. Sebastian watched, his eyes tender, as she peeked out the window.

"There is no need to worry, Ivy. You are lovely."

"What they must think…" Caught between her teeth, her bottom lip was worried back and forth. As the coach rolled to a stop, Sebastian reached for her.

"What they will think," Passing a thumb over her lip, he halted the fretful motion, "is that I am a fortunate man, and Beaumont once again has a beautiful, gracious woman to call Countess."

When a footman rapped on the door, Sebastian hopped down, turning to offer his assistance if she wished it.

Despite snapping at him earlier, Ivy was grateful for his words of encouragement. She descended the coach, holding tight to his hand.

~

THERE WERE FAR TOO MANY SERVANTS FOR AN ESTATE SO RARELY visited. Ivy recalled Timothy Garrett remarking once that both he and his mother both preferred Town, even though it was dreadfully dull during the summer months. Country life, he explained, was the epitome of dreariness, regardless of the time of year. Ivy disagreed but had kept her opinion to herself.

A hum of excitement existed at Beaumont, an air of vitality and comfort. It cascaded over Ivy all at once. *This was home.* She had yet to meet the first person, but everyone smiled warmly, pleased to welcome her. Stealing a glance at Sebastian, she felt a surprising tranquility emanating from him. He was relaxed, the smile spreading across his features genuine and real.

Her husband had been happy here. He *still* found happiness here. And Ivy loved Beaumont without hesitation simply because Sebastian loved it. The instant connection was startling. She was prepared to dislike it only because it equated with her forced marriage.

Sebastian led her to an elderly couple waiting at the bottom of the terrace. "This is Jasper and Annie Bancroft, our butler and housekeeper. Jasper, Annie, this is your countess, Ivy Elizabeth Cain, Countess of Ravenswood, Kleychord Keep, Monterey, Hammocks Glen, and Roseburn, the Countess of Somerset and Viscountess of Kinley."

Hearing all the titles made Ivy dizzy. Knowing they were now hers made her achingly aware of just how much she was now *his*...The Earl of Ravenswood's newest acquisition.

Ivy could see these two ruled Beaumont with a stern yet gentle kindness. Annie, even while welcoming her new mistress, admonished a young maid for slouching.

"Milady." Jasper's smile was broad, the wrinkles at the corner of his eyes disappearing into the edges of bushy white eyebrows. Tall and robust for his age, his hand held his wife's elbow while he bowed to Ivy. "We are most pleased to welcome you to His Lordship's home."

"Anything you need at all, milady, you just come to me. Yes, mum, you just ask old Annie and we'll see you are taken care of right and proper. No need for you to want for anything. Milord can vouch for that, we take fine care of him when he comes to stay, that we do. We always have, and we shall do the same for you, that we will!" Annie chattered, curtseying and grinning all at once. The plump housekeeper was infectiously exuberant, blue eyes twinkling. Her face hardly touched by the passing of time, her age was somewhere around sixty, the few wrinkles she possessed crafted of laughter and cheerfulness.

Ivy could not fit in a single word. Sebastian quickly realized her predicament. The housekeeper's steady stream of chatter came to a halt when he lifted a hand. "As you can see, Annie does like to go on. Why don't you both begin the introductions of the staff to Her Ladyship?"

Each servant was presented, including Lizzie, a young blonde Annie declared suitable to serve as Ivy's maid. Jasper introduced the footmen, the under-footmen and so on. Next came the kitchen staff and their leader, Monsieur Bouchard. A tall, slender elderly man with a twirling steel-colored mustache, he possessed the strange habit of clapping his hands before each introduction of those beneath his command.

Following him was the Head Stablemaster, numerous grooms, stableboys, and groundskeepers. By the time it was over, Ivy's head spun with dizziness. Although her own family's estate was large, Beaumont was enormous, with seventy-five servants in the house itself and another hundred keeping the grounds and the stables in order. Having grown up with her own servants, Ivy never had any reason for personal introductions to each one. Meeting this army of staff was overwhelming. And exhausting.

Only one person lacked introduction. Standing by the coach horses, he waited patiently to be motioned forth.

A hulk of a man, he stood a foot or so taller than Sebastian, with arms the size of oak trunks and a chest as wide as a barrel of English ale. Dressed in dark, brown breeches of fine broadcloth and a stylish waistcoat of deep navy blue, he was much more than a mere servant. Slicked into a modish cut, his hair was a thick, wonderful mixture of various browns, dark, light, golden chestnut. A woman might murder for hair the shade this man possessed naturally.

Twinkling with benevolence, his eyes were a clear shade of russet. In addition to his impressive size, his most recognizable feature was a thin, jagged white scar. Inching out from the temple, just below the hairline, it sliced his left eyebrow in two and ended just above his eyelid. The man possessed the most fearsome presence, certainly not a fellow one would cross in an alleyway on a dark night. Or anywhere else, for that matter. At Sebastian's directive, he stepped forward.

"This is Gabriel Rose. Gabriel, your countess."

Ivy caught Sebastian biting back a smile at her look of wonderment. Such a beautiful name for such a formidable man. It probably caught more than one person off guard.

"Milady." Gabriel's voice was melodic. Bowing at the waist, his movements exhibited a surprising elegance.

"Gabriel, ah, has been very busy since our return to England, which is why you've not been afforded a chance to meet him before now." Sebastian grinned. "He's what you might consider my man of affairs. I trust him with my life and now, I trust him with yours." Noting the man's fierce scowl, Sebastian threw up his hands with a chuckle. "And yes, you may take a well-deserved rest very shortly."

"Good," Gabriel grumbled, loud enough for only Ivy and Sebastian's ears. "I spent enough time carting that damn devil of horse yours all over God's green Earth, and these last few months in England traipsing back and forth on the errands you required seeing to."

The words, words no servant would dare voice aloud to an earl or master, Sebastian met with a hearty laugh. Ivy stared at Gabriel quizzically but did not feel any fear of him. His eyes were too kind. She decided she liked him at once.

"Mister Rose, if my husband places his trust in you, then I shall do the same." Ivy extended her hand, and when Gabriel took it, she shook his firmly.

"I owe Lord Ravenswood my life. Now, it belongs to you as well." Gabriel bowed, turning her hand to place a respectful kiss on the back of it. "It would honor me if you called me by my Christian name."

"I should like that very much, Gabriel. I hope I may call you as close a friend as my husband does."

"A better friend one could not hope to have." Sebastian slipped his arm around Ivy, giving Gabriel a conspiratorial wink. "You'll find it a more pleasant task to watch over her."

Gabriel's response was calm, his eyes sparkling with humor. "I expect it to be just as eventful."

CHAPTER 25

$\mathcal{B}$eaumont's interior was as impressive as the exterior. White plaster walls curved in barrel shapes, soaring high within the main entry hall. Ornately plastered medallions accented the ceiling and heavy mahogany furnishings upholstered in gray and dark blue were strategically placed throughout the massive space. A hundred people could easily fit inside just the foyer space.

Beneath Ivy's heels, exquisite Italian marble floors gleamed brilliantly white and delicate porcelain urns filled with massive arrangements of lilies, roses, and snapdragons sat displayed atop several pier tables in the hall. The heady perfume of the florals blended with the scent of lemon oil and beeswax polish, all familiar scents of a well-loved home.

Annie chattered, giving directions to Lizzie on the unpacking of Ivy's trunks as the group ascended one side of a massive, double curved iron staircase. On the opposite side of the stairs, a contingent of under-footmen carried the baggage up. Reaching the third landing, the entire group veered to the left. Annie's commentary of the manor's attributes was the only conversation as they trekked toward the earl's wing of the manor. An impasse was realized once a set of dark stained oak doors came into view. Where exactly to place Ivy's belongings?

Two huge apartments with a massive dressing room connecting them lay beyond those doors and without a mother to impart advice on such matters, Ivy had no idea what to do. Should she select the lady's chambers or would Sebastian decide for her? Everyone stood, ill at ease. Even Sebastian frowned, unsure of the correct move. When alive, his parents shared the master apartment, the other used as a makeshift nursery until he outgrew it, and then later, it was not used at all.

Annie's cheerful observation broke the awkward silence. "Here now, it is no trouble to move your trunks wherever you've a mind for them to go, milady. We will place them in milord's rooms for now. If you change your mind, then quick as a flash we'll move them again."

Ivy appreciated Annie's assurance, aware of Sebastian shooting her a peculiar glance over the housekeeper's head of grey curls.

It was suddenly overwhelming. Staring about the room, Ivy did not feel well at all. Vertigo, swift and dizzying, swooped about her stomach like swallowtails diving for dragonflies. Her bottom lip was being chewed to ribbons again. This room…it reminded her of Sebastian's suite at Ravenswood Court in London. What she could remember of it, anyway. Odd, how the walls seemed to be closing in on her. Taking a deep breath, she quickly laced her fingers together to conceal how they trembled.

"The countess and I require a moment of privacy," Sebastian said quietly.

Within seconds, the bedchamber was empty.

Ivy blinked in astonishment. Even Annie, in the midst of directing the placement of the trunks, clamped her mouth shut, rotated on a heel, and exited the room.

When the door closed behind the last servant, Sebastian leaned against it. Arms crossed, he regarded Ivy with a raised eyebrow. "Well, Ivy?"

With slow deliberateness, she removed her gloves. It gave her time to think, to steady herself and regain her balance. Which did he want her to choose? The master's suite or her own? What was a newlywed countess supposed to do? Tossing her gloves onto the lid of her trunk, she turned to him, swallowing back her nerves.

"What do *you* wish me to do?"

Sebastian grimaced, not liking the direct question. "As a gentleman, I should insist you take the other chamber. As your husband, I demand you stay here." His eyes blazed hot, like glowing sparks of coal. "What I want most of all...is that you allow me to strip that gown from your body, lay you on my bed and thoroughly make love to you. But I know you do not want that...not yet anyway. The question is what do *you* want?"

Ivy squared her shoulders, her stomach swooping again with his words. "I want you to wait... before expecting me to share your bed. I need time to adjust to this. To being your wife."

"I'll not have my rights denied." Sebastian's jaw tightened, his annoyance held in check. "I've waited too long to make you completely mine."

"Not denied." The silk of her gown was now a twisted, wrinkled mess. "Just...delayed."

Silence trembled between them until Sebastian scowled, "Damn it. How long?"

"I don't know."

He pushed off the door, shrugging out of his coat and subjecting Ivy to an unfathomable glance. Disappearing into the dressing room, he emerged with a fresh, white linen shirt and pair of dove gray breeches. Flinging the items onto the bed, Sebastian's eyes held hers as he unknotted his cravat, pulling it free so it dropped to the floor. The shirt was stripped away next, pitched into a chair with the previously discarded coat.

Bare-chested, he opened another door at the opposite end of the chamber to reveal a spacious room. Inside, Ivy saw an enormous porcelain clad bathing tub. Tracing down the wall, a streamlined network of piping attached to two gold spouts in the shape of dolphins with levers feeding directly into the tub. Close to the tub, a large basin sink sat mounted on a mahogany stand with two additional dolphin spouts jutting from the wall above it.

Taking a cloth and a bar of soap, Sebastian stepped to the sink, spun the levers and within seconds, water poured from the dolphin's mouths. Steam rose in curling ribbons as he washed away the grime of their journey from his face and upper torso. He did not care she witnessed his actions. He did not care she imagined dragging that cloth across his skin, her hands slippery with water and lather sliding over his flesh...

Ivy's face grew hot, her cheeks burning as she gazed at Sebastian's broad back, the muscles rippling as he bathed. The scent of sandalwood and spices drifted with the steam and she grew unaccountably lightheaded. The intimacy, the casualness of such ordinary things as undressing and bathing brought home an unavoidable fact. She was really and truly married to this man.

Married...

And, in the eyes of English law, his to treat however he pleased. An exercise of his husbandly rights did not require her permission. He could throw her on that massive bed, take his pleasure and she could not do a blasted thing to stop him.

Briskly drying himself with a fluffy towel, Sebastian exited the bathing room to sit on a dark blue velvet tufted bench at the foot of the massive bed. Methodically removing his boots, he allowed them to drop one by one. Ivy's rapid pulse gave an answering thud of apprehension and, God help her, excitement as each boot hit the floor with ominous thumps. She could not look away when he slowly stood to his full height, eyes dark and unreadable and locked on hers, hand resting lightly on his hips. For what seemed an eternity, he regarded her while Ivy tried remembering how to breathe, her lungs aching as if ready to burst from her chest.

Light from the late afternoon sun spilled through oversized windows, dancing about the large room to bath Sebastian in gold. He could be a pagan lord from another time, with his raised brow and wickedly sly smile. His fingers hovered over the fastening of his breeches and in slow motion, the buttons slid from their holdings, his eyes holding hers as the fabric shimmied down his hips and lower, revealing the vee-shaped indentations above his hipbones. When the breeches dipped past the point of indecency, Ivy gave a muffled cry, whirling to present her back.

A sharp bark of laughter echoed behind her. "It's not anything you haven't seen, or touched before."

There were the rustling sounds of Sebastian redressing in fresh clothing. She heard him pulling back on his boots, the slide of fabric against fabric as he tucked the shirt into his breeches. Ivy closed her eyes, heart pounding, blood thrumming through her veins. As if a charge of electricity jolted her, she tingled from head to toe. The image of his chest, the ripple of muscles, the leanness of his hips as the fabric slid lower and lower. It all burned into her brain until she wanted to shake her head to dislodge it.

Sebastian gripped her shoulders, spinning her to face him. It startled her when he released her just as fast, stepping away as if he did not trust himself to touch her an instant longer than necessary.

"Sleep where you will, either my bed or in your own. But understand this." He paused and Ivy swallowed hard, pinned to the spot by the heat of his gaze. "You have experienced the act of lovemaking twice. The first I forced upon you. The second, you were so damned intoxicated that I can't imagine you remember much at all, although the night of the Faringdon's Ball is forever burned into my brain. I know you found your pleasure; however, I assure you, the full experience of it, minus the fog of alcohol, is something you cannot comprehend. And you won't, not until I show you."

Wordless, pale, hating the memories crowding her mind, Ivy stared at him. Sebastian was wrong. She remembered. Every moment. Like a silky web, his words wrapped about her, holding her in place. A tiny victim waiting to be devoured.

"I shall convince you that my bed is where you belong. I will not force you. However, I will use every weapon I possess to persuade you. To draw you to me. To prove you belong to me." Leaning closer, his face mere inches from hers, Ivy had nowhere to look other than his stormy eyes. "I will entice and seduce and tempt you until you surrender. Eventually, you will beg me to take you. You will beg to become mine in every sense of the word. You will beg to have me inside you, plead for me to taste you, to caress you, to discover every hollow and curve of your body with my tongue and fingertips..."

Swallowing hard, his voice dropped to a husky whisper, "While patience and desire war with each other, my temper is another matter entirely. I would never physically hurt you, nor could I bear to seek another's bed, but I am merely a mortal man. Not a bloody saint." Sebastian brushed past her, jerking the door to the suite open. Giving her body one last scorching sweep of a glare, he exited, slamming the door with enough force to shake it on its hinges.

Ivy involuntarily jumped at the violence of his departure, tears stinging her eyes. His voice echoed from the hall, barking orders at the little army of servants gathered there before his angry footsteps stomped away. There was no time to regain her composure before the door cracked open to reveal Annie's weathered face.

Moving to the window, Ivy stared blindly over the perfectly landscaped grounds, not wanting the housekeeper to see her tears.

"Milady?" Annie let herself in, motioning for Lizzie to enter as well. Two footmen hovered in the hall, waiting to see if the trunks would find a home in the countess' apartments or be left in the middle of the earl's bedchamber. They whispered to each other.

"Still slamming doors," Annie chuckled, bustling about the room, retrieving discarded clothing and the used towel. "Drove his mother to distraction, it did, God bless her. Don't you go bothering your lovely self about it, my dear. Milord doesn't hardly mean anything by it, and I vow, when you see him next, he'll have forgotten why he was banging things about in the first place."

Ivy stared at the housekeeper over her shoulder, choking back a laugh when Annie gave her an audacious wink.

"Ah, a smile. That's better, it is." The older woman grinned. "The best way to keep a man's interest is give him a reason to slam a door."

CHAPTER 26

$\mathcal{S}$ebastian poured a healthy splash of bourbon into a
tumbler and swallowed it in one gulp. He poured
another.

Then another.

Gabriel watched impassively, brown eyes flickering with
amusement. While Sebastian sipped the third ration, he acquired
his own, and glass in hand, took a seat in one of the oversized
leather chairs situated in Sebastian's study.

The earl paced before the fireplace in agitation.

"I assume milady has not adjusted to the idea of being your
countess," Gabriel remarked dryly. "Or your wife." He amused
himself by counting how many times Sebastian completed the
pattern on the expensive rug.

Sebastian halted just long enough to throw a black scowl at
Gabriel. The stalking resumed for several more minutes before he
flung himself into the chair behind his desk. "Damned if she's not
going to drive me to drink." The two men, in a masculine salute to
exasperating femininity, clinked glasses across the massive desk.

"A wifely duty, some people say," Gabriel noted.

Sebastian sighed, frustration with his reluctant bride easing a bit as the bourbon unknotted him. It had been a long day. Restraining his desire would surely test the limits of his sanity from time to time. Raising the glass to examine its amber-hued contents, he said, "I hope to not make this a nightly habit. I've done too much of drinking lately as it is."

Gabriel chuckled in agreement then turned to a more serious subject. "Basford has yet to appear in London. Indeed, his family is most tight-lipped regarding his absence. They've spread the tale that the viscount was seriously injured in an accident outside the city and now recuperates in an undisclosed location. To better facilitate his recovery."

"Alan has been to Basford's estate twice. His staff claims he's not in residence. Perhaps he is at a smaller family estate else-where." Sebastian toyed with the cut glass tumbler held loosely in his hand. "We'll need to determine for ourselves if he is indeed holed up in Staffordshire."

Gabriel grimaced. "I thought you might say that. I have a man watching the estate. You still intend to go through with the duel?"

Sebastian hesitated, his first instinct to say yes. He was quickly realizing the reluctance to disappoint Ivy. She made no secret of her disgust with his methods of dealing with her abductor. "I am not sure. Perhaps it would be worthwhile to persuade him to leave the country instead. Although I must admit, I have relished the idea of killing him."

"No duel and you find yourself in milady's good graces, is that it?"

"An avenue to consider. The countess has no wish for the duel to take place. Much depends on Basford himself...he must be agreeable to leaving." Would Ivy be pleased? By this restraint? Sebastian considered her assertion a duel would create a scandal, casting a shadow on their new marriage. He did not wish her touched by any hint of gossip. It was very hard to admit, but maybe she was right. "It may be the best course, as much as I am loath to concede my wife's good sense in pointing it out."

"It appears in a few days we shall travel to Kent in search of the elusive viscount," Gabriel stated jovially. "But for now, a toast to celebrate your discovery of such an intelligent woman. How you managed it is a true mystery."

~

DINNER WAS STRAINED, BUT EVENTUALLY, THE CONVERSATION settled into a safe discussion of Beaumont and its history. Neither Sebastian nor Ivy mentioned the contentious incident earlier that day.

Ivy wore a gown the color of dark gold doubloons, the shade accenting the chestnut of her hair and deepening her eyes to a shade of luminous green. The hue favored her, drawing attention from the fading bruises on her wrists and the purple welts in the shapes of fingers on her upper arms where Brandon gripped her so tightly.

Sebastian's eyes touched on the marks. Their presence seemed to disturb him. Did evidence of another man's cruelty serve as a reminder to restrain his own? But she needn't worry. Annie's prediction proved accurate. The earl was attentive, charming and one would never guess their exchange of harsh words only hours earlier. Ivy nervously toyed with her dinner, drinking far more wine than she intended. If he noticed the tendency for her glass to be filled often, he did not comment. Their conversation remained agreeably neutral, more like their old exchanges before the terrible night that ruined things between them, changing their relationship into something hurtful and dark.

"Tell me of Gabriel," Ivy prodded when the final course of cherry tarts and fresh clotted cream was served. "He is very intriguing. How did you come to meet him? How does he owe you his life?"

"It's not a very noble story, I'm afraid. We met in a rather disgusting alleyway behind a house of ill repute in Paris." Sebastian held up his hand at her opened mouthed surprise. "I was merely playing a game of cards with an acquaintance of mine when a disturbance took place. It seems a woman had been ill-treated and Gabriel came to her defense. He and the lout abusing the female were tossed from the establishment. And as these matters usually go, the troublemaker, along with three of his friends, decided to take their displeasure out on the one deemed responsible for their removal."

Sebastian frowned, remembering the scene that night. "It hardly seemed fair to allow the four of them to beat one man to death so naturally, I stepped in. Although Gabriel was holding his own, he would not have lasted much longer. They nearly got the better of him. My friend was always ready for a tussle, so he and I easily routed three of them. Drunk as they were, it was really no contest. But Gabriel and the initial agitator were locked in a struggle far beyond fists. The other man had a knife and was atop Gabriel, trying his damnedest to slit his throat. I grabbed the first thing I could find, a piece of wood from a rubbish pile. Knocked the scoundrel over the head with it. When the others saw their companion was unconscious, they scattered."

"Then you cared for Gabriel and his injuries."

"He was in terrible shape. Busted ribs, broken nose. He'd suffered several stab wounds, and his eyes were swollen shut."

"Is that where he got the scar?" She leaned forward in her chair with barely concealed excitement. "The one on his forehead?"

Sebastian grinned. "No, that he already possessed. And I never had the courage to ask how he obtained it. But, getting back to the story, had I left him in that alley he most likely would have died. I took him to the chateau I was leasing at the time, called in a physician to patch him up. I tasked a few servants with tending to his needs and went about my business. A couple of weeks passed before my guest recovered enough to remind me of his existence. He was an Englishman, the bastard son of a nameless lord who saw fit he received an education and the scratch to make a start in the world, but little else. Gabriel had no one. No family, few friends. In exchange for saving his life, he vowed to serve me, although I assured him such devotion was entirely unnecessary." He shrugged as the tale came to an end, "Gabriel has been with me more than five years. I consider him as close a friend as Alan. Indeed, they are both like brothers to me. The man's loyalty is unquestionable."

Ivy swirled the wine in her glass, considering this side of her husband; the compassionate nature which did not hesitate to come to the aid of an unknown man. She knew of few in their social circle who would dare do the same, placing their blue-blooded necks at risk for someone they did not know, much less someone of a lower class.

"Why have I not met him before today?" A yawn was stifled behind her hand. The wine and the soothing tone of Sebastian's voice left her relaxed and drowsy.

"I've kept him very busy with important matters."

"What important matters?"

He chuckled, helping her rise from her chair. "That is none of your affair, my curious little wife. Now, you are exhausted and understandably so. It's been a long day. Much has occurred since this morning when you first woke."

Ivy leaned into him, yawning again. Their wedding seemed to have happened a century ago. *He's so warm. I wish his arms were around me. I wish he would hold me. I wish...* She wanted to feel secure. Loved. In a rational portion of her brain, she knew her fatigued state and the wine she consumed left her vulnerable to such dangerous sentiments and tender emotions. Still...she wanted his arms wrapped tight about her.

"You are right, of course," she conceded. "It's been a long day."

"Will you find your way all right?"

"Yes, thank you." As difficult as it was to ask the next question, she had to know. She tried her best to sound nonchalant. "Are you retiring too?"

"No." Sebastian smiled. "My head won't find a pillow for a

while. Sleep well, Countess." Pressing a quick, cool kiss to her unsuspecting lips, he left her standing alone in the massive hall.

～

SEBASTIAN MADE HIS WAY TO BED AND ONLY THEN BECAUSE HE WAS utterly exhausted. He attempted to work on some neglected estate accounts, but the figures merged and swam. Adding the same column incorrectly for the third time, he conceded it was time to retire.

A lamp burned on a table in the alcove next to his bed, the low light casting dark shadows. Sitting on the blue tufted bench, he tugged off his boots, tossing them to the side. He gave William leave of his duties for the next few days, so he managed his own disrobing.

It was bizarre, he thought, sliding between the sheets. Ivy's distinctive perfume lingered within the bedchamber. With tired bemusement, he wondered how he would keep from dreaming of her when her scent surrounded him. Especially tonight, their wedding night, for God's sake. It seemed unfair to spend it alone.

Settling against the pillows, Sebastian threw an arm over his eyes. A sigh of pure exhaustion escaped him. He stretched, yawning, and as the softness of the bed enveloped him, the awareness he was not alone seeped into his consciousness. A sleek figure, with skin scented of oranges and lilies and smooth as silk, wiggled close.

Ivy was in his bed, a tousled, sleeping ball of warmth. Like a kitten seeking a cozy spot, she instinctively rolled from the far side of the mattress, curling next to him, her hand resting on his chest. She wore a cloud of a nightgown, the muslin fabric sliding against his bare skin as she burrowed close to his heat. Pulled into a fat braid, her hair lay across her shoulder, and if he wished, he could grab that silken rope; use it to tug her to him, to hold her still while he devoured her.

Remaining on his back, Sebastian shifted his arm to wrap it

about her. Her sleepy sigh of contentment melted him, a sense of fulfillment and peace seeping into his bones. It had nothing to do with desire or lust. He treasured holding her. Drifting off, he realized he'd never fallen asleep with a woman in his bed without first making love to her.

What a novel experience.

CHAPTER 27

*S*ebastian faced her, stretched on his side. One arm lay tucked beneath both his head and the pillow, the other rested possessively in the curve of her waist. The weight of that arm held her prisoner, but Ivy did not mind. It was a perfect opportunity to examine him. An unforeseen gift, she mused, her gaze drifting over his features. Her husband's face was softened in slumber, his eyes hidden behind lush, black eyelashes thick enough to make any woman jealous. The sensual fullness of his lips and the high curve of his cheekbones were complimented by eyebrows dark and full like a raven's wings. She almost reached up to trace one before reminding herself to remain still, altering her breathing to light, shallow breaths so he would not realize she was awake.

His chin bore a dark shading of stubble. He would need a shave soon. Would he ask her to help with that, or would his valet always take care of such things? Did wives typically assist with such things? Ivy's eyes dropped to his chest. It was bare, a rippling expanse of hard, bronzed vastness much wider than she remembered. It beckoned exploration, calling her to outline the rigid, dark points of his flat nipples so different from her own, the skin stretching in gleaming sheets over bundles of sinew and flesh.

A vee of rough black hair commenced below his navel before trailing off to destinations better left uncharted beneath the edge of the coverlet. The fabric lay pinned to his waist by the position of their bodies, and for the briefest of moments, Ivy considered tugging it free. Lean muscles lined the slabs of his abdomen along with a long, thin scar, pale cream in color. It snaked across the lower part of his rib cage. Barely noticeable in the dimness of the room, it was damage a rapier or a knife blade might leave. Duels were practically a gentleman's hobby in France and England. Ivy wanted to trace the length of that scar, to gently press it with her fingertips, as if she could heal any residual pain with a simple touch.

The faint laceration was a sobering reminder of the confrontation Sebastian wished to undertake against the Viscount Basford. Ivy shifted slightly in renewed distress with the thought. Her movement dislodging his arm a fraction of an inch from the curve of her waist and she realized he was awake.

He watched her, the strangest expression stamped across his features. Ivy considered flinging herself from the bed before forcing herself to relax. She had placed herself there of her own accord; she would not flee. As sleep dissipated and desire sparked in Sebastian's gaze, her chin tilted.

"I'm curious how we came to be in this particular situation. Especially when I recall your strong feelings on this subject yesterday afternoon." Propping himself up, Sebastian rested his head in the palm of one hand, the other still locked around Ivy's waist. His grip tightened, drawing her closer until mere inches separated them. "Well?" His voice was rough with restraint. "I eagerly await your explanation."

Jumbled thoughts overwhelmed Ivy. Did Sebastian wear anything beneath the edge of the coverlet? His chest was naked. Was the rest of him? What the devil did men wear to bed? Anything? Nothing? Waves of heat emanated from him. The same heat she gravitated to in the middle of the night. Never was she so warm, so content, as the first night of sleeping with her husband.

His leg brushed against hers. *Oh God*. It was bare. Or did her imagination run rampant with panic? Her mind could not properly function, not when feverishly contemplating the state of his clothing. Or, lack of.

"Your silence leads me to believe you would prefer I take matters into my own hands." Sebastian's lips lifted with the beginnings of a grin as Ivy swallowed and finally found her voice.

"It did not seem right we should spend our wedding night in separate beds." Ivy cleared her throat, her heart beating so rapidly she thought it might thump out of her chest. "Regardless of everything, I did not wish that we spend it apart. I…I know it was not as you wanted it to be. Since we did not... that is to say, you did not..."

Her words trailed off into silence. Foolish, embarrassed tears swelled and she furiously blinked them back. Since meeting this man, the disturbing tendency to cry raised its head at the most inopportune times, and she hated the peculiar weakness.

Sebastian's features softened at her dismay. "I will remember our wedding night forever. Because it was *not* as I expected. You would know I'm a liar if I said I do not want to make love to you, but right now, you trust me to hold you." He brushed a wayward curl from her forehead. "Will you let me kiss you, my anxious little wife? I'm not sure I trust myself to go no further, but what matters most to me, is will you trust me?"

Hypnotized by the silky roughness of Sebastian's voice as he moved closer, Ivy waited in wary curiosity. When his hand glided to cup her jaw, fingers sliding into the tendrils of hair springing free from the braids, she voiced no objection nor did she move away.

Moving so that he loomed over her, Sebastian pinned Ivy flat to the mattress. His large hands buried themselves into the pillows on either side of her head, his lips closing the distance separating them. He kissed her deeply, slowly, leisurely dipping his tongue into her mouth until she was breathless. Desperately grasping handfuls of her own nightgown was the only way she kept her fingers from sliding into the thickness of his hair. A fire ignited within her belly, spreading flames of insidious delight. She imagined his hands touching her everywhere.

Then Sebastian stopped.

"That's probably enough for now, don't you think?"

Rolling away from the bed in one smooth motion, he reached for a dark grey robe lying on a nearby chair and Ivy had a quick glance of muscled, impossibly golden-brown buttocks before the fabric concealed his nudity. Tying the garment's silk sash, he grinned at her over his shoulder.

Why, *why* was he touched by the sun *there?* Where breeches should have covered him? A thousand questions whirled in her brain, each more confusing than the last.

"Forgive me, sweetheart. It's my habit to sleep as Nature intended, so I suggest you accustom yourself to it. Eventually, you will come to know my body as well as your own."

"I don't understand," Ivy stammered. "I thought you wanted to..."

"Make love to you?" Sebastian laughed softly at her confusion. "Oh, I do. Believe me, I do. Only this is hardly a good time. Gabriel is incredibly dedicated to being my man of affairs. It is habit to pop in quite early. He may already know you decided to take up residence in my chambers, he usually knows everything. But, then again, he might not expect you here when he comes barreling through the door. You left matters up in the air yesterday afternoon."

"Does this occur every day?" Ivy's voice was tight with mortification. Her own words made it seem as though she wanted far more than kissing. Her cheeks burned, thinking what might have followed those kisses.

"It doesn't have to be." The look he gave her was inscrutable. "If you've other ideas, I'll instruct Gabriel to come only when summoned. It would be quite awkward to be discovered in the midst of something...ah, intimate."

"You are insufferable," she breathed.

Sebastian only laughed. "Save your judgment. At least until tomorrow morning." His eyebrow raised slightly, a faintly challenging gesture Ivy could not ignore. "You could always retreat to the safety of your lonely chamber."

Ivy pulled herself to a sitting position, arms wrapped about her knees as she considered the options.

On her impulsive orders, all her clothing and personal toiletry items were placed in the dressing room and not within the personal armoire in the lady's chambers. The other apartment, spacious and feminine, lacked the same warmth and vitality as his. Ivy felt comfortable here, safe, somehow more alive in this room. There was no desire to spend even one night in that other cold, lonely, bed. Not if she were honest with herself.

Sebastian Cain was both calming and disconcerting to her senses all at once. Although she wished this marriage had not taken place, she gravitated to him. And while she hoped he would honor the vow giving her time to adjust to being his wife, the idea of not being near him was unimaginable.

Sebastian's eyes flared with victory when Ivy settled back into the warmth of his bed.

She would stay. Whatever the reason, she would stay.

A knock came at the door, saving Ivy from his triumphant remark as he called out a command to enter.

"Good morning." Gabriel smiled upon seeing her in the middle of the rumpled bed. "I took the liberty of assuming you would still be abed. I've brought Her Ladyship tea, hot chocolate, and coffee."

Slouching at the intrusion, Ivy pulled the coverlet up to her chin, although Gabriel's jovial tone indicated he was hardly surprised to find her there. With Sebastian's impatient wave, he shouldered his way into the room, carrying an ornate tray, burdened with three gleaming silver pots and two smaller vessels containing cream and sugar.

"How thoughtful of you." Ivy trembled with embarrassment from the tent of covers. "I prefer tea in the mornings, but hot chocolate is an occasional treat. There's no need for you to go to such trouble on my account, Gabriel. I always take my breakfast in the dining room."

"Do not fret, milady. I already knew your preferences, and I bring Ravenswood's coffee up, regardless. He is a veritable bear in the mornings without it. It is no trouble to add a pot of tea and some sugar biscuits to tide you over until breakfast. Milord informed me you enjoy the Rosethorne tea from his plantation, so I took the liberty of having Chef brew it for you."

"I have not had it for some time, but I do adore it." She frowned at the puzzling statement of her habits being known, then averted her gaze at Sebastian's upraised brow. How could she confess to throwing the remains of his gift into the fire during an inconsolable crying spell only two weeks ago?

Sebastian leveled a perturbed glance at Gabriel. "I have only managed to convince the countess to remain in my bed. I'd rather you not frighten her out of it by referring to me as an animal."

"Very good, milord." Gabriel gave Ivy a mischievous wink as he set the tray on a low fruitwood chest. "I'll leave this and return later."

"A splendid idea. Might I suggest you don't come back at all?" Sebastian poured a cup of coffee without benefit of cream or sugar. "And, have done with this "milord" business."

"See what I mean, milady? A real bear," Gabriel murmured, then louder he said, "Perhaps it may be best if you ring when you would like your coffee and milady's tea delivered."

"If you will abide by that, then yes..." Sebastian muttered. "Good God, all I want is a bit of privacy in the mornings. It's not too much to bloody ask, is it?"

Gabriel chuckled. "You must inform me when you wish for privacy. Damned difficult business to read minds."

Ivy smiled at their bantering. Gabriel apparently delighted in pushing Sebastian's patience, and even she was curious how far he might go before the earl snapped.

Sebastian's lips tightened with annoyance when Gabriel, wearing a devilish smile, exited the chambers.

"What would delight your heart today? Hot chocolate and tea are only the beginning of the debauchery I intend." Picking up a delicate teacup, Sebastian poured a splash of cream, followed by tea and one cube of sugar.

Ivy did not know whether to be pleased or surprised. He remembered precisely how she preferred her tea. Of course, he would commit to memory everything about her when actively pursuing her as prey. Anything which might prove an advantage, no matter how minuscule the detail...

"A bath." Accepting the tea, her eyes widened as Sebastian sat on the edge of the bed. He drank his coffee, his smile relaxed, as if this ritual was commonplace. How disturbing...that she should be so comfortable with the earl serving her a morning cup of tea in bed.

"I find it high on my agenda as well," Sebastian paused, then continued in a wry tone. "Will you accept my assistance? I vow to be the perfect gentleman. I *can* keep my hands to myself when required."

Ivy's stare was frankly disbelieving.

"I did not say it would be damn near impossible and extremely difficult, but I can do it." His eyes glimmered with something dark and intent. "Will you trust me?"

Ivy sipped the tea, allowing its warmth to trickle through her. The thought of a bath in that intriguing room with its huge porcelain tub and elegant faucets was so enticing.

Lizzie explained the system yesterday, demonstrating how the taps worked and the process in which heated water was forced up from the kitchens through the piping system, the separate faucet allowing cold water to be added as needed. Sebastian's father modified the suite's previous sitting room based on the steam baths in Rome. The inventions much impressed him as a young man; he spent a small fortune replicating them.

The tub was large enough for two adults. Ivy blushed, thinking one day she and Sebastian might share it. "I'm not sure."

Sebastian pounced on her weakness. "I'm sure. Very sure."

Ivy contemplated the intimacy of such an act. Taking another nervous sip of tea, the cup rattled against the delicate saucer when she lowered it. "I'm sure there aren't nearly enough towels..."

"The room is well stocked and your toiletry items are already in there," he interrupted. "Now, let's fill the tub, shall we?"

Taking the cup and saucer from her, he pulled back the coverlet. Ivy heard his low groan. The thinnest of white satin ribbons held the bodice of her flimsy white gown closed while the sleeves billowed full and luxurious before narrowing to tiny circles around her wrists. However, those charming details did not hold Sebastian's attention. During the night, the length of the gown had twisted around her thighs, and now, her legs flashed in the dim morning light. Ivy hastily yanked the fabric down and scrambled from the bed, ignoring the hand he held out to assist her.

Her bare feet did not make a sound as she passed from the soft Aubusson rug to the gleaming hardwood floor, her toes curling slightly against the chill. She followed Sebastian silently, reconsidering the situation.

Once inside the large bathing room, Sebastian twisted a spigot, and a few moments later, hot water began filling the tub. While Ivy stood awkwardly waiting, steam rose in curling tendrils of vapor to drift lazily in the cool air. She studied the room as the bath was drawn. Wallpapered in a pleasingly masculine style of dark and light green horizontal stripes, the cream toned furnishing provided an elegant accent. A bank of floor to ceiling windows occupied much of the largest wall opposite of the tub, with cream-colored drapes pulled open to reveal the scenery. Next to the tub was a heavily carved bench as well as a step stool to aid with getting in and out. Creamy white porcelain pitchers lined the bottom shelf of a washstand and an oversized armoire contained armloads of fresh towels and an assortment of soaps, oils, and sponges.

Sebastian filled the pitchers with water, lining them beside the tub. After rummaging around in the armoire, he produced a small vial of bath powder and poured a tiny bit into the tub. It foamed with the agitation of the water.

The frothy puffs fascinated Ivy, the scent of lilies perfuming the air. "I did not know it would do that."

Sebastian knelt before the marble fireplace. Soon a cheery little blaze burned, chasing away the slight chill of the room. "It only requires the agitation of the water hitting the powder to make the bubbles. It still softens the skin but I believe you will enjoy this immensely."

A bar of lily-scented soap, two huge soft bath towels and a tan colored sponge were set within reach of the tub. Sebastian closed the faucets.

"Milady, your bath awaits you." He gave her a courtly bow.

Wrapping her arms around herself, hiding within the folds of her nightgown, Ivy chewed her bottom lip. She could not disrobe before him. A gleam of banked desire lurked in his eyes - it hardly seemed wise to remove her clothing when he looked at her so hungrily.

Sebastian grinned in sudden understanding, nodding toward the decorative screen in the corner. Beautifully painted, a woodland scene spread across its three panels. A group of scarlet clad lords on horseback, along with a pack of lean hounds, raced across one scene, a section of woods and fields occupied the middle scene, and in the last panel, a petite red fox looked back at its pursuers, mouth open as if panting in distress.

Ivy felt a shared kinship with the unfortunate creature.

"You may disrobe behind that. If the bubbles are not enough protection, you may pull a towel in along with you." His eyes slid over her, warm and appreciative. "And should it please you, I will help you wash your hair."

Sebastian pointed her toward the screen, giving her rump a little slap and ignoring her small "Oh!" of surprise.

"Better hurry," he drawled. "Wouldn't want the water to get cold. Or even worse, from your point of view that is, for the bubbles to subside."

Rubbing the slight sting on her posterior, Ivy hurried behind the screen, taking a towel with her. Whipping the nightgown off, she wrapped the towel tight around her then rushed to the tub, scrambling over its side. Tossing the towel aside, she eased into the fluffy bubbles and once safely submerged to the tops of her breasts, she looked at him.

Sebastian stood with his back to her, arms crossed, bare legs exposed from mid-calf down. The robe stretched across the width of his muscled back.

"You may turn around." Ivy sank lower into the water as Sebastian pivoted, his eyes meeting hers over the rim of the tub. Pulling the fat braid of her hair over one shoulder, she tugged at the end of it. "This is quite extraordinary. You may never get me out of here."

Coming closer, his grin turned wicked when she sank even further into the water's depths, up to her collarbone. Her cheeks flamed with heat. Thank God for the bath powders. Mounds of sudsy bubbles concealed her body from his stare.

"Once it is mutually agreed I should join you, I may not let you out." Sebastian walked behind the tub, and taking her braid in his hands, he untied the bit of ribbon.

"I don't believe the scent of lilies would be to your liking." Ivy tensed as he deftly unraveled the plait.

"I'll take the risk." Gathering up the whole mass of her hair, Sebastian raked his hands through it. From her forehead to her temples, his fingers massaged her scalp as he gently, but firmly pulled the hair away from her face. Ivy closed her eyes at the pleasurable sensation then frowned when his hands dropped. He bent to fetch two of the pitchers.

"Lean your head back," he instructed, pouring the water over her hair until it was thoroughly drenched. Picking up the bar of soap, he worked it into a luxurious lather, his hands plunging again and again until her hair was a soapy mass.

It was a luxurious experience, the feel of his fingers scrubbing and massaging, the hot silkiness of the water lapping at her skin, the soft foaminess of the bubbles caressing her flesh. Sebastian looped her hair through his hands, swirling the slippery profusion of it around her head. At one point, he chuckled softly.

When Ivy peeked at him over her shoulder, he shrugged. "I'm not sure how you manage all this by yourself."

Her answer stuck in her throat. The sweetness of Sebastian undertaking such a mundane task was heart-stopping. What would this do to his ruthless reputation if word leaked out? His robe was open almost to his waist, revealing golden skin and sinewy muscles. His male beauty was difficult to ignore. Ivy's skin tingled. The entire experience was luxurious, sensual and uncomfortable all at the same time and undoubtedly, he planned it that way. The way his fingers slid through her hair - similar, but not quite the same, as when they glided over her body, tracing her curves, dipping into hollows and skimming over sensitive places aching to be touched.

Ivy sensed his hesitation when his hands drifted to either side of her neck, the long fingers massaging those muscles and the tops of her shoulders until she trembled.

With a faint noise of frustration, Sebastian resumed the task of washing her hair with a brisk efficiency. When it was time to rinse, he took the last of the pitchers, pouring them one by one over her head to flush the suds away.

"I'll leave you to finish your bath." With both palms up, he faced her, eyes dark. "And true to my word, I kept my hands to myself."

Ivy nodded, surprised by the tiny frisson of disappointment streaking through her.

"I shall have the fire going, and perhaps you would like to try a cup of hot chocolate. I have the cocoa brought in from Spain. It is quite decadent. We'll ring for Lizzie to come help you dress. Unless you prefer my assistance again."

Ivy knew…if he helped dress her, she'd be unable to resist him. Lips tight, she shook her head. "Lizzy will be fine."

He gave her an unfathomable look before exiting, and Ivy finished bathing in silence. Stepping from the tub and winding a towel about her hair, she frowned at her own complacency. She was making her own seduction incredibly easy. He merely washed her hair and she quivered at his touch.

After slipping her nightgown back on, Ivy returned to the bedchamber. A chair and a small table were pulled close to the fire. The pot of hot chocolate and a clean cup, along with her brush and comb rested upon the table. He had placed a soft blanket in the chair and her slippers waited beside it.

"Ah, there you are," Sebastian said cheerfully, pulling the drapes back. Early morning light filtered into the room, mingling with the glow of the firelight. He knelt down to slide the slippers onto her feet, a smile twitching his lips.

"What is so amusing?" Ivy drew the blanket across her lap.

"With your hair wrapped so, you remind me of an empress I saw once. Only you are much more beautiful. And, daring to touch you won't leave me in danger of losing my head or having my hands lopped off."

She laughed despite herself. "Are you sure about that?"

His eyebrow lifted in mock challenge. "I suppose the risk is worth it."

Gathering up a few personal items, he disappeared into the bathing room while Ivy pondered his words. A curious feeling of anticipation shimmered through her.

Kisses, hot chocolate, Sebastian washing her hair. Such a peculiar first morning as husband and wife.

CHAPTER 28

*B*reakfast was served in the impossibly large and elegant dining room at an equally impossibly large table that could easily seat a hundred guests. Sebastian then gave Ivy a tour of her new home.

There were two sitting rooms on the main floor, each decorated in complementary shades; silver and blue in the east wing; blush rose and cream in the west. A life-size portrait of Sebastian's mother, gracefully beautiful with dark hair and soft gray eyes presided over the fireplace in the rose parlor. In the blue parlor, a portrait of the old earl hung. It was easy to see Sebastian in his father's countenance, if one looked past the blue eyes and salt and pepper hair. It reflected in the autocratic and yet kindly gleam of his father's eyes, the regal lift of his chin. And certainly in their features, although Ivy believed her husband to be the more handsome of the two.

A separate corridor veered into a wing containing Sebastian's study, the library, and a music room. The study was fascinating- a well-organized, masculine space, with files and personal papers neatly stacked in shallow wood bins on the large desk. An enormous globe of Earth, held aloft on an ornate iron axis, stood before a large window. Dominating the wall above the fireplace was a painting of Beaumont from the fifteenth century, depicting the manor before a main portion of the house burned to the ground. Accented by deep green forests and open fields dotted with fluffy sheep, the manor in the painting was quite cozy when compared to its present magnificence.

And the library! Ivy sighed with pleasure, for it was grand and delicious with the prevailing scent of book leather and old paper and lavender. Mahogany bookcases stretched from floor to vaulted ceiling on three walls, and several rolling ladders made it easy to reach the volumes along the top shelves. An ornate fruit-wood bar stocked with spirits occupied one corner, and the combined lighting of several sconces and numerous exquisite crystal chandeliers overhead lit the dark wood interior with an amber glow.

"It is so lovely." Ivy ran a finger along the spines of a row of books on the shelf by her head.

Diffused morning light streamed through a wall of windows overlooking a magnificent four-square rose garden. In the late afternoon, the space would be stunning as sunlight filled it. Ivy made a mental promise to visit. With a crackling fire in the hearth and a pot of hot tea at her elbow, the multiple cranberry hued divans scattered about, it would prove a perfect spot for curling up with a good book. It would be heaven itself.

"I spent a great deal of time in here growing up." Sebastian followed her, watching intently as she traced the book titles on the spines. "I was never able to read all of them, but I tried."

Ivy smiled at him over her shoulder. "I would have believed you to be running wild over the countryside instead."

"I certainly did that. However, my mother required I read at least one book every summer, and I did wish to make her happy."

"Did you have a favorite author?"

"Shakespeare when my mother was about." He gave her a wicked wink. "Chaucer when she was not."

Imagining her husband as boy, hiding his choice of books from his mother, Ivy fought the tug of tenderness to ask briskly, "Where to next? The music room, I think you said?"

He indicated she should walk ahead of him, but as she skirted past, he caught her by the elbow, spinning her around and back up against the bookcase. Sebastian moved with the quickness of a deadly jungle cat.

Ivy's breath caught in her chest and Sebastian smiled at her surprise. "The music room can wait. I'm afraid I cannot."

Taking her hands, he raised them high, pinning them against the spines of the books behind her. The edges of the different shelves hit at her shoulders, hips and the back of her knees.

"It's been damned difficult keeping my hands off you. I've reached my limits. For the morning, at least." His eyes were hot and dark. Lustful.

Before she could answer, his mouth swooped down, his tongue delving to fence with hers, swirling around, leisurely tasting her. And she could not move, not with the weight of his muscular body pushing her against the bookcase. His hands kept hers prisoner while his mouth continued to search and give and take and request until Ivy finally melted.

Sebastian growled. A low, deep sound of want and need. Desire and frustration. Even with the layers of cloth between them, his arousal was evident. An answering spark lit within Ivy, one she wished did not exist. It was dangerous to her sanity. She tried shifting away, but he held her too tight.

"I want you." Tearing his mouth from hers, Sebastian laid a flaming hopscotch of kisses along the curve of her throat. "I want you as I have never wanted another woman. And God help me, it's only been one day and already I grow impatient with this waiting. What must I do to have you, Ivy? What must I do to make you want me with the same desperation I feel? I'm mad for you. Utterly and completely insane...but you know this."

His grip shifted, holding her wrists in one hand higher above her head while his other smoothed down her side, skimming the curve of her breast before coming to rest in the indentation of her waist. That light touch tracing her form, through layers of silk and muslin, was scorching.

"You mustn't say such things." Ivy's words dissolved into a moan of longing. Her knees wobbled, suddenly incapable of holding her weight.

"Mustn't I?" Sebastian murmured. He pressed sinful kisses to her jawline, drifting along the delicate line of her collarbone revealed by the neckline of her gown until she sucked in a sharp breath. He took great pleasure in seducing her and, shameless creature that she was, she was powerless to stop him.

Finally, he released her, allowing her arms to fall. A flounce of lace along her shoulder was flicked back into place with his index finger. "You win, my dear." Resignation rumbled in his tone, his eyes dark with challenge. "Shall we continue our tour?"

Bright and airy, the music room was exquisite. Wallpapered in cream on cream satin stripes and accented with dark blue, the woman's touch it exhibited plucked at Ivy's heart. It was both feminine and sophisticated at the same time. Another painting of the late countess hung over the fireplace. This one included Sebastian as a dark haired, grey-eyed little boy about the age of five.

"She was so very lovely," Ivy observed. The artist did a masterful job capturing the merriment in his mother's eyes as well as the mischief in Sebastian's. "You were quite the handsome little lord."

"It is one of my favorite paintings of her." Sebastian wore a tiny smile as he considered the portrait. "I never saw Mother cross, although I am sure she must have occasionally been. Theirs was an arranged marriage, but she and my father fell in love very quickly. It nearly destroyed him when she passed."

"How did she die?" Ivy asked gently. Sebastian's sadness was noticeable although his demeanor remained unchanged. Extremely sensitive to it, she could not stop her hand from finding his.

He squeezed her hand while gazing up at the portrait. "Giving birth to my sister. The babe was stillborn and Mother died a few hours later. I was twelve at the time."

"I'm so sorry." Ivy moved closer until she nearly hugged his arm.

"It was difficult for my father, although I suffered her loss with a depth of heartache almost unbearable. You must understand since you lost your own mother at the same age." Sebastian turned suddenly, taking both of her hands within his, his eyes dark. "The day is too beautiful to dwell on the sadness of the past." When he smiled, it only took a moment for the light of it to reach his eyes. "Tell me, what do you think of the music room? Does it please you? Would you like to redecorate it, put your own touch on it?"

Sebastian offered the opportunity to change a favored room of his mother's, and Ivy's heart swelled. He wished to please her, to help her feel as though at least one room in this enormous place felt like hers, but if she were honest, she would change nothing. The former Countess of Ravenswood and she shared similar tastes. The room was perfect as it was; timeless and graceful, unspoiled by the capriciousness of a society following every decorating fad until the style of a room was a hopeless mishmash of clashing trends.

"I would not change a thing," she replied and Sebastian nodded in pleasure.

"I'm heartily glad to hear that. I recall our first kiss was in your music room."

"Yes." Ivy blushed. "I busted your lip then nearly crippled myself jumping up from the piano. I was so surprised."

"So was I."

Ivy tilted her head. "How so? You knew you were going to kiss me."

"Yes, but I did not know how it would affect me." He tipped her chin with a finger. "Somewhere within my soul, I knew you were destined to be mine, only I did not realize it then. And now, here we are."

He brushed her lips lightly with his own, and her eyes fluttered shut. She swayed toward him, but Sebastian abruptly stepped away.

"Play for me. Something cheerful," he said, moving toward the piano. "When Mother was here, this room was always lively. I'm glad it will once again be filled with music and laughter."

Ivy gratefully sank down on the bench, her knees weak. When he sat beside her, she began to play the melody from the afternoon when they first kissed. Sebastian's smile told her he remembered it well and she nearly basked in the glory of his approval.

The ballroom was next. Ivy admired the white and gold gilded plasterwork, the tall, soaring fluted columns circling the highly polished light oak floor. The room could comfortably hold four hundred or more people, the space stretching like an open field. Ten huge crystal chandeliers hung from the high-coffered barrel ceiling and encompassing one wall were glass doors opening to a large terrace overlooking the parterre gardens. A fountain similar to the one in front of the manor occupied the garden center. Decorated in shades of gold, silver and blue, the entire room shimmered with light and richness in a sophisticated, unmistakable display of the earl's wealth.

"Oh, how exquisite the gardens are," Ivy exclaimed, crossing to the windows to gaze at the gardens. She fingered the heavy, gold damask of the draperies, admiring the intricate scrolling pattern of dark blue embossed in the fine fabric.

"They should be," Sebastian said. "A veritable army keep the grounds pristine even though I'm not in residence."

"It seems a shame not to utilize the beauty in this grand space."

"There is reason, now that we've wed. Come, no one has danced on this floor in almost six years, and longer than that since my mother danced here with my father." Tugging Ivy to the middle of the ballroom floor, Sebastian executed a courtly bow. "Would you grant me the honor of being the first Countess of Ravenswood to do so in more than sixteen years?"

"There's no music..." Despite the protest, her hands automatically clutched his shoulders.

"We shall make our own."

A half memory, perhaps something he witnessed his own

parents do once long ago when he was a boy, flashed in Sebastian's eyes. Placing one hand in the small of her back, he rested it there for a brief second then drew her closer into him.

Sensation, hot and thrilling, shot straight from his hand to Ivy's very core. Maybe he knew how the simple gesture affected her, but Sebastian only smiled and gathered her, his hands moving to the proper places. Humming the tune of an unknown waltz, he twirled her around the gleaming oak floor with its inlaid swirls and center medallion emblazoned with the Ravenswood crest.

They created a haunting beauty. Anyone peeking in would have been enthralled by it. Ivy's chestnut curls tumbled to feather the tops of Sebastian's hand resting in the hollow of her back. He cut a dashingly handsome figure in dark brown breeches and a simple white shirt. No pretense existed between them at that moment. No glittering crowd, no witty repartees, no clinking champagne glasses and double innuendos. Best of all, a lack of clever banter and a blessed absence of chatty gossip drifted in their wake as they floated across the ballroom. Only the two of them inhabited that moment and it was simple, perfect and honest.

Ivy hummed the tune with him until it faded and they stood in awkward silence in the cavernous room. Sebastian drew her closer, his arms wrapping completely about her waist. The corner of his lips lifted with a wistful smile. "I shall always remember this."

Ivy had the impression of being dragged into something warm and encompassing, a safe harbor she could trust if only she allowed herself to do so. "As will I." Her admission was reluctant but truthful.

"Oh, Ivy. I do love you, you know" His lips touched hers. "Too much for my own sanity, I think."

Ivy knew he felt her melt, knew he tasted her hesitation as it eased away and she kissed him back. But before, when he might have deepened the kiss, sliding into something darker, more passionate, this time he did not. When she made a longing noise low in her throat, Sebastian again was the one to step away.

Lifting her hand, he pressed a kiss to it, easing the sting of his retreat. "Little butterfly, we have so many things to explore..."

Ivy tried to gather her wits. Did he refer to something more intimate? She could not seem to think straight, and that was not likely to change if he insisted on kissing her in every room of this huge mansion. But still, she mused, glancing about the ballroom, this, this was her favorite moment of the morning.

Sebastian's expression when he said he loved her caused an odd little pang in her heart. He was destroying her defenses in the most devious of ways. Soon, she would dissolve in a puddle of weak foolishness and then where would she be in this game of cat and mouse?

Ivy mustered up a cool degree of aloofness as they continued through the house and Sebastian frowned in amusement as she skillfully kept herself out of arm's reach. He knew precisely what she was doing but allowed her to play the little game with a shrug. It was only when they entered the room doubling as both nursery and schoolroom, did her improvised strategy unravel.

A sturdy swinging cradle crafted of smooth rosewood, adorned with a few wispy spider webs, sat in forlorn abandonment in one corner. It was a piece of art, with all its intricate carvings. The crest of the Ravenswood earldom formed the head of the cradle, the split shield containing roses, trailing vines and a raven with widespread wings carved on one side, a long stemmed curved rose in full bloom climbing the other.

"Did you sleep in this as a babe?" Ivy inquired, her fingers trailing over the carvings.

"I did." Sebastian touched the side of the cradle so that it rocked gently. "So did my father. And his father. And his before him. Whatever previous Cain children slept in was destroyed in the fire. This cradle is still sturdy enough to hold a dozen children, I believe." When she blushed, his laugh was almost bitter. "Do not fret. I've no intention of burdening you with so many."

Her head tilted. Of course, he would want children. At least one. Having an heir was necessary and inevitable once they shared a bed as husband and wife. A wave of remorse swept her. Her childish efforts to maintain a distance between them was selfish. Not many husbands would allow such headstrong and foolish behavior. Nor be so patient.

Sebastian had hurt and betrayed her. Truly, she must guard her heart, but the fact remained she was his wife. Her duty was to provide his successor. She gave a vow, before God and witnesses, to be his in every sense of the word. Eventually, she must honor that vow.

Ivy reached for his hand, untangling his fingers where they gripped the side of the cradle. "Half a dozen then." Her fingers meshed with his, her mouth curving into a smile.

Sebastian blinked. He was silent for a long moment. "There is only one way to ensure such a brood."

"Yes." She acknowledged even while holding her breath.

He did not say anything else although his hand closed firmly over hers. Ivy knew he did not miss the slight sway of her body, the little intake of breath as her face tilted to his. A flash of pleased triumph appeared in his gaze.

"Why don't we make our way downstairs for lunch? Then I shall take you to the west gardens. They were my mother's favorite. I think you shall adore them as well." Sebastian abruptly turned, pulling her toward the nursery's door.

Frowning at his unexpected defection when she would have willingly allowed him a kiss, Ivy followed him from the dusty nursery in contemplative silence.

CHAPTER 29

*T*hree days passed and during the nights following their conversation in the nursery, Ivy hoped Sebastian would sweep her into his arms, to make love to her.

He did not, adhering to the vow of making her beg for his attentions. Night after night, desire bubbled beneath the surface, and night after night, each remained silently stubborn, unwilling to be the one to bend first.

Catching sight of Gabriel striding across the wide lawn, Ivy gave a desperate wave for the man to join the two of them. It was early afternoon and refreshments were set upon the expanse of green stretching between the house and the stables. A tea tray, the remnants of a few cucumber and watercress sandwiches and an awkward silence were all that remained between Ivy and her husband. Gabriel's presence was a godsend.

Sebastian leaned back in the wrought iron chair, his brow furrowed upon seeing the seriousness on the other man's face.

"I should not interrupt." Gabriel protested.

"Nonsense," Ivy said quickly. "It is little trouble to fetch an extra cup. Besides, we require more tea anyway." She reached for a little brass bell on the tray, and in rapid fashion a fresh pot, and cup, and a new plate of sandwiches were procured.

"Her tiniest desire is met and carried out with dizzying swiftness." Sebastian shook his head. The staff's eagerness to do Ivy's bidding was remarkable. Already they spoiled her, seeking her favor with almost embarrassing compulsion.

Ivy smiled at him. "I am a sorceress and have cast a spell over all your servants. They have no choice but to dote on me. Have a care, or I shall cast one over you as well."

"Too late," Sebastian replied lazily. "My fate is tied to theirs."

"It's said the bewitched are blissfully unaware and ignorant."

The earl tsked, his eyes hot as they swept over her. "I am neither unaware nor ignorant. My state of bliss however, is entirely dependent upon my countess."

A polite cough concealed Gabriel's chuckle at the scandalous statement.

Flustered, Ivy turned to him. "How do you take your tea, Gabriel?"

Polite conversation ensued for the next half hour until Gabriel set his teacup down. "Thank you, milady."

His action triggered some type of silent communication as Sebastian stood from his chair. "My dear, please excuse us. Gabriel has information to share with me, and it can no longer wait. I won't be long."

Gabriel stood as well, staring off into the distance, strangely reluctant to meet Ivy's eyes. The meaning behind the statement pounded into her awareness. Her heart clenched in painful degrees, the day growing dark although the sun still beamed bright and warm overhead.

The stormy night of her abduction was centuries away from Beaumont's lush gardens. Birds chirped merrily from all corners, the sickly-sweet scent of roses and jasmine perfuming the air. Ivy almost laughed. Strange, how roses continued to remind her of death. Only now, Sebastian's mortality frightened her beyond all reason.

"I understand." Coming to her feet, Sebastian's hand touched her elbow. "I believe I shall visit the library. I've been wanting to explore it."

"For some reason, it's filled my thoughts as well," Sebastian said in an obvious attempt to lighten her somber mood.

Ivy could barely swallow past the lump in her throat. The devil wanted her to remember every detail of that kiss in the library. Her gaze skittered away from his as an image of being held against the bookcase flashed in her mind.

His grin widened even further.

"It's an extensive collection of books, I'm sure I will find something to please me," she said weakly. She should try harder to erase that scorching kiss. She should concentrate instead on why Gabriel sought the earl out. What report did he bring to Sebastian's ears? Had they tracked Brandon down at last? Did they set the date and time of the duel?

Leading Ivy a few steps away, Sebastian's smile was wicked mischievousness, his whisper hot in her ear. "Might I suggest, 'Chaucer'?"

Unreasonable, nauseating fear choked Ivy as she pulled free of his grip. His laughter followed her as she hurried into the house.

~

"THE MAN WATCHING BASFORD'S ESTATE SAYS A DOCTOR FROM two villages over visited early this morning."

"Is he certain?" Sebastian resumed his position at the small table, waving at Gabriel to do the same.

Gabriel nodded as he sat down. "We should go while Basford is likely to still be there."

Sebastian mulled the options. How long the viscount might remain in Staffordshire was uncertain, and this need for revenge had become a living, breathing thing. Just that morning, he glimpsed yet another fading bruise on Ivy's creamy shoulder as she dressed. The rage it sparked was instant and hot.

"If we leave at once, we could be back before morning." Sebastian decided. What should he tell Ivy? How to explain this abrupt abandonment on the fourth night of their marriage? The logical course would be to explain the reason for his departure after, and not before. If things did not go to plan, his original strategy of pinning the viscount to a duel would be kept, and she would be none the wiser.

"You wish to leave right away?" Gabriel cocked a brow at him.

They were both eager for this particular task to be done and over. It was dangerous, stealing into the viscount's house in the dead of night.

"Yes. I do not wish to be away longer than necessary." Sebastian wished the matter dealt with quickly. The time was better spent seducing his wife.

Upon informing Ivy of his impending departure, explaining an urgent matter required his presence at one of his smaller, nearby estates, her eyes narrowed slightly. She did not smile in understanding nor did she ask to accompany him. Sebastian held her hands, told his lie, and when he finished, she carefully pulled from his grasp. With the primness of a schoolmistress, her fingers laced together and dropped to her lap.

"Will you be back tomorrow?" She sounded indifferent.

"By dawn, I imagine." Sebastian frowned. "My apologies for being forced to miss dinner. I've enjoyed our evenings together."

"It is of no matter." She waved in breezy dismissal. "I'm certain it is only the first of many I'll spend alone."

"Ivy..." He reached for her.

Eluding him with the grace of a bullfighter, she was at the library doors before he could stop her. "Safe travels, my lord."

Sebastian's jaw clenched with annoyance at the cavalier farewell. Then, she hesitated, a hand upon the curved door lever, shoulders squared as if accepting the heaviest of burdens.

Swinging to face him, her eyes appeared wet, as though she might burst into tears. She stood motionless, a statute in the golden lit sanctuary of Beaumont's library and she took a step toward him.

Then another, and another. Sebastian was completely unprepared as she flew across the polished wood floor. Clinging to him, standing on tiptoes, pulling his head down to hers, she pressed her mouth to his. A sigh of pleasure escaped her as his arms slid around her waist, hauling her against him.

Why she willingly initiated such contact hurtled beyond his comprehension. He only knew it felt incredible to have her in his arms. His mouth moved, shaping, molding her lips, their tongues swirling in a hesitant dance. And somehow, it was bittersweet. As if the kiss was a final farewell. Dazed by the whirlwind of it, Sebastian stood overwhelmed.

Ivy seemed intent on committing each of his features to memory, her eyes brimming with tears. Why she might cry confused the hell out of him.

"Come back to me."

Her words were so softly spoken, it was uncertain she said them at all.

IT WAS NEARLY A THREE-HOUR RIDE, THE TIME PASSING SLOWLY. Sebastian wanted to return to Ivy as quickly as possible. What did she mean by that kiss? The manner of it was so puzzling, an element of desperation lurking beneath the sweetness. Were her defenses finally weakening?

Light sizzled in his brain. *She thinks I've gone to duel with Basford. She fears I will not come back.* His heart somersaulted with possibilities and relief. Ivy *wanted* him back. He was sure of it. Regardless of her ice, regardless of the pain her heart still harbored, she cared for him.

Oh, Ivy. Have you learned nothing yet? Nothing on this earth could ever keep me away from me.

Upon his return to Beaumont, he intended to prove it.

"HELLO, BASFORD."

The viscount frowned in his sleep, rolling over the best his broken arm and busted ribs allowed. While attempting to readjust the pillow, he was jerked from the bed, his body dangling a good three feet or so above the floor. Held aloft, Basford struggled, his broken arm flapping in its sling. The hard, capable hands holding him prisoner gripped bunches of his nightshirt, like a hawk holding tight to an unfortunate creature soon to be devoured.

"What the devil...!" He kicked wildly, twisting in vain, broken ribs stabbing viciously. His eyes struggled to adjust to the blackness of the room and the brightness spilling from the single lamp.

"Shut up, if you possess any desire of saving your miserable hide." A soft, deadly voice drifted from the depths of the shadows. "I find myself extremely vexed and quite willing to rid the earth of your filth."

Basford stared into the darkness beyond the glow of the lamp. His gaze drifted down to the burly fellow holding him. The man was straight from a drug-induced nightmare with that wicked scar slashing across his face. His grin revealed even, white teeth, but to the viscount, they appeared like fangs. "He means it, you know. Don't tweak his nose any further. He's got the devil's own temper, he does." The monster holding him high with such ease possessed the achingly beautiful voice of a celestial being.

"This is obviously a mistake," Basford sputtered. "I've no idea what you want or why you are here."

Ravenswood emerged from the shadows. A sinister figure clad in black, he so perfectly resembled an avenging angel of death that Basford's mouth dropped open in astonished horror. This could not be happening. It was truly a nightmare, a by-product of the opiates that sham of a doctor prescribed.

"Really?" Ravenswood's laugh was the sound of the Devil poised to collect a new soul. "You've no idea why I've come? I warned you once. Do you remember? You should have kept your distance from her."

The viscount's mouth opened and closed several times before

he managed to squawk, "You ended things with her! You've no standing to demand a duel. No right!"

Gabriel *tsked- tsked,* his head shaking in mock disappointment. Arms bulging, he was in no danger of becoming fatigued as Basford hung suspended. "Wrong answer, my fine gent. Must you insist on annoying the earl? This won't end well, should you continue."

"No need for a warning. It seems we've passed any point of negotiation." Boredom etched Ravenswood's tone. His impassive gaze raked the viscount. "Make it appear an accident."

"Wait! Wait!" The man twisted with desperate futility. "What do you want? A duel? Good God, man! You broke my arm and three of my ribs when you pitched me out of my own damned coach. It will be weeks before I can meet you on the field!"

"You are most fortunate I did not kill you that night. And this conversation bores me. Mister Rose, proceed as you will."

Gabriel lowered the viscount to the floor, happily preparing for the 'accident'.

"Wait! Goddamn it! I'll leave the country. You won't see or hear from me, I swear it. Won't tell anyone why, I'll just go. France, Ireland, you name it and I'll go there."

Ravenswood swiveled to face the viscount. His lips twisted with a cruel smile as he considered the offer. "Strangely enough, that was an option I was willing to extend. From the kindness of my heart, you understand. It's probably terrible to give you false hope, but would you care to hear the others?"

Basford's head jerked in the affirmative.

"Very well." The earl stepped closer, his black cloak swirling in a dark cloud.

The viscount shrank back. Ravenswood truly resembled Lucifer, his eyes glowing like silver chips of hellfire in the darkness of the room. Half his face remained shadowed, the other half only dimly lit. There was no mercy in his features. No hint of civility or humanity. Only a mask of retribution and absolute possessiveness for what belonged to him.

"Option one. You leave England. I do not care where you go. I would prefer America or maybe even Spain. I have no holdings in those countries and little reason to travel there. As long as you are not on English soil, I shall be content. It goes without saying you will never mention the reason for your exile. Should I hear the slightest rumor regarding the night you abducted my wife, I shall seek you out and tear you apart. Slowly. Limb from limb. And I won't care to make it appear an accident."

Basford's features registered shock.

"Ah, you did not know. As we were secretly engaged, you must understand how aggrieved I was when you abducted her." Clasping his hands behind his back, Ravenswood was a study of nonchalant violence as he murmured low in the other man's ear, "Your second choice - stay and do nothing. But I shall still challenge you to a duel. And rest assured, viscount. I *will* kill you. Whether by sword or pistol, or my bare hands, I will dispatch you to hell and take the greatest pleasure in doing so." His voice dropped to a husky whisper, as though relishing the thought of undertaking the task right then and there.

"The last option is to avoid the duel entirely as you have thus far." His smile was tight hearing Basford's gulp of relief. "This carries its own problems. Mister Rose has kindly shown me a few of his favorite methods of disposing nuisances. And what would appear nothing more than a regrettable set of circumstances to others, would unfortunately for you, result in a very painful demise. A useful skill set to be sure, but something I doubt you want to experience firsthand. Not a pretty sight, I'm afraid."

Basford swallowed against a lump of fear, eyes wide as the earl came closer to taunt him.

"I've learned the art of entering and leaving a residence so one would never know I was there. You may foolishly believe you can hide from me. Keep me from killing you. Impossible. I will always find you and be able to reach you. That's the easy part, being able to come and go anywhere, anytime without detection. A skill perfected during my time abroad."

Gabriel chuckled, giving the viscount a rough shake to gain his attention. "Those particular adventures usually involved females, milord. You understand my meaning?" He nudged the man's broken ribs with a blunt elbow to emphasize his words, eliciting a sharp groan of pain.

"So, I will allow you a choice, although it goes against the grain to do so." Ravenswood flicked a speck of imaginary lint from his black cloak. He eyed Basford in a way clearly indicating he hoped the choice allowed the opportunity to dispatch the young lord slowly, painfully and at his leisure. "Make it now. I grow weary of the time spent in your presence."

The viscount did not consider matters for long, his choice made before option two was enumerated. "I shall leave the country. I shall go to France...to see a specialist for my injuries. Then, to Spain. I shall leave within the week."

"Tomorrow." This was murmured in a most ruthless manner.

"*Tomorr-*" Basford's protest died a quick death when a deadly light flared in the earl's eyes. "Yes, yes. Tomorrow. How-how long must I stay away?"

"A lifetime," Was the cold reply. "Or until I deem your life no longer a nuisance to the countess or myself."

"I see." The earl would allow him to live. The viscount sagged with relief; his head still reeling with the news Ravenswood had married Ivy. How the hell did he managed it so quickly?

"Excellent." Ravenswood nodded to Gabriel who loosened his grip so Basford could stand on his own once more. "Although, my man here is sorely disappointed. There are so few opportunities to hone our particular skillset." He stepped closer while Gabriel grinned in unabashed delight, subtly moving a few paces away from the viscount.

"There are a few matters I cannot, in good conscience, depart here without seeing done. If you will indulge me?" Ravenswood's tone was deceptively soothing.

"Anything. Anything." Basford gulped, nodding in furious

desperation. He wanted nothing more than for these men leave his home.

He was completely unprepared for the fist slamming into his jaw. The sheer force of it spun him around, knocking him onto the bed. His head spun dizzily before the world tilted to dump him in a painful heap on his shattered arm. The broken and cracked ribs robbed him of breath. Bile rushed to the top of his throat, the searing pain choking him until he teetered on the verge of blacking out.

"That is for terrorizing her." Ravenswood snatched Basford back up to his feet, his hands hard and hurtful before tossing him to the other man. With a terse nod, Gabriel's hand immediately covered the viscount's mouth, and he held him upright.

"And this is for hurting her, you bastard. For bruising her. For making her bleed. For daring to touch what is *mine*." Ravenswood drove a fist into Basford's flank, breaking the tenuous knitting job Nature had begun on the broken ribs. Two completely healthy ribs cracked, an agonized groan muffled behind Gabriel's huge hand. Leaning close to the sagging man, eyes burning with the fires of hell, the earl said, "Never speak of her. Not even to mention her name in passing. *Ever.* If I discover you ignored my warning, our next encounter will make this one seem like a pleasant daydream."

The viscount watched with bleary eyes as Ravenswood exited the room, a hazy swirl of black melting into the dark night. Gabriel's laughing, melodic words buzzed in his ears while he hovered on the edge of pained unconsciousness.

"I told you the earl was vexed."

CHAPTER 30

*S*ebastian expected to find Ivy in his bed. He expected to climb between the sheets and hold her close, even while his body screamed for release. Sleep would be elusive, but he expected that too.

His bed was empty; the coverlet pulled back, the sheets icy cold. No warmth lingered on Ivy's pillow. The adjoining bedchamber was empty and unused and she was not in the bathing room. Sebastian stood in the middle of the suite. Where could she be?

Perhaps the library. She was quite taken with it - his search would begin there. Then he would rouse the whole damn house to search for his wife.

The faint glow of firelight emanating from the library flooded him with relief. Securing the doors behind him, the soft click of the lock barely discernible, Sebastian scanned the room. A divan was pulled close to one of the two fireplaces. Its high back concealed the plush cushions, but a flimsy, pale blue robe trailed over one of the gently rolled arms, the edges brushing the floor. A lamp cast a feeble radiance on a stack of books piled haphazardly upon a large table beside the divan.

Ivy lay curled on the dark cranberry hued settee, like a delicious bonbon on a wrapping of velvet just waiting to be consumed. The fire snapped as he gazed down at her, the popping sounds loud in the stillness. With the drapes drawn shut on the wall of windows, only the light of the flames and the single lamp cast wild, elongated shadows on his wife. A thick, cream colored blanket covered her and one foot, clad in a delicate blue silk slipper, hung from the edge of the cushioned seat.

Her hair was not pulled into the usual braid she wore to bed. Tangled in it, tucked under her cheek, her hand cradled her face. Sebastian smiled. It was his wife's favored position when she slept. He woke every morning to find her thus against his chest. It was impossibly endearing.

Kneeling beside the settee, he used his forefinger to gently traced the stains tracking down her cheeks. She'd been weeping.

"Ivy." He brushed a honey sparked curl from her brow. "Wake up."

She mumbled something unintelligible, eyelashes fluttering as she drew the blanket closer to her chin. Sebastian leaned forward, his mouth pressed to hers. He kissed her more insistently until her eyes drifted open.

"Hello, love," he murmured.

Ivy reached out, her warm fingertips drifting over his jaw. A strange expression, something bordering on relief, flashed across her features. "You came back."

"And what else could I do? I cannot exist without you." Sebastian did not expect to find his arms filled with her.

Ivy's embrace was fierce, her arms wrapping tight about him. He moved to sit on the divan and she immediately adjusted until she was completely in his grasp, her face buried in his neck.

"I said I would be back by dawn." He tried to sound nonchalant, tried not to notice the frothy excuse for a nightgown she wore. The same pale blue, it matched the discarded wrapper and Ivy's flesh glowed through it. The sight and scent of her made Sebastian's body react violently. His hands, curled about her waist, shook as her warmth seeped through the fabric of her gown to heat his palms. He felt both hot and cold. "Did you think I would not return?"

Damn, he tired of sidestepping their issues, tired of hoping his wife might open her arms and her heart to him.

It was time to resolve matters. Tonight.

"I DID NOT KNOW WHAT TO THINK." IVY KNEW IT WAS IMPOSSIBLE to tell Sebastian she could not sleep in his bed, surrounded by his scent, tortured by memories of how gently he held her that first morning at Beaumont. How could she explain that his kisses rattled her soul when she did not understand it herself? How to explain that she could not bear to be where he was not?

She came to the library, thinking a book would help her sleep, to ease her mind. But nothing pulled from the shelves captivated her. Instead, she roamed the library until collapsing in self-defeat on one of the divans.

She could not tell him she foolishly cried herself into an exhausted slumber.

"You thought I would not return," Sebastian prodded, grasping her by the shoulders to peer into her eyes.

Ivy knew she could not answer *that*. She could not put to words how devastating it felt, knowing he was gone and might never return. Watching him ride away caused a burning, empty ache in the pit of her stomach.

Her brow knitting in confusion, she shied from acknowledging his statement. "I don't understand. Duels are undertaken at daybreak. Is the viscount dead?"

"There will be no duel. And when I left Basford, he was very much alive. Frightened half out of his wits, what little he has, but alive. More's the pity, I think." Cupping Ivy's chin, Sebastian tipped her face so the firelight illuminated it. "The last thing I want to do is discuss Brandon Madsen. I wish to speak of us and our particular situation."

"Why is there to be no duel?" Ivy believed it unlikely Sebastian would relinquish the opportunity to make Brandon pay for his crime. Why would he?

The sound escaping Sebastian was both groan and chuckle. "We won't move past this unless I explain. So, listen carefully, my love. The viscount will be taking an extended trip abroad. Indeed, he may never set foot on English soil again; at least not while either of us live."

Suspicion glinted in her eyes. "Why would he do that?"

"I persuaded him to it. There will be no duel and no talk of scandal. No one, other than those close to us, will know what occurred. You can be certain Basford will never mention it, at least as long as he values his life."

"But Basford's coachman. He -"

"Is now in my employ, happy and handsomely paid, I might add. Your next question undoubtedly concerns my aunt. The threat of exile to one of my northern estates in Scotland and the cutoff of her generous allowance gains her silence as well. Our dearest friends, Alan and Sara? You know they will never breathe a word. I have taken care of it. I will always take care of things." Sebastian's eyes held hers, burning and dark. "I will *always* take care of you."

"I know I was abducted." Ivy's challenge was soft but direct. "You cannot make it disappear as though it never happened."

He smiled. "Can't I? Are you a loose string, my dear? Shall I tie you up as neatly as I have the others? I have ways to make you forget that awful night. To erase it from your mind until it never existed."

Tugging her to him, his mouth descended upon hers in a flurry of heat and desire and for an instant, Ivy almost wrenched herself from him, the fear of giving into him almost a conditioned response.

But she did not. Instead, she melted, hot and fluid, squirming closer to the heat of his body. Sebastian kissed her almost roughly, but she loved it. His tongue swept the inside of her mouth, meeting and entangling with hers until she wanted more. She sighed low in her throat, ready to capitulate to him.

Drawing back at the sound, Sebastian appeared to contemplate his next action, and Ivy did not dare look away from his diamond bright eyes.

"Unbutton my shirt," he finally said in a hoarse whisper.

As she did his bidding, her hands trembled. One by one, the ivory buttons slipped from their moorings until at last, the garment lay open to his waist. Without his directive, she pulled the shirt tails from his breeches until the edges fluttered open, exposing his chest and the slabs of golden, sleek muscles there.

Sebastian sucked in a quick breath as her fingertips skated across his flesh. With her feet tucked underneath her, Ivy could get no closer unless she crawled across his lap or she laid back against the divan. She was not sure which she wanted. With a brazen decision, she pressed herself to him, laying across his thighs.

"I like this nightgown." He traced a pattern on her back while she huddled against his chest.

Ivy trembled with the reality of her decision. She was about to become Sebastian's wife. His *real* wife. Kissing him and touching him like this, there was no escaping the path she'd set. "Should I remove it?" She ached for him to say yes.

"There's no rush." Sebastian shifted, slipping the shirt from his shoulders to toss to the side. His eyes, dark and solemn, locked with hers. He gently pushed until she was prone on the settee and he loomed over her. The slide of her gown against the sensitive peaks of her breasts when he moved was both tantalizing and torture. Ivy wanted to arch while at the same time she wanted to pull his body down more firmly atop hers. She groaned in frustration when he placed more distance between them.

Bracing himself with elbows on either side of her head, he leisurely traced the outline of her lips with his tongue, playfully teasing the corners of her mouth before taking it fully. He swirled and teased and dipped and tasted until Ivy was breathless and straining, her hands plunging into the dark silk of his hair.

Sebastian tore his mouth away to drag kisses across her throat, down to the vee of skin exposed by the bodice of the nightgown. She held his head tight, desperate to feel his mouth upon her. Sensing what she wanted, he moved even lower, until the heat of his lips closed over her nipple, wetting the flesh through the thin cloth as he bit and nibbled.

Ivy couldn't help but moan. She wanted more. She wanted his mouth on her bare skin. She wanted his hands on her nakedness. She wanted his fingers inside her, his body inside her. She wanted him to take her to heights that left her drunk with pleasure.

She wanted him. Wanted. Needed. Craved.

Sebastian lavished the same treatment on her other breast until Ivy writhed beneath him, the hem of her nightgown riding high on her hips. He swept the bare skin of her outer thigh with his hand before settling in a firm grasp of her buttocks. She felt the ridge of his sex trapped as it nestled against the damp cleft of her body when he jerked her closer.

With an impatient growl, he whipped the nightgown over her head. Ivy's sigh of surrender echoed in the room. Clutching his shoulders, she opened to him when his hand slipped between their bodies.

A whimper of gratification escaped her. With maddening deliberateness, he speared through the chestnut curls at the junction of her legs before dipping inside her.

Ivy's body clenched around the invasion.

"Sweet Jesus, Ivy," Sebastian muttered, ravishing her mouth while she quaked with need. His finger leisurely plunged in and out of her slick passage, pausing to swirl the pinpoint of her desire, his thumb nudging the exceedingly sensitive crest there.

Beyond the point of shame, Ivy clasped his hand, pressing it urgently against her throbbing flesh. She sobbed aloud from a frenzied torrent of sensations.

Sebastian froze, all exquisite movements coming to an abrupt halt. Slowly, he lifted his head, the glowing victory in his gaze unconcealed, but Ivy did not care. She wanted him too desperately to care.

"You will recall my words, Ivy." His eyes deliberately bored into hers.

"Sebastian." A thread of panic laced through the solitary word. Not for what he might do, but because he might stop doing these wonderful things.

"Tell me," he demanded in a raspy whisper, his eyes burning like pieces of silver in the firelight. "Not because I must hear it, but so you acknowledge *you* want this. There will be no going back. No changing your mind. And I won't have you accuse me of deceiving or forcing you." He bit the words out, his voice strangled, his body taut with need. "If I must stop, if you still need time to accept the fact you are my wife, then tell me. Tell me now so I may set you from me while I still possess the strength to do so."

Ivy gazed at him, her eyes slumberous, every nerve thrilling to the feel of his finger filling her. He did not move, just waited for her to decide. Her hand, which only seconds ago feverishly pressed his palm to her flesh, came up to tentatively caress his clenched jaw.

Expecting a rapid halt to the seduction, Sebastian regarded her, wary frustration unmistakable in the hardness of his face. He started to slide away.

"*Don't…,*" Ivy panted, the glide of his fingers dissolving her insides into an inferno, "*…stop.*"

She arched to him, pressing desperate kisses to his throat, dragging him down to her, the words a breathy entreaty inflaming them both. "*Don't stop.* God, don't stop. I need you. I want you. If you wish to hear me beg, then I shall. Please, Sebastian, please *don't stop…*"

Sebastian hesitated, and with a gruff cry, claimed what was his. What was always his.

An answering thrill of wild sweetness raced through Ivy's veins. There was something wickedly carnal in the fact she was utterly naked while he still wore breeches and boots, only his chest bare to her exploration. She wanted to discover every part of him, to learn why his muscles rippled when he moved a certain way, why he groaned as her fingertips skimmed his hard, dark nipples, to know why his breath rattled harsh and hot as her hand drifted to the top of his breeches and coasted along the flat plane of his abdomen.

Sebastian had other ideas.

"Damn it, Ivy. It seems like forever since I touched you, held you. A lifetime since I made you quiver with pleasure." Capturing her hands in one of his, Sebastian dragged them above her head, and bending his head to her breasts, he took each into the wet furnace of his mouth in turn, licking, biting with restrained excitement until her nipples hardened into sensitive peaks. He resumed the exploration of the junction between her thighs, his fingers gliding in and out, over and around until Ivy trembled uncontrollably and waves crashed over her without warning.

When she cried out, he smothered it with the heat of his mouth, sweeping it away until the only sound in the room was the popping crackle of the fire and their mutual, harsh breathing. When he finally released her hands, she weakly wrapped her arms around his neck.

Sebastian sat up, pulling Ivy sideways into his lap, her legs dangling over his thighs. His palm coasted down the smooth expanse of her back, tracing the delicate line of her spine while she shivered, overwhelmed by sensations and emotions. Huddling against him, she absorbed his heat until he reached for the cream-colored blanket, settling it over her shoulders.

"I'm not cold," Ivy murmured against his neck, kissing the corded muscles there with soft, presses of her mouth. She did not make any effort to remove the blanket, wondering if he believed she needed it for modesty's sake. She would not take it away just yet. What went on beneath that blanket was secret and hot and private, a little world where nothing else existed except kisses and caresses and whispers of desire.

She alternated the kisses with little bites as he had done to her in the past. Every time her teeth raked his skin, he groaned in approval. Experimentally, she licked a spot below his jaw before lightly biting his earlobe. He tasted salty and clean, shuddering in response to her exploration.

"Is it alright to do this?" Her palms spread across his chest, feeling the powerful muscles bunch beneath her fingertips.

"God, yes." His sharp laugh was incredulous. "Touch, kiss, bite to your heart's content. If you don't kill me first."

"Even here?" Ivy whispered, her hands drifting down to the bulge in his breeches. Running a shy finger over the rise beneath the fabric, his low groan thrilled her. It was a revelation to discover she could tease and torment him as he did her.

"No. I won't be able to control myself if I allow you that," he said. "I've no intention of making love to you, our first time as husband and wife, on a damn settee in the library when we have a magnificent bed at our disposal."

"I want to touch you. To feel you in my hands. Like I did that day by the stream. Please, Sebastian." Ivy kissed him, using her mouth to persuade him while her hands worked the buttons to his breeches.

Sebastian stared at her as though he'd lost all his wits, and she continued to undress him when his hands quivered, unable to halt her progress. She explored the hollow of his throat, pressing her lips where his pulse beat in quick thumps. One by one, each button slipped free until his erection eased from the tight confines of the breeches and into the warmth of her hands. Sebastian adjusted the blanket, hiding the wickedness of her fingers as Ivy leaned back.

The breath hissed through his teeth in a desperate bid to hold tight to his sanity. She gently traced the length of him, her fingers closing about him, encircling the silky hardness and his eyes shut as if he could not bear it. Her hand moved from base to velvety tip, marveling that his skin was both soft and hot, burning her palm.

At Bentley Park, she'd not taken the time to learn the length, the shape, or the true extent of his size, but she did now. Her fingers drifted, soft at first, then with a firmer grip as he grew even larger with her touch. When Sebastian muttered a curse beneath his breath, Ivy's courage faltered. "Does this hurt? I'm sorry."

"No, it doesn't hurt." His laugh was shaky as he removed her hand from his body. "It feels good. Too damn good. But you have to stop. Before you drive me completely mad."

While he held her wrist in a grip that should have frightened her, Ivy slid to the floor between his knees. Somehow, the blanket stayed draped over her shoulders and she was glad for the little bit of concealment for what she was about to do.

He stared at her and she at him until with an inarticulate sound of pleasure, Ivy did the only thing reasonable at that moment. Lowering her head, she wrapped her mouth around his erection until its silken thickness of nudged the back of her throat.

Sebastian buried his free hand in the mass of her hair, fingers raking her scalp as if to pull her away. The grip on her wrist tightened to the point of bruising her, but Sebastian seemed unaware.

"My God..."

The oath, and the others following, were incoherent as Ivy instinctively moved her head, twisting her tongue in a leisurely exploration of his thick length, mimicking what she'd done with her hands only moments before.

He was so hard and yet the skin stretched so thin and impossibly tight over a surging of power. There was a swelling of feminine potency within her, learning that she could render him helpless. She lifted to the top of his shaft as if to stop, then filled her mouth with as much of him as possible, moaning in response when he uttered a word she'd heard him say only twice in anger.

"Fuck..."

The next thing Ivy knew, she was up in his lap once again, his eyes boring into hers. A wildness existed in those depths and Ivy felt a sense of power like nothing she'd ever experienced. It was heady and dangerous. And addictive.

Sebastian slid a palm over the curve of her hip and Ivy realized his intent to lift her away. Twisting almost violently, she shifted to straddle him. Gripping the back of the settee, one hand on either side of his head, she levered herself down. Her breasts bobbed eye level with his fascinated stare; to accommodate the width of his muscular thighs, her legs spread. If she lowered herself completely, she would be impaled. She wanted that desperately.

"For God's sake, Ivy." His breath was ragged. "Stop this madness."

"No. I won't stop," she replied, staring into his smoky eyes. "Not yet." Her gaze dropped to where their bodies almost touched. His erection strained to reach her softness beneath the shroud of the blanket.

Clasping both of his hands around her hips, Sebastian braced again to remove her from the tantalizing position. But he seemed incapable of forcing his body to obey the commands of his own mind when she rocked her hips forward.

"Bloody hell," he groaned, his body jerking to awareness as the underside of his erection slipped through the curls between her thighs.

It was not penetration, just a maddening glide through silky wet heat.

Ivy was caught off guard by the sensation. She thought it might feel similar to when he used his hands and fingers to stoke her passion, but this was altogether more exciting. This was something else, something electrifying and provocative. Quivering with the need to do it again, she slid down a second time. Then a third time. A fourth, her arousal creating a slick, easy slide. It was all wicked and wonderful and irresistible. And she could not stop. She would not stop...

SEBASTIAN FOUGHT FOR CONTROL, FOR SANITY, FOR A REASON TO haul Ivy off him; to put an end to this glorious torture. Every time she floated up, then down, he burned to bury inside her, to plunge into her heat until he was so deep within her soul she would never escape. He gripped her with the desperation of a drowning man, feeling the trembling of her body as though it were his own. Every gasp of breath she exhaled burned him as if somehow, they passed through his lungs first.

If she did not cease, he would explode.

"Ivy, we must stop. I cannot...we can't...I don't want to make love to you here, for chrissakes. It should be in my bed, where I can lay you out. I want to kiss you all over, caress every inch of you. Kiss you everywhere." His words came in a heated, jumbled, incoherent mess while she ignored him, sliding up and down. Again and again.

Until finally, Sebastian gripped her hips tight, holding her in position to prevent a downward stroke. Held open by the muscled width of his thighs, the entrance to her body bare and ready for him, she was undaunted by his callousness.

"Damn it, Ivy." The words were a growl. "I said we are not doing this here."

With a flash of something dangerous in her eyes, Ivy reached up to her shoulder. "We aren't?" She dragged the blanket away.

Sebastian choked. And cursed.

Damn her. For all her innocence, she knew precisely how to tip the scales in her favor, to drive him past the point of no return. The abrupt exposure of his countess, riding him with the supreme confidence of a beautiful pagan goddess, backlit by the firelight's glow, hair streaming in dark waves over her shoulders, curling around her breasts, tumbling to the small of her back, after she just wrapped her lips around his cock, was too much. He was only a man after all, and he had wanted her for too long to reject what she so sweetly offered now.

He was lost.

"Make me yours, Sebastian. Now. I don't care where we are... do it now. *Now.*" She kissed him, her tongue swirling to touch his.

His groan was one of defeat. He could not fight the power of Ivy's arousal for it fueled his own to dizzying, scorching heights.

His blood sizzled with the need to claim, to possess, to conquer. She was his. Every sweet inch of her.

"Except her heart." Came a sly voice inside his head. *"She has yet to give you her heart and probably never will again."*

Sebastian ignored that voice to focus on the exquisite creature in his arms. Now, he held her steady, guiding her down upon him and every heartbeat brought him closer to pulsating warmth, the silky tightness of her body almost more than he could stand, more than he thought it possible to bear. Once he was fully inside her, they both became motionless as Ivy adjusted to the full, burning pressure of his possession. Sebastian felt unaccountably dizzy, his body acclimating to the feeling of her holding him deep within her. He could not breathe. He gripped her with almost hurtful fingers attempting to keep her still upon him because her buttocks resting atop his thighs was both heaven and hell.

"What do I do now?" She whispered mischievously in his ear and he grinned.

"Little hellion. Now you ride."

CHAPTER 31

*I*vy grasped the carved wood top of the divan and using it for leverage, her hips began a slow, tantalizing rise and fall. The sensations were exquisite, although there was an intense compulsion to rotate against Sebastian. She had no control over her body. It instinctively knew what to do to create immense pleasure for them both.

He did not object. His hands roamed over her curved rear, then gripping her waist before drifting further upward. He rubbed tantalizing circles over her sensitive nipples then cupped her breasts, the weight of them filling his palms. Wherever his fingers trailed, tingling explosions of sensations burst until Ivy thought she might actually go up in flames.

He splayed his hands below her shoulder blades, his mouth locking on a peach crested breast, her nipple sucked and twirled into scorching heat. Ivy gasped as he raked the bud with his teeth, flicking it repeatedly with his tongue until it puckered. Her breath quickened, her skin warming by degrees until she was a burning flame beneath his palms. When he lavished the same care to her other breast, Ivy abandoned her hold on the divan. Her head fell back until her hair brushed against the tops of his thighs and she realized with a dazed sort of bemusement that he still wore his breeches, the garment pushed down to accommodate her naked body straddling him.

Sebastian held her hips, helping her rise up and down upon his body. Ivy braced her hands against his broad chest, trembling at the sensation of being filled so completely. When she moaned, his hand pressed against her lips to stifle the sounds of her mounting pleasure. Without a second thought, Ivy took his fingers into her mouth, twirling her tongue around them as her body stiffened.

"Damnit, Ivy," Sebastian choked, captivated by the sight of her lips wrapped about his fingers. And Ivy knew...he was thinking of his erection in her mouth. Because she was thinking of it too.

The pleasure was too piercing, too great to bear. It overwhelmed her, sucking her into a dark whirlpool. Nothing kept her from drowning in the depths of obsession as she struggled to breathe, to comprehend the tidal wave of feelings flooding her. When she bit him, it was sheer reflex, a primal way of balancing out the intense pleasure when the climax shattered her. Sebastian grunted as her sharp teeth scored his index finger.

The flurry of her body tightening around him, the pulsating intensity of the tremors and her high, restrained sob of satisfaction sent his lust spiking to summits never before reached. Ripping his hand away, he pulled her down, hard, forcefully, until he exploded inside her with a muffled shout.

As Ivy quivered, still riding her own wave of pleasure, Sebastian crushed her to him, devouring her mouth with fierce kisses, silently telling her she belonged to him and no one else. He kissed her until she was soft and compliant in his arms; until she kissed him back so gently, it made him aware just how tightly he held her.

His grip loosened slightly. Ivy sighed, burrowing into his chest. Pressing languid kisses to his neck and the tops of his shoulders, she huddled close while Sebastian exhaled slowly, catching his breath. They dozed off to sleep while he was still buried deep within her, Ivy's soft breath fanning his jaw.

~

Sebastian roused himself from a surprisingly comfortable position. An overwhelming giddiness permeated his entire being. He lay prone on the settee, arms folded about Ivy's waist, his head against her temple. She sprawled over him like an imperious kitten. Half aroused, his erection waited inside her, twitching in response to the feminine scent and heat surrounding him.

For God's sake, he still wore his breeches and boots. Biting back a rueful grin, Sebastian slid her from his lap, using his shirt to wipe the stickiness from her thighs and from herself. When he drew the blanket over her, Ivy mumbled in her sleep, curling her legs on the settee while trying to wrap her arms around his neck.

"Sweetness, we must go up to bed. It would not do for the servants to discover us here in the morning." He smiled when she frowned in drowsy disagreement.

"Mmmm, lock the door."

"A brilliant idea, my love, but I did that before. Come now. I'll help you dress."

Sebastian fastened his breeches, fingers fumbling as he gazed down at her curled on the cranberry colored velvet. The fire burned low, making it difficult to make out her features, but he knew every sweet curve and angle of her face. Tracing the pertness of her nose with a forefinger, he slipped an arm beneath her to pull her upright.

Ivy's eyes never opened as he slipped her nightgown over her head and pulled her arms into the matching wrapper. "It's inside out," she murmured, swaying in drowsy acceptance of his assistance.

"That doesn't matter, love." He located her slippers under the divan.

"For a countess it does," Ivy yawned.

When the slippers were on her delicate feet and the robe wrapped securely, Sebastian stepped away to make sure the fire was properly banked. Once that was done, he twisted about to find

Ivy slumped back onto the seat of the divan, her hands curved beneath under her cheek.

"Oh, for the love of..." He bit off the remainder of a bemused curse then scooped his exhausted wife up into his arms.

With a fervent hope no insomniac servant roamed the halls, he carried her through the darkened mansion. Upon reaching their bedchamber, he laid her gently on the bed then tended the fire until it burned merrily in the hearth. Hastily stripping off his breeches and boots, Sebastian climbed between the sheets and Ivy immediately gravitated to him, curving against his side, her legs twining with his.

Sebastian pondered Ivy's surrender, the willingness to make their marriage a true one. Did she truly believe he would not survive a duel with Basford? Or, had she finally accepted the inevitability of being his?

Whatever it was, Sebastian decided, settling back against the pillows and pulling her closer, he was grateful.

CHAPTER 32

*S*ebastian gently pushed the hair from her face and a faint smile lifted Ivy's lips. Resisting the urge to stretch, images from the library flashed in her mind, awakening her body in ways she never thought possible.

"What are you thinking, Ivy Cain? Some new way to shock me?" Sebastian's bemused voice was low and husky as she nestled her cheek into the palm of his hand.

It was close to dawn, the light dim, the fire long ago reduced to embers. She had a vague memory of Sebastian carrying her upstairs while she clung to him. Swallowing a laugh, Ivy wondered what might have happened if a servant crossed their path.

"If you must know, I thought the whole experience amazing." Her gaze didn't waver as Sebastian's brow rose in astonishment. "And I wonder, if there are other places we could…"

"Your recent change of heart intrigues me," Sebastian murmured, caressing her soft cheek before sliding his hand along her jawline. His fingers eventually ended in her tangled mass of hair.

Ivy could not fully explain this sudden willingness to be in his arms, and the justification of providing a Ravenswood heir was not the sole reason. Only she was too cowardly, and maybe too prideful, to admit it.

"I'm not complaining, mind you." His soft laugh was wicked. "Maybe I like being surprised. Now, it's my turn."

"What do you mean?" Rational thought was difficult with this gorgeous man wrapped so completely around her. When he rolled over her, Ivy's legs parted with distressing eagerness.

"Let me show you." His lips pressed against the curve of her neck. Nibbling his way up until he reached her lips, Sebastian coaxed her mouth open. When she obeyed, his tongue slipped inside to begin long, languid sweeps, encouraging Ivy to kiss him in the same manner. It was an unhurried, persistent assault.

Ivy became caught in that kiss, aware he was slowly edging her nightgown higher. The fabric bunched at her waist, at her breasts then, in a fluid movement, was whipped over her head. Bare at last, with only heat between them.

Sebastian held there. Unmoving and silent. Just stillness, two bodies molded together, legs tangled, skin burning, hearts pounding in an effort to find a common beat. Ivy's eyes widened as her body slowed to accommodate his and Sebastian's accelerated for hers until one steady thump existed between them.

"I've dreamt of this since the first time I saw you, warding off your damn Pack, steadfastly ignoring me. I wanted you then - wanted to press myself against you. To imprint myself on your soul as you have imprinted on mine." His lips pressed to her temple. "Do you feel our hearts beating as if it were one, Ivy? Do you feel me waiting to come inside you? My sweet, sweet little butterfly. I won't ever let you go again; you are too precious to me. I love you. Too damn much."

Ivy did not say anything, frightened by the power he held over her. She could not risk laying bare her heart so easily and so soon after having it trampled and broken.

No. She could not say the words yet.

If her silence angered or upset him, Sebastian did not reveal it. His lips were gentle when he kissed her, his hands smoothing over her skin in reverence. He made love to her so tenderly and so expertly that by the end, when she sobbed his name in release, Ivy miserably suspected it was only a matter of time before all of her was completely and utterly his once more.

Including her treacherous heart, which he just proved he could easily control.

~

DAMNIT, WHAT STEPS MUST I TAKE TO ENSURE NO ONE DISTURBS US IN the mornings?

Sprawled against his side, one leg hiked and riding his thigh, Ivy's arm lay carelessly thrown across his waist. Her cheek rested on the muscles of his bicep; her hair was a wild, tangled mess streaming away on the silk pillows. They made love as dawn broke then fell asleep. It was well past morning now.

The knock came again, a bit more insistent, and this time Ivy did stir. Her brow pulled into a disapproving frown and rolling away from him, she burrowed beneath the covers. With a grunt of annoyance, Sebastian rose from the bed and threw on a robe. "Whoever is beating my door at such an ungodly hour, there'd best be a goddamn good reason for it." He jerked open the door.

"I've obviously committed a grave error this morning. Or I should say, afternoon. It is, after all, the noon hour. Do you and milady plan to stay abed all day?" Gabriel stood in the doorway, holding the usual tray loaded with coffee and teapots, along with a plateful of sugar biscuits and a vase containing a single cream-colored rose.

Sebastian glared at the man before taking the platter. "You would do well to remember our agreement. Return when I ring for you. In the meantime, have Chef prepare a light lunch."

"Very well. I thought you may be interested to hear our friend did indeed vacate his manor this morning. He is en route to Bristol to catch the next ship leaving for France. And milady's gift arrived this very morning." Gabriel laughed as Sebastian nodded, and using his foot since he now held the platter, unceremoniously shut the door in his face.

Placing the tray next to the bed, Sebastian poured coffee for himself and a cup of tea for Ivy. Almost gingerly, he sat on the edge of the bed to awaken his wife.

She turned to him with drowsy eyes when he shook her shoulder. Staring at each other, each remembered the events from the night past. And that morning.

"Good morning, love," he said, as Ivy smiled and pulled herself to a sitting position.

Clutching the coverlet to her naked body with one hand, she accepted the teacup. "Is it still morning?"

"Truthfully, it's noon and there is no rush to jump from bed. I vow that's the best sleep I've had in months."

Ivy's aqua eyes smoldered with a mischievous light. "And I as well. Do you think lovemaking to be the cause for our perfect slumber?"

Sebastian chuckled, his gaze dropping to where she held the covers to her bosom. With her sparkling eyes and that wild tumbling hair cascading over creamy bare shoulders, she looked sinfully delicious. "I've no doubt that's true, and on that subject, would you care to undertake a little experiment this morning?"

"Afternoon." Ivy automatically corrected, her voice high with nervous excitement. "What do you have in mind, my lord?"

Taking the teacup from her, Sebastian set it on the tray. Slowly, inch by inch, he tugged the covers from her grasp until she was bare. Ivy shivered, but let him gaze his fill in the soft light. "Have you wondered if that tub is big enough for two?" he murmured, reaching out to brush her hair back from one soft shoulder.

"I have." Ivy did not look away from the possessive light in his eyes. "And is it?"

"I'll let you determine that"

CHAPTER 33

*T*hat same afternoon, Sebastian led Ivy to the stables. Samuel, the stable master, met them in the entranceway, his smile warm with welcome before making an excuse to disappear quite abruptly.

Ivy gave Sebastian a quizzical glance at the man's odd behavior just as he reemerged from one of the aisles, leading a dappled grey mare. The horse's polished hooves danced a delicate tattoo on the cobblestones, her head high as the stable master grinned with pride. Ivy's eyes lit up, a longing on her features that could not be concealed.

"Her name is Spring," Sebastian said, taking the lead rope from Samuel. The horse gazed at them with dark, sweet eyes then butted a finely molded head against Ivy's shoulder in curiosity.

Ivy ran a hand down the sleek neck. "She's perfect. And so beautiful."

"No denying that," Sebastian agreed. "She's one of Raven's get. I bred him to one of Bentley's finest mares before I left England and to our surprise, that mare threw twin foals. Alan gifted the filly over to me and kept the colt." He ran his hand over the mare's flank, pleased when she did not nervously dance away.

371

She was a good mount for Ivy; spirited and gentle. "She's yours, if you would like her." Smoothing his hand over Spring's rump, he gave it a light, affectionate slap. "Or, if you rather, you may have your choice of any horse in our stables. We can even journey to Tattersall's...I will purchase whatever horse you..."

"Oh, I love her, Sebastian," Ivy interrupted, her face glowing. "She reminds me of my pony, Heather. She's retired at Somerset Hall, the old girl. They are almost the same color, although Spring is certainly taller, nor as plump. I shall go change into my riding habit at once."

Sebastian shook his head in regret, smiling at her impulsiveness. "Have you noticed the lateness of the hour, love? It will be nightfall soon. Tomorrow, we'll set out and explore the estate and you can ride her then. It pleases me that you like her but she only arrived this morning, so a bit of settling is best on her first day."

Ivy glanced out the double doors of the stables. The afternoon had quickly slipped away. Stable boys lined up buckets of oats for the evening rations while high overhead in the lofts, other lads tossed down hay into the individual stalls. She stroked Spring's velvety nose, leaning to breathe deep her sweet horsey smell. "You are right. It's so hard to wait, but tomorrow will be a lovely day to ride. Thank you, Sebastian. Thank you for gifting her to me."

Sebastian handed the mare's lead rope to her and crossed over to Raven's roomy corner box. Slipping inside, he ran a hand down the stallion's legs, checking for any lingering effects from their late night ride. Giving the restless horse an identical pat on the rump, Sebastian's words drifted to Ivy standing outside the stall.

"I rode Raven fairly hard last night, but he'll be itching to get out tomorrow. He's not one to appreciate confinement."

Sebastian leaned over Raven's stall door, his eyes dancing. Ivy's cheeks were pink. Studying Spring's dappled pattern, she traced the curve of the mare's slightly dished nose before sneaking a glance at him. Her sudden silence must be in response to the unspoken reminder of what occurred in the library and that morning. Exiting the box, he retrieved Spring's lead rope, guiding the mare back to her stall with a clucking sound.

"Why doesn't he like it?" Ivy asked, an odd breathiness to her voice.

Sebastian shot her an inquiring glance as he closed the stall door, throwing the iron latch to secure it.

His wife was truly dazzling. Like a sweet piece of fruit, she stood in the center of the cobblestone aisle way. The apple green dress turned her eyes to a sparkling shade of emerald, dust motes dancing about her, caught in shafts of late afternoon sunlight. The stable boys, busy with their chores in anticipation of the end of the workday, buzzed about her like industrious bees, unable to take their eyes off her.

"Samuel," Sebastian called out, his eyes never once leaving her face as the man came jogging up. "We require the use of your office. Her Ladyship feels a bit faint. Just the excitement of the new horse, I'm sure, but a moment of privacy will be appreciated."

Ivy stared at him in amazement when he took her arm. Before she could voice an objection, Samuel wholeheartedly offered the use of his office for as long as necessary, although everyone understood Sebastian did not need to provide an explanation for its use. The Earl of Ravenswood could go and do whatever he desired.

Sebastian directed Ivy to the opposite end of the building and into a spacious room. It was an orderly space. A battered and scarred oak desk containing various stacks of paperwork relating to the operation of the stables took up most of one corner. Pieces of bridles and snaffle bits were interspersed among the papers, with some used as paperweights. Against one wall was a narrow cot, useful for when the mares were in foal, and a spot was required to rest.

Shutting the door behind them, Sebastian lit a lantern to supplement the golden light streaming through the upper gallery style windows. A traditional window just behind the desk was open to the late afternoon breeze. Pastures were visible through it, the green grass gilded gold as the sun began to descend behind the trees.

"What devilry are you are about?" Ivy watched Sebastian lean against the functional desk. "I certainly don't feel faint."

"Don't you?" His eyebrows soared. Folding his arms across his chest, legs stretched and crossed at the ankles, his expression was curious. "You appeared quite pale for a second there. And you sounded a bit shaky."

A nearly invisible shiver ran through Ivy.

"What is the matter, love?" he murmured. "You know, I can always tell when something is vexing you."

She stared at him, eyes wide. "You can?"

Sebastian shrugged. "You are quite transparent. At least to me. Don't you know that?"

"No," she responded slowly. "All of London believes me to be made of ice. Perhaps you are right. Perhaps only you see through me. Regardless, I don't know why you think anything could be wrong. I only thought Raven must enjoy his rest, considering the hour you returned...and we rose so late this morning..." Her voice trailed off while another unfortunate blush colored her cheeks.

His smile was perceptive. "Come here to me, darling." Ivy accepted his hand, allowing him to tug her against him. Widening his stance so she fit between his legs, she squirmed at his perusal as he asked, "Are you remembering what we experienced together?"

The flush on her face was answer enough as she remained silent and stiff in the circle of his arms.

"Are we moving too quickly?" Sebastian dreaded her answer. He did not intend to give her up, but he possibly could control himself so he was not making love to her three times a day. Besides, even with his renowned stamina, he doubted his ability to keep such a pace. Especially with Ivy. Every orgasm experienced thus far was soul draining and exhausting. She wrung him dry and he loved every minute of it. An insistent voice in his head immediately screamed his endurance would be maintained as long and as often as necessary. Clearing his throat, he asked, "Do you regret making love?"

"No."

Her husky little whisper was surely designed by the Devil himself, designed to drive him mad with want. Tilting Ivy's chin, Sebastian recognized a spark of yearning in the gold flashing depths of her eyes. "Do you wish me to kiss you?"

Her eyes fluttered shut for a heartbeat, thick, sable lashes brushing like delicate fans against her skin. She sagged a little in his arms then steeled herself. "Yes," she whispered, almost angrily, eyes snapping back open. "I shouldn't, but I do. I should have some control over myself and my emotions."

Sebastian chuckled, wrapping both arms about her, pulling her as close as her full skirts would allow. Soft and restless, her fingers traced the shape of his shirt's buttons and he found himself filled with bemused desire. "There's no need for restraint. In fact, I forbid it. Anytime you want to be kissed, sweet little wife, you need only say so. Or, better yet, you kiss me."

When his lips settled on hers, Ivy melted into him without hesitation. Her hands gripped the front of his shirt, twisting the fabric. The aching sweetness he tasted on her lips fired his blood. With a little growl that came from somewhere in the back of his throat, or maybe his gut - he wasn't quite sure, his hands moved to cradle her face.

The loud bang of someone dropping a feed bucket on the cobblestones broke them apart.

"That's probably for the best," Sebastian ground out. He eased her away as she gazed up at him in wonder. "I can't seem to control myself when I'm with you. Another minute and I'd have you on that cot...or maybe even across this desk..."

Exhaling slowly, he closed his eyes and willed his body to a more manageable state. Ivy's words from that morning regarding different places he could make love to her needled and pricked him like a thousand bees. Suddenly, it was all he could think of.

He could make love to her here, in the stable master's office.

Oh, and the hedge maze, hidden behind a wall of glossy, emerald green boxwood. He would lay her across one of the many decorative concrete benches and push her skirts high, exposing her to his gaze and the deep blue sky. The orangery would be perfect too, surrounded by lemon and orange trees, the air perfumed with citrus. Butterflies would flutter about, paying tribute to Ivy, to the countess of butterflies, as he took her amongst the lilies and the roses, the scent of her, the lushness of her filling his head.

Or, perhaps the century-old apple orchard. Sweet, green grass would serve as their bed and fragrantly soft apple blossom petals would shower their naked bodies every time a warm breeze sifted through the trees...

"Sebastian?" Ivy's soft voice snapped him from his pleasant daydreams, her expression quizzical. "You are suddenly a million miles away. Where were you just now?"

Staring at her, feeling a bit dazed, a broad grin slowly spread across his face. "Do not worry, my love. In time, I'll take you there and show you."

CHAPTER 34

*I*vy practically skipped along the gravel path leading to the stables. Walking in a dignified manner proved difficult in her excitement. Clad in a plum-hued riding habit and matching hat with jaunty pheasant feathers of rich auburn and gold, she hoped her appearance pleased Sebastian.

Glancing back, she pondered his somewhat distracted mood. He'd met with Gabriel last night before retiring, and his preoccupied manner manifested as they prepared for bed. Feeling self-conscious enough, she wondered if Sebastian now found some fault with her. He made love to her with great care, but she still worried at his reticence when during the night, she brushed her lips against his and he held her away.

"I've ill-used you for the past two days," he explained. "I'm only thinking of your comfort. You're hardly accustomed to this sort of activity, and I've no wish for you to suffer from my attentions."

The gentleness of his words failed to ease the sting of his rejection. Ivy felt it quite keenly. She had just given herself to him. Had he tired of her already?

When he wrapped those steel corded muscled arms around her,

Ivy tried to hold herself aloof. Eventually, however, she curled into him like a sleepy kitten, basking in his warmth. Tangled in his limbs, she'd fallen back asleep with his breath stirring her hair.

It was so easy, slipping back into what they shared once before, this comfortable yet curiously charged atmosphere. Ivy did not realize how much she missed it, how much she missed his smile, his hand on her elbow. The way he tilted his head to listen to her. Intimacy added additional layers to the feelings unraveling in her half-frozen heart. Telling herself it was her duty to provide the next heir to the Ravenswood earldom rang patently false. Her pulse leapt to life any time he touched her, no matter by accident or by design. She was obsessed with him.

Sebastian cut a fine figure in his casual garb of charcoal grey breeches, ivory linen shirt and favored Hessian boots. He wore no coat or ascot today. The weather was growing warmer, and the informal style of clothing suited him well. Ivy longed for such comfortable attire. The riding habit was her winter one; it was sure to grow uncomfortable as the day wore on. Removing the jacket would allow her to ride in the blouse and skirt, but the boyish apparel she wore at their country estate, Somerset Hall was far more to her liking.

Seeing Gabriel at the entrance to the stables, Ivy called out a greeting. "Good morning, Gabriel. Shall you ride with us this morning?"

Finishing his conversation with the stable master, Gabriel executed a bow for Ivy's benefit while Sebastian rolled his eyes at the courtly gesture. "Good morning, milady. Sebastian."

All turned as a pair of stable boys, each carrying full buckets of feed, collided with one another. Oats spilled across the cobblestones as the two, embarrassed by their clumsiness, argued over who was at fault. With a cluck of his tongue, Samuel excused himself to intercede in the fray.

"Regrettably, I leave for London today," Gabriel explained. "Ravenswood requested I personally oversee matters before your arrival in Town."

Reminded of their short time remaining at Beaumont, Ivy felt a bit of joy evaporate from the day. In two weeks' time, she and Sebastian would return to London to finish out the social season and she did not wish to go. Did not want to face the curious stares and wagging tongues speculating on their shocking marriage. And, truth told, no desire to face Lady Rachel Garrett.

Despite Sebastian's assurances on the matter, Ivy knew the woman despised her. How unpleasant it would be to reside in the same house. Clashes were inevitable. No matter how disagreeable Rachel might be toward her new niece-in-law, it was unlikely Sebastian would banish his aunt from her own home. Ivy sighed. At least for half the year it was possible to live at Beaumont. And Lady Garrett despised the country, so she would not accompany them. It was a small pleasure to look forward to.

Gabriel scowled. "Ahh. Here comes that devil of horse now."

A young groom led the horses up and Raven, typically quite standoffish, pushed past the mare to lean heavily against Ivy. Resting his head against her chest, the stallion heaved a great sigh, cocked his rear hind hoof and promptly dozed off.

"Devil horse? I don't believe it. He's a lamb." Ivy rubbed the space between Raven's perfectly formed ears. "See?"

"Yes, Gabriel, see?" Sebastian repeated with a grin. "Perhaps the countess might lend you a bit of her perfume. It seems to have a strange effect on horses, turning them into quite docile creatures."

"Indeed." Ivy caught her husband's eye and the current passing between them was so charged even the sleepy groom blinked. "All manner of beasts appear to be affected."

Gabriel laughed aloud, slapping Sebastian on the back. "Obviously, a private matter better left unspoken."

Unable to think of anything witty to add to the conversation, Ivy took Spring's reins from the confused groom. "I wish you a safe journey, Gabriel. We shall miss your morning visits-" she ignored Sebastian's snort of disbelief. "-and look forward to seeing you again in London."

Annie had packed a picnic lunch for them in a small duffle, and while Samuel tied it to the back of Raven's saddle, Sebastian pulled Gabriel aside to exchange a few private words. When Ivy entered the stable courtyard, he followed her, motioning for his man to follow.

"See to it in all haste. Before we arrive," Sebastian said to Gabriel. He shooed the groom away from the mounting block, holding Spring by the bit until Ivy was settled upon the mare's back.

"I shall attend to it immediately." Gabriel nodded. "Don't worry. Matters will go as planned."

The earl threw a leg over Raven, pulling the edgy stallion under control. His laugh was sharp. "I've no doubt they will. Until London, then."

With a wave of farewell, Sebastian and Ivy nudged their mounts down the gravel lane, past the east pastures where the other horses would be turned out from their stalls. They rode in companionable silence, enjoying the sweetness of the air as the morning sun burned the dew off the grass. A light breeze tickled the napes of their necks and the horses pranced in high spirits.

"You were angry just now." Ivy was the first to break the silence.

Sebastian glanced up in surprise. "I've yet to say anything, although I was about to launch into a scintillating description of where we shall ride first."

She tilted her head as he maneuvered up alongside her mare. "I'm referring to your rather cryptic exchange with Gabriel."

For a split second, his face altered into a mask of hard, secretive lines before smoothing into a pleasant expression. "Only a business matter." His hand waved dismissively. "Gabriel has it under control."

Ivy almost pressed the issue but the day was too beautiful and their remaining time at Beaumont too short to mar with unpleasantness. Gabriel's need to travel to London with such haste and her husband's secretive, distracted manner were obviously related.

Although she was nearly dying of curiosity, she said, "I know that is not the truth, but I've something to ask of you, if I may."

"You know I will do anything for you," Sebastian replied slowly. "What is your request?"

Gathering up the mare's reins, Ivy gave him an impish grin. "Race me to that elm at the top of the hill?"

Before he fully comprehended the challenge, her long-legged mare took off like a cannon shot.

Raven bolted sideways; had he not been so attuned with the stallion, Sebastian might have been unseated. He could not contain his laughter as Ivy cantered away. Even riding sidesaddle, she possessed an excellent seat, her hands skilled in directing the responsive mare. After giving her a ten-second advantage, he nudged Raven into a hard gallop. The stallion snorted in frustration, the bit in his teeth as he tried to pull ahead but Sebastian kept the reins short, and for the length of the open field, the two horses raced side by side.

Ivy bent over Spring's neck, her fingers meshing in the silky black mane as the mare surged to a faster pace. Glancing back, she saw Raven tossing his head. Clearly, his master controlled his stride.

"Let him go!" She did not want the advantage although the chivalry was very sweet.

"It's hardly fair to do so," Sebastian edged Raven even further off the lead.

"There's a kiss for you, if should you win!" Ivy's wide smile was full of promises.

Sebastian evaluated the distance remaining on the field, then with a jaunty salute and an apologetic grin, he loosened Raven's reins. The dark grey stallion flamed past like a comet.

Her mare squealed in dismay while Ivy whooped with the abandon of a wild Indian in her delight. The stallion was incredible to watch, his powerful beauty a staggering counterpoint to an amazing speed. While Spring was certainly fast, she was no match to the stronger, muscled physique of the other horse. Raven quickly left them far behind, his long legs sweeping across the late spring grass.

When Ivy finally arrived beneath the canopy of the elm, Raven danced with excitement, sides barely heaving, tossing his head as if greatly amused by the outcome of the contest.

"Oh, if a horse could gloat, I believe Raven is doing so now!" Ivy exclaimed, her cheeks flushed with the exhilaration. Her stylish little hat having been knocked askew, she reached up to secure the pins in her hair.

"I'll have that kiss now," Sebastian demanded once Ivy was done repairing herself.

"To the victor go the spoils of victory." She grinned, nudging Spring to where Raven pawed the ground.

"I didn't encourage you to challenge me…and I did try to give you the win."

"I would not have claimed victory if you gifted it to me upon a silver plate. But, I would have given you the kiss no matter who reached the tree first," Ivy admitted.

Charmed by her unexpected playfulness, Sebastian seized his prize as soon as her face lifted to his.

At noon, they reached a large meadow dotted with sweet yellow flowers and inhabited by a herd of black and white sheep and several new lambs. A low stone fence covered with wild red and white roses enclosed the meadow with a rustic wood gate providing entrance. Sebastian indicated an old trail led into the woods on the backside of the field and they would follow it after lunch.

At the top of the rise stood a small grove of ancient oaks and while Sebastian took care of the horses, Ivy unpacked their lunch, setting everything out on the edge of the shade trees.

"Annie is absolutely wonderful," Ivy exclaimed. "Look, she had Chef include strawberry teacakes. My favorite."

"The teacakes were Annie's idea." Sebastian grinned, plopping onto the grass beside her.

"And the wine?" She held up a bottle, brow raised at the inclusion of the beverage.

"Mine, of course. I intend to get completely intoxicated so you are better able to take advantage of me. You may have all the lemonade you desire."

Ivy giggled. "And if I prefer wine instead?"

"We'll work something out." He winked.

Chef had also packed thick, salty slices of ham, fluffy biscuits, and a mixture of cut up fruit. Pickled cucumbers provided a tart compliment to the salted meat and the teacakes were a sweet finish to the meal. While they ate, a small herd of sheep ventured close, the baby lambs curious to explore the strange creatures invading their meadow. The sweet little dears wobbled closer until finally, Ivy got upon her knees, stretching a hand to touch the wooly softness of one bi-colored lamb. Tottering forward, it collapsed in her lap, a tangle of spindly limbs, as its mother watched, ready to take action if necessary.

"You darling thing," Ivy crooned to it as Sebastian refilled their wine glasses. "I've never touched one before. It's so soft." Ivy took a sip of wine then set the glass down in the grass so she could better cradle the lamb. Gazing out over the meadow, her expression turned wistful. She was silent for a few moments then sighed. "I do wish we could stay at Beaumont forever."

"The endless balls and soirees in London no longer hold any appeal?"

"I enjoy the dancing, but usually not the company."

Grimacing with mock pain, Sebastian held a hand to his heart. "You wound me, love. I thought the times we waltzed were as precious to you as they are to me."

Ivy lightly slapped his arm. "I am not referring to you and you well know it. I'm sure I appear quite besotted by your attentions. Anyone with eyes could see I despised dancing with anyone other than you."

Sebastian could not stop the flash of memory from the last ball they attended, when he so grimly watched from the shadows while Ivy whirled in the arms of countless men. Jealousy - bitter and ugly - darkened his features. Thankfully, Ivy did not see it as she nuzzled the lamb's neck.

She'd been far from happy during those awful weeks of their separation, suffering as much as he. At the mercy of those who took advantage of her weakness and sorrow. Men like himself.

What would Ivy think of the ruthless plans he recently set into motion? He had carefully plotted to bring significant financial burdens to a particular set of predators. Those pursuing her at the Faringdon Ball deserved a great deal of discomfort, worry, and angst. Would the exhibition of her husband's malice please her? Or disturb her?

Sebastian had neither forgiven nor forgotten those involved that night. While the gentlemen would not be completely destroyed, their losses would prove devastating. It would become blatantly obvious who orchestrated those monetary damages when the Earl of Ravenswood gained from their misfortunes. Sebastian did not desire anonymity. He *wanted* them to know. Only the future Duke of Richeforte danced beyond Sebastian's reach.

Ivy laughed as the lamb softly butted her in the chest. She did not know Sebastian was engaged in a complete analyzation of that night once again, counting friends and enemies. Reluctantly, she untangled the baby's ungainly legs, setting it in the direction of its bleating mother.

"It's breathtaking here. Like a fairy tale. Or a dream," she murmured, watching as the herd gradually began to move away. "With all these roses, you would have held the advantage in London this past month."

Sebastian reached for her hand. This grove of trees grew on a slight swell, making it easy to see much of the land stretched between them and the manor. The sun had burned off the early morning mist, and now, puffy white clouds drifted lazily across the blue of the sky. Combined with the light and dark greens of the grasses, the low, stacked stone fences, and the cascading profusion of red and white wild roses, the huge house far off in the distance resembled a work of art.

"You've never told me why you dislike roses so much," he remarked quietly.

Ivy ducked her head. "I don't mind them so much anymore. My previous aversion to them is difficult to understand."

"I'd like to try." Sebastian settled closer to her. "If you do not wish to…"

"No, I don't mind telling you." Ivy took a deep breath. "My father had the habit of sending roses whenever he and my mother were at odds. When she fell ill, and later, when she was dying, he sent them every day. Even if he was out of the country. Now, I understand what the roses meant. To her. To him. I used to think them a paltry, sympathetic gesture, something he sent from guilt. But I was wrong. Those roses gave my mother a measure of comfort and reminded her of their love." She smiled at Sebastian. "And of his sorrow in his failings of our family. Every time he sent his roses, he begged Mother's forgiveness and reminded her that he loved her. But, I only saw them as a symbol of death. Betrayal and pain. Loss." Her aqua blue eyes sparkled with tears. "I don't see it that way anymore. Father explained how things were…and then there you were, with your endless bouquets, and I realized how silly I was for hating a simple flower. Especially knowing your own mother loved them too."

"I'm very glad you changed your mind about them," Sebastian breathed. "Because you are astoundingly breathtaking wearing rose petals and nothing else." He pressed a soft kiss to her lips.

"Scoundrel," Ivy gave him a light push. "I won't fall for it, you know. Not out here. No matter how many rose petals you might cover me in."

"Pity. I must imagine you then, on this hillside, in the deep, green grass, blue skies overhead. White and red petals covering you, while I decide what to uncover and what parts of you to kiss."

His eyes blazed, sweeping her body with such heat her clothes should have caught on fire.

Ivy's breath was decidedly quicker as she admonished him. "You, my lord, are wicked."

"Hmm, one of my better qualities, don't you agree?" Taking mercy on her, Sebastian reclined on an elbow to gaze over the countryside.

"Shall this be our residence when we are not in London?" Ivy asked a few moments later.

"Do you wish it to be?" He was still contemplating making love to her there on the hillside, thoughts of her naked firing his imagination. He knew she was worried about their return to London, but was unsure of its reason. "This is the closest of my residences to Town. I have an estate near the border of Scotland and a plantation in the Caribbean, should you ever desire to visit the tropics. As well as a small chateau on the southern coast of France."

"Is this why you are brown all over? From visiting the tropics?"

"Why, my dear countess," Sebastian teased. "Have you been peeking beneath the covers?"

Ivy's brow arched. "It's difficult not to notice when you refuse to wear a stitch of clothing to bed."

"I did warn you our first morning here, remember?"

"You're not answering my question."

He chuckled and with Ivy's help, began packing up the lunch items. With everything gathered, she followed him to the horses and watched as he secured it all to the back of the back of Raven's saddle. They walked down the hill to a second gate, the horses held loose by their reins. As they traipsed through the yellow flowers, the same lamb, which before sat so contentedly in Ivy's lap, stumbled away from its mother. With a plaintive baa'ing it attempted to follow them, Sebastian and Ivy watching in bemusement before the mother ewe emitted a distinctively stern sound that made the little thing turn back.

After passing through the gate and remounting the horses, they turned to the path leading deeper into the woods. Sebastian resumed their conversation.

"Before I returned to London by way of Paris, I spent nearly a year at Rosethorne. If I was not working the plantation, I lazed the days away on the beach. You cannot imagine the color of the water, Ivy, it's such a beautiful blue-green. Your eyes are nearly its exact shade, you know, and the sand is so white, it's almost blinding. It's very hot, although it rains nearly every afternoon to cool things off a bit. When the sun sinks down over the water, it's such a gorgeous sight, you wonder how God could create so many colors."

Ivy's head tilted as she regarded him with a contemplative eye. "How lovely. Still, it does not explain why you are so tan."

Laughing at her determination, Sebastian confessed, "Because I swim as I sleep. The Caribbean sun is quite strong; it bronzes the skin quickly. The same would probably happen to you, my little English butterfly, ruining that rose and cream complexion of yours. I'm afraid you'd turn color of a walnut. Then I'd have to call you my little brown moth."

"I would hardly be running about on the beach with no clothes on, Sebastian." Ivy blushed. "Someone might see."

Sebastian saw little sense in mentioning that he and his mistress spent hours cavorting on the beach and in the surf and no one ever violated that privacy. That other woman, he could not recall neither her face nor her name.

A silent promise was made in that moment to take his wife to Rosethorne one day. They would spend their days swimming, making love, on the soft white sand and in the jade green sea. All memories of any woman before her would be forever blotted out until only his butterfly countess existed.

"No one would dare intrude," Sebastian replied softly, his eyes glowing with half-made plans. "And yes, we may reside here at Beaumont, if you wish. My parents did."

"I would like that. We would be close to Lord Bentley and Sara after their wedding, should they choose to reside at Bentley Park. If you've no objections, I would like it a great deal."

Bringing Raven to a halt, he leaned over to press a kiss to Ivy's lush mouth. She tasted of tart strawberries, wine and cool lemonade. "You only need ask, my sweetness. I will grant your every wish."

"I'm pleased to hear it." The grin she gave him was cheeky. "For the moment, however, I shall settle for another kiss."

Sebastian happily obliged.

CHAPTER 35

This corner of Beaumont was dense, almost primeval, with dark, cool woods and hilly terrain, but as the afternoon passed, even the forest's coolness did little to combat Ivy's discomfort. Removing the smart little jacket of her riding habit was necessary. Soon, even the long-sleeved shirt beneath became uncomfortably warm.

"Will you melt?" Sebastian asked. Sunlight filtered through the tree canopy and Ivy sighed with visible relief every time a shady patch appeared.

"I should hope not." The heaviness of her apparel exasperated her. "I don't know what Molly was thinking by not packing my summer riding habits."

"We can go back if you like."

"No, I'm enjoying this immensely." She slanted him a glance. "If I rode in breeches it would be a great deal cooler."

"And a great deal more dangerous."

"Dangerous? For whom?"

Sebastian's brow rose. "For you. Myself. The mere thought of you in breeches does horrendous things to my sanity. I would ravish you before you stepped foot outside our bedroom. Should you make it downstairs or - God help me - outside, well, I have a vast appreciation for those I employ. To slaughter a man because his eyes lingered on you would greatly disturb me."

Ivy waved her hand in disbelief. "You exaggerate, of course."

He gave her an odd half-smile. "Do I?"

Unfastening three ivory buttons on the delicate shirt, she closed her eyes in delight when a slight breeze discovered the newly exposed skin. "Nevertheless, were it any warmer, I would happily risk your displeasure to defend the poor servant, whomever he might be." Smiling, eyes still closed, Ivy swayed in cadence with Spring's even gait. "I'd visit you in the Tower before you swung for murder and plead very prettily for your life."

When no response came, her eyes opened to see Sebastian leaning forward in the saddle, his gaze bright with speculation and riveted on her bare skin.

"I have the solution." He grinned.

"Unless you've an extra pair of breeches and a shirt hidden somewhere, I fail to see this situation improving. I cannot believe how warm it is. We barely had a spring." Ivy squinted up at the sun from under the brim of her hat.

"My intention is that you remove articles of clothing. Now, the path is around here somewhere..." Sebastian studied the trail ahead, considering trees and the vegetative twists in the overgrown path. Ivy watched in bemusement as she rode silently behind him.

A gnarled, century-old oak tree with low, sweeping branches brushing the ground grew about twenty feet from the path, served as the landmark for their unexpected detour. "Come along," he directed, nudging Raven into the overgrowth.

Ivy gave Spring her head, allowing the mare to delicately pick her way through the soft underbrush and knee-high dark green grass. "Where precisely are we going?"

"You'll see."

They passed the huge oak, the terrain growing steeper the further they ventured into the forest. Very soon after locating the trail Ivy heard rushing water. The mare's ears pricked up in confirmation just as the woods opened to reveal a wide stream. It did not seem deep but the water plunged from a much higher rise of huge rocks and boulders, the fall creating a crystal clear pool which appeared bottomless. The stream meandered to the banks, snaking between larger boulders gleaming ghostly white in the sunshine. The water was quite shallow and gentle around the boulders then gained momentum to tumble noisily around the bend. Where it flowed from there was beyond Ivy's view.

A mixture of elms and river oaks hugged the banks along with clumps of wildflowers and lilies, the blooms a mixture of buttery yellow and white. In a broad swath of sunlight, a bleached sand beach stretched like a glittery ribbon. A few of the boulders in the middle of the stream were flat enough for two or more people to climb up and lay on.

Ivy slid from Spring's back, giving Sebastian a pleased smile. "You own a magical, secret water garden?"

"I've heard it said fairies cast love spells from such places. This looks as though such creatures might reside here, doesn't it?" Dismounting, Sebastian took the reins from Ivy's hands to lead the horses a few feet downstream. He allowed them to drink their fill before tying the mounts to the low branch of an oak. As he removed the saddles, he glanced back at Ivy. "I thought you would want to wade in the water. Take off your boots, sweetheart. There's no one to see you other than myself."

"I couldn't possibly..." Ivy stammered.

The heat in Sebastian's stare interrupted her protest more than his response. "Of course, you can. Take off your boots."

Dropping to the soft grass, she did as he asked then ventured into the water, the coolness of the stream swirling around her ankles eliciting a sigh of pure pleasure. "Oh heavens, that feels good."

Sebastian chuckled, tossing his own boots aside. A second later, his shirt landed on a low tree branch, his fingers already working the buttons of his breeches.

"What are you doing?" Ivy's voice trembled.

"Cooling off. Remove your clothes too, Ivy."

"You - you're going to be naked?" She squeaked. *"Outside?"*

"It is as remote now as it was when I last swam here. Do you recall my mention of a stream I hoped to show you one day? I promise, my vision did not involve you wearing so many damned clothes. Now, do as I say and remove that hot, scratchy riding habit."

Toes wiggling in the stream's sandy bottom, skirts bunched in her fists to keep them high above the clear, cold water, Ivy shook her head. "I'm feeling refreshed, thank you."

Sebastian peeled his breeches off and Ivy felt pinned to the spot when he swept her with a heated glance, from head to bare toes.

It was so very hard to gaze at the blatant, male beauty of her husband without thinking of him making love to her. To recall the touch of his hand on her skin, thinking they might make love by this stream was dangerous. It was reckless, wondering what it might feel like in the warm sunshine...

Her husband waded into the water then dove with graceful precision toward the emerald pool where the waterfall pounded and splashed the rocks in an unsteady rhythm. Ivy watched as he swam through the current, his golden shoulders bunching and lengthening with movement. Reaching the falls, he hoisted himself onto a submerged ledge. With the water hitting behind him, his head tilted back so it could drench him.

Tearing her eyes away from his perfect form was impossible. When he slicked his hair back from his forehead, Ivy admired the muscles rippling in his arms and along his chest. Spellbound, she stared as the water ran over the slabs of his ribs, down the muscled bisection of his abdomen, trailing in tiny individual streams across the chiseled leanness of his hips and thighs. Her face flamed hot and suddenly, the cold stream did not feel invigorating anymore. It felt surprisingly warm, as though the heat of her flesh somehow caused the water's temperature to rise.

Sebastian shook his head, causing water to fly in glistening drops. "Remove everything but your chemise, Countess. Keep it, if you require some semblance of modesty."

"I don't know how to swim." Ivy wavered with indecision. The waterfall would be a delicious experience if she dared to try it. That is, should she dare remove her clothes with the sinful temptation Sebastian presented. Such a scandalous thing, swimming naked in the middle of the afternoon. Her heart beat so fast she felt lightheaded.

"I'll teach you." Calling out to her, his smile flashed white, but underneath was a current Ivy could not ignore. "Do not make me ask you again, my dear."

She made her way back onto the bank, her legs unsteady. Tossing her hat to the side, she removed her hat, skirt and various articles of undergarments until nothing remained except a thin, champagne-hued chemise. It barely reached the tops of her thighs and just skimmed the edge of her breasts, but at least she was covered.

The last thing she did before walking toward him and into the water, was remove the pins from her hair. The heavy mass tumbled to her shoulders.

Sebastian was strangely quiet as he slid from the waterfall's edge. He swam to a spot where the water swirled just above his waist then stopped, waiting for her. Ivy knew her chemise revealed far more than it covered. He could probably see the shadowy vee between her thighs and the dark circles of her nipples through the flimsy bit of silk. As the garment grew damp, it became a second skin on her flesh, molding to her curves, highlighting every asset. It took all she possessed not to cross her arms over her chest. Her intent was to stay to the shallows, but the moment he held out a hand to her, Ivy immediately went to him, into the deeper water.

"I did not lie when I said I could not swim. I-I am afraid to go any further." Ivy glanced down, checking her footing in the water. Here, the stream's bottom consisted of both larger pebbles and sand. She rolled her toes over the round stones, momentarily distracted by their smoothness and lost her balance. Submerged to her shoulders, Ivy floundered in panic until Sebastian lifted her up.

"Shhh," he soothed, his arms slipping around her waist. "I won't let anything happen to you." With the buoyancy of the water, held firmly against him, Ivy bobbed in his embrace, her toes now barely touching the stream bed.

"You'll teach me?" Her smile was self-conscious, her heart racing madly. "What should I do? Lie back or...?

Sebastian's eyes were dark and serious. A lock of his hair fell across his forehead and Ivy reached up to sweep it back for him. "Later," he said in a hoarse voice just before his mouth swooped down to take hers in a mind drugging kiss.

He tasted her thoroughly, sweeping the inside of her mouth until Ivy clutched his shoulders to steady herself. Sliding his hands down, Sebastian cupped her bottom, lifting her, holding her against his erection as the kiss blossomed and desire erupted into an inferno of want and need and lust.

Without warning, he sloshed to the middle of the stream to deposit her on one of the sun-drenched boulders. After being clasped against his body, Ivy's chemise now clung to her, the silk molding itself until every inch of her was glaringly obvious. But as she settled atop the boulder, Ivy reached for him, beyond shame, beyond self-consciousness. Her hand entwined with his. Bringing it to her mouth, she pressed a kiss to his rough palm.

Wild hope soared in Sebastian's eyes. He seemed to steel himself, slowly pushing Ivy back until she had to brace herself on her elbows. A glazed expression washed over his face as he rubbed his thumbs over the hardened peaks of her nipples. He slid his hands down to cup the fullness of each breast in his palms.

Ivy swallowed a helplessly excited moan, her back arching as she thrust into his touch. Replacing his thumbs with the wet heat of his mouth, Sebastian bent forward, tonguing her nipples with delicious intent, one by one, the smooth friction of silk adding a wicked layer of sensation as he licked and bit her through the cloth.

When she gasped, he forced her to lie prone on the warm rock, placing a large hand on her stomach in order to hold her flat. Moving his palm to the flesh between her thighs, he found her hot and moist. Agitated and growing restless, Ivy tried capturing his hand.

"No. Stay like this, love, and do not move. No matter what I do to you, you will stay here. In this position." A smile emerged in the tone of Sebastian's words while he stared down at her. "Holy hell, I may keep you here, like this, forever. If only you could see how beautiful you are..."

Biting her lip, Ivy remained as Sebastian placed her, arms stretching obediently above her head at his murmured directive. With the sun warming her face and the hardness of the stone beneath her, she felt like a pagan offering to the gods. Sacrificial and wanton. Closing her eyes, she was unaware of holding her breath until Sebastian chuckled softly.

"Breathe, my little love. Otherwise, you will not last through what I have planned for you." A trembling moan escaped her as he explained in a scandalous whisper, "I'm going to taste you now, Ivy. From one end of your delicious body to the other, I'm going to lick...bite...suck you. I'm going to place my mouth on you. Over you. My tongue inside you. Anywhere I damn well please, for as long as I please. No. Stay as you are. I'll tell you when you shall move. Keep your hands there. Open- open your legs for me, Ivy. Open. Yes, that's it. If you are a good girl and do as I say, you'll find the reward well worth it..."

The words were hot, liquid honey pouring over her, into her, melting any reluctance or embarrassment she possessed. Sebastian pulled her thighs apart when she failed to respond quickly enough in her languid haze, his large fingers shoving the flimsy barricade of the silk chemise up. It clamped against the soft skin of her lower belly as he held her open with the flat of his palms. When she was bared to him, he stared at her for a long moment, as if he could not believe she was his.

Then he bent and put his mouth upon her.

A shudder shook Ivy from the top of her head down to her tiniest toe, a muffled sob of amazement escaping on a gasp of air. She almost reached down to grip his hair - to pull him away or drag him closer - she wasn't sure. A low growl of warning reminded her to keep her hands where they were.

She melted into him and tried to shrink away at the same time. But Sebastian would not allow a withdrawal. His mouth became a branding iron on her sensitive flesh. Drawing his tongue over and across the slick heat of the soft folds centered every nerve in her body on the spot he possessed with his mouth, all the sensations pooling into a tangle of exquisite pleasure and quivering need.

Her craving was used as a weapon against her. When she inhaled with delight, he pushed further. When she tightened, legs stiffening, her body coiling, he eased off. He licked and teased her to the point of madness, then moved so he was no longer at her sex but the soft skin of her flat stomach. Ivy moaned in protest, limbs trembling as she receded from the peak he intentionally drove her to. He was prolonging her satisfaction with deliberate intent. He wanted her panting for his touch, trembling for him. If she wished to climax, he required her total surrender.

Gliding over the curve of her hip, his lips explored the inside of her thigh. He raised one of her legs to trail leisurely kisses down its length, stopping to trace the curves and hollows of her knee before discovering her delicate ankle. Using his tongue, he swept away drops of water, his teeth lightly raking her bones until Ivy flinched whenever his lips touched her.

Each time she whimpered in frustration, Sebastian chuckled. How difficult it was to remain in the position he placed her! Oh, her hands remained above her head, fingers alternating between gripping the smooth stone of the boulder for support and lacing with themselves to keep from grabbing him, but her entire body undulated for him. Her cries were for him. And the wet, slick honeyed sweetness of her arousal was for him.

She was completely his.

Sebastian lowered her leg, only to pick up the other and dive into a new adventure involving her skin. The actions repeated in reverse earned several muttered curses from Ivy. Moving from her ankle, up to her knee, then the inner side of her creamy thigh and back to her center once more, he ignored all of her swearing.

Again, his mouth fastened on her sweetness. It would take only seconds to bring her to completion. She nearly sobbed with need. When Sebastian raised his head to murmur, "Lower your arms now, sweet," Ivy's hands plunged into the thick waves of his hair, holding him to her pulsating flesh. Arching into his mouth, she shamelessly sought the expert strokes of his tongue, his name falling from her lips, punctuated with the word, "please,". She would have killed an army of marauding invaders for him when his finger slid into her, pushing against a hidden spot on the inner wall of the silken passage. With his finger deep inside her, and unrelenting teasing flickers of his tongue, he pushed her into a kaleidoscope of oblivion.

Ivy flew apart, crying out as pleasure shimmered through her. Sebastian savored every single pulse as she clenched about his finger until he slowly removed it. And as she shuddered, the rippling pleasure sharp and new, while she floated boneless on a cloud far above the little stream where he had her laid out like food for the gods, Sebastian thrust inside her. Holding her hips aloft, the stream curling around them, he delved deep, pulling her legs up until she wrapped them about his waist. Whispers filled her ears; love words, words of adoration, words of need and lust.

"I love you, Ivy, love you, love you." With restrained impatience, he whipped her damp chemise over her head, his hands molding her bare breasts to the shape of his palm before skating down her waist and flanks to grip her hips again. Holding her tighter so she was not injured on the smooth surface of the boulder, Sebastian stroked in and out, hard, then soft, then hard once more, carrying them to a place where desire, love, and lust jockeyed for position and intertwined with the other.

Ivy teetered on the brink again before he skillfully nudged her into dark, sweet depths. His lips covered hers, his mouth taking hers, swallowing her cry of fulfillment. When Sebastian found his release, she held him close, her hands soothing and warm. Their souls surely mingled on some mystical level, Ivy thought, raining kisses on his face, sighing as the whirlwind of their passion subsided and the world intruded once more.

But never once, in this magical, secret water garden, could Ivy bring herself to say she loved him. The fairies failed them both in that regard.

CHAPTER 36

Sebastian's London home was a smaller, more intimate version of Beaumont, with darker wall colors and a heavier, more masculine feel. The furnishings were expensive and tasteful, their weightiness making Ivy feel small and delicate in comparison. The vast space contained a somberness, an unhappiness which seem to linger behind every door and in every cranny. Ravenswood Court did not possess the lightheartedness of Beaumont and this saddened Ivy. Knowing Timothy passed away within these very walls might well be the source of the uneasiness, but even that could not explain all of it.

Ivy was so glad to see Brody's face when the ornate doors swung wide, she impulsively embraced the man, ignoring the bemused frown Sebastian threw her. Her old butler's grin and familiar wink bolstered her spirits, and he too, appeared unfazed by the earl's faint objection to their unorthodox greeting.

Molly's welcome was characteristically unreserved. Chattering gaily of the details in moving their belongings to Ravenswood Court, she enveloped her mistress in a warm squeeze then dipped an absent-minded curtsey to Sebastian. Arranged in a formal line to meet their new lady, the other servants observed the going-ons with raised eyebrows, horrified by this informality. Only after meeting the lady who'd snagged their beloved earl did the servants sigh amongst themselves in collective relief. Their new countess, it seemed, would be very pleasant to serve.

Gabriel was not present to welcome them. Attending to business, Sebastian informed her while Ivy found herself wishing for another familiar, friendly face. And when Lady Garrett glided downstairs like a silent, dismal raven dressed all in black, Ivy wished it all the more.

"I'm sure you will be happy here, my dear," Rachel said, taking Ivy's hand in a gesture of politeness.

"Thank you, Lady Garrett." Ivy was jittery and Sebastian frowned, both at her nervousness and his aunt's definite coolness. The remaining conversation was a stiff replay of their journey to London, and after a few moments, Rachel excused herself to check on preparations for the evening meal. Saying nothing in regard to his aunt's flat reception, Sebastian dismissed the servants. He took Ivy's elbow to give her an abbreviated tour of the home's receiving spaces before leading the way upstairs. Once inside the privacy of their bedchamber, he pulled her into his arms.

Only a fraction of Ivy's tenseness eased as he held her. Facing Rachel drained her, the animosity rolling from the woman nearly tangible. Could Sebastian not see and feel it? Maybe he did. It was still so difficult to know what went on behind those slate hued eyes of his.

"It'll be alright, love," Sebastian said. "If she does not warm up within a reasonable timeframe, I shall have her moved to another estate, if you wish."

Ivy's lips tightened. *That* decision should not be hers. But instead of saying so, she shook her head. "I do not want her forced to leave her home. I'm sure things will grow easier." Only, time would not help at all. Indeed, time would probably worsen things.

The next morning, her father came to have breakfast with them and Ivy suspected his visit was to determine her contentment. What he saw must have pleased him, for he undertook a lengthy discussion with Sebastian regarding the details of a new business venture. Had Jonathan Kinley any misgivings of this marriage, Ivy hoped he would never consider such a proposal, regardless of his admiration for his new son-in-law.

Midweek, Sara came for tea and Ivy was relieved to see a friendly face. Sebastian was buried in his office with Gabriel, and Lord only knew where Rachel had taken herself off to. The woman was determined to avoid Ivy as much as possible; with the exception of that first night, Lady Garrett declined to take meals with them or spend time with them at all. Ivy was glad.

Agnes, the bustling, businesslike housekeeper poured the tea, and once the elderly woman exited the drawing room, Sara gave Ivy a wide grin. "This is a far better welcome than the last time I visited."

Ivy smothered a helpless giggle. "Sara Morgan, you are terrible. When I think of you barging through the front door, pushing the poor butler aside, not to mention Lady Garrett, even I am shocked." She reached to squeeze her friend's hand. "But I am so glad you did. And I never thanked you for that night. After the way I treated you, for you to come to my aid means so much to me."

"Nonsense. I love you and I did what needed done. Besides, things seem to have worked out for the best. You look very happy. In fact, you are glowing, my dear."

Sara's statement carried an unasked question. Had Ivy forgiven Sebastian?

It was a question difficult to answer. A month of marriage hardly seemed enough time to forgive such deep betrayals, but deep inside, Ivy knew the answer. Only her damnable pride prevented her from admitting it aloud.

"You believe I'm glowing?" Ivy skirted the issue. "Careful, Sara. Should Lady Garrett hear of my contentment, or the earl's, she'll vow I've employed witchcraft to twist events to my benefit."

Sara grimaced. "How I detest the fact you must live with her. Oh, Ivy, has she been terribly unkind?"

"Just in spirit and demeanor. That first night was a nightmare of awkward silence and Ravenswood attempting to make civilized conversation for the three of us. I understand her unhappiness, Sara, but I too, dread the thought of living with her six months out of the year."

"I hope Ravenswood will make her mind her manners. I can't imagine that he won't. The man seems to worship you. Is it true he gave you one of his stallion's offspring? And full possession of the estate jewels? They're said to be worth a king's ransom and all yours now. Is that brooch from the coffers? It's beautiful and quite different."

Ivy traced the tiny, gold filigree and diamond butterfly pinned to her shoulder. The collection of rings, necklaces, bracelets and brooches, tiaras and hatpins, bejeweled haircombs, all meticulously catalogued and stored within a huge safe in the master dressing room, was astounding. When Sebastian showed it to her, that first afternoon at Ravenswood Court, she'd been overwhelmed. Her interest was piqued by the butterfly jewelry, and hearing the story behind the understated piece, Ivy knew she could not allow it to be locked up in the safe again. It was one of the earliest pieces of jewelry commissioned by the first Earl of Ravenswood, presented to his new bride in 1067, the year after William of Normandy over-took the throne of England, pairing those loyal to his cause with the daughters of his enemies.

The brooch was not particularly delicate, due to the craftsman-ship of its time, but it was intricately wrought and sturdy; the diamonds cut and placed so light was captured from all angles inside the filigree cage. During dinner that evening, Aunt Rachel had stared at the pin, a fixed smile on her features, and Ivy couldn't help but wonder if the woman secretly coveted the item.

Sara took another sip of tea, frowned slightly and Ivy grinned. Whatever Lady Sara Morgan wished to say would not stay contain for long.

"This tea is rather strong. It's from Ravenswood's own planta-tion, you say? How interesting, but I'd prefer a different brew, if it isn't too much trouble." Sara waited until Ivy rang for another pot before readdressing the subject at hand. "Have a care around Lady Garrett, Ivy," she advised, taking Ivy's hand and forcing her to meet her eyes. "Ravenswood will keep you safe, but please, do not lower your guard down around that woman. Is it possible she could live elsewhere?"

"And give her yet another reason to truly hate me? The best course is to stay out of each other's path in the attempt to maintain civility." Ivy managed a brave smile. "But you are right. Sebastian will never allow any harm to come to me."

Sara laughed sharply. "I've learned the lengths he will go to that end. It's said Viscount Basford departed England with no plans to return in the near future."

Ivy bit her lip in silent frustration. "A far better solution than a duel."

"True, but you know the earl will have vengeance on those who cross him. The latest rumor concerns the men from the Faringdon Ball. Each gentleman finds himself teetering on the verge of financial ruin. Whether at the races, the gaming tables or the Exchange, Ravenswood gains from their misfortune." Sara's gaze was unwavering. "Some whisper a plan was devised; the infliction of pain where it is felt most keenly - in their pockets. Only the new Duke of Richeforte has been spared. It cannot be mere coincidence."

With a flash of understanding, Ivy realized what Sebastian had done; the mission he sent Gabriel on that morning from Beaumont clear now. He was punishing those involved the night of the Faringdon Ball. She did not know whether to be appalled or grateful, but the blaze of jealousy searing her heart was merciless. What reward did Lady Veronica Wesley receive for her assistance that night?

Ivy sought to steer the subject to something less volatile. "Landon's father passed away?"

"Just after your marriage, God save his soul. He was a miserable man, wasn't he? And lingered forever, it seemed. He was in great pain during his last days. It's rumored Landon refused to visit his bedside, although he wasted no time taking control of the estates. Alan told me the barristers waited outside the old duke's bedchambers, quills in hand, ready to take possession of everything and Richeforte's last breath was to curse his son's very existence." Sara bit into a teacake, chewing reflectively. "Now Landon is the duke and Ravenswood will never be able to exact revenge, if that was his intent. Richeforte is too powerful."

Ivy sat so quietly that Sara leaned squarely back against the brocade cushion of the divan. She too was silent for a few moments, noting her friend's pale features before wisely changing the subject.

"I find myself wildly curious, my dear, as to the nature of marital relations," Sara's lips curled into a smile when Ivy's eyes met hers in shock. "What is it truly like? Will you tell me? Kissing is quite exciting, as are the caresses, but should the rest of it exist purely for a man's pleasure, then I'll exercise control until the wedding night. What are your thoughts on the matter?"

Ivy swallowed hard, unsure how much to reveal and infinitely grateful they no longer spoke of Sebastian's revenge and his victims. Especially since it was only recently she'd been counted in those numbers. "Wait for the wedding, darling. Succumbing before bears its own set of problems."

"The act itself is painful? Should I be afraid?" Sara's blue eyes held a fierce determination. "I must know more. Blast it. You're the only one who can tell me the truth of such things. Mother blushes and stammers and always manages to change the subject. I have failed miserably to get any information out of her. And as we recently decided to move the wedding to the end of the summer, I would appreciate the time to prepare myself for what will occur on our wedding night."

Ivy knew the depths of her friend's love for Bentley, and she knew she should tell Sara a falsehood. She should not say the act of making love was magical and so deeply poignant that many times she was moved to tears by Sebastian's touch.

To say the pleasure of kisses led to even greater delights would be a grave mistake. It would most certainly have Sara wishing to experience it herself. Doing so before the wedding, before vows, before rings, but most importantly in the deepest of shadows, would result in tangled complications. Sara and Alan had the opportunity to do things properly, not hopelessly muddled like she and Sebastian.

Ivy recalled the relief experienced last week when her monthly courses appeared. A few days late, but they came. The discomfort was a welcomed nuisance even with the recurring bouts of nausea she suffered. It ensured their tale of a romantic elopement remained untinged by salacious rumors of pregnancy. He'd not said so, but she suspected Sebastian was vastly disappointed she was not with child.

Plucking at the threads of the cushioned seat, Ivy constructed a reasonable argument. "Sara, do you recall our conversation that day at tea when we spoke of marriage? Marry well and provide heirs. That is expected of us and we both know this. I will admit the marriage bed is not unpleasant, but my role is to provide Ravenswood his heir. It is a duty I am bound to honor, regardless of what led to our hasty wedding. Dearest, wait until Bentley makes you his wife. Your way will be so much easier than mine; you love him and he adores you. You will understand what I mean on the night of your wedding, I promise."

SEBASTIAN WAITED OUTSIDE THE DOOR FOR AN APPROPRIATE moment to join the two women. Chivalry prompted a delayed entrance until the conversation turned to something less intimate, less intriguing. Now, his stomach clenched as if suffering the most vicious of knife jabs.

Stalking down the hall, cold sickness rose in his throat. Is this why Ivy succumbed? Why she yielded that night in Beaumont's library? It could not be the misguided belief he needed an heir to secure the Ravenswood legacy. Performing her wifely duty and providing him a son would not excuse her from his lusts. A small part of him had believed her capitulation to be a form of gratitude for not killing Basford, but now, Sebastian realized it was something else entirely.

There must be more than duty between them. When he brought her to climax after quivering climax; when she clung to him so sweetly, kissed him softly as they drifted back to earth - there had to be more. There was affection in Ivy's voice, a shimmer of love he thought flashed again just below the surface in her eyes. These were not indications of a wife just performing her obligations, as she just so patiently explained to Sara.

At least Sebastian believed he saw something inside those turquoise eyes, something easier to recognize every time they made love. Was that elusive emotion truly there? Fluttering below a thin shell of mistrust? For all the talk of waiting for Ivy to love him again, to trust him, Sebastian realized he was becoming decidedly impatient. He hated himself for it.

And now to discover she was merely doing her "duty".

He could not allow himself to believe it.

He misconstrued her intent. Or, perhaps misheard her.

"...a duty I am bound to honor..."

Sebastian brushed Brody aside when the butler scrambled ahead of him in grand foyer. There was a perverse pleasure to be found in wresting control of the door away from his new butler, *his wife's old butler,* and even greater pleasure when the massive oak door slammed behind him. The resulting shudder of it undoubtedly alarmed the two women, sitting in *his* damned drawing room, discussing sex and marriage and birthing sons to carry on the Ravenswood and Bentley names.

Sebastian staggered out into the warmth of London's early summer.

Damn her.

The words, *"a duty,"* reverberated in his brain as he hailed a hansom cab, having no desire to wait for one of his own carriages brought around. Barking out directives, he sagged against the torn leather seat of the musty vehicle. He needed a drink - several in fact- to erase everything pounding in his head.

He needed lightning bolts to crush the betrayal stabbing his heart.

A TERSE NOTE ARRIVED LATER INFORMING IVY THAT SEBASTIAN was called away on business. Urgent, he claimed; he could not tear himself away. He would not return until it was time to set out for the ball they had pledged to attend in their honor. Puzzled by the curt tone of the missive, Ivy put it aside and settled in the library with a book. Her solitude was short lived.

"I thought I might join you." Rachel glided, taking a seat in a taupe shaded chair. It was opposite the settee where Ivy just tucked her feet on. Jumping with guilt, she almost slid her feet to the floor before steeling her spine with a sudden resolve. *She* was Countess here. This was *her* library now, her settee, and if she wished to place her feet upon it, she possessed every right to do so. Nodding at Rachel, Ivy kept her feet right where she pleased, although she did curl them under the hem of her gown.

Rachel's brow lifted, but she only rang the bell, giving instructions to the maid that arrived. "Tea, Mary. No, not the Rosethorne blend. Prepare the selection Cook picked up at Market last week."

When they were alone, Rachel's sharp blue eyes, raked Ivy. "I must admit you are quite beautiful." Her tone was dispassionate.

Rachel Garrett greatly resembled her deceased son. She bore the same black curly hair and blue eyes, the same mouth and chin. But whereas with Timothy, these attributes created a charmingly boyish face, on his mother, those same features created a hard countenance of angles and severity. Ivy resisted the urge to squirm, feeling a sudden desire for Sebastian to be near.

"Thank you," Ivy murmured, unsure how to respond to a compliment that was not truly a compliment.

"It certainly explains why Ravenswood could not resist you."

Rachel studied Ivy as though she were an experiment gone awry. Something to be examined, dissected, then quickly labeled and stored away; a danger to mankind. "Nor Timothy, for that matter."

Tracing the lettering of the book's cover to conceal her mounting annoyance, Ivy remained silent as the tea was delivered and poured. She was glad Rachel did not wish to drink her Rosethorne tea. It might be selfish, but she did not want to share it with someone who disliked her so intensely.

Rachel continued. "I suppose my nephew says he loves you. Although men will say anything to gain the prize, especially one wanted so desperately."

Ivy bristled. "Whatever led Sebastian to marry me is between us, madam."

The other woman's laugh was dry. "Calm yourself, my dear. Let us remain civil. After all, we must share this house for periods of time. While I am not happy you are here, I cannot change the fact it is so. And we shall endeavor to make the best of it. Don't you agree?"

Ivy's lips tightened. A thread of insincerity laced Rachel's tone, a note of calculated planning, but the olive branch she extended must not be ignored. Sebastian would want it accepted. He would be so disappointed if it was not.

Rachel sipped her tea, her tone conversational. "I've noticed you are wearing the Butterfly Brooch often. As the new countess, the Ravenswood jewels are yours, but my dear, I do hope you realize, while somewhat humble in appearance, it is one of the more valuable pieces. Please take care of its handling, won't you? I hoped that Timothy would be allowed to choose a few heirlooms for his own bride but, unfortunately…"

Ivy swallowed past the lump in her throat. "Lady Garrett, I've wanted to tell you for so long how Timothy's passing was tragic." She touched the brooch as if to protect it. "I understand your feelings toward me, but I want you to know, I never encouraged him in the manner you believe. Never. And, I do wish to put the past behind us. I hope we can reach a level of understanding."

"Please, my dear." Rachel's half smile practically reeked of satisfaction as she ignored Ivy's hesitant words regarding her deceased son. "You may call me 'Lady Rachel,' and if you do not object, I shall call you...Ivy."

Ivy bit her lip. The word "poison" trembled on the tip of Rachel's tongue before it was swallowed back. Then Lady Rachel sipped her tea and smiled at her over the rim of the cup.

The truce existed in words only.

A GLEAM OF SYMPATHY EXISTED IN GABRIEL'S DARK BROWN EYES, his manner subdued, but he would not reveal Sebastian's location, only relaying the earl's delay was longer than anticipated. He sat with the coachman as they drove Ivy to the Graham residence and he was the one to help her down from the coach. Before she disappeared into the manor however, he murmured, "Do not fret, my lady. He will be here to accompany you home, I promise you that."

Two hundred guests turned to watch as Ivy entered the ballroom alone. A chorus of chattering voices, excited to see the Earl and the new Countess of Ravenswood, exclamations over the outrageousness of their elopement, fell abruptly silent. Ivy cursed the Graham's and their antiquated penchant for announcing guests. Someone should inform them it was no longer the thirteenth century.

Snickers of laughter brought her chin up. Her fingers rose to trace the filigree butterfly. For an eternity, Ivy stood, and her gaze, glittering with anger and embarrassment, cut the crowd like a queen through vagabonds.

The Earl of Bentley, the dear man, appeared at her side to twirl her into a waltz the musicians apparently forgot how to play. The notes were jarring, with stuttering half-starts, but Alan's kind actions opened the floodgates. Other gentlemen sought her attention following that initial dance. Without Ravenswood's glowering visage to stem the tide, Ivy found she was in even higher demand than before her notorious wedding.

It did not seem to matter she was newly wed to one of the most feared men in all of England. She was a woman to be conquered for different reasons now. Gentlemen who carefully steered clear of the Marriage Mart eyed her with consideration. If Sebastian deserted her with such haste, it was a reasonable assumption the new countess was open to discrete advances.

For nearly an hour, Ivy danced before excusing herself. Several Pack members approached her, offering congratulations on her marriage, comically diligent in their efforts at avoiding mention of Viscount Basford. Count Phillipe Monvair gave her a lackluster wave from across the ballroom, his arm occupied by a lady most definitely not an heiress. Ivy bit back a smile at his air of resignation.

Declining Lord Longleigh's entreaty of a second dance, Ivy found refuge near a cluster of young ladies enjoying their first season. Like busy, fluttering sparrows dusted in white, they flocked together, giggling behind gloved hands. One girl in particular calmly returned Ivy's perusal until the contingent of men from the Faringdon's Ball snagged her attention. The Earl of Clayton boldly met her eye for the briefest of moments, a spark of interest evident in his hungry stare, but the others were noticeably subdued. Was it true? Had the dissolute lot of them been punished for that fateful night? It seemed a bit unfair. She should bear some blame for her own rash behavior.

Her gaze next landed on Lady Veronica Wesley as she was announced by the Graham's majordomo.

An awful rumor had already circulated the ballroom twice over, preceding the lady's late arrival. Lady Wesley was recently the recipient of an inheritance of some sort. An obscene amount of money, someone whispered. Subsequently, she dismissed Lord Alimar as her sponsor just two days before. It was all quite secretive; no one really knew where the funds originated from. Someone said a great aunt living abroad in Italy had died, leaving her fortune to Veronica, but Ivy knew better. Sebastian was her mysterious benefactor. Veronica was rewarded after all.

A lump of sour tasting jealousy rested in the hollow of Ivy's throat. Was the lady Sebastian's current favorite once again? Had her husband spent his day in her bed? Where was he now? In another paramour's arms? The thoughts swirling about her head left her nauseous. Sebastian would not do that to her. He couldn't.

He loves me. I know he does...but still, men are such fickle creatures...

Ivy stared at the glittering blue topaz ring on her finger. It felt impossibly heavy. As if it weighed a ton. Focused on her own misery, she failed to notice Veronica approach until the woman's husky voice sounded in her ear.

"Begging your pardon, Lady Ravenswood, but are you alright?"

Ivy pasted a smile on her dry lips, her response wooden. "Of course, Lady Wesley. Why do you ask?"

Veronica smiled. "Just that you did not appear yourself for a moment. My felicitations upon your recent marriage. I understand it is agreeable to you both, which I'm glad to hear. How I love elopements - so very romantic. Is Lord Ravenswood about? I'd like to offer him my congratulations as well."

The lady exhibited genuine inquisitiveness. Her tone held no cattiness; no snide implications underlying the words. Glancing about the ballroom, Ivy realized wildly curious eyes now fixated on the two of them - the new wife and the former mistress. The situation was simply too delicious to ignore.

"Oh, they do adore a good scandal, don't they?" Veronica murmured, her lively eyes dancing with amusement.

"I beg your pardon?" The woman was making a concerted effort to be pleasant, but Ivy still wondered at her motives.

"None of it is true, you know. The rumors you've undoubtedly heard. Your husband has not sought my attentions." Veronica's smile was serene. "Ravenswood has not visited my bed since the day following his return to England. And that was before he ever saw you. Lord knows he was ruined for any other woman after that. But you probably realize that."

Accepting a glass of champagne from a liveried servant, Ivy resisted the urge to toss back the contents in one gulp. "Why are you telling me this?"

"Because you know about the money." Veronica's head tilted, gauging Ivy's reaction to her bluntness. "I trust you will repeat the same story he instructed me to relate. However, it is an insult to your intelligence to pretend it came from a great aunt. He gifted it to me. I was rewarded, the others punished for the Faringdon incident. It's the earl's way. There is still Richeforte to be considered, although I confess I do not know Sebastian's plans for him. He was instrumental in your rescue, but that man's motives are always suspect, regardless of circumstance. Richforte's callousness is renowned. There is sure to be a cold-blooded, utterly ruthless motive behind his assistance." Her smile twisted as she sipped her champagne. "Or, maybe he wished to claim you as his next mistress and I thwarted his plans too. Be glad Sebastian did not allow Richeforte to have you. The duke possesses a rather short attention span. Unfortunately."

Ivy did not reply, her fingers twisting nervously about the stem of the fragile champagne goblet.

The lady touched her arm. "I see doubt in your eyes, Countess. You must know Ravenswood is devoted to you. He would not have married you otherwise, and he is so different with you."

Ivy's heart was doing funny things within her chest. She took a deep breath to still its wild thumping. "I'm not sure what you mean."

Examining her as if to determine Ivy's secret power in holding Sebastian's attention, Veronica chuckled. "Don't you? There is a visible hunger in his gaze when he looks at you, a desperate sort of craving. As though you calm him and yet, he fears your hold on him. It is most fascinating. I've known him for simply ages so I can verify his legendary indifference toward women. I've never seen him so captivated. His eyes look nowhere else but at you."

Ivy laid an impulsive hand to Veronica's arm. "Thank you, Lady Wesley. For your kindness now and that night."

"Ravenswood loves you, perhaps more than you realize. He would burn to the ground anyone who harmed you and gift you with the cinders, if you only asked him, I think." Veronica offered one last bit of advice as she took her leave. "Do take care to steer far away from Clayton, my dear. He is quite the vindictive sort."

Sara came up as Veronica glided away. Bristling with protectiveness, her arm slipped about Ivy's waist, and together they watched Lady Wesley slip through the crowd. "What was that about? Was she unpleasant? I swear I'll ..."

Ivy's reply was contemplative. "No, no, nothing like that. She and I merely discussed our mutual connection. She was quite lovely, actually."

"I can scarcely believe that..." Sara snorted, her eyes skating to the ballroom's entrance. A commotion was causing people to crowd close. A guest of some importance was making a late arrival.

"The Earl of Ravenswood." The magnificently uniformed and embellished majordomo announced in grave tones.

"Blast it all," Sara muttered. "Speak of the devil..."

Ivy drew up, the bones in her body rigid enough to snap in two. *He was here.* He had come and he would be looking for her.

"He is here," Ivy finished Sara's sentence, the three words containing enough frost to put the vastness of Siberia to shame.

CHAPTER 37

*S*ome type of internal honing instinct existed within Sebastian, tuned exclusively to the sight of his wife. A dizzying sense of déjà vu jolted him, seeing her across the ballroom floor with Sara standing at her side. It was a flashback to that first night, when he savagely sliced Ivy Kinley to ribbons for the perceived stain on his family's honor.

A crescendo of whispers and snippets of conversations bombarded him. His Aunt Rachel, in the midst of a small group of matrons, wore a faintly satisfied smile. Guilt assailed Sebastian as he weaved his way toward Ivy. *Damnit.* His failure to escort her to their first event as husband and wife would have gossip running amok of a rift between them. It looked bad. It *was* bad. Why had he left Ivy to face this alone?

Expressionless, she watched his approach and as he drew closer, she whispered in Sara's ear. Sara shook her head, lips tight with disapproval. Ivy whispered again, her features never changing although the conversation became obviously heated. Finally, throwing her hands into the air in a gesture of frustration, Sara stalked away to take up a position at Alan's side.

When Sebastian reached Ivy, he found his wife's eyes alit like twin pieces of blue-green coals. She had a right to be furious. He abandoned her and she had no idea why.

Gripping her arm before she flitted away, Sebastian gave what others would describe as the most mocking of bows then reeled her into his embrace as though she were a prize trout, hooked and landed.

"Good evening, Countess."

Sebastian took advantage of Ivy's astonishment by dropping a light kiss upon her slightly opened mouth.

Guests laughed in shocked delight. Ravenswood's public display of affection was deliciously scandalous.

"You're drunk," Ivy hissed. The bitter-sweet fumes of bourbon filled the space between them. "Where have you been?"

Where have you been?

A splendid question, one Sebastian could answer in the physical sense. But it was difficult to say where he was mentally. His soul was shattered by the conversation overheard that morning. He was so angry; emotionally twisted into a very strange place.

Ivy's emotions were equally high. Fury and embarrassment were a lethal combination in a woman. They should tread lightly, but Sebastian doubted this was possible for either of them.

"I spent the day at my clubs. Then an hour or so with my barrister, seeing to the responsibilities and duties required of an earl." Sebastian stressed the term, *"duties"*, but Ivy failed to react. "I'm not entirely drunk, my dear, but I am bored with this conversation. I prefer to be engaged in other activities, if the truth is known." He hated the almost petulant note his voice carried. "A pity I currently have only one viable option and must settle for it."

Ivy's form, displayed so enticingly in a champagne-hued ball gown, was subjected to his scorching appraisal. The fabric glittered, an intricate design of crystals and seed pearls sewn throughout the satin and the decadently low bodice displayed her assets to exquisite perfection. She had begun wearing the filigree butterfly every day; sometimes as a brooch, sometimes even as a hair ornament, fixed into her coiffure. Tonight, a gossamer piece of bronze ribbon threaded through the pin mechanism so it could be worn as a choker. It glittered against the pulse of her neck and Sebastian swallowed hard. She was so lush and seductive. His wife, oh, his beautiful, heartless wife managed to affect every one of his senses and it was infuriatingly magical. With an arm wrapped about her waist, he yanked her onto the ballroom floor where a waltz was just beginning.

Rather than struggle in his steel-like grip, Ivy allowed herself to be dragged along. She seemed to understand resisting would only create further scandal. Setting her focus somewhere over Sebastian's shoulder, she refused to meet his gaze as other couples joined them.

"Aren't you happy to see me?" His tone remained bland as he maneuvered her through the steps. It grated upon his nerves that she would not look at him.

"I'd be a great deal happier had you troubled yourself to escort me tonight."

"I am unavailable to attend your every whim, madam." Damn her for pointing out his transgressions, especially when he knew the full measure of each one. He should have been by her side. That was his duty. Just as hers was to provide him a son.

Ivy's gaze collided with his. With a choked sob, she said, "I cannot pretend to know your mind, Sebastian. Indeed, I find it difficult to understand what occurred from this morning, when you held me so tenderly, to this moment when you slice me to ribbons with your cruelty." She attempted to pull away, but he jerked her back, their bodies molding in a manner so indecent, Ivy gasped out loud.

Their behavior was snagging the attention of others, whispers spreading like wildfire. Sara hovered on the edge of the floor, eyes wide with uneasy anger. Bentley, arms crossed, a frankly concerned frown on his handsome features, seemed to debate what course to take. Either step between the couple, risking even more gossip or allow the crisis to play out.

With a moan of desolation, Ivy drew back.

"Don't you dare walk away from me, Ivy," Sebastian ground out between clenched teeth. He hated himself for the tears welling in her aqua colored eyes. He hated causing her pain. He would let her go in a moment. As soon as he explained things. He promised... promised he would let her go.

But something had snapped inside Ivy. Something frightening. The heat of her skin nearly burned his palm. She trembled in his hands.

"You are truly unbelievable," Ivy breathed. "Why should my humiliation come second to your embarrassment when I walk out on you, Sebastian?"

Several couples on the ballroom floor, attempting to eavesdrop before, now began to twirl in widening circles away from what appeared to be an impending explosion.

"You wouldn't dare," Sebastian growled. "It is your duty -"

Ivy's eyes flared with murderous intent.

"*My duty? My duty!* Don't you lecture to me about duties. You forced me into this marriage. You made promises you never intended to keep. And now you speak of duty? Do you know what you can do, Ravenswood? You can go straight to hell, you... you bloody liar!"

A wooden heeled slipper stomped the top of his foot with enough force to dent the polished ebony boot. Sebastian lurched back, losing the grip on her arm.

In a spinning flurry of champagne colored satin, Ivy escaped, her stony glares spawning enough heat to send guests skittering every whichaway. Whispers of a fire-breathing countess trailed in her wake, the crowd parting as if sliced with a sword and knitting back together just as quickly.

Infuriating barricades hampered Sebastian's pursuit. Those same guests who were so careful to steer clear of Ivy now crowded about him and even after shoving his way through a tangle of elbows and full skirts, Sebastian found himself drowning in a handful of debutantes.

Little birds of white surrounded him, all chirping high voices and dancing hands, intent on preventing the chase of his wife. His murderous stare cleaved a path through them, but one girl was determined to bar his way. Whenever Sebastian made to step around her, she glided in the same damn direction.

"We've not been introduced, my lord." She gave a soft laugh as they performed this strange, silent dance three times. "But, perhaps now is not the opportune time to point out our familial connection."

"Excuse me if I cannot linger." Sebastian muttered, barely comprehending the young woman's words. Peering over her head, he spied Ivy's gold gown disappearing through a side door.

The blonde blockader smiled. "I have only recently arrived for the remainder of the season. It is expected my guardian shall arrange introductions but I hoped to circumvent matters." Looking past him, the girl abruptly scowled, dipped an almost mocking curtsey and stepped aside. Sebastian saw a pretty brunette, a horrified expression etched on her face, barreling toward them. Upon reaching them, she clutched the blonde's elbow in a severe grip, and a fiercely whispered conversation ensued.

Sebastian, with a sigh of thankfulness, brushed past them both.

A formidable gang of five matrons threw themselves into his path next, clinging with offers of refreshments and frivolous conversation. Gritting his teeth, he responded with terse politeness to varied questions regarding rainclouds in Kent and the heat in London, and did he think the lemonade required more sugar. Only when he nearly tossed a full glass of lemonade back at one determined old hen, muttering a foul curse, did they finally relent and allow him to pass.

Only one gauntlet remained.

Sara.

Sweet, calm Sara. Sara, armed with words that sliced like knives and that fierce temper she kept hidden beneath a beautiful, china doll exterior.

She declared him an ass of magnificent proportions; a heartless cad who did not deserve a treasure like Ivy Kinley. He was unfit to lick her boots; too lowly in nature to clean her chamber pot. The attack was scathing, the girl holding tight to his coat sleeve, forcing him to hear every word before letting him loose with a scowl of disgust. Half of the ballroom bore shocked witness to the set down and it was only by the grace of his friendship with Alan that Sebastian did not physically remove the petite woman from his path. Eventually, Lord Morgan came to his aid, pulling his daughter away from him with a murmur.

Snarling with frustration, Sebastian burst into the main gallery. He must find Ivy. Somehow, he must undo this unholy mess.

A hand landed heavily on his shoulder.

Gabriel's brown eyes contained the chill of the moors. Alan stood nearby, fingers twitching no doubt with the desire to land a series of punishing blows to Sebastian's chin.

"Let her go, my friend." Alan gave his advice calmly, but the steel in his voice would have given any man reason to pause.

Sebastian rounded on them both. "Gabriel, if you wish to keep that hand, remove it. Now."

Gabriel's smile was hard and unfriendly, fingers tightening in direct contradiction to the warning. "You placed milady's safety in my hands. I'm following your directive. Keeping her safe."

"You are too angry to go after her," Alan echoed, moving to block Sebastian's path.

"I am warning you both." His own friends now betrayed him? Rage had him stuttering ineffectively. "Goddamn it…this is insane."

Gabriel's chuckle contained no mirth. "I swore to protect her. An oath you laid before me. And I will honor it, Sebastian, even if it means protecting her from you."

THEY KEPT SEBASTIAN AT THE GRAHAM BALL FOR TWO HOURS IN an effort to diffuse his anger. Only when he demonstrated full control of his emotions did the men accompany him home in

Alan's coach. Gabriel left Sebastian in Ravenswood Court's front hall, his unmarred brow raised in unspoken warning.

The flames from the low fire revealed his bed was empty; the covers drawn back, unrumpled. Ivy thought to sleep elsewhere tonight, did she? Sebastian did not blame her. Throwing off the black cutaway coat, he loosened his cravat, tossing it to the side. Boots were yanked off, left in a careless heap, his shirt landing in a crumpled pile on the floor. On bare feet, wearing only trousers, he tried the connecting door between the suites and found it locked.

The rap he gave the door was as sharp as his irritation. "Ivy. Open this door."

There was no response so he banged harder. Finally, a slight rustle could be heard on the other side. She was in there. She was in there and she wanted nothing to do with him. His voice vibrated harsher than his fists against the wood. "Open the damn door. Before I break it down."

After a long silence, her weary voice muffled by the thickness of the oak, Ivy replied, "Go away."

Stumped by her quiet resolution, Sebastian stared at the door, thinking what to do next.

It took a minute to recall the location of the key. For years, it sat in the drawer of the bedside if ever needed and pushing open the door to the countess's suite of rooms, Sebastian felt a rush of satisfaction. On bare feet, he padded silently forward until he stood where the lamplight formed a pool of illumination.

Ivy sat in the middle of the bed, a pale, yellow counterpane clutched to her bosom. Huge and liquid, her eyes followed him, bottom lip catching between her teeth when Sebastian held out the key, dangled it, then dropped it into his trouser pocket. She did not appear surprised or even alarmed that he gained entry with such ease. She seemed to expect it.

Crossing his arms, Sebastian prepared for the battle to come, and despite his previous anger, he was relatively calm. The evening was a disaster, but one of his own making. He possessed an unfortunate tendency to react in the worst possible manner with

Ivy, each incident only pushing her further away from him. Eventually, she would be so alienated as to be unreachable, and that reality was destroying him. He did not know what to do to make things better. He'd made the Devil's bargain when promising her that it was possible to wait until she loved him again.

In the weeks since their marriage, he had not succeeded in changing Ivy's heart. This failure, *his* failure, was slowly killing him.

~

IVY TURNED UP THE BEDSIDE LAMP AT THE SOUND OF THE KEY IN the lock. She watched in grim resolution as the door swung open and Sebastian prowled into the room. He waggled that key at her and dropped it in his pocket, mocking any effort to keep him locked out.

Drawing her knees to her chest, Ivy clutched them hard. Nearly three hours had passed since she fled from the Graham's ball. Where had Sebastian been? He wore only trousers, the muscles lining his ribs flexed with each deep breath. Seeing the tic in his jaw, and the way it clenched, Ivy knew it was only by the thinnest of threads he kept himself from snatching her up and shaking her.

From forehead to chin, Sebastian rubbed his face. "Never lock a door to me again, Ivy. Ever." His tone was blanketed in restrained composure.

"It did little good, obviously."

"Come to bed. *My* bed. Where you belong."

Her eyes narrowed. "You cannot be serious."

"It would be unwise to doubt my sincerity at the moment."

Ivy's teeth hurt from being clenched so hard. She shook her head. "If you think I shall jump at the snap of your fingers, you are a bloody fool. And I repeat my words directing you to go straight to hell." What motivated her husband to such irrational behavior was a mystery, one sure to bewilder her for many nights to come.

Sebastian's smile was faint, as if suddenly amused despite

everything. "You also called me a liar. No one has ever said that to my face and lived to tell the tale."

Ivy stared straight ahead. "Should you wish to call me out for the insult, I'm waiting."

"My intentions are quite different."

"I do not know your intentions, my lord. However, if you meant to demonstrate your disregard for me, you succeeded. You deceived me, Ravenswood, when you forced me to this marriage."

"I apologize for tonight." A frown darkened his features. "I was not in my right mind."

"Well, fortunately for the both of us, I'm in my right mind. I won't allow you to continue to use me." Ivy flicked him an icy glare. "You may take your apology, shove it up your arse and go straight to the devil."

"Ivy, I'm warning you."

She laughed at him. "Really? Or you'll do what? Make me mind my tongue? *Force* me to your bed? You are my husband. You may claim your rights any time you bloody well please, but this does not mean I must be agreeable in my heart and mind. My body may allow it, but I vow I will not be willing."

Sebastian appeared both distressed and furious at her words. Ivy hoped they struck at his heart, but she despised the truth hidden deep within her. While she hated him for his unexpected cruelty, and even if she submitted for the sake of duty, her body loved what he aroused in her.

Lashing out to grip her arm, Sebastian dragged her from the bed. Ivy did not resist.

"I can change your mind. You know I can," he said in a hoarse whisper, nibbling at her lower lip with a soft persuasiveness. "And I don't want to hurt you. Because we both know I can do that too."

Ivy shrugged. She had already decided to slip away from herself. "Do as you wish, my lord."

A confection of a nightgown, the fabric soft and billowy, flowed around her form. It was new, one of many Sebastian special ordered for her before leaving Beaumont. The extravagant parcel arrived at Ravenswood Court only the day before, and her squeal of delight at the unexpected gift pleased him. Simple ribbons held the pale, blush-hued garment together along the sides; should they come loose, the entire thing would fall to her feet. Damn her haste in grabbing the first one in the wardrobe. It would be the easiest to remove.

Sebastian's fingers did not move to those bits of silk. Instead, he kissed her with growing insistence, and Ivy hated him when her eyes became wet with tears.

"I should have considered how my actions would affect you," he murmured, hands cradling her face, his thumbs gently swiping away the dampness on her cheeks. "I did not think…"

"Whatever you are going to do, do it quickly and leave me be."

Grim determination settled over his features and Ivy shuddered, abruptly realizing what she just gave him permission to do. He would not allow her to detach herself, would not allow her to deny her own pleasure. Resignation froze her in place as he gently unplaited the braid of her hair until the shiny chestnut strands flowed over her shoulders. A wounded doe, she had placed herself at the feet of the wolf and dared him not to devour her.

His thumb brushed the curve of her jaw. "Shall I show you how sincere I am in my apology?"

Ivy arched to avoid contact, but it only made it easier for him to touch her. He cupped her breasts through the cloud of fabric, filling his hands with her flesh and like heated sugar, her insides melted. "You and your apologies be damned." A moan, tiny and helpless, drowning in the back of her throat, revealed everything.

Sebastian smiled at the sound of it.

He abruptly spun her around, pulling her against him until his hips cradled her bottom and she was anchored in place. Keeping one arm locked around her waist, he swept the mass of hair off her neck while his other hand moved to her breast. Teasing her through the delicate cloth, he applied slight pressure to her nipple, pinching harder before those wicked fingers moved to torment the other.

Ivy lurched away, but Sebastian's arm tightened, forcing her to feel every part of his muscled form and the rigid proof of his desire. Rocking against her, his hand drifted to the junction of her thighs, and then he was cupping her there. When he nuzzled her ear, Ivy quivered. She *could* resist him. She must resist him! But that seemed impossible when he ignited every nerve ending in her body.

Sebastian's fingers moved away from her center, wandering up along her flanks. She gulped in relief that his hand was no longer between her legs until there was a slight tug on the ribbons. A flutter of fabric and the gown fell away as if commanded by unseen forces. Ivy braced herself, knowing what was to come, the sweet and savage wildness of it all as his hand slid over the silky skin of her stomach to nestle again at the apex of her thighs. His fingers delved into her heat, his other hand stroking her breast.

Between kisses to the slender column of her throat, Sebastian's laugh contained a rueful softness. "Look down, Ivy. See my hands upon you? How you tremble...so violently...your little pants of breath, the heat of your skin. The way your pupils dilate when I touch you here...like this." He pressed two fingers against the throbbing button of flesh and Ivy gasped. "Knowing how I affect you drives me crazy." Running his tongue in a swirling pattern on the sensitive skin at the back of her neck elicited another whimper from her. "I am sorry for tonight, my love. How shall I prove it to you?"

"Be quick then leave me alone." Ivy sagged against him. Blood rushed through her veins so hard and fast she felt faint. His mouth on her skin was an awful reminder of his power over her and the delight she found in it.

Glancing down, she immediately wished she had not. Against the creamy hue of her flesh, the darkness of his hands was hypnotic. "Please." Her ability to resist was near a breaking point, the whisper a desperate plea. "Just do what you must..." She felt his smile as he nuzzled her.

"Oh, Ivy. My very heartbeat. It's not that simple. Not between us. Don't you realize this by now?" Spearing his fingers through the soft curls between her thighs, his mouth fastened on the nape of her neck. With just enough pressure to trigger pain, he bit her.

A thrill flashed straight to the center of Ivy's soul.

Keeping a steady tempo with his fingers, his teeth repeatedly sank into her flesh in different places along the line of her shoulder and neck. The pain was almost too sharp, the pattern of nibbles and full mouth tastes of her skin always followed by a sweep of his tongue to soothe the sting.

The overload of stimulation was too much. Ivy came apart, intense pleasure leaving her on the point of collapse. Sebastian held her tight to prevent her from sinking to the floor in a puddle of satisfaction. The sensations coursing through her were too dangerous, too powerful, too much of everything to fully comprehend or absorb.

She was barely aware when he scooped her up. Carrying her to his room, he laid her diagonally across the huge bed, and he appeared to hover on the edge of indecision. Then slowly, Sebastian turned her on her stomach, gathering her hair off the nape of her neck. Weakened, confused, Ivy remained as he placed her, listening as he divested himself of his trousers. When his warm hands smoothed over her buttocks, a nervous jolt of awareness streaked through her. She tried to roll from the bed, but he quickly prevented any hope of escape.

"Shhh, little butterfly. Do not flutter about so. I swear there will be only pleasure. Trust me, sweet Ivy. God knows you've reason enough not to, but trust me in this. I won't harm you…"

The words were dark whispers, his large hands roaming the twin mounds of her bottom. With exacting pressure, he pushed her shoulders until she was once again flat on her stomach then seizing her by the hips, he tugged her to the edge of the bed to stand between her legs. Ivy pressed her cheek against the coverlet, her arms tucked beneath her body until Sebastian gently dragged them high over her head.

"Stay," he murmured, and Ivy did as he ordered, trembling,

waiting, hating herself for the anticipation strumming through her veins.

She did not like this position, the helplessness of it. She did *not* like being unable to see what Sebastian intended to do. Still, she did not move, not even when his hand swept into the heat between her legs, causing her to moan in distressed delight. When two of his fingers pressed deep inside her, she choked back a cry and did as he commanded. She stayed.

This unfamiliar position was intoxicating. And confusing. Her body did not know whether to bear down on his hand and the firmness of the bed, or rise up to meet the slow plunging. Her hands twisted the coverlet as his fingers sank into her again and again, the sensation so different from when he stroked her to completion, when the focus centered on the tiny bit of flesh at the apex of her center. Those strong, clever fingers delved deep, drawing her moisture out, the unrelenting movements driving her closer to the edge of heaven. Her hips undulated with the pace he set.

"Are you ready for me, Ivy?" Sebastian murmured, tracing the outline of her spine with his tongue. From the nape of her neck to the hollow of her lower back, he blazed a trail of fire before his teeth raked over the twin globes of her buttocks. His fingers never stopped the relentless surging in and out and Ivy was unable to stop her body from mimicking the motion of his hand. "This is your duty, after all. To submit, to do as I bid you. Sweet love, you are so wet, so hot. You will not deny your responsibility to this. How can you when you need it as much as I?" His low voice contained an undeniable note of bitterness.

"Stop..." Ivy trembled uncontrollably, the sensations becoming too much to endure. She was going mad, insane, her skin coming loose from bones. Despite begging him to cease, her hips continued to rise and fall, her body writhing against his hand, clenching on his fingers in greedy demand. *"Please....please..."*

Sebastian ignored her, laughing softly. Hardly missing a beat, his fingers were replaced with the smooth fullness of his erection. The heat and width of his body, stretching her, only half-buried inside her and yet filling her so unequivocally, sent her soaring. He whispered a hoarse command, "Let me in," impaling her until she opened to him completely.

His harsh groan of conquest echoed in the room and Ivy exploded with a shuddering cry, her flesh clamping around him when he thrust harder, burying himself to the hilt. A rushing wave of intense pleasure covered her. Disoriented, she could only gasp helplessly.

Sebastian let the sensations wash and ebb before gripping her hips with hard, needy hands. Lifting her, he placed her in the position he desired, on her hands and knees. Shaken by her powerful response, Ivy attempted to edge away only earn a cautionary slap to her rump. He bent over her, caging her with his body and preventing escape.

"Again." The demand was a cajoling hiss against the nape of her neck. He nipped her ear and she writhed against him, her rounded bottom hitting the lower portion of his belly in a tentative rocking motion. Keeping one hand on her flank, Sebastian guided her, fisting a handful of her hair in the other, tangling his fingers almost painfully in it. Dominating her, mastering her, he plunged into her body as though she were specifically crafted for his lust.

Ivy welcomed it. Even as he pulled her hair until her face turned to his and their mouths sealed together. Even when he kissed her with brutal possessiveness, taking her like a stallion mounting a mare, the act and position a primal reminder she belonged to him. He would do to her as he pleased. And she allowed it.

Because she loved him. She had always loved him. She would always love him. Only him. She would love him until her heart stopped beating. Until the world and everything in it fell apart around them. The knowledge destroyed her. Inside, she wept as Sebastian pushed her with relentless authority to the glittering edge then tumbled over with her, at the end of his own endurance.

Their climaxes drained them both. His body sagged over hers as they sank into the mattress, melting into the bedclothes. His muscled chest pressed like a heavy weight against her back, but Ivy did not care if he crushed her. She was too lethargic to care, too fragile and emotionally bruised. Confused by her own emotions and feelings for this man, this man who trampled her so brutally and caressed her with such aching tenderness at the same time. What was wrong with her? Why did she allow him to do such wicked things and secretly thrill to have them done? How had he managed to corrupt her to the point she craved his touch even when he hurt her so terribly?

"I don't give a damn if you believe this is merely your duty," Sebastian abruptly rolled to his back, pulling Ivy to him, his lips touching her temple in a fleeting caress. "I won't allow you to keep yourself from me."

～

IVY TURNED ON HER SIDE, AWAY FROM HIM, TREMBLING. EVEN after that rocketing encounter, when it seemed he'd reached into her soul, she was icy as ever.

"What are you thinking?" Sebastian swallowed around the sharp pain in his throat. It devastated him that she would not bend. Why would she not allow him inside her heart?

"You said this is my duty." She sounded sleepy and unexpectedly heartbroken.

He could not hide his bitterness. "Yes."

"Is that all this is to you?"

"What is this to *you*, Ivy?" Silence fell between them until he rasped, "I overheard you with Sara." She did not respond. Did his eavesdropping offend her? *It's my damned house…I will listen to any conversation I damn well please.* "You think sharing my bed is a responsibility until you give me my heir." His voice cracked with restrained vehemence. "Ivy, no matter how many sons you give me, one or a dozen, I will still want you. With every breath of my soul, I crave you. My hunger, my appetite for you, is insatiable. I suggest you accustom yourself to that fact."

Rising to a half - sitting position, Ivy's eyes flashed in the dim light. "What would you have me tell Sara? That Lord Bentley should have her before marriage?" She laughed softly at Sebastian's frown. "The consequences for a woman are so much greater than a man can comprehend. If only it were a simple matter of indulging our desires without a care. Shall I advise her not to wait? Throw all caution to the wind? To take her chances and pray a child is not conceived before vows are exchanged? "

"You said *this* was a duty, to provide my children. I need more from you than a damned heir to my estates." His words dripped with ice. "I want more than that."

Ivy's lower lip trembled. "This *is* my duty. I swore a vow before God, and I will honor it. Sebastian...how could I possibly tell Sara how *this* feels? That every time you touch me, I shatter. That I am turned to liquid, your kisses leave me weak, wanting more. When I feel most alive is in your arms. Should I tell her that sometimes my heart feels so full of emotion I believe it may burst? Do you think this will keep her from her beloved's bed until they wed?" She choked as the confession tumbled out. "The scandal would ruin her and I adore her too much to wish my experiences upon her, to have the *ton* rip apart her soul with their viciousness. I know too well how it hurts."

The reality of the truth, hearing it from Ivy's lips, stung more than Sebastian ever imagined. Knowing she felt so deeply for him, even after his many abuses of her, twisted his gut. He'd done things, things impossible to undo. And it seemed he could not stop making the same mistakes.

It was unwise, returning to London so soon after their wedding. At Beaumont, matters were simplistic, their relationship becoming a passionate, sweet yearning neither could resist. But in this house, it was altogether different. Sebastian imagined he felt the ghost of Timothy Garrett lingering between them and his aunt's thinly veiled censure coated the air like a poisoned fog. The heavy eyes of the *ton* watched their every move, reporting all with glee. It left him with a heightened sense of betrayal and an unfortunate tendency of overreacting. He was the very Devil, here in London.

Ivy was right. What else could she have said to Sara? What other advice was there to give? Sebastian felt sick. Good God, how could she abide him when he continued to torment her like this? He caused her such heartache. He truly was a monster.

"Is this why you abandoned me tonight?" Ivy asked quietly.

"Damnit, Ivy, I apologized."

"Your apologies are used to bend me to your will. You do and say what you wish and pathetic creature that I am, I forgive you. And allow you to do far worse the next time. You proved your mastery over me. Congratulations."

"Bloody hell, it's not like that." Sebastian slumped against the pillows, an arm resting across his forehead while he struggled to find the right words. "I want you in my bed because you wish it. I want you with me because you love me. Not because you believe it is your duty to be here. I want you, Ivy. All of you. I will not rest, damn it, I *cannot* rest until I have all of you. I'm going mad trying to find a way to make you mine."

Ivy crumpled. Unable to keep from touching him, one small hand came to rest upon his chest, right on his heart and Sebastian covered it with his own, trapping her slender fingers.

For a long time, they lay in silence, each wrestling with despair. Just when he believed she must have fallen asleep, Ivy gave a deep sigh.

"Sebastian, don't you understand?" she said, soft and drowsy with exhaustion. "I've always been yours."

CHAPTER 38

*S*ebastian watched Ivy donned a riding habit. She did not bother to ring for Molly's assistance. "Where are you going?" A flare of panic ignited in his eyes.

Waking from a restless slumber to find one's wife entirely dressed, ready to escape, was surely an unnerving sight and regret stabbed Ivy. She'd grown accustomed to their mornings together; sharing tea, coffee, and sugar biscuits while discussing their plans for the day were now treasured moments. But not this morning. Her emotions were too tangled and raw to face him without bursting into overwrought tears.

Her boots were yanked on with fierce tugs. "Riding." Taking a deep breath, she clarified, "Alone. I... I need time alone. To think."

Sebastian's gaze morphed into cool steel. "It's not safe at this hour."

"I'll take a groom." Ivy finally dared to look at him reclining against the pillows, bare chested, sheets twisted about his waist. A lock of raven black hair tumbled over his brow; she almost crossed over to brush it back before catching herself. Considering her intention, his jaw clenched with annoyance.

"Stay close to your escort. And Ivy, when you return, you and I will have a necessary conversation on what is to be done."

Tears springing to her eyes, Ivy ducked her head and hurried from the room.

No one was stirring in the stables at this time of the morning so Ivy saddled Spring herself and led the mare to the curving gravel path in front of the stables. While wondering if she possessed the bravery to defy Sebastian's order, Gabriel rounded the corner of the building. Even in the grey predawn light, his broad form was recognizable.

Ivy's lips tightened. "He rang for you the moment I left, didn't he?"

"Of course. Which is why I must ask where is your groom, milady?" Gabriel's brow rose high as Ivy climbed the mounting block without answering him. He held Spring by the bit while she mounted the mare and gathered the reins. The leather was buttery soft in her bare hands; in the haste to escape Sebastian, she forgot both riding gloves and hat.

"There's no one to ask."

"You cannot ride unaccompanied." He held up a hand as Ivy made to argue the point. "He'll have my head on a platter, as well you know."

Ivy met Gabriel's calm amber-hued stare. "Try to keep up, but do not get too close. I desire privacy this morning and after last night's fiasco, I deserve it."

At first, she kept a sedate pace, contemplating the evening before. The fact Sebastian overheard her comments to Sara muddled things in their fragile relationship. Did she truly mean those words now? Sebastian pressed for something she could not give him... a declaration of love, a surrender of her soul she could not bear to actually forfeit. He wanted to possess all parts of her. She shivered, thinking of the previous evening. The dominant nature of Sebastian's lovemaking was worrisome, containing some element of male governance she had yet to unravel.

Ivy wished herself a million miles from London, from England, away from the troubles twisting her inside out. She was shattered from fighting her husband and her own emotions; mentally exhausted in these attempts to outfox him. She craved blankness, a tiny sliver of time where she could wipe her mind clean. When her knees touched Spring's flanks, the mare shot forward, eager to gallop at the speed her mistress demanded and Ivy realized that peace was attainable, if only for a short time, riding in the early morning fog.

Racing through Hyde Park's open fields, Ivy ignored the carefully manicured gravel pathways where London society rode in aimless, pointless circles every afternoon. Had Sebastian chanced upon her, witnessed the dangerous pace she set, he would have tossed her skirts to give her rump a furious blistering. Thoughts of his anger proved incentive enough to drive the mare faster, the speed almost violent. Riding hard and fast emptied Ivy's mind of the issues crowding it. Soon, there was nothing other than the muscles of the horse beneath her, the whip of the mane against her face when she bent over the mare's neck, and the crisp morning air stinging her cheeks until her eyes watered.

There were few souls who ventured into the park this early and they were mere silhouettes in the misty distance. Spring tossed her fine head as Ivy loosened the reins to urge a speed bordering on perilous. Gabriel did not intervene, but undoubtedly her pace frightened him. As she entered small groves bright green with early summer leaves, he would catch up then fall behind once she reached open fields. As long as she was visible, he gave her the freedom to go where she willed, as fast as she desired.

Exiting a strand of trees, Ivy caught sight of two riders and one, streaking toward her on a flashy sorrel, was much closer than she initially thought. The other rode a huge bay with one white stocking, and shouted in a voice rough with irritation, "S*low down!"*

Ignoring the command, the smaller, faster rider was soon racing alongside Ivy and Spring gave a familiar squeal of anger at the direct challenge. For nearly a half mile, the pair thundered along as if a queen's fortune in diamonds lay at stake. Chunks of turf flew in all directions from flashing hooves as the headstrong gray mare outstripped the sorrel with ease.

The sound of feminine laughter made Ivy tug back on the reins. Pulling the mare into a half circle, she brought Spring to a snorting halt. Eager to continue the race, the gray cantered and spun in place, hooves churning up the soft grass as the other rider drew close.

It was the girl from the Graham's ball, the one who had captured Ivy's attention by standing with, but somehow apart, from the group of debutantes. She wore fawn-colored breeches and a white linen shirt, topped with a man's style black riding coat cut to exacting trim proportions. Ivy noted enviously that she rode astride, her long legs encased in scuffed brown boots gripping the horse's flanks. The gelding heeded every subtle command of the girl's knee. A black cap covered her head and when she swept it off, a cascade of stick-straight, sunshine blonde hair was released. The girl's mouth curved into a wide grin almost disturbing in its lushness.

"You ride magnificently, my lady. Is it not shameful women are barred from the Newmarket Races? I vow we could set the place on its ear if only allowed to show those arrogant men how it's done!"

Both horses pricked their ears. Husky and feminine with an intriguing lilt, the girl's voice held the power to effortlessly arrest the attention of both men and beast. Her admiring gaze passed over Spring. "That mare is splendid. She must be from Ravenswood's own stables. My guess is an offspring of that devil of a stallion he owns."

Ivy nodded in silent agreement. She noticed Gabriel corralling the girl's companion and following a brief conversation, the two men set toward them at a more leisurely pace.

"I'm Lady Grace Willsdown." Leaning over the blowing sorrel, the girl offered her hand as a gentleman would. A rueful bark of laughter escaped her at Ivy's surprise. "Sorry. A dreadful habit. I do forget that not everyone is forging business deals when excellent horseflesh is around." Her head cocked in an inquisitive manner. "But it's damn difficult to curtsy while on horseback, don't you agree?"

Charmed by the girl's blunt manner, Ivy grinned. "I am-"

"Lady Ravenswood, of course. You and the earl seem to be the subjects of choice this season." Grace's honey gold eyes flashed with both sympathy and instant regret. "Forgive me, my lady. I have a distressing tendency to say things quite improperly. What I meant is, everyone knows of you."

Ivy was unoffended by the girl's candor, for there was no artifice in Grace Willsdown, no cruelty lurking behind her smile.

Grace reached up, ruffling a shock of hair on her forehead so the silk strands fell into place, pieces of it framing her face in an appealing manner. It was quite long, tumbling to her waist. Although some might consider it boyish in nature, the fringe across her forehead somehow made her features more feminine.

She was not gently beautiful, at least not by the current standards dictating women be soft, wispy creatures speaking in demure tones. There was something brashly irresistible about her, a genuine sweetness, and when combined with bronze hued eyes and skin touched with the sun's rays, it all made Lady Grace quite stunning.

Realizing Ivy was assessing her hair style, Grace chuckled. "Never let anyone curl your hair unless they first practiced on their own." She ran her fingers again through the blonde pieces. "My guardian's daughter, Celia, burnt off what was wrapped about the iron, then mourned my loss for two days. No matter, it's only hair, and it does grow back. If only you'd seen it three months ago! Oh, it was beyond dreadful."

Ivy choked on a laugh before composing herself. "Have you been in London for the season? I confess I do not recall making your acquaintance."

With a glance over her shoulder to determine her companion's whereabouts, Grace nudged the sorrel closer. "One month. One long agonizing month." Her sigh was intentionally dramatic. "My guardians have only allowed me to attend certain functions as apparently, I lack a certain decorum deemed necessary for London Society. I've been trying so damnably hard, too. Gaining this social polish." Grace brightened. "Every morning I've ridden in this park and it's been the only cheerful spot during my time here. However, today I saw you and knew I must introduce myself. I wished to do so last night, although the situation was not appropriate. Even I, with my deplorable lack of refinement, realized that." Her tone brisk, she continued, "You see, Lady Ravenswood, I confess to ulterior motives. I own a rather magnificent stallion, and my fervent hope is to persuade the earl to consider a breeding venture. Or, in the alternative, introduce his Raven to one of my fine mares. My guardian would have my head if I approached Ravenswood with a suggestion of breeding horses, though. Quite the delicate subject, you understand. The earl was distracted last evening but I do hope he'll listen to my proposal. Being we *are* cousins, it is not completely beyond the bounds for us to converse."

"Wait." Ivy frowned in confusion at the twisting conversation. "What?"

"I've shocked you," Grace crowed in delight, her lush mouth stretched into an infectious grin. "Was it the indelicate subject of horse breeding or the fact we are indeed cousins? Ravenswood and I, that is. Fourth cousins. Or is it fifth? Do forgive me; I forget... yes, I believe it is fifth. When my father, the Earl of Willsdown died, the title ceded to Ravenswood. And, when my dear mother passed, their friends, the Earl of Darby and his wife, were named my guardians. It's all so devilishly complicated. Men tend to do these things when they are in control of a woman's future. I find it quite maddening and wholly unnecessary, don't you?"

Grace seemed not to notice Ivy's open-mouth shock and continued with a merry breeziness. "When I reach the age of twenty-one, I shall return to my Bellmar Abbey in Cornwall. And, social polish be damned, I shall ride my horses when I please, how I please, dressed as I please. I'm very fortunate my majority was not set at twenty-five, as most young women in my situation find themselves. Bless my mother for that… she obtained a special petition to allow it. I shall have full control of my inheritance and my horses and won't be forced to ride at the crack of dawn so as not to be seen in my scandalous breeches. Do you think one was meant to wear a skirt and sit sideways on a horse, Lady Ivy? It puts one at a terrible disadvantage. How is it possible to control your mount if you are unable to utilize your legs, your calves and both heels? It's what they respond to. Much more so than a bit. I daresay a sidesaddle is the silliest invention created by man…with the exception of a corset. I've refused to wear one when riding, a corset that is, not a sidesaddle. Lady Darby believes it very wicked of me, and while I do hate to disappoint her, they are devilish things."

"Please, you must call me Ivy." Caught off guard by the girl's outspoken views on saddle equipment and women's fashion, Ivy nearly stuttered. "I'm so sorry for the loss of your parents."

Undeniable sadness crossed Grace's features. She ducked her head in appreciation of the condolences, and then brightened, as though a shadow passed from in front of the sun, leaving everything joyful once more. "Thank you. Please call me Grace. After all, as I said, we are cousins." She threw Ivy an admiring look. "I do wish we'd met upon my arriving in London. Things would not have been so dreadfully dull."

"Lord Longleigh was remiss in making introductions last night," Ivy said slowly. "He also failed to mention the family connections."

Grace grimaced, blowing the hair off her forehead with an outward puff of her lips. "Yes. I certainly mean no offense, but my assumption is Tristan sought your favor in a misguided attempt of provoking my jealousy. You see, he's only recently decided he is in love with me and I believe it is more of a physical attraction than anything else, much along the lines of what stallions feel for mares during the first part of spring. I've told him as gently as possible I am not interested. Neither Lord nor Lady Darby has encouraged him in this, for which I am ever so grateful. It would be an awkward situation if his parents did wish such an alliance."

Hoof beats boomed in the distance, and hearing them, Grace's chin tilted. A stubborn glint to her golden eyes, she said to Ivy, "Please say nothing of what I divulged. He's yet to accept it, and squeals like a rejected stallion when reminded of my indifference."

Ivy clearly saw the desire in Longleigh's eyes. That, and a fair amount of annoyance.

"Grace." A muscle ticked in his stern jaw. Astonishingly handsome, with deep chocolate-tinged eyes and dark brown hair glimmering with glints of auburn, his broad shoulders fit his navy blue riding jacket to perfection. Long muscular legs in buff colored breeches gripped his horse's flanks with just the precise amount of pressure. "I realize you insist on riding pell-mell whenever the opportunity presents itself, but for God's sake, you will end up breaking your neck."

Undaunted, Grace rolled her eyes. "Do not accompany me if you cannot keep up."

Tristan drew up ramrod straight, his face darkening as he bit out, "My concern is for your safety."

"That, and my neck, are my own to worry over." With careless aplomb, Grace steered the conversation to Ivy instead. "Aren't you pleased to see the Countess of Ravenswood?"

Longleigh gave Ivy a tight smile, his frustration with Grace still readily apparent. "Lady Ravenswood. How wonderful to see you this beautiful morning. I trust Ravenswood is well? He did not seem himself last evening."

Ivy grit her teeth. "My husband was uninterested in an early morning ride, sir, but his health is fine. Grace was just explaining her connection to my husband. It would be lovely for Lord and Lady Darby to pay us a visit so that formal introductions may be undertaken. Or perhaps the earl and I may come to call?"

"I believe my mother intended to wait until the summer season was upon us." Tristan nudged his gelding closer to Grace's mount, ignoring when her lips tightened in exasperation.

"Perhaps once we've settled at Beaumont, you could all come

for an extended visit. Grace, you might be particularly interested in seeing our stables there." Ivy offered.

"I would indeed." The girl's features lit up with the sparkle of a firefly while Tristan groaned in obvious dismay.

"Lady Ravenswood, do you even realize the danger of your offer? You'll never be able to convince Lady Grace to leave your estate."

❦

SEBASTIAN WAS ABSENT FROM THEIR ROOMS WHEN IVY RETURNED. As Molly assisted her with a bath, she learned the earl was in his study, but left instructions that she was to join him for breakfast when she was presentable.

An hour later, Ivy slipped into the dining room, taking a seat at the head of the table, opposite the end Sebastian and she usually occupied together. While servants carried in breakfast platters, she fidgeted, and when a footman opened the door to admit her husband, her stomach dropped to her feet at seeing Sebastian's frown. She'd seated herself so far away they might as well have been on opposite ends of the earth. With an unconcerned shrug, he stalked to her end of the table, hauling a chair closer until his elbow touched her own. Fordham raised a brow and without comment, relocated the earl's place setting and poured the coffee while Ivy shifted on the hard, wooden plane of her chair.

It simply wasn't done...the seating arrangement highly improper. The earl should be at the head of his table - not to her left, as if she occupied a place of honor.

A curious detachment clung to Sebastian while he gazed at her with eyes of flint. He seemed to have trouble deciding how best to deal with her and the issues raised the night before. And although outwardly calm, every nerve in Ivy's body prickled with aware-ness. She was so tightly wound, waiting for him to say something, she thought she might shatter into a million pieces.

"How was your ride?" His voice, so abrupt after so long a silence, had Ivy nearly dropping her teacup.

"Fine."

Sebastian's eyebrow rose at her one syllable answer. With a single glance toward the servants, his unspoken command was obeyed. In a matter of seconds, the room cleared.

Elbows on the table, he sighed, resting his head in his hands, raking fingers through his hair until it stood on end. "Tell me, Ivy, what do you want of me? Tell me what to give you and I shall do it. Tell me what to say, and I shall say it. I was wrong...not giving you a chance to explain your position." His voice dropped so low, Ivy strained to hear his words. "What happened between us - I shouldn't have been so damned rough with you. Should not have used you like that...last night was a disaster, but you know I don't want this to be the way of things."

"I don't know what you want, my lord." Ivy's cold hands curled around the teacup, wishing its warmth would seep into her.

He took the teacup so his fingers could twine with hers. "Ivy. I want you. But I can't have you, can I?" With one hand, he rubbed his eyes again. "Maybe you will never be mine as you once were. Maybe this was a mistake."

Ivy regarded Sebastian with despair. "I told you this would happen when you forced me to marry you. When I feel my heart opening to you, it is crushed beneath your heel."

His eyes sparked with guilt, recognizing the truth in her words. "But your heart is not open to me. Tell me what I must do to change it.

"I don't know. I don't wish to quarrel. I...I just want to be happy."

"You don't believe I can make you happy, my love?"

"At Beaumont, it seemed possible. Everything was so much easier there. But now, I'm not sure. Sebastian, I want to be where you are, but we are both miserable. Don't you see?" Ivy's lips clamped together in a hard line, abruptly breaking off the desolate confession. "I don't know what to do."

"Little did I realize what a poor husband I would make. I know that is of no comfort to you, when I must atone for my actions time and again. But even if I were able to let you go, Ivy, I would not," Sebastian declared quietly. "I told you once, you are mine. What is mine, I keep. That will not change - it will never change. You belong with me and here you will stay. I love you with every breath of my soul. If you were to leave me, I would not survive without you."

CHAPTER 39

$\mathcal{I}$vy avoided Sebastian for the rest of the day, taking her meals in her room. Suffering bouts of revolving nausea, she only picked at her lunch, sending the tray back to the kitchens practically untouched. However, by the time dinner rolled around, she was ravenous and cleared the plate of every morsel.

It was late evening when she made her way to the library and having neither seen nor heard from Sebastian since their conversation that morning, Ivy thought he might have slipped out to one of his clubs. Obviously, he did not wish to see her and that hurt more than she cared to admit.

Hearing voices coming from within the library, Ivy steeled her shoulders, moving silently as she entered the cavernous space. She would not scurry away like a frightened mouse. Peeking around a column, she saw Rachel seated near the fireplace, one hand pressed to her chest as if greatly pained.

It was shocking to see his aunt. With the exception of the Graham Ball, neither Ivy nor Sebastian saw much of her. Rachel tended to a full social calendar with a few other matrons and when at home, she kept to her rooms.

"Sebastian, it is for your safety. Please, send her elsewhere... for your own sake."

Sebastian gave his aunt a cold stare. "Madam, I'd cut off my own arm before sending Ivy away from me."

Rachel's lips flattened into thin lines of bitterness. "There is no understanding your fascination. She's dangerous. You need protection from..."

"Don't." His hand rose in warning.

"But I-"

"Cease!" Sebastian's voice quivered with barely leashed anger. "Or it is you I shall send away."

Rachel's mouth snapped shut, then with a deep breath, she ignored her nephew's cautionary words. "Because of Timothy, I must voice my concerns. You are as obsessed as he, and just as blind. You will suffer his same fate."

Sebastian leaned against the dark oak mantle of the fireplace, swirling a crystal tumbler in his hand. Only the barest hint of amber colored liquid remained in the glass. Hidden by the massive columns, Ivy sagged against the wall. Yes, it was eavesdropping, but she could not find the willpower to leave.

"Your relationship borders on toxic. How can you ignore your suspicions? Gabriel told you of her meeting with Longleigh this morning. She danced with many men last evening; he was just one of her partners before your arrival. At one point, the two of them disappeared onto the terrace together. They were absent so long, I almost ventured after her. To stem the inevitable gossip. Sebastian, the girl is playing you a merry game, just as she did with my Timothy and all the others."

"Aunt Rachel, you are my father's only sister and I have an interest in your well-being. I shall repeat this one more time. The last time," Sebastian advanced upon his aunt with fists clenched, his features twisted into a mask of reserved violence. "Say another word against my wife, and I will, without hesitation, have you permanently removed from this house. Is this clear?"

Rachel abruptly nodded her head, standing to take her leave. "It is unfortunate you will not listen to reason, just as my son would not. If you'll excuse me, I shall retire now." Whirling on her heel, her face oddly pinched, she hurried away from him as Ivy stepped from behind the column.

Sebastian's eyes slid to her then back to staring at the fire.

"I did not mean to intrude on your conversation," Ivy murmured. "I only came to select a book." Her face flamed at Sebastian's cutting dismissal of her presence, tears stabbing like hot pokers at her eyes. She walked blindly toward the nearest set of shelves. It could hold the history of astrology in regards to the ancient Greeks or the bawdiest of Irish limericks and she would not care. She only knew she would not cry. *I will not! Not in front of her! Or him!*

"You walk as silently as a cat, my dear. One never knows when or where you might show up." Rachel followed Ivy, her tone conversational. "Ravenswood Court has acquired many fine works of Shakespeare over the years. From comedies to tragedies, you'll find them on that shelf. I have my favorites, if you care for a recommendation."

Ivy did not trust herself to say anything, did not even dare turn around, since her palm fairly itched to slap the older woman.

Rachel came closer, perusing the shelf Ivy stared at blindly. "Try *Hamlet,* my dear. Complicated, but a true masterpiece."

Although she ground her teeth at the subtle jab regarding the infamous play centered on family and multiple poisonings and suicides, somehow, by the grace of God, or maybe the Devil, Ivy's calm demeanor remained in place as her fingers glided over leather spines, tracing the titles etched in gold.

Realizing her prey refused to take the bait, Rachel sniffed in defeat and floated from the library in a cloud of black.

"I honestly did not know you were in here," Ivy murmured as the silence stretched until it became a living, breathing entity inhabiting the library's mahogany paneled walls. Deliberately skipping *Hamlet*, she slid *The Tempest* from its place. How difficult it was, ignoring Rachel's insinuation she was little more than an interloper in Sebastian's household, or, even worse, that she might seek an affair with another man. Her fingers clenched with both anger and hurt, the pain a thousand times sharper because her husband failed to dispute his aunt's suggestion.

"Why did you not tell me you rendezvoused with the Viscount Longleigh?"

Ivy turned, holding the book to her chest as though it were a tiny shield. "I met Lady Grace Willsdown during my ride. Lord Longleigh's father serves as her guardian and the viscount provided her escort this morning. I did not meet them by previous arrangement."

"Didn't you?" The question was soft. "Was the mysterious Lady Willsdown at the ball last night? Is she now tasked with making your assignments? Longleigh was not one of the Pack, nor part of Clayton's group. Why his sudden interest in you? Or does he simply facilitate your meeting someone else? He is very close to the Duke of Richeforte, although I'm sure you know that."

"Lady Grace Willsdown is your fifth cousin and her father's title passed to you years ago, had you bothered to take notice of it. I had no idea either she or Longleigh would be in the park this morning - "

Sebastian interrupted her with a snarl. "Damnit, Ivy. Do you take me for a fool?"

"It is the truth, or Gabriel would have told you otherwise," she said flatly. "You are welcome to question Longleigh. Or, your newly discovered cousin, should you like."

"Why did you not tell me you met him there?" The question was repeated just as gently as before, his voice containing a strange quiver.

Ivy's eyes narrowed. "Because, I did not *meet* him. There, or anywhere, for that matter."

Sebastian's hands shook the tiniest bit as he swallowed the rest of the brandy. His fingers clenched the glass hard enough to crack it before he tossed it into the fireplace with a muttered curse.

The sound of the glass shattering and the fire popping from the droplets of brandy was abnormally loud in the library's stillness. Ivy's heart twisted in abrupt recognition of Sebastian's distracted jealousy. Perhaps Rachel Garrett was right. Perhaps her husband needed protection from her after all. Her own iciness, her unwillingness to melt; it was destroying him. She was doing nothing to erase his doubts. She was making things worse.

She was ruining them both.

Regret flooded Ivy. Flinging aside the book, she flew to him, her arms wrapping tight about his waist.

Breathing in the sweet, clean fragrance of her, Sebastian gave a broken sigh. His forehead dropped to rest against the top of her hair. Molly had pulled her curls back into a simple braid, the thick rope of it reaching to the small of her back and he toyed with the end of it as Rachel's warning echoed in Ivy's mind: *You need protection...*

Perhaps he believed his aunt. Maybe his obsession would lead to his downfall and she would provide the catalyst for yet another tragedy. A tear trickled down Ivy's cheek. She buried her head against his chest until his shirt absorbed the bit of wetness. She did not want to be the reason for his heartache and she had no desire to intentionally wound him. Could he understand how terrified she was that he would hurt her?

When his arms tightened, Ivy drew in a deep shuddering breath of relief. Her emotions were so tightly strained that the slightest bit of kindness from him was enough to shatter her fragile composure. Stroking her back in rhythmic silence, Sebastian had no idea how close she was to crumbling.

~

LATER THAT NIGHT, CURLED AGAINST SEBASTIAN'S SIDE, IVY LET her arm rest lightly across the width of his abdomen. The rise and fall of his chest below her cheek and his steady breathing was calming. Unconsciously, her grip tightened around his waist. She snuggled closer.

But, even while holding her, she felt the faint chill in his embrace. He would not send her away, as evidenced by his own words, but he remained eerily distant.

Pulling herself to a sitting position, Ivy saw his eyes glittering in the dim light cast by the fire. "Do you believe I would be unfaithful to you?"

Sebastian's voice was emotionless. "Many women find the constrictions of marriage to be a heavy burden. Some seek pleasure outside the boundaries of wedding vows, and there are men who will believe you to be one of those women. You should not encourage them, Ivy, no matter how innocent their intentions may seem. Fulfilling your duties to the Ravenswood title should keep you busy enough."

Ivy stared at him. Beneath the carefully chosen words lurked the unspoken accusation. Sebastian believed she would strain against the reins of duty, rebelling against a marriage she never wanted and the responsibilities thrust upon her. He was suspicious, questioning if her escalating unhappiness might force her to another man's arms. If she came to his bed out of a sense of obligation, she would abandon it just as quickly. She would betray her husband. Eventually.

"The same is said of men, although it is common for them to find pleasures elsewhere, both before and after vows are exchanged," she pointed out. "Do not mince words with me, Sebastian. Do you believe me capable of betraying you?"

He was taut as a new bow awaiting its first arrow. Her accusation did not meet with denial as his gaze slid to focus once more on the ceiling. His jaw clenched so tight, she saw a muscle ticking in it, even in the close darkness of the room. They were both worn down to delicate shells of raw emotions, a state where every imagined slight carried the potential to erupt into a full-fledged battle. These two issues, obligation and betrayal, were so horribly entangled there seemed no rational way of dealing with one without confronting the other.

Ivy slumped, the tears impossible to stem. "Send me away,

Sebastian. Please. Send me away before we destroy any feelings we have for each other with hurtful words and accusations. Send me away before I hurt you, before you hurt me. I cannot bear this any longer."

Sebastian's arm snaked about her so quickly Ivy exhaled in relief. Warm and naked, he surged against her, and although she wept with heartache, she welcomed him. No matter the argument between them, the fact he held her, his erection prodding her stomach, his lips gliding over hers, shot a thrill of excitement through her bones. He pulled her beneath him, sinking into her softness.

"I wish it were that simple, Ivy. I wish to God, I could send you away. I wish I could live without you. I told you - and I will tell you again and again, if I must. You are the very air I breathe, my heartbeat and my love. I cannot set you from me - damn you, I cannot. Do not ask it of me again, I beg you. No matter the different ways you demand it, I will always give you the same answer. No. You are mine."

DEEP SLUMBER WAS DAMNABLY ELUSIVE. IVY'S DESPAIR TORE Sebastian's heart to pieces and he lay awake until dawn, attempting to find a solution to the coil he had created.

Aunt Rachel delighted recounting, in exacting detail, every one of his wife's waltzes at the Graham Ball, how she laughed and flirted over lemonade and champagne. How many times she strolled the terrace and visited the exotic attached garden conservatory, and the different gentlemen lucky enough to accompany her before his arrival. Jealousy stung him, but his finger, tracing the curve of Ivy's soft cheek, did so gently.

These moments of doubt were despicable. He loathed the insecurity he felt, the nauseating punch to his gut as Gabriel reported the events of his wife's morning ride. Ivy could not possibly betray him. She did not want to marry him, but she possessed too much honor to be unfaithful. He was the worst monster to think it, even for a moment. Ah, he was so goddamn awful to her at times - could he blame her if she ever did turn to someone who treated her kindly?

"Mmmm…" Ivy snuggled closer. "Is it night still?"

"Nearly daybreak." He shifted so she fit more comfortably in the circle of his arms. "I did not mean to disturb you. Go back to sleep."

"Were you sleeping?"

Sebastian let out a weary sigh, dropping a kiss to her temple. "No."

"Oh. Then, will you - will you kiss me awake, Sebastian?" Her face lifted to his, aqua eyes alight with invitation. "Kiss me and make love to me as the sun comes up?"

How could he resist her? She was so lushly sweet and warm and pressing against him. Oranges and lilies enveloped him, the headiness of her scent swamping him as they made love with an odd tenderness never present before. When Ivy wept at the end, holding onto him as if nothing in the world would ever make her let go, Sebastian couldn't help but hope he was finally breaking through his wife's fragile barriers.

Flying from the bed, a hand clamped over her mouth, Ivy barely made it to the commode room. Molly hurried to her, pulling her mistress's hair, sticky with sweat, away from her shoulders and flushed face. When the violent retching spell was over, she wiped Ivy's cheeks with a cool cloth.

"Tis the eighth time since you arrived in London, milady," the maid stated matter-of-fact. "It could be a babe."

Ivy took a shuddering breath, blotting her lips with the cloth before accepting the cup of water Molly offered. Swishing the liquid around her mouth, she spat into the sink. "Impossible. My monthlies were less than three weeks ago."

"Tis not uncommon. To bleed and still carry a child. My mum

told me once the two could overlap. We should call for the doctor…each time is worse than the last."

Ivy drank the remaining water before trusting herself to answer. Thank heavens Sebastian was not there to witness these bouts of illness. It usually did not happen this soon following breakfast - the last two times occurring just after she'd had afternoon tea. *Oh, God.* Just thinking of tea made her queasy.

"I would know if it were a baby. At least, I think I would know." Steadying herself before exiting the commode room, Ivy made it as far as the bed before needing to lie down. The dizziness was intense, the room whirling like a child's toy top. "I do not need a doctor and the earl does not need to know of this either."

"But he will find out, milady. Especially when you start to grow," Molly said with her usual stoic, Irish pragmatism.

"Molly," Ivy's voice grew sharp with irritation. "It's not a baby. Now, please, bring something to quiet my stomach. It feels like a basket of seagulls, all swirling about. And, God, my head. If only this dizziness would cease."

"I'll ring for fresh tea."

Swallowing hard against a second wave of daunting nausea, Ivy groaned. "No. I cannot stomach it. I wonder if perhaps that batch has gone bad."

"I'll see what Cook suggests, milady. Maybe some ginger water and something soft to eat. You can't be sick like this and not eat. You've lost weight as it is." Molly bustled about the room, pulling the drapes against the bright sunlight although she'd drawn them open just an hour before.

When the door closed behind the maid, Ivy sank against the pillows with a heavy sigh, her eyes closing in fatigue. She pulled the coverlet up to her shoulders, appreciative for the coolness of the silk pillowcases against her flushed cheek. Blissful silence ensued until the door creaked.

Waving a hand, Ivy's eyes remained shut. "For God's sake, Molly, do not bandy it about in the kitchens. Miss Agnes concocted some manner of foul tonic for me last time. It was dreadful, awful stuff…"

"Last time?"

Ivy's eyes snapped open to see Sebastian framed in the doorway, his brow pulled into a fierce frown. "What's this about the last time? I passed Molly on the stairs - she was scared as a rabbit to see me."

"I-I thought you left to meet with Bentley."

"He can wait. I hoped you would be agreeable to a ride in the park. Raven and Spring could use the exercise. And I wanted to spend the day with you." Crossing to her, Sebastian placed a hand on her forehead. He frowned again at feeling how warm she was. "You are ill. I gather this is not the first time?"

"It is nothing. Something I ate or perhaps the tea from Rosethorne. I adore it, but maybe it has spoiled." Ivy leaned into his hand, grateful for the soothing motions against her scalp as his fingers brushed her hair away from her forehead. "I do not wish to burden you."

"Ivy, you are mine. Mine to care for and to take care of. You are my wife. *Never* a burden. How many times have you been ill? When did this begin?"

After hearing her explanation, he nodded. "It may be the tea, although I've never heard of this happening before. I'll have it disposed of and procure a new batch from Beaumont's cellars. But, should this occur again, you will tell me immediately."

Sebastian demanded Ivy stay abed the rest of the day and she reluctantly acquiesced. Her claims she felt much improved went ignored. When the noon meal came, he watched while she ate weak chicken broth and a small bowl of fruit. Later, she polished off a small plate of biscuits Molly snuck up to her, along with a cup of coffee, complete with extra sugar so she could abide its bitterness.

The next day it was as though Ivy was never sick and she convinced Sebastian it was perfectly safe to ride Spring at a sedate walk. That afternoon all of English society witnessed the Earl of

Ravenswood, courteously, and with all the mannerisms of a besotted husband, attend to his wife as though the two had never quarreled so fiercely just the week before.

Ivy's smiles and laughter were most puzzling to those watching from a distance. The countess did not appear miserable, and the Earl could not keep his hands off her. He constantly touched her arm or her hand, sometimes leaning over to give her a kiss, all of which the countess welcomed with a smile. If they were indeed angry at each other, they gave magnificent performances to indicate otherwise that afternoon in Regent Park. Perhaps, interested parties grumbled, neither was quite ready for the type of affair one engaged in when bored with marriage.

An unspoken truce emerged between Ivy and Sebastian. A truce not formally agreed to, but one both readily clung to. It was a fragile, sweet thing and they strove not to break it, treading lightly around each other. The days were filled with soft kisses and the nights with such passionate lovemaking, that the remaining time in London glowed with a hazy, dreamlike quality.

The final balls of the Season had begun, the streets of the city filling with Society's exodus eager to escape the heat of town for the cooler climes of the countryside. Household staffs were shifted and rearranged in preparation of the summer's whirlwind of events. The ormolu clock on the fireplace mantel chimed two o'clock as Sebastian closed the ledger book with a decided snap.

Ivy was home from an afternoon spent visiting at Sara Morgan's. Stepping to the door of his study, he overheard her giving Brody instructions to serve tea in the west drawing room and to inform his lordship she would meet him there after freshening up. Humming an Irish waltz just slightly off key, she ascended the stairs while holding onto the banister for balance, giggling when she lightly tripped upon a step.

When Sebastian ventured into the foyer, Brody grinned and quickly explained the situation. "Her Ladyship, Lady Morgan, and Lady Willsdown did a bit of celebrating, milord, to toast the end of the season. A tradition of sorts, you see."

"I see." Sebastian chuckled as he heard the sound of a piece of furniture being bumped against and a second later, his wife's enchanting laughter. "Would you hazard a guess on their beverage of choice? I suspect something a bit more potent than tea."

"Champagne. Most definitely, milord."

"Hmmm." Sebastian still had a few items of correspondence to attend before he could make his way to the west drawing room and it took everything within him not to follow Ivy upstairs to lend his assistance in "freshening up." Thinking what might occur if he acted on that impulse, he smiled. "See to the tea, will you, Brody? And Brody- no champagne."

"Of course not, milord."

"Lady Garrett informed me that new batch of the Rosethorne blend arrived this morning. Will you have Cook prepare a pot? Her Ladyship will be most pleased. I know she's missed it."

Sebastian was mildly surprised Ivy was not in the drawing room when he arrived. Wolfing down two sugar biscuits from a small platter, he prowled the confines of the elegant room. When ten minutes had passed, and there was still no sign of her, he went ahead and poured himself a cup of the tea.

A slight bitterness was detected toward the end of the brew and he frowned to discover it. Pouring another cup, he sipped this one more slowly, rolling the liquid over his tongue. A strange flavor was certainly there, tempered with a delicate hint of something fruity and bitter. It was a taste difficult to place but not enough to ruin the tea.

It was a half hour before Sebastian deemed it necessary to investigate Ivy's delayed appearance. Thinking perhaps she had lain down for an impromptu nap, an irrational grin broke over his face. With unseemly haste, he hurried from the drawing room, taking the stairs two at a time.

A surge of abrupt dizziness swelled inside him before he reached the landing of the second floor. He clutched the balustrade for stability, nausea choking him. Stunned, Sebastian held in place, breathing hard until the spell passed. He ate very little at the noon meal, a mass of paperwork preventing much concentration on the rumblings of his stomach. This wave of vertigo, quickly followed by excruciating paroxysms across his lower belly, was credited to nothing more than severe hunger pangs. Although he was left shuddering in its aftermath, he continued toward their suite of rooms.

Ivy lay on her back, sprawled across the middle of their bed in a heap of turquoise silk. She'd kicked off her slippers, unfastened a few of the bodice hooks and fallen asleep. Her head was turned to the side, one hand tucked under her chin and the butterfly brooch twinkled from a gold chain around her neck. It nestled in the hollow of her throat, as if it were a real butterfly sipping from a tiny pool of nectar. Sinking beside her, Sebastian smelled the faint bubbly aroma of champagne mingling with her perfume and when his arms folded about her, she turned, burrowing into him. Sebastian thought it quite possibly the closest thing to heaven on earth. How he adored this enchanting, dazzling creature.

The night Ivy begged him to let her go, the same night she clutched him as though he were a lifeline, crying as they made love, she had unknowingly convinced him of something she could not yet admit to herself. She loved him. She could not, or would not, say it aloud, but she loved him. His eyesight grew blurry, thinking of the next step in wooing his wife.

Sebastian's vision contracted even further, everything growing smaller and smaller until Ivy was hardly more than a pinprick of light at the end of a black tunnel. Unexpectedly, his mouth could no longer form words, his throat sealing tight in a raw grip of agony. Forcing himself to swallow, he panicked, straining to say her name.

"Ivy..." It came out in a guttural rasp.

"Hmmm." Her lips just inches from his, Ivy stirred but did not awaken. Her breathing remained steady, the moist warmth of it brushing his cheek. Sebastian struggled to rise but found his limbs paralyzed and horrifyingly useless. His arms, draped about Ivy's waist, suddenly dropped away like lifeless sticks.

What was happening to him? He was tossed into a dark pit, while from a rim far above a thousand pair of eyes stared back at him. All glowed with aqua fire, flashes of deep gold candlelight melting into empty, hollows. Slowly, they spiraled into gaping caverns as he slithered further into the pit to be swallowed whole. He wanted to grope and scratch his way to the top, but he could not move, could not breathe nor cry out for help. Ivy lay close enough to kiss, but she could not save him. Inside his head, Sebastian shrieked but she slept on, oblivious as he slid away.

The world grew darker, the universe weaker, all light diminishing until everything wasted to a blue-black night.

CHAPTER 40

The bed shook, as if a mighty earthquake had descended upon their fashionable corner of Mayfair. Ivy mumbled, moving closer to the blazing heat beside her. She reveled in the warmth before coming to a hazy realization it was actually uncomfortable. Droplets of sweat trickled between her breasts, and restless, she scooted further away. Her eyes drifted open as the bed quivered.

A vague memory of returning from Sara's after a morning of champagne and too many toasts to the end of the season rose in her mind. While undoing the buttons on her gown, she became a bit dizzy and decided to rest for only a moment. She must have fallen asleep.

The bed wobbled again, a tortured moan jerking her upright, setting her heart pounding. Sebastian lay beside her, making that awful noise. Ivy touched her palms to his forehead then his cheek and he trembled at her touch. His flesh was like fire burning her and she stared at him in utter confusion. With a small cry, she scrambled to her knees. Sweat drenched Sebastian, heat rolling off him in waves, yet he shuddered as if bared to the wilds of Northern Scotland during the depths of winter. He moaned again, eyes feverish and bright, opening to gaze through Ivy as though she were not even there.

"Sebastian," Ivy choked. "Dear God, you are ill."

Help. She must get help. Gabriel would know what to do.

Mid-tumble from the bed, Ivy found her arm caught in an unyielding grasp. With the strength of ten men, Sebastian held tight, fingers digging into her flesh. His face glowed the same pristine white as the pillow casings and between lips dry and cracked, a single word finally croaked out.

"S-s-sick."

Somehow, Ivy managed to wrench away. She hurried to the bathing room, locating a porcelain basin in the dimly lit room. Sliding back onto the bed, she tipped the bowl toward him just as he rolled to his side to become violently ill. Bracing his shoulder, she supported his weight the best she could while the meager contents of his stomach emptied into the shallow bowl.

When the spell was over, Ivy set the basin on the floor and helped him onto his back. She procured a fresh cloth, a glass of water and set about cleaning him up, passing the cloth gently over his face. Murmuring soothingly, even though Sebastian seemed unaware of her presence, Ivy reached over, yanking hard on the servant's cable that would summon Gabriel.

WITH A RUSTLE OF FABRIC, LADY GARRETT GLIDED THROUGH THE open doorway, her brow furrowed as she took in the bustling scene. "Whatever is going on?"

Ivy did not answer. Taking a new basin of cold water and fresh cloths from Miss Agnes, she dabbed at the newly formed rivulets of perspiration on Sebastian's forehead and upper lip.

"Is the earl not feeling well?" Rachel stepped around Gabriel where he'd taken up a post at the door.

"He is terribly ill," Ivy replied. "Where have you been?"

"To lunch at the Countess of Latham's, and tea at old Lady

Danbury's. Poor old dear suffers terribly from gout. I thought a visit would cheer her, although she barely remembers who comes to call. Feebleminded, you know." Rachel gazed at her nephew, a strange gleam in her eye. "I was under the impression you two were hardly on speaking terms. Although after that display in the park, and your antics this past week, I'm not sure what to believe. One must keep up appearances, I suppose."

Ivy could barely breathe past the guilt choking her. "He is my husband, madam. Regardless of everything else, there is that. It is my responsibility to care for him."

"How very admirable." Rachel murmured, stepping back as Sebastian began to thrash restlessly. She bumped into an immobile, unsmiling Gabriel. "When did he become ill?"

"This afternoon." Ivy dipped the cloth again in the cool water. "We are awaiting Dr. Callahan's arrival to learn more."

"Let us hope it is a passing illness. I confess I've never seen Sebastian ill before," Rachel replied.

When Dr. Callahan arrived, he too, was perplexed. The possibility of food contamination was put forth, or perhaps some manner of blood poisoning. Had the earl recently suffered an insect or animal bite?

"A dangerous situation, Lady Ravenswood," he intoned. "Extremely serious. You must prepare yourself for the worst, as the earl is very ill. Should he not awaken by morning, then I fear… well, let us pray circumstances are better by morning."

Ivy sat frozen with terror during the doctor's examination. It could not be explained how or why her robust and healthy husband was so vital that morning, but at Death's doorstep by nightfall. There was her own perplexing illness to be considered, but Dr. Callahan did not believe the two to be related as the symptoms were not precisely the same.

The doctor left instructions; rest and cold compresses to be applied to the earl's forehead and body to keep the fever down. Should the fever spike higher, ice baths would become necessary. A bloodletting was recommended, but when the instruments were pulled out for the procedure, Ivy quietly informed the man the only blood to be shed would be his own.

The devices were hastily packed away and the doctor took his leave.

Late in the night, for a few blessed seconds, Sebastian woke. A transient, lucid awareness lit his face and he stared at Ivy as if shocked to see her weeping so softly in a chair beside the bed. Remorse etched his features as he said in a gravelly whisper, "Ah, my little butterfly. What the hell have I done to you this time?"

He brushed his mouth across her knuckles until Ivy pulled away to pour cool water for him. As shudders rolled through him, she smoothed his hair from his fevered brow, holding the glass's rim against his parched lips. "Sebastian...please, do not talk just now. Drink this."

"Forgive me, love. Seems I'm always begging your forgiveness." Moisture brightened his eyes as he drank his fill, then his head sagged forward in a struggle against the inevitable skid into unconsciousness.

"You must be strong, darling. For me." Ivy pressed her lips to their tangled fingers. His skin was so hot, like a bright flame against her mouth.

"Ivy, promise me." Fever left Sebastian twisting with pain. He brought her hand up to press it to his face.

"Anything, Sebastian." Against the stubble roughened plane of his jaw, the coolness of her palm seemed to soothe him. She kept it there, willing to do anything to bring him comfort. "Anything."

"Don't leave me...don't want...to be alone. Oh god, stay...Ivy, you must promise me. Stay."

Ivy was frightened. More frightened than she had ever been in her life. This awful pain Sebastian suffered and her powerlessness to do anything for him eclipsed everything. Even the agony of losing her dear mother did not compare to this. She held his hand tight while his tears scalded her knuckles and she kissed his forehead until he drifted into a restless sleep plagued by nightmares. She could lose him forever this time. No matter how tight she held to him...he might slip away. Before she could tell him how much she loved him. *I cannot live without him.* Why did she continue to deny what was in her heart? She was so tired of fighting it. Tired of walling herself off from the love Sebastian repeatedly gave her. Sebastian loved her. She loved him. She never stopped loving him, even when he crushed her heart and destroyed her.

"Come back to me, my love." Kissing his cheek, Ivy found his skin clammy and hot against her lips. "Come back to me."

~

WAS IT A DREAM? A NIGHTMARE? OR A HALLUCINATION.

Sebastian's stomach clenched with excruciating spirals, contracting with such painful sharpness he could only gasp. Icy torrents of his own musky sweat drenched him. He tried pulling his hand from the loose grip, to caress the soft mane of chestnut colored hair spilling across his forearm, but he was too weak. Frustration mounted as the pain in his belly grew into an unbearable ache. It hurt worse than anything he'd ever experienced before, but he welcomed it. He needed it. To feel something...something real. *Tangible.* It meant he was still alive.

Was Ivy really here? Holding his hand? Were those her tears splashing his fingers? Every drop scorched him, burning like salty acid on his skin. Then her lips brushed his flesh, the caustic blistering soothed by sweet coolness. Her kisses were numbing flecks of ice dousing waves of fire. She whispered something, words he could not quite make out. It was a struggle to keep his eyes open, to focus on the dark head bent over him. Oblivion encroached once more to envelop him within a silky, inky darkness. Long, black fingers reached for him, grabbing his face and his body, his hair...

No, no, no... He struggled to hold as the tunnel sucked him down. Ivy's face floated above him, blue-green eyes wide. Terrified. For him

Please, Ivy, Ivy, don't let me go. Don't let me go...keep me with you.

CHAPTER 41

Sebastian drifted in a no man's land of unconsciousness and elusive lucidity. A high fever gripped him despite the cold compresses and numerous soakings with ice cloths. Incessant nausea meant nothing substantial stayed on his stomach, although he held down sips of water for periods of time. The discovery of a strange, pale rash erupting on his stomach and thighs the next morning proved cause for great concern.

With the breaking of dawn, Lady Garrett was the first to visit the sickroom, slipping in with the maids as they arrived to carry away soiled bedclothes and linens. Distressed over Sebastian's lack of recovery during the night, a distinct shade of green discolored her pinched features. Mumbling something about increased prayers for her nephew, she rushed back out, and Ivy was not saddened to see her go.

The doctor was scheduled to return sometime after breakfast. Ivy swallowed against the flip-flopping in her stomach at what he might say. The rash inflaming Sebastian's body alarmed her more than she cared to admit; even more so when Gabriel blinked twice at the sight of it.

Dr. Callahan did the same. Blinked twice, then reached for his bag to pull out the same instruments Ivy demanded be put away the day before.

"What are you doing, Dr. Callahan?" The position placed Ivy between the elderly man and her husband. Molly, William and Miss Agnes, stood to the side, watching the impending confrontation. Gabriel, sitting guard again by the door, narrowed his eyes.

"Lady Ravenswood, I had my suspicions yesterday. This rash confirms it. His Lordship is the victim of poisoning. Whether intentional or not, I cannot say, but if the infected blood is not removed, it is unlikely he will survive another day. As it is, the earl is tremendously fortunate to have lived this long." Running a hand through a shock of white hair, Dr. Callahan subjected Ivy to a stern glare over the rim of his wire spectacles. His mouth no longer curved with a sympathetic smile and there no were soft murmurs of comfort for the wife of his patient. His manner turned brisk and cool. "It is only speculation, but I believe His Lordship's exceptional physical condition has enabled his survival thus far."

"Poisoned?" Ivy stuttered in shock. "That's - that's impossible."

"Is it?" Dr. Callahan placed a small canvas bag on the table, rolling it open to reveal an array of lancets, tubing and a small box with tiny, razor-like blades protruding from it. "We rarely travel in the same social circles, my lady, but even I've heard rumors of His Lordship's enemies. Is it that unreasonable to assume someone wished him harm, and took steps to see the deed done?"

"But how?" Ivy's arms and legs felt as if they were suddenly carved of stone. Enemies? The Earl of Clayton and Lord Danbury. Brandon Madsen. The new Duke of Richeforte. Oh God...there were more than a few to consider. The room seemed so tiny all of a sudden, every bit of the air sucked out until she was dizzy and lightheaded.

Her eyes latched on the lancets, mesmerized by their shiny, cruel beauty. Behind her, Molly choked on a little hiccup of a sob; Miss Agnes crossed herself and whispered a prayer.

Bloodletting was an accepted practice of curing many diseases and ailments, although Ivy never quite believed in the concept. Her mother insisted upon the procedure during the last few months of her illness, convinced it would restore her health. But every visit by the doctor only resulted in an increasing fragility until Caroline eventually faded away, like a pale golden light slowly blocked out by a bigger, brighter world. This was not the answer to making Sebastian well. Ivy believed with every thread of her soul this treatment would weaken him, depleting his body and strength until there was nothing left.

Dr. Callahan noted the grim loyalty of the servants and Ivy's stricken features, unwilling to completely dismiss the fact Her Ladyship had tended her husband faithfully, and with the utmost care, for the past forty-eight hours. She appeared ready for the sickbed herself, but it was no secret this couple quarreled in full view of the *ton* just two weeks prior. "Perhaps someone intimately associated with milord might be the culprit?"

Like a mountain unfolding, Gabriel's huge form was both sheltering and intimidating when he moved to Ivy's side. "It's time the doctor took his leave," he growled. "Another physician can be procured, milady. One with yours and His Lordship's interests at heart.

Dr. Callahan swallowed hard but still busied himself drawing stark white bandages and other items from the bag. "If I don't remove the blood poisoning this man's body, he will die. It's only a matter of time."

"If you do this, he will die. Perhaps even quicker," Ivy argued.

Molly and Miss Agnes stepped closer to William while Gabriel brazenly took up a stance beside the bed, guarding it like a bulldog. Brody, arriving to check the earl's prognosis, paused in the doorway, a last-minute witness to the scene. Judging from the ominousness expression on his face, he'd heard enough. Catching Ivy's eye, he gave an infinitesimal shake of his head.

It was all Ivy needed. Surrounded by those who cared she felt infinitely stronger. Still frightened half out of her wits, but stronger. And more resolute. She was doing the right thing. She must be. Without realizing it, she touched the gold butterfly pinned to the lace at her neck.

"Dr. Callahan, I have no idea who may have poisoned my husband, but I intend to find out. If you wish to be helpful, put those things away and tell us what to do to help His Lordship. There must be another way. And if there isn't, I suggest you come up with something quickly."

CHAPTER 42

The room was dark, the bedside lamp providing the only light. Ivy was unsure what woke her. Stirring, she opened her eyes, allowing them to adjust as she straightened in the chair.

The clock on the mantle began to strike. She counted out nine chimes as she reached for the cloth draped over the basin's edge. The water was still cool but a new bucket of ice was needed. How she hated to disturb any of the servants. They were as exhausted as she, running back and forth for the past three days tending to Sebastian's needs.

With a half hysterical sob, Ivy tried to recount the order of the days, what happened when, but things were so desperate, and she was so fraught with worry, it was all a blurry mess. She recalled bits and pieces, people bustling about, caring for Sebastian, and for her too. There was the awful visit by Dr. Callahan, his diagnosis of poisoning, although he could not say with definitive certainty what served as the lethal substance. Sebastian's symptoms did not fit with known elements of readily available poisons. That he could keep down a substantial amount of water was in his favor. Dr. Callahan's consultation with various colleagues led to a recommendation of a small cup of salted water as a strengthening aid. The elderly man administered it, although he clearly held no faith in its value as a medical tool.

Both her father and Alan had taken a turn watching over Sebastian earlier that day while Ivy met Sara in the west drawing room, taking comfort in her sympathetic embrace. Her friend wiped her tears away, made her eat something more substantial than broth and forced Ivy to lay down on a settee, promising to wake her immediately should Sebastian's condition change.

But worry and fear twisted her restless sleep until Ivy apologized to Sara and hurried back to Sebastian's side.

She ran a gentle hand down her husband's sunken cheek. Poor Sebastian. The things they'd done to hurt each other. Should he ever wake from this fevered nightmare world, where he fought invisible monsters and sobbed and cursed for reasons unknown, she would tell him over and over of her love for him. Until he tired of hearing the words from her mouth.

"How touching."

With the stealth of a deadly spider dropping from an unseen web, Rachel emerged from the darkness to stand at the shadows at the foot of the bed.

"Good evening, Lady Rachel. Sebastian is resting comfortably at the moment." Ivy rose automatically, a strange sense of protectiveness trickling in her veins. "His condition has improved somewhat."

A ghost of a smile played on the older woman's pinched lips. Hovering at the edge of the lamplight, her blue eyes assessed the earl before she slit her gaze at Ivy. "My dear nephew has disturbed my plans." The light glinted off something she held in her hand.

At first, Ivy did not comprehend Rachel, neither her words, nor the pistol she held. The information processed at a much slower speed than normal, a result of her exhausted state. Why did Rachel require a weapon? Did she fear Sebastian's enemies might come for him here? Inside his own home?

Rachel waved the dueling pistol at her. It was a beautifully crafted piece, with intricate metallic etchings on the curved oak butt and a tarnished silver barrel in need of polishing. "Sit down."

"I don't understand." Ivy sank into the chair, her mouth so dry the words escaped in a hoarse whisper.

"It's quite simple, really." Rachel held up the second bottle of laudanum Dr. Callahan left behind earlier that day. "It's you I meant to poison, not Sebastian."

"What are you talking about?"

"Do you think I can allow you to live? After what you did to Timothy?" Rachel's breath burst out in a hiss. "What sort of mother would I be, if I did not bring you to some manner of justice? This latest development is unfortunate, and I've no doubt, should Sebastian recover and learn what I've done, he'll pack me off to one of his God- awful lesser estates where nothing exciting ever happens and nobody of importance ever goes."

Ivy shook her head in disavowal. "Lady Rachel, I won't let him do that. And Sebastian will get better, he must. He's improved already. Should you wish, we'll help you obtain your own house, here in London..." The feeble attempt to placate the woman trailed off, doused by the spark of madness in Rachel's eyes.

Dressed in a black silk ball gown of severe lines, hair scraped into an austere bun, Lady Garrett's features were accentuated by the harshness of her coiffure. Coldly elegant, thin and pale, the past year had changed her. As if she'd wasted away from the inside out, devoured by grief and a hidden madness.

Rachel tilted the bottle so the light reflected off it. "I've mixed apricot leaves into your Rosethorne tea since the day you arrived. Wilted leaves will make a person deathly ill. Only a few at a time, of course, as it would prove too suspicious if done all at once. You're the only one to drink the tea, so no one was ever in any danger. How fortunate he sent for more after throwing the old batch away. As soon as it arrived, I mixed in all the leaves but never expected Sebastian to drink it. He so rarely drinks tea."

Ivy traced the filigree butterfly, somehow drawing strength

467

from it. "Sebastian loves me. It will hurt him if you harm me. Don't you even care?"

"I did care. Once. Before he chose you over his family. Over blood." Rachel frowned. "Sebastian is very stubborn. He refused to send you away. He wouldn't listen to me, although I rather expected it."

Ivy thought of the strangely painful episodes experienced over the last weeks...her illness following breakfast or teatime. She remembered Sara's distaste for the Rosethorne tea and her complaint it was too strong. There was the occasion Lady Garrett called for a different brew, claiming she did not care for the plantation blend. His aunt intentionally attempted to poison her and now, Sebastian's life hung in the balance. She *could* be with child at this moment, its life equally in danger. Bile rose in Ivy's throat.

"This will not solve anything..."

Rachel laughed. "Of course, it does. It eliminates you. And how I've enjoyed knowing you suffered from my actions. I *want* you to suffer. As Timothy suffered. As *I* have suffered." Her voice turned pensive. "Do you know how desperately Timothy wanted you? Had he won you, he was to borrow funds from Sebastian to purchase his own home. To move away. Away from me."

"You hate me simply because your son wished to marry me?"

"Oh, my dear. There's more to it than that." Lady Garrett's eyes flashed harder, colder. "*My* darling Timothy. Every time you rejected him, his condition worsened. Timothy always took far too much medicine when those headaches came upon him." She stared through Ivy, back to a stormy night the year before. "He cried so bitterly for you. And blamed me for it. He said you rejected him because I would not allow him to become a man. It was *my* fault you did not love him - *my* fault you refused him. Everything you did to him, he blamed me. He was crazed with pain the night he died. He wept at how terribly he'd ruined things; how I ruined him and destroyed his chance for happiness. I'd never seen him in such a state..." Rachel's eyes narrowed, her fists clenching the bottle of laudanum so tight, Ivy feared it would shatter.

"He believed if he sent me away, he could win you back. But he needed me to take care of him! He did! He needed me to ease the pain caused by your heartless actions." Rachel's voice lowered to a whisper. "I gave him too much. He had taken nearly half a bottle already...I thought he was drunk and he did not stop me when I gave him more. I - I only added a little extra. To calm him...he was so distraught."

Staring at Rachel in shock, Ivy did not comprehend the confession then the world tilted. "*You* gave him too much."

"It was an accident." Rachel snarled, hands wringing, her mind churning to make sense of what transpired that night. "How could you possibly ever take care of him? If he sent me away, there would have been no one."

"I was blamed for his death. But, it was you. All this time." The last bit of guilt deep inside Ivy washed away. She took a deep shuddering sigh. Sadness, relief, elation, fear; every emotion crashed into her as if she were strapped to an out of control carousel. "Oh, Lady Rachel, let us help you, please. You don't have to do this..."

A fog of insanity appeared to roll over the woman and Ivy knew the moment of pressing Rachel to accept either help or her own guilt had passed. Now, only a steely resolve existed within her to make Ivy pay for the imagined crimes.

"Don't you understand, you dense creature?" Rachel bit out. "None of that matters now. You will swallow this, go to sleep and never wake up. I'll be rid of you for good."

"If I don't?" Ivy trembled.

"I will put a bullet through your head. If Sebastian recovers, he will think you killed yourself, perhaps because you thought you would be discovered as the one who poisoned him. I will put the apricot leaves in your possession, and he'll think you betrayed him, just as Marilee did. This will no doubt drive him from England again. Or push him to depths of despair as great as Timothy's."

Fear for Sebastian's safety surged through Ivy. That he might believe she betrayed him cut her with the agony of a thousand knives. That he might think she could harm him hurt even worse...

"Drink the laudanum. Things will go on as they did before you bewitched my nephew." Rachel moved closer, her eyes fixed on the butterfly pinned to Ivy's shoulder. "Of course, I won't have my Timothy, but it will be as it was before Sebastian met you. Everything returned to its rightful place and their rightful owners."

Ivy's pulse thumped in her veins, the strength of it pounding a mad drumbeat in her head, making her dizzy. If Rachel came close enough, perhaps she could knock the pistol from her hand. She might even have time to make it to the door. A slim chance, but worth a try.

Rachel leveled the pistol with a sickly smile and a steady hand. "All the very best balls are happening tonight. Once you are dealt with, I plan to attend several of them and I imagine I won't return before dawn. You'll be dead by then. Such a tragedy. Sebastian will weep, but I'll be happy to be free of you."

Ivy shook her head. "No one will believe I committed suicide, or that I would harm Sebastian."

"Won't they, Poison Ivy? They believed you capable of driving my Timothy to his death."

Ivy's gaze locked with Rachel's. "You killed Timothy."

Rachel's hand trembled. She thrust the bottle at Ivy. "Drink it. All of it."

Ivy flung her arm up, knocking the bottle away while launching herself at the older woman. Crashing to the floor, they both lay motionless, the breath knocked from their bodies.

Smashed upon impact, the contents of the vial began spreading in a wide black puddle across the hardwood. Horrified, Rachel stared at the shards of glass, and retaining the grip of the pistol, she sat up, her movements sluggish.

Ivy lurched forward, attempting to wrest the weapon away. A hoarse cry ripped from her throat when Rachel knocked her back to scramble atop her. In a matter of seconds, Ivy was pinned to the floor, the weapon and her wrists held in Rachel's iron-like grip.

Despite her exhaustion, Ivy was slippery and desperate, kicking and bucking until Rachel lost her balance and toppled partly off her. Scuttling away, Ivy knew a momentary triumph as her foot connected with Rachel's ribs and her muffled shriek echoed in the room's stillness.

The flash of victory was short-lived. Rachel latched onto Ivy's ankle, using it to crawl up her body. Like fierce tigers, they rolled about on the floor, gowns tangling about their legs and hindering any efforts to gain a steady footing.

"I'm going to enjoy killing you," Rachel hissed. With a sudden, twisting motion, she straddled Ivy again. For all her thinness, the woman was wiry, a crazed fury giving her astonishing strength. Her venomous expression was unlike anything Ivy ever witnessed before on another human's face. Hatred lit the blue eyes, an insanity that chilled to the bone. With one hand, she reached down, ripping at Ivy's dress, tearing at something...

A scream finally poured from Ivy. High, foreign and so full of terror, she did not even recognize that it came from her. It seemed to go on forever.

~

IN THE DEPTHS OF HIS NIGHTMARE, A SOUND REACHED SEBASTIAN. To his fevered brain, it called, rousing sluggish blood to beat in frantic rhythm. Consciousness flooded him, making him dizzy, a shower of sparks inside his head touching off fires. Clarity rushed in with a punishing vengeance.

A scream reached a heart-stopping fullness then died away, buried in the muted sounds of a violent scuffle beyond the cool comfort of the bed he felt bound to with hidden ropes. Giving a massive shove of his shoulder, Sebastian raised himself. He must be hallucinating. Caught in a nightmare...because he thought it was Ivy screaming.

Peering over the mattress edge, he tried making sense of what he saw.

Locked in struggle, two figures were highlighted by the small pool of light thrown by the bedside lamp. His aunt straddled Ivy, their hands entwined around a dueling pistol Sebastian hazily recognized as one of Timothy's prized possessions.

"I'm going to kill you," Rachel grunted. "For Timothy. For me. I don't care if it looks to be an accident or not..." Both strained for control, a desperate fight the older woman was winning. Ivy sobbed, forcing the gun away from her face. She was drowning in the full black skirts of his aunt's gown.

"What the hell..." His astonishment was a weak whisper.

"Sebastian!" Ivy's eyes filled with gut-wrenching horror. "No...*NO!*"

Rachel's thin lips curled. With inhuman strength, she jerked free of Ivy's grasp to level the weapon at her nephew.

With the fierceness of an angry hornet, the gold butterfly stabbed Rachel, the long needle burying into the flesh of her forearm. She shrieked in pain.

Sebastian launched himself from the bed while at the same instant Ivy shoved Rachel back. Her fist connected with flesh; there was the sound of bone cracking and Rachel's moan. Maniacal laughter and a gunshot...

The echo was deafening and yet it amplified everything, every sound, every noise. Stunned, Sebastian stumbled back, staring at his shoulder and the tiny, emerging stain. From a great distance, he heard people running, doors slamming. And a scream which slowly dissolved into a long, low wail of anguish.

Ivy. His Ivy.

Was she shot? Oh God, was she hurt?

The sound rang in cadence with Rachel's crazed glee as Sebastian sank to his knees. Hard footsteps thumped behind him. He needed to comfort Ivy, needed to reach her, to ease her pain, to wipe away her sorrow, but he could not seem to move. Never had he heard such agony. Except the night his mother died. His father made the same gut-wrenching sound that night... Sebastian remembered it so clearly, those horrible cries. The torment of someone's heart sliced in two.

Something large and solid passed by with a whoosh. Sebastian crumpled in its wake, befuddled, staring at Gabriel's back as the man appeared then disappeared from the pool of light. The subdued sound of a hefty fist striking flesh underlay the sobs and the laughter.

That laughter abruptly stopped; dying away into the shadows like a terrifying nightmare fades with the morning light. Everything grew grey, an eerie silence falling over the room.

Sebastian drifted for a moment, or maybe many moments, alone, untethered from earth. Until the aching sweetness of Ivy's lips brought him back. Dampening his cheeks were her salty tears, her soft hands cradling his face and pushing against his shoulder. The silky darkness of oblivion beseeched him but he fought its insistent appeal.

I can't go...not now. I won't go...

Ivy embraced him, saying things he did not understand. He focused on her lips, watching them shape words he never thought to hear again. Now she sobbed them.

"Sebastian, I love you. *I love you.* Do you hear me?" She kissed him again and again, tears splashing everywhere and Sebastian wanted to drink her tears. Like wine of the gods, their magic would sustain him, keep him alive. "Sebastian, my darling...my love, I love you."

His breath escaped in a gasp of pain when Ivy pressed the heels of both palms against his left shoulder, blood seeping through her fingers. In the lamp's glow, it appeared as inky ribbons of black streaking down his body. There was no color to the fluid. No color to anything, not even something as important as one's lifeblood, he mused. Only black, white and grey.

Sebastian's eyes closed, his body limp and sagging as Ivy shifted to support his head in her lap. She held him together with just her tiny hands. Holding him. His heart. *His life.*

"Please don't leave me, please...Sebastian. *Sebastian!*"

He could not muster the strength to answer her fading call. He wanted so badly to touch the beautiful face hovering above his own, but for some damned reason he could not get his arms to move. *You're an angel,* he wanted to tell her. An angel with freckles and unruly chestnut hair. And the sweetest lips he could kiss for all eternity…*my angel. Little butterfly...*

Sebastian floated far above the earth. *"I love you,"* she kept saying. He held those words close and Ivy's eyes, shining bright as stars, were the last glittering lights visible as the world spiraled to black emptiness.

She loves me…she loves me again, at last. She loves me. Thank you, God.

She loves me…

CHAPTER 43

Sunlight filled the room. Curled beside him, her head tucked beneath his chin, Ivy lay with one hand wedged between her cheek and the fluff of a pillow. The other rested on the side of his neck, her fingers tangled gently in his hair. Her palm lightly cupped the corded muscles leading to his bandaged shoulder. Sebastian drank in the sweet beauty of his wife, reflecting on how he nearly lost her.

And how close she'd come to losing him.

Drifting in and out of consciousness, for God knows how long, Sebastian knew Ivy rarely left his side. Maybe he dreamed everything else, including her confession of love, but whenever his eyes opened, day or night, she was there.

While he contemplated the possibilities of a miracle, Ivy's fingers curled, drawing his attention. She stared up at him, smiling that radiantly beautiful smile that always stole his breath.

"Hello," she murmured, green-blue eyes sparkling.

Sebastian's heart swelled, nearly bursting with gratitude. Nothing could be as lovely as his wife at that moment. He was alive and she was smiling at him. He wanted to kiss every single golden freckle on her beautiful nose simply because he could. He wanted to shout his love from the rooftops of London. Twice now, he cheated death, given another chance to prove his worth. Never would he squander such a precious gift again.

"Hello." Realizing he held his breath, Sebastian released it slowly. There was so much to say, so many questions to ask. He did not know where to begin. One of the last awful memories of that night was of Rachel screaming, the antique butterfly brooch protruding from her forearm like a glittery, vengeful dagger. The other was Ivy kissing him, weeping while life leaked from his body to stain the floor black.

A wave of weakness surged over him when he attempted to sit up. "Thank God, you are safe..."

Ivy laid a finger to Sebastian's lips, gently shushing him. With a tiny shake of her head, her hand curved along his jaw, the unshaven stubble rough against her palm. She gave him a quick kiss, then slid from the bed. With quick, efficient movements, she assisted in caring for his basic needs; a drink of cool water, tooth powder on his toothbrush. As he rinsed his mouth she held a basin for him, handing over a clean cloth moistened with soap to wipe the grime of the sickroom from his skin. She fluffed the pillows behind his head before climbing back up alongside him, cuddling close as if unable to bear parting from him.

Sebastian grinned at his wife's foresight. He felt much more like himself.

"Before you ask what occurred, I must tell you something. Something I should have told you long ago." Ivy's fingers lightly traced Sebastian's chin before drifting to the angles of his cheekbones. She swept back the lock of raven hair that was forever tumbling into his eyes and biting her lower lip, gathered her words. "I love you, Sebastian. I love you with all of my heart and soul and being. I have loved you from the moment you kissed me on that piano bench and I have never stopped loving you. Even when I hated you," she laughed ruefully, "even when I cursed you, which I have often, I loved you."

Sebastian placed his hand in the curve of her waist, masterfully hiding the grimace of pain the movement caused his injured shoulder. But he must touch her. She drew him like a moth to candlelight. If his arms fell off his body, he would still find a way to hold her. Ivy sighed, moving closer, her eyes never leaving his.

"I should have told you I loved you the day you rescued me from Basford. You hurt me, and I did not trust you not to hurt me again. But, I still loved you. Perhaps things would have gone differently had I just admitted it." Ivy pursed her lips, recalling the unpleasantness of their time in London. "I hate myself for not trusting you. I hate that I did not trust you to take care of me." Her finger traced his cheek. "Had I not pushed you away, Rachel would have been unable to do what she did."

Ivy gave a quick accounting of his aunt's actions and the reasons for it, the truth of Timothy's death.

Sebastian's jaw tightened. His hands shook with anguish and anger. "I'm so sorry, my darling. I should have sent her away at once. It is my fault you were in danger, my blind arrogance that nearly cost your life."

"It is the past now. If we are to move on to our future, we must keep it in our past." Ivy said. "You almost died. Twice. I thought I would lose you. That you would not know how much you mean to me. I thought I would never see you laugh again, have you kiss me, hold me. I thought I would never bear your children." She blushed, eyes sparkling. "And I do wish to have your children, Sebastian. Not because of silly things like duty or responsibility. No, there are far more important reasons. Love and hope and happiness. Sebastian, my beloved. My darling, my very heart." Ivy smiled through her tears. "I love you beyond all reason. I always will."

A mixture of relief and happiness rushed through Sebastian. He soared, around the world and back in an instant to this warm bed, his love by his side, her hand on his cheek. Burying his face in her fragrant hair, he knew the entire universe consisted of this tiny space between them and it was breathtakingly perfect.

"Ivy, you vexing, magnificent creature." An exasperated groan escaped him. "It appears we both won the game we started." He captured her lips, fusing their mouths in a tender kiss. It was a pledge to put aside the bitterness of yesterdays, a promise to focus on the future and the happiness to be found there. They would meet it together.

Ivy finally leaned back, eyes dancing with sultry promises. "I propose a new wager, dear husband. I shall leave the details to you, but should a divan appear as part of the bet, I won't complain. Or perhaps the stream where I discovered stars shining in the bright light of day." Her whisper turned mischievous, "Our wagers can be quite intriguing."

Sebastian burst out laughing, his mind sparking with a thousand possibilities. "My love, I should like nothing better. Be forewarned, though. I do intend to let you win."

"You wouldn't dare," Ivy murmured, pulling his head to hers for another kiss.

EPILOGUE

*I*vy sliced through the water, legs flashing. Heeding Sebastian's previous instructions, she swam with determined resolution toward the waterfall and the rocky outcropping. Upon reaching the ledge where the waterfall tumbled, she let loose an unladylike whoop of triumph and hoisted herself up. Standing beneath the onslaught of water, she cupped her hands to hold the liquid, laughing in delight as it streamed through her hair.

The water sluiced over her. "If you could have something just like this installed in our chambers, I'd be so grateful." Turning slightly, Ivy expected to see him near the shoreline. Today was the first time braving the swim from shore to waterfall and breathless with exhilaration, she wanted to share her accomplishment. "Sebastian? Where are you?"

He was not along the sandy bank or anywhere near the large boulders where they laid earlier, soaking up the warmth of the summer sun. Stepping carefully to where the mist drifted up from the rocks below the ledge, she peered into the churning depths of the blue-green water. Concern wrinkled her brow.

"Lose something?" Sebastian's amused chuckle tickled her ear. Pulling her against the hard security of his body, he held her tight.

"Oh!" Ivy turned to wrap her arms around his neck. "Sebastian Cain, just what do you think you are doing?" With gentle fingers, she traced the red scar on his shoulder. "Swimming that distance? Your wound hasn't fully healed..."

"My shoulder is fine." Sebastian silenced the admonishments with a kiss. "I would not have attempted it otherwise." Tugging Ivy closer, his hands rested lightly on her waist. The thin silk of her chemise barred his fingers from touching bare skin. "How should I divest you of this? It's in my way."

"Oh no, you don't," she giggled, squirming closer so it was impossible to lift the chemise over her head. She wore the flimsy garment when they swam although Sebastian pointed out with a wicked grin he almost liked it better when she did.

Seeing his eyes flare with ardent purpose, Ivy knew if she did not find a way to block him, she would find herself devoid of clothing. Sebastian's singular objective was to divest her of garments every time they came to the stream, while he scarcely conceded to wearing anything at all. Only her insistence he must wear *something* resulted in an undergarment which by itself was almost indecent. Hanging low on his hips, the cream colored linens created a tantalizing image of sheer maleness hovering on the verge of wild abandonment, drawing attention to the pale gold rows of muscles lining his abdomen above the drawstring closure.

"I've no intention of allowing whatever you have planned." Ivy's hand rested against his chest, playfully blocking him.

"Well, you've gone mad," Sebastian murmured, kissing the tender curve of Ivy's neck where it met the slope of her shoulder. "You, my love, will allow anything I wish. Won't you?"

Ivy trembled. Sebastian was right. She would give him anything. And she was mad. Insanely, utterly, madly in love with her husband. She ran a careful finger over the puckered scar marring his flesh. An inch over and he would have died, Dr. Callahan said. He very nearly did, weakened by the poisoning and blood loss.

Shuddering at the thought, Ivy stood on tiptoe to gently kiss the mark. The specialist called to render an opinion expressed amazement that not only did the earl escape with relatively minor repercussions, he also failed to suffer the customary bone fragments common with such shoulder wounds. A miracle, everyone claimed.

Once treated for her bruised jaw caused by Gabriel's blow, a broken nose courtesy of Ivy's fist and a puncture wound from the brooch, Sebastian ensconced Rachel at one of his most secluded estates. A well-paid, dedicated staff of nurses attended her day and night. Although Sebastian wished to have his aunt incarcerated, Ivy did not. No, Rachel would live out her days in relative comfort. Comfortable and banished, knowing the genteel treatment she received was due to Ivy's mercy and intervention on her behalf. Living in isolation with the knowledge of what she had done to her own son.

Within their small circle, everyone believed it a foolish proposal, considering Lady Garrett's peculiar state of insanity. But eventually, Ivy gained the stonily opposed Gabriel to her side, her father, and even Sara. Sebastian was the last to be convinced forgiveness was the first step in moving forward with the rest of their lives. Ivy thanked him with a thousand kisses when he finally agreed.

"Hmm," Sebastian sighed, drawing her back to the present. "I've something to show you, should you care to see it."

"You are wicked." Ivy laughed softly. "I know precisely what it is. I feel it against me."

"You've a naughty mind, my love," he replied indignantly, tweaking her nose. "Come along and careful now. It can be slippery here."

They moved along the rock ledge to a point where the waterfall and the wall met. Stepping through a curtain of rushing water, Sebastian disappeared then reached back to pull Ivy by the hand into a small cave.

Hidden behind the waterfall, the secret space was illuminated by captured sunlight. Reflections of the arrested sunbeams shimmered and danced upon the rough walls, rainbows of color captured and held. Natural outcroppings of stone eased away from the walls of the cave, smoothed by eons of moisture, ledges carved out and smoothed until they were as comfortable as seats. Ancient, bizarre symbols marked the stone, some representing the sun, moon and stars. Ivy wondered who might have chiseled them so many years ago.

"Why did you not tell me of this before?" Ivy breathed.

There was no time to explore or ask further questions because with impatient hands, Sebastian stripped away the wet chemise, yanking it over her head to toss it to the side. Warm hands cupped the fullness of her breasts, his thumbs rubbing the hardened points of her nipples. Ivy quivered, desire roaring through her veins. She forgot about the drawings.

"Discovering new things has its own rewards." His whisper was dark. "Don't you agree?"

Ivy's hands rested briefly on the band of his drawers before she pushed the linen down. With a little shimmy of his hips, the garment fell to the floor and was kicked aside. Sebastian captured her mouth, drawing her in, tasting her. He walked backwards, dragging her to a ledge along the wall closest to the light filled entrance without breaking the kiss.

A natural seat existed there, molded from stone and high enough to sit upon. Sebastian sank on it, pulling Ivy so she straddled his lap. With no pressure on his shoulder in this position, she would control the pace, at least until he decided the pleasure too much to bear. Without preamble, he surged up, his erection filling her, swallowing her startled cry until nothing but low moans escaped her.

Ivy braced her hands against the wall of the cave behind his head, her fingers sketching the rough lines of the rock and carvings of what might be butterflies or maybe birds. The aching quickness of Sebastian's possession was a reminder of his impatience that very morning. She had teased and taunted him with softly voiced concern for his injury until Sebastian finally rolled from the bed with a growl. Very easily, he had yanked her to the edge of the mattress and before Ivy could scramble away in a giggling escape, he slid into her. His hands held her hips, high and steady, until her legs wrapped about his waist and she surrendered all to him.

The experience that morning was a decadently wicked experience; her arms stretched above her head, desperately gripping at the sheets while her husband drove her to a fierce climax before finding his own release. The remembrance sent a sharp thrill singing to Ivy's core as Sebastian filled her now. Breaking off the kiss, she stared down into his eyes. Pools of silver in the reflected sunlight, they gleamed with love, adoration, and honor. For her.

Overwhelmed, Ivy's movements stilled, and Sebastian instantly responded. He understood her so completely she did not even need to speak the words aloud.

"I know, little butterfly, my love," he whispered, his large hands coasting down her back. "Sometimes, it truly is too much to contain- all the happiness, the joy. Despite my wickedness, God decided I deserved you and I'm so damned grateful. I will always love you, Ivy, but you already know that."

Ivy's voice trembled. "I don't want to contain this joy, Sebastian. Ever. I don't care if all of London, all the world, believes us to be crazy fools, I adore you. I'll never hold back from showing it, saying it, shouting it. I thought once you had destroyed me, but you woke me from a dreamless sleep, a dull existence in a colorless world. You woke me to perfectly ruin me and I would not wish it any other way." She kissed him fiercely, their mouths fusing as their bodies surged together.

When she whispered *"I love you"* over and over in his ear, Sebastian echoed the words as the world spun away, shattered and knit itself back together until only the two of them existed.

THE END

AFTERWORD

You can find April Moran on the following media sites. Please stop by and say hey! She can't wait to meet you and is so thankful you gave her book a try!

Facebook:
https://www.facebook.com/authoraprilmoran

Goodreads:
https://www.goodreads.com/Author-AprilMoran

Instagram:
https://www.instagram.com/aprilmoranbooks

If you loved Taming Ivy, please don't hesitate to leave a review on Amazon and Goodreads!

ABOUT THE AUTHOR

April has been writing since she was in elementary school. She still has those old notebooks, and for a giggle, might let you read them. Her style has sharpened since then, but the belief in the power of romance never changed. Readers will always find a happy ending at the end of her novels –but only after their favorite characters endure great angst!

April lives on Florida's Emerald Coast and has been married for 30 years to her high school sweetheart. They have one grown daughter, Alyssa, who they love dearly. April is adored by a goofy German Shepherd, tolerated by a sassy Quarter Horse and suffers a severe rock-n-roll addiction. When not writing romantic tales about dashing, alpha heroes and confident, loving heroines, she and her husband attend concerts and plan trips to Disneyworld and Nashville with their daughter and son-in-law.

11673239R00286

Printed in Great Britain
by Amazon